KU-033-821

Justin Hill was born in Freeport, Grand Bahamas Islands, in 1971. He grew up in York, attended Durham University, and spent seven years as a volunteer aid worker in rural China and Eritrea.

His travel book, *Ciao Asmara*, was shortlisted for the Thomas Cook Travel Award and his acclaimed first novel, *The Drink and Dream Teahouse* (translated into ten languages and banned in China), was awarded a Betty Trask Award and won the Geoffrey Faber Memorial Prize.

Justin Hill currently lives in Connemara, Western Ireland.

Also by Justin Hill

A Bend in the Yellow River
The Drink and Dream Teahouse
Ciao Asmara

Passing Under Heaven

Justin Hill

An *Abacus* Book

First published in Great Britain by Abacus in 2004

Copyright © 2004 Justin Hill

The moral right of the author has been asserted.

*All characters in this publication other than those clearly in the public domain
are fictitious and any resemblance to real persons, living or dead, is, unless otherwise
intended, purely coincidental.*

All rights reserved. No part of this publication may be reproduced,
stored in a retrieval system, or transmitted, in any form or by any means,
without the prior permission in writing of the publisher, nor be otherwise
circulated in any form of binding or cover other than that in which it is
published and without a similar condition including this condition being
imposed on the subsequent purchaser.

'In Memory of W. B. Yeats' from W. H. Auden's *Collected Poems*
reproduced by kind permission of Faber and Faber Ltd.

A CIP catalogue record for this book is available from the British Library.

ISBN 0 349 11739 X

Typeset in Garamond by Palimpsest Book Production Limited,
Polmont, Stirlingshire

Printed and bound in Great Britain by Clays Ltd, St Ives plc

Abacus
An imprint of
Time Warner Book Group UK
Brettenham House
Lancaster Place
London WC2E 7EN
www.twbg.co.uk

For elle, of course,
and the candlelight
at Sugiyama.

By mourning tongues
The death of the poet was kept from his poems . . .

Now he is scattered among a hundred cities
And wholly given over to unfamiliar affections;
To find his happiness in another kind of wood
And be punished under a foreign code of conscience.
The words of the dead man
Are modified in the guts of the living.

'In Memory of W. B. Yeats', W. H. Auden

Prologue

AD 903

The day Minister Li retired from office, he lay on his bed and felt a great sense of release, as if the values and morals that had controlled him through his life were as frail as the morning dew. For a moment he felt he was hovering an inch above the mattress and gripped the sheet. He took a few long, deep breaths and relaxed enough to wipe the cold sweat from his upper lip. Get up, get up, the insistent birdsong seemed to say: you have many years yet.

It was nearly ten before Minister Li finally stood up into the day. He threw back the furs, lowered his legs over the side of the bed. The fire beneath his brick bed kang had gone out in the night. The clay still felt warm. There was a smell of ashes in the air. He pushed himself to the edge. His feet nosed into their slippers. He stood up and limped towards the chamber pot, set it on his writing desk, moved the paper to the side in case he should miss, dragged up his robe.

The urine came in hesitant spurts; the smell was not healthy, nor the colour. Minister Li let his robe drop to the floor, limped back towards his bed. As he took his blue silk robe from its bamboo peg, a line from a poem came to mind. *She plays her anger on the red lute strings, only a bud when he taught me.* He ignored it and tied his belt and folded back his sleeves, reached for his comb. *The doorstep's carpeted red with leaves.* He combed all the thoughts and worries away, tied the winter-grey hairs into a bun, let a few strands fall fashionably in front of his ears. He turned his head to admire them before he stepped towards the door, made ready to start his day.

Unswept till he returns, the words came, but as always he clenched his teeth and ignored them.

The servants had already eaten, and a stack of bowls and chopsticks stood by the door as they finished the final packing, sacks and chests heaped in the corner. Minister Li cleared his throat, spoke in his ministerial voice.

'Fang,' he said, 'when will all this be ready?'

The young man flapped across the room in his straw-sandalled feet. 'Tomorrow,' he said. 'At the latest.'

'Tomorrow is too late,' the Minister said. 'I wanted it done three days ago.'

'I know,' Fang apologised, but however much Minister Li swore and fumed there was nothing he could do to change the world. 'It was difficult to find enough men,' Fang explained. 'There were rumours about conscripters. All the village men stayed away. I had to pay these men double.'

Minister Li looked at the foreigners: hooked noses, deep-set eyes, dark skin. What were the armies for if not keeping the barbarians out? he thought. But now the armies were foreign, their generals were Mongols and Kazaks; only the servants were still Chinese.

'Well,' Minister Li's tone turned almost conciliatory, 'we can't wait. I want you to leave this and see that everything we need is ready. I'm leaving today. I can't bear to stay here any longer.'

Fang bowed low and ran off into the yard, bristling with orders. He was already shouting at his team when Minister Li went to take yet another last look round. He thought of admiring the ornamental fish, but they were frozen into their pond. They stared up through the ice, and waved up at the world with their long trailing fins, but the old man's eyesight was never strong. All he saw were smudges in the ice. Leaves, he thought.

The paint was peeling off Moonlight Pavilion. In his room he tried to conjure up a vision of his younger days – but all he could see were the tattered windows, dusty floor, and long cracks in the plaster, inching curiously up the walls.

Minister Li shut the door and walked back towards the main hall. Fang was waiting in a cloud of his breath, his hands tucked into his sleeves for warmth, his face drawn and anxious.

'Minister,' he said, 'your chair is ready.'

The minister walked out of the main hall on to the steps. A troop of uniformed men were standing around, blowing on their fingers, coughing in the cold. His sedan stood in the centre of the yard, the gold and red silks worn and faded, flapping wearily in the breeze.

Minister Li stepped down the stairs. His mind's eye joined the watching men, an unseen face in the crowd, saw himself as others saw him: a retired official in blue silk gown and red felt boots leaving the capital.

The picture of the Li family tomb came to mind. He had taken his mother's body there when he was a young man. Memories of that time returned for a moment, as vivid as a silk painting. He paused to let Fang hold open the curtain, then bowed his head low and stepped inside.

The headman of the chair bearers clapped his hands and the men moved towards their places. Fang pulled himself up on to his horse. He watched the bearers take the weight of the poles on their shoulders, then stand. The sedan rose awkwardly, like a camel. The vermilion gates bent slowly open and the procession marched out into the streets.

The Avenue of Heaven was jostling with people and traffic. 'Out of the way!' Fang called to the crowd beneath him, as he steered his horse through the throng. 'Make way for Minister Li!' he shouted, and felt the blind hands of the crowd pulling his horse back.

Fang kicked his heels and the horse pushed forward, the sedan following in their wake.

As they marched to the south gates they passed the Large Goose Pagoda on the left. The temple bells were ringing and the monks were chanting for compassion and freedom from the world's sorrows. Minister Li gave a snort of contempt, but when they passed the Small Monk Monastery he pulled the curtains of the chair back for a moment.

He had studied Daoism there in his youth. They had a revolving library, a huge cylinder of scrolls. He looked at the ruins, watched farmers ploughing between the crumbling walls, turning the frozen clods. The 'Greatest City under Heaven' was crumbling back to farmland. He nodded silently to himself and stared down into his open hand. Who would have thought the world would disintegrate so quickly?

As the Small Goose Pagoda came into view the minister let the curtains hang closed. His name was carved on that pagoda. He did not want to think of the excited young man who had written his name that day, paid the stone carver to chisel it into posterity, but the image leapt into view. Was she there that day?

Minister Li thought for a long while and decided, no, she wasn't. His memory had her there – laughing and

4

clapping her hands – and he could see the glossy sheen of sunlight in her hair, her teeth as she put her head back to laugh, but he hadn't met her yet.

No, he thought to himself. Not yet.

AD 850

At the Last Fort Under Heaven the water-clock marked the changing of the watch. Off-duty conscripts went to the wine shops and then the mess hall, where steamed buns and simple dishes of cabbage and pickles were served out by the ladleful. A few thought of their homelands where their memories of happiness waited. In the mornings they went to the Temple of Guan Gong, burnt incense to carry their prayers heavenward: a fat wife and fat children, rich fields – far away from tax collectors.

'Mountains have peaks,' the second Tang Emperor's treatise on government read, 'so order has its limits.' His advice on barbarians was to subdue them with 'goods, learning and marriage'. Folk still remembered the Chinese princesses: doomed to spend their life in a chieftain's yurt, not a tranquil garden, far away from the beacon of learning. Concubine Hua sang the 'Lament of Wen Cheng' to her daughter as she waited for the marshal to return; sang as she spun raw wool into thread, *clack! clack!* as the loom turned thread into cloth.

'There!' she said, when the cloth was finished, cut it from the loom and held it up.

Little Hope's face was cold in the candlelight, her eyes bright.

'When will Father be back?' she asked.

Concubine Hua put the cloth down. 'When the Emperor returns him,' she said.

Little Hope nodded. The Emperor lived far away in Changan; he sent officials into each village to rule them according to Heaven's laws; sent soldiers north, south, east and west; defined the border between civilisation and barbarian with watch towers and customs houses; kept her father away, left her mother sad.

'Why did he go?'

'To capture horses.'

'Why?' Little Hope asked.

'Because the army needs horses,' Concubine Hua told her, 'to keep the barbarians out.'

That night Little Hope lay in bed as her mother sat and stitched mallard ducks into a new mattress cover. A pair of ducks was a sign of fidelity: they mated for life, like husband and wife. Blue silk thread for the duck's wings, the midday sky and the core of a candle flame. Little Hope looked away from the candle and up at the rafters – there were faded gold dragons on faded red, half hidden in shadow. She thought of her father's scraggly beard, of being lifted up, of him feeding her fat pork dumplings, carrying her to bed. She thought about when Father would return. She would never let him leave again. She would keep him safe at home. When summer came they could go south to his home town, leave the cold grasslands behind.

Concubine Hua trimmed the rush wick, sat on the bed, close to her daughter.

'What are you thinking about?' she asked, but Little Hope shook her head.

7

'Shall I tell you a story?'

Little Hope nodded.

Concubine Hua told her a story about the fantastical west, but Little Hope's attention wandered.

'I want to hear about Father's hometown,' she said.

Concubine Hua didn't know much about the marshal's hometown, except that it was south of the capital, in Wushan Prefecture. She knew little more about his family. His father was a censor in the local government. He had a brother who was a magistrate, a sister who had died giving birth to her fourth child.

'Your father's father is very kind,' Concubine Hua told her daughter. 'You'll eat meat every day, wear silken slippers and marry a fine young scholar.'

'What's Father's hometown like?' Little Hope said and Concubine Hua half-laughed.

'Well,' she said, and began to imagine aloud: wide avenues and broad streets; high ramparts with tall gatehouses; in the centre of town a huge drum tower with a kettledrum so large it took ten men to lift. Little Hope listened wide-eyed, but the next day as she played Little Hope remembered the story of the western deserts, not the story of the marshal's hometown.

'In the west the sands are so vast that they swallow whole rivers!' her mother had said, and Little Hope imagined rivers sinking into the desert, puddles so sandy the fish jumped out to breathe, magnificent dragons turning into puffs of steam, sunlight like a furnace flame. Dragons were dangerous beasts, Little Hope knew, proud and playful and violently destructive. Her mother had grown up near the Yellow River, so she knew all about dragons and the trouble they could cause. Each year the river flooded, and each year families drowned. Once, when her mother was a child, her family had to climb a tree. Her father had

8

tried to haul the family pig up as well, her mother said, but it was too heavy and they left it squealing in alarm as the yellow waters rose, rose so high the squeals turned to gurgles, and the gurgles to bubbles, and then the bubbles stopped altogether. They watched a buffalo swim to a tree, still pulling its plough, and lost count of the pots, wheels, pitchers, cauldrons, barrels and bins that went spinning past in the endless water.

The river shifted course that year, kept her mother's family's fields for good. That was why her mother had become a concubine, not a wife. Little Hope knew that story well. Her mother's family gave everything they had to the dragons: that was why they'd sold their daughter.

'I'd been promised as wife to the son of one of my father's friends,' her mother told her one afternoon, as she was hanging out their mattresses in the fine spring weather, 'but he died young and I became a concubine.'

Wives had status, Little Hope understood. They ruled the family when their husbands died, were obeyed by children and servants, had their names entered in the family genealogy. Concubines were less than servants: they could be bought and sold like slaves, didn't even own their children.

'Will Father's wife take me away?' Little Hope asked that night.

'I don't think so,' Concubine Hua said.

'No?'

'No,' Concubine Hua said, as she worked the loom.

There was a long pause as the candlelight flickered against the whitewashed wall.

'Why?'

'Because you are a girl,' Concubine Hua said.

Little Hope turned away, and Concubine Hua felt she had spoken a little too harshly. She stretched out a tickling hand but Little Hope refused to smile. Concubine Hua had to pick her daughter up and hold her. 'You'll never be a concubine like me.' Concubine Hua kissed the top of her daughter's head. 'I'll find you a husband, I promise.'

'I don't want a husband,' Little Hope said, and her mother laughed.

When it was time for sleep Concubine Hua snuggled in next to her daughter and blew out the candle: her brightly lit face, the room, the embroidered mallard ducks gone in a puff of breath. The glowing wick watched them for a moment, then shut its eye, and Little Hope shivered, cuddled close to her mother.

What would happen if her lover did not return? Concubine Hua thought, as she tossed and turned and tried to sleep. For each man there is a patch of sky, the saying went, but it said nothing about woman. Women were nothing more than overcoats: tried on for size and then discarded. If the marshal did not return, she must find her daughter a good husband, Concubine Hua told herself. She would find Little Hope a good husband, then travel south, attach her destiny to that of another man.

———

When the marshal had been away five months, Concubine Hua visited the captain. The captain's wife spent her days at the rear of the house, in a private courtyard, but he entertained visitors in the front yard, bounded on three sides by yellow-tiled halls with carved lattice windows, painted in gaudy red, yellow and blue.

The captain sat in the main hall, brazier coals rippling the air; his youngest son, fat and hungry and sprawled in his lap. Another chair was brought, the braziers moved to be close to his guest. The captain poured the tea himself, handed across the cup, with a smile.

'No news?' he said, after the pleasantries were over.

'None.'

'Don't be worried.'

'I wasn't,' Concubine Hua said. 'The marshal said to worry when the autumn was here. Not before.'

The captain laughed. 'Yes, that's true. They should be on their way home now.'

Concubine Hua tried to smile but the fact he was already telling her to not worry made her uneasy. She remembered the story about rivers drowning in sand. It seemed an unlucky tale to have told.

'I mean to go and visit the White Water Falls,' she said to the captain. 'To pray for the marshal's safe return.'

The captain looked up and nodded. 'I will send my servant with you,' he started, but Concubine Hua cut him off.

'I will go alone,' she told him. 'All I need is a horse.'

Little Hope was still asleep when Concubine Hua lifted her from bed, carried her, wrapped in a blanket, to the fort stables. A cavalry pony snorted in the morning chill. They mounted and trotted out of the south gate, the road paved with grooved slabs of quarried stone. Little Hope dreamt of dragons flying and goddesses floating on long silken scarves. One of them lifted her in her arms and they flew west, out over the sea: the goddess's upper body was naked, her hair was tied in a top-knot.

'I'm taking you to see the Fire Mountains,' she told Little Hope, and Little Hope tried to push her off but she held her close and lifted her clear of the ground. The clouds swirled all around them; the sensation of flying was like riding a horse.

The five miles were long and quiet and empty. To either side they could feel the mountains, folded one on top of another; clouds and forests mixed together – grey and black – under a lavender sky. After a while they passed a staging post on the left – a hut with a stable larger than itself – around which the smell of horse dung lingered.

'Are we going to the capital?'

Concubine Hua laughed. 'No,' she said. 'We're going to the monastery.'

'What monastery?'

'White Water Monastery.'

'Why?'

Concubine Hua explained that in Heaven there was an emperor with ministers and officials just like on earth. 'The officials in Heaven are as interested in bribes as those on earth,' she said.

Little Hope thought deeply. 'Is it expensive to bribe the gods?' she asked, and Concubine Hua smiled.

'Ma?' Little Hope said after they had gone a little further.

'Hmm.'

'Is it far?'

'No,' Concubine Hua said, and Little Hope looked deep into the forests of pine and cedar.

The temple was in a narrow gorge a few miles north of the town of Diyi. Concubine Hua could see the distant haze of dust trodden streets, imagined the noise and bustle, and wished she had never been sold, had never met the marshal. A woman married to a dog will follow the dog; she who marries the chicken will follow the chicken. Sayings were all very clever, Concubine Hua thought, but what happens when the chicken is cut up and boiled for soup?

They turned off the road, along a mountain path that followed a mountain stream. To their right was a mossy cliff: as it bent, the path and stream bent with it, coiling into the forests. Soon they were out of sight of the road, only the hoof prints in the mud to show that they had passed. The further they went the colder the air became, the louder the water, the thicker the ranks of pines. Pines were like fathers, Little Hope thought, tall and proud and upright.

Around another corner they could see the thatched roofs of White Water Monastery, huddled together under a tall cliff, where a single ribbon of water fell into a dark pool. Concubine Hua tied the horse to the stone pillar. Little Hope kept away from the pool. In the still forest air, the waterfall splashing sounded melancholy, like sobbing.

'Be careful,' Concubine Hua said, but when her back was turned Little Hope ran over to see the stream, stopped an arm's reach away from the edge. The water and rocks were dark against the splattered white foam. Spray chilled her face.

'Come away!' Concubine Hua said and pulled Little Hope well away from the stream, but when she went inside Little Hope wandered back, thought of the pig the Yellow River Dragon had stolen, how the stream would seize her as well if she went any nearer. 'Tell the Yellow River Dragon,' Little Hope shouted at the white foaming water, 'that he made my mother a concubine!'

The temple porch was painted with all kinds of terrifying demons. One had a bull's head, a screaming man in one fist and a halberd in the other. Little Hope looked at them and paused. 'Ma?' she called, the dark doorway swallowing her thin and small voice.

'Ma?'

Little Hope looked at the blue-skinned monster and wanted to cry.

'Ma?' she called again and felt the tears bubble up. Little Hope imagined her father taking her hand and leading her inside. 'Come along,' his grip seemed to say. 'Let's see Mother.'

Little Hope stepped forward, eyes on the blue-skinned demon all the way. 'Ma?' she said, voice trembling, waiting for her eyes to get used to the dark.

Little Hope's mother was kneeling in the corner of the room, where gold glimmered in the splash of candlelight. 'Ma!' Little Hope said as she ran over, but her mother kept kowtowing. 'Ma,' Little Hope said, but her mother wasn't listening: she was praying to the Laughing Buddha. Little Hope stared at the sticks of incense leaning on each other for support, sandalwood smoke threading itself up through the beams. After a while she got bored of waiting, knocked an incense stick into the ash, knocked over another, began to hum a tuneless melody.

'Ma-a?' she said again, took hold of her mother's sleeve. 'Ma-aa?'

'Ssh!' her mother said and gave her a stick of incense and helped her light it in the candle flame. When the flames had taken root she held it in front of Little Hope's face.

'Blow it out,' she said, but Little Hope didn't want to so Concubine Hua blew it out herself.

'Bow three times,' her mother told her, but Little Hope refused.

'I don't like him,' she said, and pointed at the Buddha.

'Put the incense in the pot,' Concubine Hua said, in her this-is-your-last-time voice, but Little Hope threw the incense on to the floor and started crying before Concubine Hua had even raised her hand. The Buddha's expression did not change as Concubine Hua slapped her daughter on the back of the legs. The noise was muffled by the thick padded trousers, but Little Hope fell on to her bottom and wailed.

'Get up!' Concubine Hua said but Little Hope refused to stand.

'I'm leaving!' she said but Little Hope kept crying and the Buddha still chuckled at the sorrows of life, double chin and fat cheeks and robes flowing over his enormous gut.

'I'm going,' Concubine Hua called over her shoulder but Little Hope paused only for breath. 'The gods aren't interested in tears,' Concubine Hua shouted from the doorway and Little Hope sniffed a little while longer, then rubbed her eyes and wished that her father would come back to take her hand again. Come along, let's see Mother, she thought, as if they were the magic words – even though she didn't want to see Mother any more. Come along, let's see the horse, she thought, eyes squeezed shut, but the feeling of his presence didn't come back to her. She tried to see her father's face but she couldn't picture him, only the Western Desert, waves of sand and a dried-up riverbed.

When Concubine Hua returned the horse to the stables the captain of the fort was there, talking to the stable boys. He himself had been riding, a boy was scraping the mud from his grey gelding's legs; steam was rising from the sweaty flanks.

Concubine Hua handed her daughter down, dismounted, let the captain take the reins. 'How was she?' the captain asked as he patted the horse's neck.

'Fine.'

The captain patted the horse's neck again, scratched at the base of the mane.

'Autumn nights are long and cold.'

'So I hear,' Concubine Hua said.

The captain's hand brushed her sleeve and she gave him a warning look, hurried home.

Concubine Hua hugged Little Hope to her chest. After the candle had been blown out Little Hope asked, 'When will Father come home?'

'Maybe tomorrow,' Concubine Hua said, but each tomorrow was as empty as yesterday, or today.

Maybe tomorrow. Little Hope played day after day. Maybe tomorrow, maybe never, kept chanting in her head till the words lost cohesion and meaning.

In the ninth month the hillside forests turned a deep red. The hillsides appeared to be on fire – not even the chill misty mornings could extinguish the flames. In the narrow lanes of the fort village the autumn leaves toppled over each other. They piled up against the stacks of gorse kindling and dried sheep dung. Little Hope played with them, picking up armfuls and dropping them back to the ground. She tried to avoid the main road, which was long and empty and stretched all the way to the Diyi. She remembered how her mother had said it ran all the way to the capital.

All roads led to Changan, Little Hope remembered, just like all lives led to Heaven.

'How far is the capital?' Little Hope asked one day after dinner.

'Two weeks,' her mother guessed.

'Walking?'

'No,' her mother laughed, 'by boat. By foot it'd take at least a month.'

'Can we go there?'

'No,' Concubine Hua said and Little Hope stretched her legs and looked at her worn cloth shoes, embroidered with tiger faces. 'We don't know anyone,' Concubine Hua told her. 'Imagine that big city. We'd be lost inside it!'

Little Hope did imagine the big city: five times as big as the Last Fort Under Heaven! It was just like her father's hometown, but larger and more magnificent. There was a drum tower and a bell tower, temples and palaces and tall brick pagodas. The Emperor lived in his palace with ten thousand concubines – all young and pretty like her mother. Maybe Little Hope would go and join them as a wife, not a concubine. She imagined herself as the Empress, eating dragon and phoenix soup every day, sitting in a room hung with crystal hangings, ten serving girls to play soft music.

The next day dark clouds wandered south from the grass-lands, bringing long, cold rain. Little Hope stood at the open doorway, watched the thatch drip-drip on to the floor, thought of the White Water Dragon thundering to the Eastern Sea.

'Ma,' she said, after a long while.

'Hmm.'

'I'm bored.'

Concubine Hua pulled a book of simple calligraphy out from under the folded bedsheets. 'Practise,' she said.

Little Hope let out a long sigh and fetched her brush. The handle was worn and the tip was split, but she dipped it into water and wrote neat girl characters. 'Ma!' she said after a few minutes. 'Watch!' Concubine Hua made a show of watching as Little Hope dabbed her brush, wrote clear water strokes on the stone steps, the characters drying and fading before she could finish the next.

'See how much better their handwriting is.' Concubine Hua pointed at the wet bird tracks, scribbled in the mud. 'That's because you do not practise.'

Little Hope sat back on her heels and stared. She hadn't known that her characters were so bad.

* * *

Winter came hard and hungry and ruthless, like returning brigands. Each morning Little Hope had to practise her calligraphy and recite simple texts. Sometimes there was a word that she didn't know. Her mother would bring the paper close to her face and squint, but usually she didn't know it either.

'Go ask someone else,' she said and Little Hope ran out into the lane to find someone who could read. Sometimes she forgot what she was going for and wandered through the fort, watched the cold birds descend on scraps of food – ran at them screaming, laughed when they flapped up in alarm.

One day Little Hope was returning with the word in her head when she saw a fat woman, leaning on a carrying pole, eating a cold steamed bun. Old Fart had spent the night helping the captain's wife give birth. The smell of blood lingered in her mouth as she chewed the fatty pork and watched the little girl walk towards her.

The captain's wife had screamed and cursed Heaven and Earth; she was a city girl, unused to hard effort. In Old Fart's village the women squatted in the fields to give birth, like dogs. They only called on Old Fart when something went wrong. She would stand over them and watch their lives run out in puddles of blood on the floor – like pigs when their throats were slit. You could get a bucket of blood in a matter of seconds. Then there was nothing that could be done. It was hard for peasant girls, Old Fart thought, but the Heavenly Census was meticulous: when their time came, their time came. If they were not due to die the Provost of Heaven sent their spirits back. It was all decided in Heaven.

'He'll make a soldier like his father,' the captain's wife had said, and Old Fart grunted. Why bring more soldiers into the world to cause more suffering she thought, then thought of the money she had been paid, two strings of a thousand copper cash, and smiled. For each man Heaven produces, Earth provides a grave.

Old Fart watched the little girl with the book in her hand and took another bite.

'Girl,' the woman called out and Little Hope stopped. 'Who's your father?'

Little Hope pointed north. 'The marshal.'

'Where does he live?'

'He's in the grasslands.'

'Where's your mother?' Old Fart asked.

Little Hope pointed towards their lane.

'Is she in?' Old Fart asked, put the half eaten bun back into her bag.

No, the girl shook her head, she's not.

Old Fart looked at the girl and smiled a toothy smile, ruffled the little girl's head. 'I like you,' Old Fart said and Little Hope bit her lip and turned away, carrying her book carefully, not sure what she should have said.

News of the captain's third son spread through the fort. Little Hope celebrated by holding a little feast on the table, where she poured the wine and served the food to her guests. She climbed on to the bed to reach the bag of offcuts her mother kept, pulled a scrap of striped silk out, spread it over the bamboo table like a picnic cloth. The soy pot was the captain, the chilli the captain's wife, her mother was the vinegar. Little Hope took a handful of unmilled wheat and put it on to the table. She handed the grains out one by one, giving the captain's wife extra for her son.

Concubine Hua was not in the mood for picnics. 'Stop making such a mess!' she scolded, when she came back with a half frozen cabbage in her basket, frail snowflakes sticking to her shoulders and hair.

Little Hope scooped up the wheat kernels and ran to the

door, watched the white feather flakes falling softly to the ground, imagined them filling the mountain valleys with silence.

'Come inside!' her mother snapped, and Little Hope wished she could watch the snow fall as her mother slammed the door shut, dropped a few more lumps of charcoal into the fire.

Little Hope practised her writing slowly and unhappily, wishing she could go out and play. But all the while the snow kept falling and she had to write out stupid characters. When her mother went behind the screen in the corner to squat over the chamber pot, Little Hope ran to the window, stuck a finger through the paper and put her eye to the hole. Each time her mother was distracted Little Hope returned to the hole. After a few hours the snow was so deep her excitement was too much to contain. 'Ma!' she called, the words misting around her head as she peered through the hole. 'Come and look!'

'Go see how deep the snow is,' Concubine Hua said to stop her daughter playing.

Little Hope looked up from the wheat kernels, ran across to the doorway and reached up to the latch. 'Knee high,' she said, enjoying being useful, skipping back to the bedside.

'Why not go and play,' Concubine Hua said.

'Outside?' Little Hope said and her mother nodded.

'Outside,' Concubine Hua said.

Little Hope ran outside, left Little Hope footsteps in circles in the snow, laughed out loud when the circles kept following her through the gloom. She laughed down the alley towards the parade ground, the footsteps always just behind – however fast she ran. From the barracks a flute sounded. Little Hope stood with her mouth open, catching flakes on her tongue, the sad tune clear in the white cold.

When she got back Little Hope started to tell her mother

about the snow but Concubine Hua said abruptly, 'Mother is tired.'

Mai-bee-tom-aw-row. Little Hope hummed tunelessly as she drew invisible words with her dry brush. *Mai-bee-tom-aw-row*.

Concubine Hua tried to ignore her as she warmed a pot of wine on the fire, watched the dark shadows of flakes fluttering in front of the window paper like windblown petals. *Mai-bee-tom-aw-row*. Concubine Hua poured herself a cup of wine; poured herself another. *Mai-bee-tom-aw-row*. After half a pot Concubine Hua couldn't swallow her feelings any more. 'Shut up!' she snapped, and Little Hope sat down and picked at her nails. *Mai-bee-tom-aw-row*, she thought. After a while she started to cry. The noise was worse than the humming and Concubine Hua had to pick her up.

'Mother's sorry,' Concubine Hua said. 'Mother's sorry.'

At last Little Hope sniffed and wiped her eyes.

'Can I go and play again?'

'Alright,' Concubine Hua said, 'but don't be long.'

When Little Hope came in that night she was so hungry and cold that even her shadow shivered. Concubine Hua hugged and kissed her and scolded her, piled the brazier full of charcoal, took it outside and fanned it till the flames began to crackle and dance. She stood in the snow, let the acrid smoke burn off, then carried the brazier back inside.

Concubine Hua held her daughter's hands over the fire and rubbed her body up and down. When her daughter had stopped shivering she boiled some soup with dried seaweed, added a smear of pig fat, stirred it in to make the liquid shine.

'Mother is sorry,' Concubine Hua said and Little Hope drank the broth slowly and deliberately.

'Will you tell me a story?' she asked when she was sitting tucked in bed.

'Not tonight,' Concubine Hua said. 'Mother is too sad for stories.'

Little Hope sniffed and wiped her nose, waited for her mother to tip the coals into the stove under the bed, the hard earth kang slowly warming.

'I don't think your father is coming back,' Concubine Hua said and Little Hope looked up. 'I think he's dead.'

Little Hope wanted to tell her mother that she had asked the Yellow River Dragon to let her father go, but her mother didn't seem to be in the mood to listen. Little Hope sniffed and wiped her nose again, curled a lock of hair round her finger and sucked it, thought of the pines in the forest, slowly bending under the weight of the snow.

That night, as Little Hope slept, Concubine Hua lay awake, thinking of the fate that had led her to this. She thought of the captain coming to tell her the marshal was alive; thought of the ambassador a Tang emperor had sent to the Western Barbarians who married the daughter of some wild chieftain; took fifteen years to return to court. He was honoured for his services to the throne, but Concubine Hua knew that she would never wait that long. She didn't have the strength to live all alone.

The grasslands knew a hundred ways of killing a man: the steppes soil was stained red. Concubine Hua thought of the man she had held at night out on the open plains: blades of grass piercing his eye sockets, a ladder of white rib bones in the green spring grass. In her head Concubine Hua could hear the marshal joking that beheading was just a bowl-shaped wound, but now it no longer seemed so funny. There was no poverty worse than begging, no disaster greater than death.

That winter was hard and lonely. Concubine Hua stopped combing her hair; stopped hugging her daughter; stopped

22

telling her stories. It was sad that she and the marshal would never share hardships again, she told herself, as she sat and drank warm rice wine; it was sad she was young and alone and son-less.

Little Hope went out and walked the narrow lanes alone.

'Poor child,' the other women of the fort said to her, gave her candied crab apples. 'Poor orphan child!'

Little Hope took them without saying thank you and ate them straight away. If she took them home her mother became angry and shouted that now her daughter had become a beggar. Heaven was kind, some people said, but during those cold dark months, it seemed to Concubine Hua and Little Hope that Heaven was very high and very far away.

With the spring and the paired swallows, Old Fart returned and knocked on Concubine Hua's brushwood gate. There was no answer so she pushed inside. The brass chain rattled as she stepped over the threshold and into the yard, saw thin smoke coming from the mud-brick chimney, noticed how low the woodpile was. Old Fart sniffed contentedly and spat, stumped across the yard and knocked on the doorway. She could hear the clink-clank of a loom.

'Hello,' she called, pushed the door open.

Concubine Hua thought it was the captain's wife at first, then saw an unfamiliar shape and stood up flustered, pulled out a stool.

'You are the marshal's concubine?'

'I am,' Concubine Hua said. 'And you are?'

'Old Fart.'

'The midwife?'

Old Fart chuckled. 'Yes,' she said. 'That is true.'

The two women stared at each other amused and perplexed.

'I am not pregnant,' Concubine Hua said and Old Fart slapped her hands together and cackled.

'I did not think you were!'

There was a long silence as Concubine Hua got up, took the lid off the soot-black cauldron, used a copper dipper to pour them both a cup of clear warm water. Old Fart took a long sip, took a packet out of her sack, handed it over.

'This is for you.'

Concubine Hua opened the oil paper, found a catty of dried lamb, cut into strips. The meat was spiced with hot pepper oil; the oil was red, the streaks of fat were orange. Concubine Hua had not eaten meat for weeks, but even so she folded the paper back down. 'This is too kind,' she said, and handed the package back, 'but we are not so poor.'

'Take it!' Old Fart insisted, but each time Concubine Hua tried to give it back Old Fart pushed away her hands till at last Concubine Hua gave up, stared at the packet in her lap.

'I can't take this,' she said, but Old Fart put a hand out and touched her arm.

'Take it. I have a son who needs a wife,' Old Fart explained. 'We could join our families.'

'My daughter?' Concubine Hua asked and Old Fart nodded and sat back.

'But she's only seven,' Concubine Hua said.

Old Fart could see the confusion in Concubine Hua's face. 'Teach a child when an infant,' she advised. 'Teach a wife when she is young.'

Concubine Hua understood. She stared at a spray of white peach blossom Little Hope had brought home that morning, still speckled with dewdrops.

'I was five when I was bought.' Old Fart smiled. 'My husband and I were playmates. Daughters stay no longer than spring flowers. Sons are like houses – they shelter you in your old age.' Old Fart sat forward and spoke confidentially.

Concubine Hua kept nodding but she was wondering how low had she sunk that peasants approached her for her daughter. It was only when Old Fart said, 'You are young and pretty, but who wants to adopt another man's daughter?' that she knew the sense of what the midwife was saying. A single woman is much prettier than a mother and child.

A few weeks later the leaves were budding and the swallows began to build their mud-nests under the eaves and in the corner of the fort walls. Little Hope sat on her bottom and looked up at a nest above their doorway, the tiny bird appearing from the hole, then flying off and flying back, adding another beakful of red dirt. Concubine Hua sat in the doorway and threaded a needle. 'I had a visitor,' she said, and Little Hope looked across the threshold. 'She wants you to marry her eldest son,' Concubine Hua continued. 'She is kind and wealthy. She will treat you like her own daughter.'

Little Hope's pet grasshopper crawled out of her pocket. She felt the movement and cupped the grasshopper in both hands, nodded seriously. The grasshopper crawled free from her sweaty grasp. Little Hope flicked it gently, thinking it would fly, but it lay on its side, waved its antennae as a sign of weary capitulation. Little Hope flicked it hard this time: *crack!* as her nail connected with the green shell. It sailed off across the yard.

'Does that mean I will leave?' Little Hope asked after a long pause.

Concubine Hua looked back at her stitching.

'We will still see each other,' she tried to sound cheerful, 'and when you are old enough you will become a *wife*.'

That night Little Hope lay and looked at the faded dragons on the ceiling and thought of the Yellow River Dragon who had swallowed her mother's family's fields.

'Ma, when I get married, will you come to the wedding?'

'Yes,' Concubine Hua said.

There was a long silence.

'Ma?'

'Hmm.'

'On my birthday will you still cook long life noodles?'

'No,' Concubine Hua said but this time she didn't turn.

'Will you,' Little Hope began again, but her mother put her hand to her face and her body started to shake. Little Hope looked back at the swirling dragons and didn't know what to say or do. 'I love you Ma,' she said, but her voice seemed far away, even to herself.

———————

It was past noon when Old Fart arrived at the outskirts of the village, large and fat and hungry. The little girl was strapped to her back like a trussed piglet; Old Fart adjusted the cords, made sure that they were not slipping, drew one arm across her forehead, wiped away the sweat.

'Look!' she said and the face in the bundle looked. The village was set half way up a hill to the east of the main road, a collection of thatched houses huddled on top of each other. The spring ploughed fields were set out like cloths on the mountain slopes, neat and regular; the path to the spring was well trodden and steep.

'Wang Family Village,' Old Fart declared. 'And your father is the headman there.'

Little Hope wanted to say that her father was a marshal and that he was in the grasslands and that he was never coming back.

'When you are old enough to marry we will build you a house,' Old Fart sniffed to clear her nostrils, spat once more, 'and you will give me many grandsons.'

Little Hope said nothing as Old Fart grinned over her shoulder. 'Hungry?' she asked but Little Hope didn't answer. 'You must be!' Old Fart told her, stomped up the path to her house, banged on the gate. There were voices inside, shouting and footsteps running in the snow. The bolts were drawn back, the wood scraped on the yard's brick floor, the doors swung wide. Old Fart barged through and saw her three sons. Number One and Number Two saw her and ran inside. Number Three ducked too late. Her hand caught him on the back of the head, knuckle hard. She followed the blow by grabbing him by the nape and swatting him again.

'I thought you were supposed to be looking out for me!' she snapped and Headman Wang came running out of the house, a sheepskin blanket wrapped round his shoulders, his bare feet poking out underneath his homespun trousers, black shin hairs standing up in alarm.

'I've been walking all day!' Old Fart shouted.

Headman Wang stammered something, but stopped just out of range and ran back into the house.

'Water!' he shouted at Number One and Number Two. 'Heat the water!'

Old Fart adjusted the straps on her back, listened to the shouts and threats of her husband with a snort of satisfaction, then stumped round the corner, found the black sow snuzzling in the snow.

'Who let the pig out?'

Headman Wang appeared in the doorway. He stared at the pig – took Number Two Son by the scruff of his coat and thrust him into the snow. Number Two Son kicked the sow towards the hut. Old Fart would have kicked him in turn, but being angry had lost its initial pleasure. She was cold and hungry and wanted to get inside.

'Is the kang warm?' Old Fart demanded and her husband rushed to the mud-brick bed, and made a fuss of checking the fire underneath. He shoved more charcoal inside and slammed the grate shut.

Old Fart let the bundle slip from her back on to the bed. She set it in the middle, then slid herself next to it, first one buttock then the other, folded her legs up and crossed them in one single movement.

The bundle had a face and hands.

'What's her name?' Headman Wang said.

'Little Hope,' Old Fart said.

The three grubby boys came closer to peer in at the little girl, and the little girl peered back. Number Two Son asked, 'How much did you pay for her?' and Old Fart laughed. 'Only twenty strings of cash.'

The first night in her new home, Little Hope snuggled up close to the unfamiliar bodies. There was no one to tell her stories at night, no one to watch her practise calligraphy, no one to tell her not to go out. The next morning Old Fart and her sons were up early to stoke the fire and draw water from the well. Little Hope lay in bed with Headman Wang, pretended she was still asleep and listened to the rumble of slow boiling water. After a while Headman Wang sat up and coughed. Little Hope kept her eyes shut and burrowed deeper into the warm blankets, but Headman Wang put his hand under the sheets and found her foot, moved up past the ankle, up her leg, squeezed her thigh. 'She's thin,' he announced to Old Fart. 'We'll need to fatten her up.'

Little Hope thought of her mother and wished that she were there. 'I will come and see you at times,' she had promised. 'They will treat you as a daughter,' she'd said. 'You go and be a good girl.'

Little Hope squeezed her eyes shut. Ma, I will be a good girl, she promised. I will be a good girl.

The Wang family ate quickly and noisily; Old Fart distributed food as she saw fit, taking one dumpling from Number One and giving it to Number Three; one from her husband and giving it to Little Hope.

Headman Wang grinned down the table at Little Hope, lumps of dumpling between his teeth, flying across the table as he spoke. 'You're in the Wang family now,' he grinned. 'We have lived in this village for over a thousand years!'

'This is Number One Son!' he said and pointed with his chopsticks. Number One Son looked down into his earthenware dumpling bowl, chipped and unglazed on the outside. 'You'll marry him.' Headman Wang spoke louder than anyone else Little Hope knew. A lump of chewed dumpling skin landed in Little Hope's bowl. She picked it out, didn't feel hungry any more.

Number One Son caught Little Hope's eye, then blushed and looked down at his bowl where a single fat dumpling looked back up at him. 'Here!' he said and reached across and put his last dumpling in Little Hope's bowl. Little Hope looked at the dumpling and didn't want to eat it. Number Two Son and Number Three Son both sniggered; Number One Son's face went red.

'Eat it!' Old Fart told her and Little Hope put her head to the bowl and chewed slowly.

When they had finished Old Fart lit a single stick of incense at the family shrine, made Little Hope kowtow nine times as they presented her to the ancestors. That night they told her stories of all the Wangs who had lived there before them. 'My people came from Weinan County,' Headman Wang told Little Hope, 'in the time of the Qin Emperor.'

Little Hope tried to hold back a yawn as stories followed one another, like generations. She clenched her jaw to keep the sleepiness inside, prayed that her mother would come and take her back home. At one point the door rattled and Little Hope bit her lip and hoped, but when Old Fart went out to get more wood there was nothing outside but cold and dark and stars.

'You'll know all the stories soon enough,' Old Fart told her as she went to bed. 'I remember the first night I came here. I was only just a little younger than you.'

Little Hope wondered whether Old Fart's mother had ever come back for her. 'Oh, no,' Old Fart chuckled, 'and even if she had I'd have never left the Wang Family Village. Life here is good and plain and simple,' she said. 'My old village was poor, the people were not kind. We were so poor that my mother used to smear us all with lard to keep us warm in winter.'

That night Old Fart tried to remember her mother's face and could not. All she remembered was a smell of pig fat, long hair and two arms picking her up to kiss her goodbye. 'You go with the lady now,' Old Fart's mother had said and let go of her daughter's hand. 'Be obedient and hard working. Obey your father-in-law and your husband and your husband's mother.' And she had, Old Fart told herself, and put one arm round Little Hope.

Old Fart's arm was heavier and thicker than her mother's. In fact everything was different: the smell of the sheets, the cramped bodies, the way the food tasted. I will be good, Little Hope told her mother and imagined her mother getting very angry with her and slapping the back of her legs. I promise I will be good, Little Hope thought and when tears began to spill, she wiped them away and used the blankets to stifle any sound.

Life was not too hard at the Wang Family Village. Old Fart treated Little Hope with all the kindness she possessed: instructed her how to sweep the floor, haul the bucket up from the well without spilling it and how to wash and clean cabbage for pickling. When the warm weather came the bleak fields sprouted green stubble. Old Fart gathered the silkworms as they hatched, spread them out on wide wicker trays and gave Little Hope the job of feeding them mulberry leaves. Basket after basket of green leaves turned the small pale worms large and fat and bloated. When the worms began to weave their cocoons, Little Hope sat and rested, watched the hillsides brighten with wild flowers, heard the orioles singing to each other, tried to pretend she was back with her mother.

Mai-bee-tom-aw-row, she hummed to herself, forgetting what it meant, but sometimes Little Hope daydreamed that her father came home and both of her parents came to the Wang Family Village. But by the beginning of summer no one had come for her and she helped gather up all the pale cocoons and heat the fire. 'More wood!' Old Fart shouted, and Little Hope ran from the door to the wood-pile. 'Quickly!' Old Fart called, and Little Hope teetered under the stack of wood, trying to be quick and trying not to spill any. She dropped the pile at Old Fart's feet and knelt down to throw the split wood into the grate, the glow of fire hot on her cheeks.

The list of jobs was never ending. After a few weeks it was time to unpick boiled cocoons and spin the thread. Little Hope fed handfuls of the cold dead worms to the sow, who scattered scraps of half eaten worms around the yard; a few brave birds hopped in close enough to feed. As the days got longer and warmer, the green stubble in the fields grew knee high, and Old Fart sat in her yard with Little Hope, entertained the other women with stories as they sat grinding wheat, and spinning silk threads, which turned into cloth on Old Fart's loom, *click-clack, click-clack*, all day long.

'Can I go outside?' Little Hope asked after lunch but Old Fart would have none of it.

'Come and sleep,' she said. 'Come here and sleep with me.'

Little Hope didn't mind being told not to go out. She didn't mind because she got to snuggle up close to Old Fart, large breasts and fat arms. Old Fart's breath smelt of raw garlic. Close up, she saw a birthmark on the back of Old Fart's hand; a single black hair, growing long and straight. Moles were good luck, Little Hope remembered. Long mole hairs meant long life, her mother had told her.

After a while Little Hope could hear the little boys running back from the fields for their afternoon naps. She waited till she thought Old Fart was asleep, then began to climb down from the bed.

'Come back here!' Old Fart told her, sitting up enough to catch Little Hope by the shoulder. 'You need to rest, my child,' she said kindly, pulled her back into her bosom.

In midsummer there were odd, quiet days when the hours drifted aimlessly past, like white summer clouds. When Old Fart was away helping at a birth and the men were out in the fields, Little Hope ran to the top of the hill and looked out. Sometimes she lay down on the grass and talked to her mother.

'I am practising,' she lied. 'Yes, I can read all the characters now.'

It was difficult trying to keep up the conversations all alone. Sometimes she found herself talking to Old Fart instead and squeezed her eyes shut to concentrate, but her mother was less a person now than a patchwork of memories, propped up like a scarecrow – coarse stuffing coming out like the dummies at the fort. At night Little Hope dreamt that she helped to push the stuffing back in, but each night her mother came to her with more and deeper holes, and there was never enough time to repair all the damage. After a week Little Hope didn't like to dream any more, didn't like to wake to the feeling of helplessness, remembered the flute that had played on the day it had snowed, and understood why it had been playing with such pain.

———————

After Little Hope left, Concubine Hua sat alone, prayed that the Lord Buddha would be compassionate. There was more to karma than eating vegetables; she told herself that she had the child's best interests at heart.

After a few weeks Concubine Hua spent some of the money Old Fart had given her on powder and a few hairpins, started to pretty herself, went out to greet the new officers, cast shy seductive glances. 'She's the marshal's old concubine,' the captain of the fort told them later that day. 'He's been missing for a year now. In the grasslands. She just sold her daughter to a peasant.'

The men stopped looking at her then: the facts of her life seemed too misfortunate; ill-chance incarnate.

As the weeks and months slipped past, Concubine Hua wondered how she had aged so in the last year. Once she had picked through suitors, like vegetables in the market; now she looked for scraps, found nothing. She wished that Little Hope was still there to keep her company at night, but then she thought of the child with husband and fields and

33

family all around and consoled herself. It was for the best, she thought as her head lay on the pillow.

One autumn morning Concubine Hua woke up and found a basket of charcoal at her door. A week later there was a ball of good wool, then a catty of mutton and a bowl of innards, all cleaned and prepared for frying. Concubine Hua imagined that her daughter's spirit had brought them, but after a few more visits she looked out to see who her benefactor was – sat up late at night, got up early in the morning – saw no one.

Concubine Hua lay in bed and hoped it was an admirer. One afternoon the captain came to check on her and Concubine Hua knew it was him, almost clapped with delight. She stoked the fire, heated water, offered him a piece of Old Fart's mutton jerky.

'How is your daughter doing?' he asked after a while and Concubine Hua looked down at her hands.

'She is well,' she said.

'You are a good mother,' he said, took a sip of tea.

Concubine Hua blushed. She did not feel like a mother any more.

'How are your sons?'

'They are well.'

'And your wife?'

'She is tired these days,' he said. 'Babies need so much attention.'

'It is tiring work,' Concubine Hua admitted, and smiled again.

'You must miss the marshal,' the captain said.

Concubine Hua blushed and looked away, but when the captain stood up to leave Concubine Hua got up and showed him to the door. He paused in the half open doorway and touched her sleeve and she said nothing as he slid his fingers up the back of her arm, shut the door and stayed inside.

'Please,' Concubine Hua said, her voice hoarse, but she did nothing to stop him as he led her to the bed, untied her sash, let her gown fall open.

Concubine Hua continued to receive gifts at night, continued to receive the captain, let him use her as he would a common whore. One night she pulled at his jacket and asked him to stay the night.

'I can't.'

'Why not?'

'My wife will be suspicious.'

'You have not told her?'

'No,' he laughed, 'of course not.'

Concubine Hua lay awake that night thinking about what he had said and what he meant. Of course he had not told his wife, she convinced herself, because accepting a concubine into the household was a delicate matter. When the time was right he would tell his wife and take her in and she would be a concubine again. There were worse fates in the world for a woman.

Concubine Hua turned over, heard footsteps in the yard, then pushed herself up on her elbow.

'Darling,' she whispered, 'is that you?'

There was no answer. Concubine Hua raised her voice.

'Darling Captain,' she called, 'have you come to warm my bed?'

The captain's wife put the bowl of ginger down on the doorstep and hurried from the yard, wondering what 'darling captain' had meant.

The captain did not come back that week, or the next. Concubine Hua stood in her doorway in the morning and in the afternoon, but however much she looked for him he did not come. There were no more gifts for her on the doorstep.

Eventually Concubine Hua threw on the marshal's old otterskin coat, went to the captain's house and asked for him, but the servant said he was out.

'Is the mistress in?' Concubine Hua asked, but the old man shook his head.

'Everyone's out,' he said, and shut the door in her face.

Concubine Hua's period did not come that month. She went to the captain's office but he would not see her; when she went to his house he was always busy. He must have a good reason, she told herself, but still she wished that he had come to explain himself. He must have a reason, like a mantra, he is a good man.

Concubine Hua waited another month. She ate spicy food, drank too much wine, slept little, did not comb her hair. When the moon waxed full again she felt giddy. Her breasts were larger, her stomach felt bloated, her tiredness was unmistakable. This time it will be a son, Concubine Hua thought, imagined life as a concubine again rather than as a marshal's used slipper.

That night Concubine Hua heated some wine, dressed her hair, shook the folds from her best silk gown and battered on the captain's gate and refused to leave till he came in person.

'What do you want?' the captain hissed.

'Open the door!' Concubine Hua banged.

'My wife is here,' he told her.

'Then come to my house.'

'I can't.'

This time it was Concubine Hua who lowered her voice. 'I'm pregnant,' she whispered through the crack. 'I'm pregnant with your child!' She spoke as quietly and urgently as possible. 'He will be your son.'

'What do you mean my son?' the captain hissed back. 'It could be anyone's!'

The captain shut the gate and bolted it, left her standing outside, as unwanted as a pile of pig-shit. Concubine Hua kicked the gate and called the captain's personal name. 'You can't leave me out here!' she shouted. 'Without vengeance there are no gentlemen!' she told the heavens, hoped the marshal's ghost was listening.

'Is it your slut?' the captain's wife called back, her voice loud enough to carry over the wall. 'Why don't you tell her to go and jump down the well?'

That night Concubine Hua sat in her yard and wept, wailed and caused such a fuss that the neighbours came to see what was the matter. 'I've been raped!' Concubine Hua screamed, and the neighbours asked for the man's name. When Concubine Hua refused to give it to them they laughed at her. There were no waves without wind. A dog never mounted a bitch, they chuckled, unless she turned her back for him.

In the days that passed the neighbours shunned Concubine Hua's yard. She wept alone and cursed the Yellow River, cursed the marshal, cursed the captain of the fort and cursed Heaven for giving her this cruel fate. When she went to bed she wished she had Little Hope with her, and cursed the fate that left mothers without daughters. Day by day despair seeped under the door, filled her days and nights, choked the room right up to the rafters where the painted dragons whirled, round and round, in faded gold.

She slept all day, did not bother to comb her hair. After a week Concubine Hua could lie in despair no longer. She took out the few clothes she still had to pawn, found her jewellery box at the bottom of her chest, the hairpins and

37

earrings all rattling excitedly as she carried the box to her dressing-table. Her face was flushed as she picked out a green jade hairpin wrapped in fine gold leaf, gently unpeeled the gold from the cool carved stone, picked up the fragments and laid them down in the candlelight. She picked up a piece of foil between finger and thumb – the candlelight caught the crumpled facets of gold as she put it on her tongue: an oily texture and a strange warmth. She poured herself a little wine, washed down another piece, watched herself all the time in the polished bronze mirror as if it wasn't *her* eating gold, but her reflection.

When Concubine Hua had eaten all of the gold foil, she licked her finger and used the damp to gather all the crumbs together, licked it clean. When she had finished she took a deep breath, poured another cup of wine, drank it slowly, sat back on the bed.

She remembered the time a girl in her flower house had eaten gold. As soon as the madam had found out what she'd done she had taken a pillow and smothered the girl. It had taken two others to hold the pillow down. Dying people were so strong. She remembered the way the girl's hands had turned to eagle claws on the bedsheets, tearing at the cloth as she grappled for purchase. Even when her bladder had spread a pool of yellow urine across the bed, they had still pressed down with the pillow.

Concubine Hua had seen the girl's face as they removed the pillow: bruised and desperate, eyes and mouth open like a wild beast. They had shut her eyes and weighted them down with copper coins, tied her sash round her head to keep her mouth shut.

It was quicker that way, the madam had said. No one argued. There was no family to demand compensation. No one cared that much about a flower girl.

Concubine Hua poured more wine, felt her palms prickle with excitement and alarm. She stood up and walked around, then started laughing out loud. She drank another cup of wine, clapped her hands, felt almost like singing. She tipped the pot and toasted the moon in the branches, danced a few steps, all alone except for the moon and her shadow.

We are lodged in this world as in a great dream, she sang to herself.

Why let our lives cause us so much stress?

Concubine Hua danced with her shadow, wine cup in hand. She laughed at one point, her voice very clear in the still night air, kept dancing, unaware of the darkness growing around her. When she stopped to pour herself another cup of wine she saw that the moon had set down through the branches, she raised her cup and emptied it, picked up the pot but it was empty. She thought of the marshal's ghost, windblown across the steppes, and let out a long sigh.

'Years and months flow like water,' the monk, Han Shan, had written.

'then, in an instant, we're old.'

So close to death, Concubine Hua felt very old. She raised the empty wine cup to her lips and waited for the last drops to fall on to her tongue.

An hour later the pain began, like trapped wind, slowly twisting knots in her guts. Concubine Hua hunched over and moaned; her hand was unsteady as she opened another pot of wine and began to pour, but the cup was too small for the amount of wine she wanted. Her hand shook as she picked up the cup but instead of drinking she threw it across the room. It shattered into earthenware fragments – blue and white on the floor – left a cup-shaped dent in the plaster. Concubine Hua threw the wine jug after it, dashed her jewellery box across the room, all the precious contents scattering across the floor. What would happen if the marshal returned tomorrow? She thought of her daughter and the marshal and the captain, slowly crawled to the bed, began to wail.

As soon as the neighbours heard the commotion they came rushing in.

'You've swallowed gold?' they screeched, and began to lament and wail as if Concubine Hua were already dead. 'She's swallowed gold!' they told one another. 'The marshal's concubine has swallowed gold!' till the whole fort was awake, hurrying with paper lanterns for help, running for medicine, or standing in groups and passing on the news.

After a few hours the pain was so intense Concubine Hua squirmed like a snake at their feet. 'Don't touch her!' one woman cautioned, and they all stepped back when Concubine Hua raised a hand to them, but no one understood her.

'The well!' someone shouted at last. 'We should take her to the well!'

They dragged the marshal's concubine by her feet, down the narrow alleys, between the stacks of firewood, a wet trail as the concubine's bowels voided. The yellow candle-light cast shadows across the neighbours' faces as they peered over one another, watched the marshal's concubine pull herself to the well's edge, look down into the darkness. The air was cool and it smelt of water, as if the Yellow Springs were down there. The crowd stood back as Concubine Hua tipped over the edge, dropped into the hole in a flutter of silk and an echoing scream and a silent prayer in her head to the Lord Buddha. Her scream ended with a splash. The splashing continued for a few more minutes. When she had finished drowning she swam slowly to the bottom, where her body rested on the pebble bed, waiting for coins.

No fish to pick her bones.

When Old Fart heard the news about Concubine Hua she kicked the fat sow and slapped Number One Son across the face, cut his lip for his impudence. The only person she didn't assault was Little Hope, who stood gazing up at her with terrified eyes, too frightened to move.

Old Fart looked at the child and took a deep breath, let all her anger out in one long sigh that seemed to deflate her vast torso, like a punctured pigskin. 'Come here,' she said, and Little Hope put the bucket of water on the floor, not daring to spill any. Old Fart lifted the child on to her knee and pressed her close. 'Your mother's dead,' she said, and put one fat arm round the child's shoulders. There, there, Old Fart rocked back and forth to soothe her but there were no tears. Little Hope's body was hard and rigid, locked into Old Fart's bosom, rocking back and forth, like a rudderless boat.

'The officials of Heaven will deal her justice,' Old Fart said, trying to sound reassuring. 'Your mother was a good woman. It's not your fault,' she said, rebuked herself for making such a match, then took in a deep breath and wondered how she could have foreseen this bad luck.

When Headman Wang came home that night no one dared talk. Old Fart sat on the kang, sipping wine, Little Hope was peeling garlic.

'Did you hear?' he said.

Little Hope turned round, damp traces of tears beneath her eyes, but she saw that he was not talking to her.

Yes, Old Fart nodded. I heard.

'We can't have her marry our son now,' he said.

Old Fart nodded and looked sadly at her new pretty little daughter. 'I know,' she said.

'I don't suppose anyone in the village would want her.' Old Fart let out another long whistle of air.

'There is always someone looking for children,' she said, and Little Hope looked away, returned to stripping the hard cloves of garlic.

AD 852

On the fourth day of the fourth month, Scholar Yu hired a pony and walked north out of the city gates, turned off the road to Wang Family Village and climbed the steep path. He paid thirty strings of cash for the child, and Old Fart promised to use the money to make sacrifices for the girl's dead parents' ghosts.

'It would not do for them to be angered by the adoption,' Scholar Yu said. Old Fart nodded and smiled, slipped the looped cash into her sash and wiped away a few unexpected tears.

'What's your name?' Scholar Yu asked the little girl when they reached the bottom of the hill.

The girl didn't answer.

Scholar Yu leant down, looked her in the face. 'What did your father call you?'

The girl didn't answer. 'Come,' he encouraged, 'how can you not know what your father called you?'

'My father is,' she said in a small voice. Scholar Yu couldn't make out the last word.

'Dead,' the little girl had to repeat, her words coming out almost silently.

'Your father's dead?'

She nodded.

'What did your mother call you?'

The girl mumbled, and Scholar Yu made her repeat it: Little Hope.

'That's not a very pretty name,' Scholar Yu said.

The little girl swung her shoulders from side to side. She didn't know if it was a pretty name or not. It was the name her mother had called her. She didn't know what her father had called her. Her father was dead, and they had called her Little Hope and she didn't know if it was a pretty name or not.

'I'll call you Little Flower,' Scholar Yu said.

The little girl nodded, still swinging her shoulders from side to side.

You will call me Little Flower.

Little Flower sat on the pony, Scholar Yu holding the reins as he walked along. He was very different from Headman Wang, shorter and broader. He seemed kinder as well, even though he didn't speak much. Little Flower wished she was back with her mother at the fort, but her mother was dead and her father was dead and now she was called Little Flower. She felt the short thick pony fur at the base of the mane, remembered the far-off day that she had gone to visit White Water Monastery, remembered the feeling of cold fat silkworms.

'Where is your hometown?' Scholar Yu asked but Little Flower didn't answer. 'Where is your hometown?' he said and stopped the pony, but she stared at him as if she didn't understand.

'The Last Fort Under Heaven,' she said at last, as if it were a secret.

'That's not your hometown.'

Little Flower's dirty face looked back at him.

'Where are your family from?'

Little Flower didn't know. 'Wang Family Village,' she tried.

'Where are your real parents from?' Scholar Yu spoke slowly to get through to the child but she stared back at him and shook her head. In the end he took up the reins again, pulled the pony south.

'Are we going to Changan?' Little Flower asked as the sun began to set, but Scholar Yu kept walking, didn't answer. They walked in silence the rest of the three-hour walk. It was late when they saw the walls and gates of Diyi. The sun slipped from yellow to orange, then a deep, dull red, and Scholar Yu hurried along as they passed buried mounds to either side, weed-grown slopes where the kings of long-forgotten dynasties mouldered.

Traders were already boarding their shops and taking down their painted banners when Scholar Yu led the pony under the low arched gateway of Diyi. The evening streets were quiet and dark; only chinks of light showed through the shutters, the muffled sound of families sitting down to dinner: chopsticks on bowls, the hiss of frying oil, the shouts of parents to children. Scholar Yu's stomach grumbled at the continual walking, the smells of food made him think of home and his wife and the son that they had lost, and with him all their dreams of the future: buried under a pregnant swell of disturbed soil.

When they reached Scholar Yu's home, Little Flower's head was drooping in sleep. Scholar Yu carried her inside and laid her on the bed. His wife took the lantern shade off, held the candle close to her face. Scholar Yu waited for her to say something, but she didn't. She put the candle down and undressed the girl and then stared at her as if looking for some sign that this was her son, reincarnated in the body of a girl.

'Well?' Scholar Yu said but his wife turned away and said nothing. It was not until they were sitting down to a simple meal of noodles and dofu that they spoke again.

'She seems healthy,' Scholar Yu's wife said and poured him more wine.

Scholar Yu served himself more noodles, shovelled them in, chewing all the while. 'She's called Little Flower,' he said through his mouthful. 'She came from the fort.'

'Which one?'

'The Last Fort Under Heaven.'

Scholar Yu's wife nodded. There were so many forts, so many passes through which the winds blew.

'Do you think that she'll be hungry?' she asked, but her husband shook his head and took a slurp from his wine cup.

'Let her sleep.'

They sat in silence. Scholar Yu sipped his wine; his wife picked a stray thread from her gown.

'How old do you think she is?'

'Can she read and write?'

'Does she seem clever to you?'

Scholar Yu sipped his wine and shrugged.

'I wonder what happened to her parents,' Scholar Yu's wife mused.

Scholar Yu finished his wine. 'They're dead,' he said, the words sounding hard and final.

Scholar Yu's wife refilled his cup, then stood up and bolted the door, tipped coals into the grate of the kang.

'You must be tired,' she told him and Scholar Yu stood up, then went to lie down. When the table was cleared Scholar Yu's wife blew out the lantern, fumbled through the darkness and lay down on the bed, on the other side of her new daughter. Scholar Yu was so tired he fell asleep without hesitation, but his wife lay awake, listening to the child breathe. It was a long time before she reached out her hand and touched the little girl's foot, held on to her big toe, kept hold of it all through the night even though it was cold and thin and not yet family.

The next morning Scholar Yu and his wife left Little Flower lying in bed, her legs curled up to her chin, a shrimp with the lotus-embroidered quilt tucked up to her chin. Scholar Yu's wife picked through the child's clothes with a look of disgust. 'We can't let her dress in these,' she said and dropped them by the grate.

Scholar Yu's wife fed the embers of last night's fire with a few tightly wound balls of bramble kindling and blew gently on them. The flames nibbled slowly. She added twigs, and soon the flames were chewing on the thickest branches. When the wood cracked and popped like gnawed bone, she took the clothes and stuffed them into the grate. It was a few moments before the flames flared up in excitement, began to chomp and devour, and a thick white smoke billowed out in the still morning, hung in the outside air like a winter mist. The smoke had an acrid taste, of loneliness and poverty and an abandoned child. It also smelt of a childless woman and a dead baby. Scholar Yu's wife shut the door quickly and Scholar Yu went outside into the yard.

'I'll go to the market and get some more,' he said.

Before he left, Scholar Yu's wife put an extra string of coins into his hand, and when she turned her back on him

47

he touched her elbow. 'Heaven has been kind to us,' he told her. 'We have food to eat and a roof to shelter us from the cold and sun and rain.' Scholar Yu's wife nodded. I know, her sigh seemed to say. She looked back to the house where their daughter was asleep. Neither of them talked about any of their misfortunes.

Scholar Yu's wife sat and watched the child for a long while, swimming in dreams. After a long while she cleared her throat. 'Little Flower,' she called softly. 'Little Flower.'

Little Flower's eyes flickered briefly open.

'Little Flower,' Scholar Yu's wife called again, and Little Flower opened her mouth, yawned and stretched, and rubbed her eyes clear.

'Hello, Little Flower,' Scholar Yu's wife said. She smiled when the little girl shut her eyes again and stretched her short arms and small hands wide. Little Flower did not speak as Scholar Yu's wife pulled back the bedsheets, left Little Flower naked: short legs and round stomach, thin bony arms and ribs. 'Come on,' she said and Little Flower took the lady's hand and walked outside into the smoky yard, goose pimples alert to the cool outside air.

'Shut your eyes,' Scholar Yu's wife said and poured a copper ladle of water from high. Ladle after ladle splashed down, clouds of soapsuds fell to the floor. 'Didn't they feed you in Wang Family Village?' Scholar Yu's wife said, and Little Flower shivered.

'You're all just rags and bones,' Scholar Yu's wife continued, pulling at the knots in Little Flower's hair, and Little Flower didn't know if she should answer or not.

When the soap had been washed away Little Flower stood trembling, hair plastered to her skull, still trembling until she stepped into the dry hug of a towel. 'Brrrr,' Scholar Yu's wife said.

Brrrr, Little Flower thought, and Scholar Yu's wife

rubbed her down till her flesh burnt pink. A trickle of water ran down her back and Scholar Yu's wife took a cloth and wiped it away, rubbed her hair again till the drips had all gone.

'Better?'

Little Flower nodded, but it didn't stop another round of scrubbing and buffing. When it was finished Scholar Yu's wife stepped back from the bed and took her new daughter in, bones and skin and ribs and all. She pursed her lips and shook her head. Everything about the child, even the flea bites on her legs and elbows, made her precious. 'There's nothing to you!' Scholar Yu's wife chastised her. 'Look at you!'

Little Flower hung her head, silently wished that she wasn't so thin.

Little Flower sat wrapped in the bed as Scholar Yu's wife put a black earthenware pot on to the stove. She searched her shelves for all the ingredients, cracked an egg into a bowl, pricked the yolk with her chopsticks, swirled the water and dribbled the raw egg into the whirling water.

'Here!' she said, adjusted the blankets and pillows so Little Flower was firmly propped up. 'Eight Treasure Soup was my son's favourite,' she said, and Little Flower nodded seriously.

Scholar Yu's wife fed Little Flower spoon by spoon, and then she laughed at her silliness. 'I'm sure you can feed yourself.'

Little Flower looked a little disappointed, but she took the bowl and the porcelain spoon, carefully counted out the eight treasures, ate them one by one, sipped so slowly that the last mouthful was cold, scraped the bowl clean.

'More?'

Little Flower nodded. Scholar Yu's wife brought the bowl

back, brimming once again. Little Flower worked quicker this time, and the next. This was a bowl that could never be emptied, just like in stories.

'Like it?'

Little Flower finished the fourth bowl.

'This was my favourite soup when I was your age,' Scholar Yu's wife said, not sure what else to say.

This is my favourite soup too, Little Flower's expression seemed to say. She only stopped eating when Scholar Yu came home and he unwrapped trousers of undyed wool, padded cloth shoes stitched with yellow phoenixes and a child's red padded jacket, embroidered butterflies and flowers swirling green and blue and turquoise.

'It's beautiful!' Scholar Yu's wife said. 'Isn't it beautiful?' she said, turned to her daughter and Little Flower saw the beautiful jacket and put the spoon down and swallowed.

When she was dressed, Little Flower looked at herself in the mirror. The silk thread changed colour as she moved, her hair was still damp, it stuck up from her head in two pony-tails. She didn't make faces but turned her head from one side to the other, stared at the face that was hers and yet so much older and thinner than the girl in the Last Fort Under Heaven.

'That's you!' Scholar Yu's wife said.

Little Flower reached out to feel her reflection – but the brass surface was cold to the touch and she pulled her hand away and looked at her new mother, held out her arms and Scholar Yu's wife picked her up and carried her outside. She took her across the yard, through a doorway into their eastern neighbours' yard, where Scholar Yu's aunt lived. There was an infirm old house, walls leaning precariously under the weight of the thatched roof. The doorframe was skewed – the door had been trimmed to fit the irregular shape; holes had been patched with bits of plank, hammered in with brass spikes.

Scholar Yu's wife stood nervously at the doorway and took a deep breath. 'I have something to tell you,' she announced as she stepped inside, but Granny Pig and Uncle Jia were still in bed, dressed in padded winter clothes. The old couple both looked up in surprise. To Uncle Jia's fading eyesight, Scholar Yu's wife was just a shadow in the blue glow of the doorway. Granny Pig squinted to see more clearly.

'Who is it?'

'It's me!'

'Who?'

'Scholar Yu's wife!'

'Ah – I thought it was you,' Granny Pig said, smacked her gums together, licked her old lips.

'I have something to tell you,' Scholar Yu's wife announced again.

'What?' Uncle Jia always shouted because he couldn't hear himself otherwise.

'She has something to tell us,' Granny Pig shouted back.

'What?'

'I don't know!'

Scholar Yu's wife had to cut through the old couple's conversation. 'I have a daughter!' she declared, and pushed Little Flower forward.

Granny Pig put her prayer beads down and Uncle Jia's eyes blinked cataract white. 'What did she say?'

'She says she has a daughter,' Granny Pig told him.

'What does she mean?'

Granny Pig didn't know what she meant.

'What does she mean?' Uncle Jia shouted again, feeling lost and helpless because no one was talking to him.

'Be quiet!' Granny Pig told him, put her hand on his arm. 'Is this her?'

Scholar Yu's wife pushed Little Flower again and she fell to her knees, as Old Fart had taught her, began to kowtow like she was greeting all the Wang ancestors, stiff and awkward. Uncle Jia squinted to make out the movement. He started to speak but his wife squeezed him, her bony fingers pressing deep into the sagging skin of his forearm. Little Flower kept kowtowing, her buttocks high in the air, grit pressing into her forehead as she showed them her deep, deep respect.

'We have adopted a daughter,' Scholar Yu's wife said and Granny Pig pushed the quilt back, climbed down from the bed, hobbled quickly across the room, smacking her gums with obvious pleasure. She took the child's chin and peered into her face for signs of good karma, then took Scholar Yu's wife's hand and squeezed it.

'Such compassion will be rewarded,' she said. 'Ah me!' She sighed. 'Buddha's blessings!'

Uncle Jia felt stranded on the bed, and began to feel his way to the edge, blind hands floundering in the air in front of him. Granny Pig pushed him back from the edge and shouted in his good ear: 'She's adopted an orphan!'

'A girl!'

Girl was said with special emphasis.

Uncle Jia looked in their general direction. 'Ah!'

'Such compassion!' Granny Pig told him, and pulled out the guests' chair and poured Little Flower a cup of warm water sprinkled with tea. It was as if a new life had been added to her own: an extra lifespan to remember her when she was gone. She hobbled over to her chest of spices and picked out one of the cinnamon sticks she had bought for the Scholar's son, then hobbled back. 'There you go!'

'Go and play!' Scholar Yu's wife told her but Little Flower stood close to Scholar Yu's wife, sucked her cinnamon stick and held on to her leg, trying to understand what was being said about her.

'She's quiet – aren't you?'

Little Flower sucked diligently.

'She's shy,' Scholar Yu's wife said, then thought that she knew almost nothing of her new daughter. Granny Pig smiled down at the child but Little Flower's forehead remained creased with concentration.

'What a strange child,' she said and Scholar Yu's wife stiffened slightly. 'Strange but pretty, very pretty,' Granny Pig added, and Scholar Yu's wife managed a brief smile.

'Isn't she?' she said, and Uncle Jia waved.

All that morning Scholar Yu's wife was busy with Granny Pig, chopping and cooking up a feast. Instead of trotters and offal, Scholar Yu came back from the market with juicy spare ribs and a lump of ham. He even brought a Yellow River carp, a looped cord tied through its dorsal fin for him to carry it home. The fish was still flapping lazily when Scholar Yu's wife lifted it to the chopping block. Little Flower stood close as Scholar Yu's wife put two chopsticks into the fish's mouth, then rammed them through its body. The fish didn't swim any more. It was gutted and scaled and simmered with ginger, the eyes congealed white and staring on the plate.

When all was set and ready, Scholar Yu took Little Flower's hand and led her to the seat of honour, opposite the door. Scholar Yu's wife introduced the dishes to her and Little Flower stared at them as if they were fantastic animals: sweet and sour lotus root, spiced jellied mutton, red boiled ham, butterfly fish, fermented dofu, and white congealed ginger fish eyes.

Scholar Yu picked treats out and Little Flower held the bottom of the bowl in one hand, chopsticks in the other, and carefully chewed. She tried to remember all the names and fragrances, but there was too much to take in. Scholar Yu's wife monitored her table manners, was pleased the child didn't do anything too offensive. A child wouldn't learn manners from a place like Wang Family Village, she thought, reassured herself that the girl must have come from a good family.

'Here!' Scholar Yu said and put a piece of mutton into his wife's bowl. 'Eat!' he told her, and Scholar Yu's wife blushed as she lifted the mutton to her mouth, chewed in time with her daughter.

Scholar Yu grinned all afternoon as he took Little Flower around Diyi, meeting friends and stopping at houses, telling them the story of how his wife had adopted the daughter of a distant relative. He started by taking her to meet the other men who worked for the magistrate: thin poor scholars like himself. They bobbed and bowed and quoted the *Analects of Sage Kung* to each other in a desperate attempt to appear the most learned. Only fat Clerk Bai smiled and patted the little girl's head. 'Blessings come from Heaven,' he said.

Little Flower didn't know what he meant. 'I came from the Last Fort Under Heaven,' she said and everyone laughed.

That night the neighbours insisted that Scholar Yu drink a cup of wine with them. It was good to have a child who could continue the sacrifices when you were gone. If she married they could adopt her husband into their family and then they would have grandchildren and great-grandchildren, if Heaven chose to bless their ghosts. No one talked about the other dead child.

Scholar Yu drank so many cups that night that the neighbours all teased him for his red face. 'Not even the Emperor wants to talk to a drunk!' they said and gave the wide earth-enware cup to Little Flower instead, but it was too large and unsteady, and half of the wine tipped down the sleeve of her new red jacket. She tried to dry her sleeve, but the men were all pushing and shouting and they lifted the half-filled cup to her mouth, and she opened her mouth and choked on the taste. Her sleeve was wet and the men were laughing and shouting and Little Flower felt her lower lip tremble.

'Look!' the neighbours teased. 'You're drunk and she is frightened of you!'

Scholar Yu's face was red but his manner was serious.

'Come here,' he said, and picked up Little Flower, a little unsteady. He held her gently, jigged her up and down, tried to make her smile. She held out her arm and he touched the cloth and jigged her once again. 'It'll dry,' he assured her.

Little Flower made another show of wiping her sleeve. 'Are you angry?' she asked, almost inaudible.

'No,' he laughed. 'Not angry.'

Little Flower stopped looking as if she was about to cry, but her face still seemed downcast. 'Drink removes all sorrows,' Scholar Yu whispered in her ear, loud enough for all to hear, and gently lifted another cup to Little Flower's lips, who took a mouthful and said, 'It tastes like Eight Treasure Soup.'

When everyone laughed Little Flower laughed too, but after another cup, instead of becoming drunk Little Flower was tired, then fast asleep. Scholar Yu stumbled home, tipped the child into bed and fell in behind her.

Good night, Little Flower thought after the candle was blown out, Mother Hua, Mother Yu and Father Yu.

Scholar Yu and his wife lay on either side of her, Scholar Yu slipping straight from drunkenness to sleep, his wife stroking Little Flower's hair, eyes open to the darkness. At last Scholar Yu's wife fell asleep as well and the three of them lay together, dreaming their separate dreams as the heavy silk floss quilt pressed them down into a family.

The next morning Scholar Yu's wife shaved Little Flower's hair down to the scalp, left a long tuft at the front and let all the severed locks blow round the yard like winter leaves.

'Her mother's ghost will never recognise her now.' Granny Pig smacked her gums in satisfaction and Scholar Yu's wife tried to smile. She thought of her son's ghost, howling lost and lonely through the afterlife. 'Come here,' she said to Little Flower and gave her a hard squeeze.

When Scholar Yu's wife had gone outside to draw a bucket of well water Granny Pig licked her lips and called, 'Little Flower!'

Little Flower turned and saw the outstretched cinnamon stick and ran to the old woman.

Scholar Yu worked in the magistrate's yamen all day long, transcribing reports, recording verdicts, supervising the punishments of those found guilty. The most common sentence was beating with a bamboo rod. Severe crimes deserved the thick rod, light transgressions the thin. Sometimes Little Flower would watch as the men were held down and thrashed, their skin splitting open like overripe fruit, blood running thin with sweat, black blood drops scattering over the soil like constellations.

As the days passed Little Flower's answers turned from nods to yesses, shakes to nos; and the long watching silences grew shorter and shorter. After two weeks she was talking in short sentences, and after a month she ran out through the gate with all the confidence of a child who knows home will still be there when she gets back.

'Be careful!' Scholar Yu's wife told her each time she went out into the street, but the streets were too full of novelty for Little Flower to listen. Instead of chores or grasslands there were bustling markets, meandering alleys, honey glazed crab apples, street performers, fortune tellers and diseased beggars. She joined the other street children and threw stones at the cripples, stared at a woman whose six-year-old son was horribly deformed and teased the smelly old hags.

One day at the yamen a case was brought against a woman for refusing to obey her mother-in-law. The woman was sentenced to ten strokes of the thin bamboo, and to wear the cangue for a week with 'Unfilial Daughter' written on a sign round her neck. There was a large crowd to see her come out of the magistrate's yamen. They set about her with fists and kicks, threw clods of dirt and vicious insults.

Little Flower joined the other children who followed the mêlée all the way down the street, laughing and excited, but when she turned for home the roads seemed strange and unfamiliar. She took one turn, and another, stood in the street and bawled like a baby, but people knocked into her or pushed her aside. Mother Yu and Father Yu did not appear, only more strangers, pushing and busy. At one point Little Flower thought she saw Old Fart and hid; then she thought she saw the back of Mother Yu and ran across to her, but when the woman turned round her face was unfamiliar.

'What's wrong?' the woman asked, but all Little Flower thought of was being sent back to the Wang Family Village.

'Mother Yu! Granny Pig! Scholar Yu!' Little Flower wailed, but the woman didn't know who she was talking about.

'Where do you live?' the woman asked. 'Where is your home?'

It took a while for the child to speak loudly enough for the woman to hear, all the while threatening to break into a wail again.

'Magistrate's yamen?' was all the peasant woman heard.

'It's not far,' she said, but the little girl's face was all red and contorted with tears. 'Look, you can see it from here!' the woman told her, and pointed down the street to the crimson gates. Little Flower abruptly stopped, wiped her eyes and looked. 'Come along,' the woman said, took Little Flower's hand and led her through the bustle.

When they reached the gates of the Yus' home Little Flower was almost skipping. The woman asked if she wanted her to come inside, but Little Flower shook her head and ran off round the corner. She pushed inside and found Granny Pig and Scholar Yu's wife sitting and smiling on the kang, and Scholar Yu sat by the light of the papered window, reading through notes from the day's procedings. 'See! She's back!' Scholar Yu said and his wife wiped her nose and held out her arms. Little Flower ran into them and held on tight.

'She's back, isn't she,' Granny Pig said, as she sat and waited for the right moment to take out the cinnamon stick, and Little Flower grabbed it and ran out.

'Where are you going now?' Scholar Yu's wife called, but Little Flower's answer was so distorted by the cinnamon stick that no one could understand what she was saying.

'Where are you going?' her mother demanded from the doorway, and Little Flower took the cinnamon stick out.

'Uncle Jia!' she said simply, disappeared round the corner.

One afternoon the spring rains were dripping the sprouts out and they were sitting with the door open to the yard, listening to the rain.

'Have you ever been to the grasslands?' Little Flower

asked after Granny Pig had gone inside to sleep.

'The grasslands?' Scholar Yu's wife said. 'No. Never. Why?'

Little Flower concentrated as she practised a new character with the tip of her finger.

There was a long pause.

'I've been to Hanging Monastery.'

'Really?' Little Flower didn't seem too interested. 'Why?'

Scholar Yu's wife looked for an answer. 'Because there were lots of monkeys,' she said.

'Monkeys?'

'Yes.'

'Did you see the King of the Monkeys?' Little Flower looked up.

'No,' Scholar Yu's wife said. 'Do you like monkeys?'

'My mother used to tell me stories of the Monkey King and his journey to the west.' Little Flower rubbed the last character out and started again.

'Mother Hua or Mother Fart?'

'Mother Hua,' Little Flower said.

'Did you like the Monkey King?'

'Yes.'

'They were my favourite stories when I was a child,' Scholar Yu's wife said.

'You were a child?'

Scholar Yu's wife laughed and nodded and Little Flower laughed as well.

As the days passed Scholar Yu's wife found how much Little Flower loved stories of any kind. She loved the one about how the Scholar and his wife met, and how they were married, and the son they had had.

'I'm sorry your son died,' Little Flower said at the end and Scholar Yu's wife tried to smile.

59

'He would have been your Little Brother.'

'I would like a Little Brother,' Little Flower said and then there was a long pause. 'I will be your daughter,' she said as if she had long debated the subject.

The house where Scholar Yu and his family lived was like any house in Diyi – three rooms around a south-facing courtyard. The central room was a hall, a shrine and bedroom all in one. On special days the scroll of the appropriate god was hung opposite the door, and when Little Flower was awake early she would watch the dawn sunlight slip down it. On the east wall near the kang there was a metal stove, and above Little Flower's head was pasted a picture of the Kitchen God and his wife – splattered with cooking fat.

One day Little Flower traced the outline of other Kitchen Gods' prints: where there were lines in the grease, shadows in the pattern of splatter.

'Careful!' her mother warned and slipped a small ham into the wok.

The oil spat and hissed and bubbled over; a drop caught Little Flower on the hand. She licked it and then walked out of the door, round the corner to the patched doorway where Granny Pig and Uncle Jia lived.

'Granny?' she called as she pushed inside, holding up her scalded hand. 'Can I have a cinnamon stick?'

When lunch was finished and Little Flower lay down to nap, Scholar Yu sat at the black wood desk, under the window, and studied the set texts for the civil service exams: I Ching; *Analects of Sage Kung*, *Life of Sage Meng*. When Little Flower woke up she stood by the desk and stared at the page that had neat rows of characters. Sometimes Scholar

Yu would look up from his books and show Little Flower a new character.

'What's this?'

'Man!'

'What if he has his arms out wide?'

'Big!' Little Flower said.

'And if he stands with his arms to his side?'

'Little!'

'What's this?' he asked.

'Woman.'

'Woman under a roof?'

'Peace,' Little Flower said.

Scholar Yu sat forward into the lamplight. 'What is this?'

Little Flower didn't know. 'Happy,' she guessed.

'No,' Scholar Yu said. 'It is a pig.'

'Pig!' Little Flower said.

'And what if we put a roof over a pig?'

Little Flower thought of Old Fart's black sow. 'We don't get hit,' she cackled and Scholar Yu gave her a strange look.

'Don't be silly,' he said. 'What do we get when we put a roof on a pig?'

Little Flower didn't think she was being silly.

'A house,' Scholar Yu reminded her. 'Yes?'

Yes, Little Flower nodded. Not a hit but a house.

As the sun set and the drum tower sounded the closing of the city gates Little Flower ran home and bowed before the stone rubbing of Sage Kung. Scholar Yu's wife heard the rustle of straw, turned her head as she peeled a bitter gourd, chopped it into bite-size chunks.

'Home,' her mother said and Little Flower jumped up and peered up to see the chopping board.

'What's for dinner?'

'Dofu soup,' her mother said and Little Flower curled her lip.

'Err!'

In the evening, when the city gates were shut and the streets were dark and empty, the family all sat close together on the kang. When the sun was warm they all sat in the courtyard, Scholar Yu's wife and Granny Pig with their sewing boxes full of needles and scraps and thread, the two men sipping tea and discussing the news in the market-place. At mealtimes everyone smelt the steaming food and talked excitedly. The men didn't wait for Scholar Yu's wife to sit down but tapped their chopsticks on the sides of the bowls, picked from the dishes and began to scrape the insides out into their mouths.

Scholar Yu's wife stood by the stove with her bowl of food and chewed slowly as the men ate. She always gave Little Flower the choicest pieces of meat, always treated her as if she were an honoured guest. If she ever finished the food in front of her Scholar Yu's wife would fry an egg with a little chopped spring onion and dark green garlic shoots and serve it to her hot and steaming. 'Still hungry?' she'd ask and Little Flower would shake her head.

'Enough?'

62

Enough, the child would nod, and only then were the bowls and plates cleaned away.

When the water was being boiled to wash the pots, Granny Pig would hand Little Flower a shiny brown date or a handful of dried plums. 'Go play,' Granny Pig told her, and she would take the fruit and go to play in the yard, happy to be Little Flower.

When the pots had been washed and stacked on the shelves, the family would gather on the kang, listen to the paper windows inhale and exhale, the lantern flames flicker with lovestruck moths.

Once a moth flew into the flame, put the lantern out.

'Aya!' Granny Pig exclaimed, smacked her lips with pleasure at the seven days' bad luck that the dead moth would bring.

For those seven days Little Flower was not allowed outside the compound. She sat bored and frustrated, Granny Pig sitting by the gateway, ready to grab her if she tried to run outside. 'No you don't,' Granny Pig told her, bony fingers pressing into Little Flower's arms. 'You stay here.'

'I want to go out!' Little Flower stamped, but Granny Pig and Scholar Yu's wife were immune to tears and tantrums and pouting looks. There was no point in tempting fate.

Some nights neighbours would come for wine and conversation, or to ask the Scholar to write a petition or letter on their behalf. Little Flower sat in her mother's lap, playing with a simple bronze hairpin, watching them stand and bob and keep thanking the Scholar as he ground the inkstone, added water till it was the right consistency. When he took his brushes out Little Flower pushed herself off Granny Pig's lap to go and watch as her father dipped the tip into the ink and on to the white sheet, draw wet black words that quickly dried.

Sometimes he gave her the brush to play with and she left black smears across the wall that made Granny Pig exclaim.

'Aya!' she wailed, and cleaned the brush in water, gave it to Little Flower to play with as she wiped the smears away.

Each time Scholar Yu refused payment Scholar Yu's wife banged the pots and pans on to the shelves, waited for the guests to leave. 'It only costs me a little ink,' he said but his wife refused to listen.

'You have ink in your blood,' she swore. 'You should take all that writing silk and use it to stuff a quilt!'

Scholar Yu picked up a book and refused to listen and Granny Pig took the brush from her and Little Flower didn't know what she had done wrong.

'You don't even care,' Scholar Yu's wife snapped. 'We could all starve!' but Scholar Yu kept turning the pages. That night Scholar Yu poured himself a cup of wine, raised his cup to the Kitchen God.

'All worry in life begins from learning to read and write,' he told Little Flower, and drank the wine down in one.

On evenings when Uncle Jia had drunk a few cups of wine, he would clear his throat and spit, then begin a tale in a half-shouting voice that carried outside the hut, deep into the night.

According to Uncle Jia, the four sins of the world were wine, women, wealth and wrath. Filial duty was the top of all the virtues. In one story he told them how he had warned his eldest son to never take a concubine, and how he had and how he had died soon afterwards of the pox. The link was clear. Disobeying his father had killed him. That was how Uncle Jia had ended up living next to his nephew.

'When a weak man is clothed and housed and fed,' the old man lamented, 'his energy turns to lust.'

The adults all sat and nodded. It was true. Affectionate couples never lived long together. The key to a good marriage was respect and duty, each carrying out their correct role.

The old man had a lifetime to recount. There was a story to explain everything: the way the world came to be; the laws that Heaven imposed; the history of the Han people, how they came together in the Yellow River basin and how the Yellow Emperor taught them the secrets of agriculture and irrigation and the craft of weaving silk. There was a week's worth of stories about China's Sorrow: the Yellow River, which had nine bends, six in the lands of the Tibetans and three in China. Little Flower blurted out the story of how her mother was sold as a concubine, but everyone looked away, except Granny Pig.

'Poor child,' she said and licked her gums with pleasure. 'Ah me,' she sighed, but then the silence returned and Little Flower didn't feel like talking about her real mother again.

Uncle Jia's favourite stories were about the days of his youth when the world seemed a simpler and safer place. Government was strong and honest; the empire was sound; the country was drunk on an age of peace. Those were the days before Lu Anshan's rebellion of course – the fat Sogdian who danced the whirl like tumbleweed, and who had almost destroyed the empire.

Uncle Jia always sighed and wiped imaginary tears from his milky white eyes when he remembered how much the country had lost. 'It was Yang Guifei's fault, the Precious Concubine,' he said with a sigh. 'The Emperor loved her too much. When in love, even great men lose ambition.'

The tale of the Emperor and his Precious Concubine was far longer than one evening allowed. Uncle Jia saved the full telling for the cold of winter, when wine was cheap and the nights were long. 'This is the story as I remember it from the marketplace storytellers,' his voice boomed and Little Flower sat on the very edge of the kang, scratched the stubble on her scalp to keep herself awake.

Each evening when the drum tower in the centre of town signalled the closing of the city gates, Little Flower ran home for dinner, bowed to Sage Kung, ate up her rice and climbed on to the kang.

'Hungry?' her mother asked, egg ready.

'No!'

'Are you sure?'

She nodded vehemently, waited on the kang.

'Granny Pig's not finished her rice,' Scholar Yu said and Little Flower let out a long frustrated sigh.

The Emperor first saw Yang Guifei as she climbed from her bath.

> Her hair like a cloud
> Her face like a flower
> A gold hairpin adorning her tresses
> Behind the warm lotus-flower curtain
> They took pleasure in the spring night.

Each night Uncle Jia picked up where he had finished the night before.

> The first of all women under Heaven,
> carried with her lord in the same sedan,
> on white horses rode her handmaidens
> champed and frothed on bits of yellow gold.

Uncle Jia's eyes were shut as he chanted, and Granny Pig stared off into the distance and Little Flower clapped with excitement.

> Dancing the whirl like uprooted tumbleweed
> out-flung earrings of paired pearls
> bewhirl his eyes, bewitch his heart
> turning Heaven and Earth upside-down.

The next day Little Flower played Yang Guifei games with the other children: they marched up and down in fantastical parades of horses and trumpets, forced one of her friends' little brothers to be the Emperor. When he cried and called for his mother they kissed his dirty cheek, told him not to be a baby.

> On Mount Li through dusk snow
> In Shangyang Palace on spring mornings
> Each night she had his bedchamber
> all to herself.

Such was the Emperor's love for Yang Guifei that he raised her relatives to positions of power. Her father, uncle and brothers were all given noble rank; their carriages, clothes and mansions matched royal ones for wealth and ostentation. Uncle Jia told how the men of Yang Guifei's family abused their power, enriched themselves, excess without limit, so that there was more of the royal dinner service in their houses than in the palace. The Emperor was deaf as he watched his concubine dance the empire to pieces, and the Sogdian general, Lu Anshan, marched on the palace, defeated the loyalist armies at Chentao Marsh and Greenslope.

In the first month,
the sons of ten provinces
gave their blood
to fill the marshes of Chentao.

The Emperor fled as far as Mawei Pavilion on the road
to Chengdu, but there his soldiers refused to go on until
Yang Guifei's uncle was executed. The Emperor agreed,
but still the soldiers were unsatisfied, and demanded that
the Emperor also execute his Precious Concubine.

Little Flower sat, mouth wide, as Uncle Jia chanted, his
voice low and sad:

Where are they now, her bright eyes
and sparkling teeth?
Flowered hairpins fell to the earth,
    no one to pick them up.
Peacock quilts cold; living and dead
    — torn asunder.

Uncle Jia raised his arm to his cataract eyes, spoke in a
whisper:

With silken sleeves he covered his face
unable to dull his ears.
She threw herself back and forth in panic
tresses all dishevelled.
In the lotus-embroidered tent
the concubine's struggles were stilled by the
    strangling cord.

The next night Little Flower came home late and forgot
to bow before the rubbing of Sage Kung. She didn't want
her dinner, and when the family sat together on the kang

she fidgeted and when Scholar Yu's wife told her off she threw the scholar's brush across the room.

'There is a story that Emperor Xuanzong and Yang Guifei met again,' Uncle Jia raised his voice.

'Ssh!' Scholar Yu's wife said and nudged her daughter. Little Flower stopped and listened as Uncle Jia told how the Emperor was sought out by a magician who had the power to talk to the dead.

'Past the rainbow clouds and the sapphire seas there is a golden tower with a gate of jade.' Uncle Jia leant forward. 'She came to the Emperor in his sleep.'

> In Heaven we will fly like birds together,
> on Earth we'll be like branches entwined.
> Heaven lasts, Earth endures,
> death resolves all troubles.

That night when she slept, Little Flower pushed Yang Guifei on the pear tree swing. The Precious Concubine was just a shy little girl. Little Flower took her hand and they sat down together in the corner of the yard, where autumn leaves still gathered on windy nights.

'I'm frightened,' Yang Guifei said.

Little Flower tried to console her. 'Stories change,' she said, but from the sadness in the other girl's eyes she could tell her friend did not believe her.

'Not mine,' she said.

The next evening Little Flower sat on her mother's knee and her mother spoke gently to her, and the sadness at the end of the story didn't seem so bad. That night Little Flower dreamt she was with Emperor Xuanzong and they were eating bowls of Eight Treasure Soup as they listened to Yang Guifei's throttled gasps. It wasn't the voluptuous female beauty who had bewitched the Emperor and escorted her favourites into power: it was the little girl she had sat with in another dream. It didn't seem strange that her dreams connected random nights like this.

'What's it like to be killed?' Little Flower asked Emperor Xuanzong, who was a little boy and looked like a young Uncle Jia, except that his eyes were black not white. He reached out and she remembered that his hand was young and smooth; smiled and ruffled her hair affectionately. 'You don't need to worry about that,' the Emperor said in Uncle Jia's voice. 'You're still young.'

In the spring of 853 Scholar Yu began to prepare for the civil service exams. He stopped working at the yamen, spent each day hunched over his desk, unwinding long scrolls of text, learning them by heart. Sometimes the pages had line drawings of Sage Kung and his disciples, their names neatly in seal script. 'Look!' Scholar Yu said and Little Flower looked and then looked away. Sages in books looked so similar to each other; whatever they said sounded the same.

Little Flower played in the yard, stood guard over the airing quilts or took her afternoon nap as Scholar Yu crammed his head with books. Soon he had mastered all the important passages, stood to recite them to the blank whitewashed wall. Let each man – peasant and Emperor – know his place and fulfil his position in society to the best of his ability. Farming is the fundamental occupation on which all other people depend. It enriches the royal treasury; supports the nobility; supplies official salaries; maintains armies; funds public works. The Emperor writes laws to provide the peasants with a level of comfort, ensures their well-being with a three-yearly census of people and land.

Clergy are exempt from tax, Scholar Yu recited. According to the 845 census, there are four hundred thousand monks and nuns in the empire; their wealth depends on land and mills and tenant farmers. Some are bogus, do not practise celibacy: they live with their families, reap profits from other business. They indulge in pawn-broking; lending money and seed grain; oil presses and mills. Only Chan monks work the land; the rest are afraid of hurting living creatures – their religion prohibits killing or violence.

While he studied, Sage Kung's quotes sprinkled his speech. First is Heaven, then the Emperor, his officials and the peasants. Next are the artisans. Lowest of all are merchants and traders. Merchants produce nothing, but live off the surplus of the peasants. The pursuit of wealth is contrary to the good of society.

When Scholar Yu had mastered the classics he learnt the glosses. Wise people are like water; kind-hearted people like mountains. If the name is not right the word cannot be appropriate. Those who labour with their minds rule; those who labour with their bodies are ruled. Since this is your life be content with it.

Little Flower listened to him and played with an old hairbrush Scholar Yu's wife had given her and thought how nothing her father said made any sense.

When the day came for Scholar Yu to leave to take the exams, his wife sat down and refused to speak.

'I'm going,' Scholar Yu said and Little Flower stood by Mother Yu and looked at him as well. 'Wife, I'm going.'

Granny Pig pushed Scholar Yu's wife up from the bed. She hung her head and looked down at her feet. 'Good winds,' she said and sat back down. She would not go outside.

Little Flower didn't believe that her father was leaving. She refused to let go of Scholar Yu's hand as he walked down the street, refused to go back to the house. In the end Scholar Yu stopped at the corner of the road that led to the main gate and spoke to her sternly. 'Go to your mother,' he said but she followed him through the streets and stopped in the arch of the city gateway, stared south as her father grew smaller and smaller, turned once, not to wave, but to signal her away.

Little Flower stayed staring south, as Mother Hua had once stared north. In the end Scholar Yu disappeared from sight and she put her hands into her armpits to keep her hands warm, walked slowly home, kicking stones, as if he would never return.

While Scholar Yu was away, sadness flavoured each day. At dinner there was always an empty space at the table, and when they talked to each other there were things that Scholar Yu would have said that were missing. The hardest step is the first, the I Ching said, but although it was hard to set out on a journey, for Scholar Yu's family it was harder and sadder and more lonely to be left behind.

Little Flower didn't like to go out so much: she sat with Granny Pig and Scholar Yu's wife and played quietly in the yard. Spring turned to summer and the summer heat rose, then fell a little; the sound of insects lasted long into the night. Occasionally travellers and pilgrims who had met the scholar on the road came to pay their respects, but Little Flower didn't really believe them.

'Will you send me off to get married?' she asked one day and Scholar Yu's wife pulled her close, pressed her hard.

'Never!' she whispered, and kissed the top of her daughter's head. 'Never!'

At the end of summer news came that Scholar Yu had finished the exams and was on his way home. Days passed, the dead cicadas were brushed up and burnt with the crisp leaves, and as they waited for Scholar Yu's return, Little Flower imagined what it would be like when he walked back through the autumn smoke.

'Maybe tomorrow,' Granny Pig said, and Little Flower nodded, kept writing words into the dirt.

Scholar Yu reached the gates of Diyi on the seventh day of the ninth month. The gates had been shut for the night, but a side door was open so he showed his papers and stepped inside, saw familiar streets again. There were street stalls set up all along the main road, lamps and candles and bobbing lanterns lighting his way home. Friends ran on ahead to tell Scholar Yu's wife that her husband was back, and by the time he turned into their street Scholar Yu's wife was there, holding Little Flower's hand, two silhouettes waiting for him in the gloom.

'Husband,' Scholar Yu's wife said.

'Wife,' he said. 'I'm back.'

'You'd better come in,' Scholar Yu's wife said, served a dinner of chive and mutton dumplings, dipped in vinegar.

'Eat up,' her mother said to Little Flower. 'They're going cold.' But Little Flower stared at Scholar Yu.

'Daughter, Father's back,' he said but Little Flower didn't want to hug him.

'We missed you,' his wife told him, like an accusation.

Scholar Yu lifted a dumpling to his daughter's lips, but she shook her head.

'Eat!' Scholar Yu's wife said and after a little more encouragement Little Flower took a bite.

The next week was full of people coming to visit the scholar and ask him about his trip, about the things he had seen, about the state of the world.

'The roads were good all the way to Changan,' he said.

'There were no bandits after Taiyuanfu,' he said and the people smiled. His news sounded hopeful: order had returned to the world at last. Scholar Yu did not mention the days he had spent travelling through Linfen Prefecture – where the damage of the 812 rebellion still showed. Ten thousand acres of ruined villages, forested fields, weed-grown towns where whole districts had crumbled back to farmland. He told them about the capital instead, where rot and ruin were harder to find. 'It is larger than twenty Diyis!' he told them. 'It is very peaceful. The curfew is strictly enforced. I was never once set upon by robbers.'

Each answer he gave them led to more questions. 'How about the exams?' they asked at last. 'When will you dress in the blue robes of an official?'

'I have to wait till they have all been marked and the results are posted. Then I have to see if I have passed.

'They're posted at the south tower of Chongzong Temple,' he explained, 'and then the results are sent out to the provinces.'

Oh, the people nodded, losing interest at last: the south towers of Chongzong Temple too far beyond their imagination.

That night Scholar Yu sat by the fire and watched the flames fade to embers. I have a good life here, he told himself, if I do not pass it will not be the worst thing on earth.

But with each day back in Diyi it seemed as if Scholar Yu had never been to Changan, had never seen the capital. Each morning he picked up his clerk's black coat as a slave might gather his chains.

Clerk Bai and the other functionaries tried to cheer him up. 'Don't fear a long road,' they told him. 'Fear short ambition.' Scholar Yu smiled – he thought of the frog that

74

was thrown down a well, and tried to recall the size and beauty of the moon-dappled ocean – said nothing.

It was more than a month's travel to Changan. The autumn days were damp and cold; at night the insect sounds ceased, but still no news. At length the results did arrive, and after they had been formally presented to the magistrate in a yellow silken case, the senior monks and generals and government officials of Diyi were summoned to hear them. There were four men from Diyi Prefecture who had taken the exams, but only Scholar Yu had passed.

As soon as Scholar Yu heard that he was invited to the capital again to take the civil service interviews, he ran to the Temple of Sage Kung and offered apples and pears and a large bag of dates. That night all his friends came to congratulate him but Scholar Yu's wife said nothing. She did not want to lose her husband for another five months; did not want to leave Diyi.

'I have decided that we will all go to live in the capital,' Scholar Yu announced one lunchtime, when there were just the three of them together.

Scholar Yu's wife choked.

'All of us?' she asked.

'Yes,' he said and pretended everything was normal as his wife stood up and walked to the door. Little Flower ate her noodles and didn't know whether to feel sad or not, but she knew that she did not want to leave her friends, did not want to say goodbye to Granny Pig and Uncle Jia.

'And what will you do with them?' Scholar Yu's wife said, referring to the old couple.

'I don't know,' Scholar Yu said.

'You haven't thought it through,' she told him. 'It's just a stupid idea.'

* * *

When Granny Pig heard that Scholar Yu wanted to take his family to the capital she walked out into the middle of the street and collapsed in a heap. 'We'll be abandoned!' she declared. 'Who'll soothe our old age?!'

A crowd of people gathered and laughed. Scholar Yu rushed back from the yamen and picked up the old lady from the dirt.

'Of course you will come with us,' he told her. 'How could we leave you behind? When my parents died you raised me as your own child. I'm no dog to eat at your house and then leave!'

It took a while for Granny Pig to hear what he was saying, and only when it was repeated to her several times did she desist. 'I can stand up!' she snapped, as she pushed away his arms. She dusted down her trousers, walked back to her yard, wiped the shame from her face. Don't worry about hardships when you are young, worry about them when you are old. To think that she had had to demean herself like that. It was too much.

'Where have you been?' Uncle Jia shouted.

'We're going to Changan,' Granny Pig shouted back.

'Why?'

'Scholar Yu is going to take the civil service interviews.'

'I can't go to Changan!' Uncle Jia shouted but Granny Pig would have none of it.

'When you are too old to move we will put you in a box and bury you,' she told him.

When there were no more reasons to prevent them leaving, Scholar Yu's wife collapsed in tears. She wanted her husband to become a civil servant, but she had never thought she would leave Diyi. It was suddenly too much to consider. 'Who will care for the grave of our son?' she sniffed. 'Who will perform the sacrifices!'

Scholar Yu went into the yard, poured himself a cup

of wine, drank it down, refused to involve himself any longer. Little Flower didn't know if she should watch or not. She felt guilty and uncertain, as if there was something she had done wrong. At last she stood up and walked to her mother.

'Leave her alone!' Scholar Yu snapped, but Little Flower stood next to her and tugged at her trouser leg.

'Mother Yu,' she said, 'I will stay behind and sweep the grave.'

Scholar Yu's wife sobbed even more. Little Flower tried to put her arms round her mother but her mother was too large to hold. 'Mother,' Little Flower began again and Scholar Yu's wife couldn't bear to hear that she might leave them as well, pressed Little Flower's face into her womb, started to silently cry.

It took a few months to put everything in order, get travel papers and letters of commendation from the local magistrate, perform the necessary sacrifices on their son's grave. The day they had buried him the soil was piled up, like a full stomach. Now it was flat and dry, small bones digested by the filthy soil.

'We're leaving now,' Scholar Yu's wife told the small patch of ground. But when she tried to picture him it was no longer easy, as if his memory was wearing away from too much use. Sometimes she mixed Little Flower and her son up; sometimes she forgot that Little Flower was adopted, not her own child. Scholar Yu's wife felt foolish standing over the flat earth, bit her lip and silently thought of all the things she had wanted to say. She made a short prayer up, turned slowly away. She left behind a final treat for her son's ghost: candied crab apples and a small bag of haw jelly, half hidden in the long summer grasses.

* * *

Scholar Yu waited for the heat of summer to pass and then one morning they set off, following their shadows southwards. Scholar Yu's friends met him three miles from the town gates. A white felt tent screened a table and two cooks worked to fan the coals; their faces were clean but their hands were dirty. The scholar's friends feasted him and toasted him, sent him, a little unsteady, on his way. Scholar Yu kept turning back but they waved him on.

'Don't think of us!' they shouted. 'Diyi's not going anywhere!'

The cooks clattered and banged as they cleared up. Scholar Yu's friends stood and watched him stroll down the road, under the mountain slopes, and eventually out of their sight.

'Strangers in the road are no companion!' they teased him.

'There are no gentlemen in the wilderness!'

'Success is as ephemeral as floating clouds!'

It was a week's walk from Diyi to Datong, a great city set in the middle of a plain, ringed by mountains; guarding the passes that led south. There were fields and settled country where bamboo and houses dotted the landscape, the soil sculpted in regular patterns by years of farming. They stopped for two nights and set off again, well rested.

In the fields the peasants were beginning the barley harvest. Granny Pig and Uncle Jia shouldered their carrying poles, balanced themselves between the load of years, tottered along, proving that they were not too old to travel. But after only three days Uncle Jia took ill and they had to hire a mule from the local villagers, ended up hiring one for Granny Pig as well. The old couple sat on the stubborn beasts, clutching felt blankets around their bones, wishing for their thatched cottage.

It was another week's travel from Datong to Taiyuanfu. If Datong had looked impressive, then Taiyuanfu was majestic. The walls were higher and larger, the banners more inspiring – they flapped more excitedly in the wind.

Hometown to the Tang Emperor's Illustrious Ancestors, Taiyuanfu was capital of the north: temples, markets, palaces and magical hills from which the people dug black rocks that they burnt for fuel. Along the roadside they passed temples to the Black Stone Sage at which miners prayed for forgiveness for digging up the earth, and where the farmers poured libations of ale.

The Black Stone Sage was also said to be able to cure infertility. 'The black rock has been given as a gift for sentient beings,' a Buddhist pilgrim, on his way to Wutai Mountain, told Little Flower, but later that night when they sat huddled in their single room, their bags and packs piled around them, Scholar Yu explained how the black stone happened when lightning struck the earth. 'The black rock is a gift from the Emperor of Heaven,' he told them all, but Uncle Jia was asleep, Scholar Yu's wife was preparing the beds, and Granny Pig put a hand on Little Flower's shoulder and yawned. It seemed that only Little Flower was interested, but eventually she yawned, and the scholar yawned too.

'Bed,' he said, and they lay down together, pulled the blankets over them, dreamt their separate dreams.

From Taiyuanfu the government roads were broad and smooth, the dykes freshly dug, the messengers busy with news from north and south. There were post-houses; inns and military villages; ranks of soldiers practising war; ready to repel nomadic incursions.

Autumn came early that year, the rain washed the green

from the leaves, and the long north wind swept down from the steppes and made them all pull their coats close round them. The thought of the next night's hostel kept them going all day, and only Little Flower stopped and turned to look north with a quizzical expression on her face.

'Daughter!' Scholar Yu's wife said and Little Flower turned and blushed and hurried along.

Three days south of Taiyuanfu they took a barge down the Fen River, stopped at Linfen, Xiezhou and Reicheng, reached the shores of the Yellow River at last, where a sandy ribbon of dykes lined the banks, lifted the river twenty feet above the surrounding farmland. It had taken generations of public labour to keep the river from flooding, but even with effort and sacrifices it was impossible to keep the river in the clouds for ever. Scholar Yu's wife looked at the farmers who worked in the shadow of the dykes and wondered how it must be, each autumn, wondering if the dykes would break, living without the possibility of tomorrow. No wonder so many men left, went south to where the landlords were fewer and the weather was kinder.

As they approached the dykes Little Flower held on to her mother's hand and refused to let go. The Yellow River was brown and thick with soil, like soup not water. They crossed the river on a pontoon bridge, two massive bronze oxen keeping each rope taut, continually straining against the lure of the river.

At one point Little Flower peered over the edge. Come swim with the dragons, the swirling water seemed to say, come swim with the pots and pans and people, come play in your mother's fields – but Scholar Yu's wife tugged Little Flower well back.

'It's dangerous!' she said sharply.

* * *

The road to the capital led north of Flower Mountain, where five great petals of granite sheltered in the clouds. Daoists and Immortals lived in the highest slopes, too steep for any man to climb. Little Flower remembered the story that Uncle Jia had told them and wished she could climb up among the swirling cloud scarves and meet the goddesses who wore rainbow coats and kingfisher hair-pins, rode on cranes and steeds of pure white wind. But as they trudged along, the clouds began to bruise and darken and spots of rain landed in the fine loess dust. They took shelter in a roadside temple, whose rotting thatch was beginning to fall to the ground, the bones of the roof exposed to the sky.

When they had finished their lunch of dried meat and water, the showers had faltered and stopped. Scholar Yu wrote a couplet to accompany the other literary graffiti left by travellers and Little Flower watched and laughed at his poem, lingered to read some of the others.

The one she liked best was a poem called 'At the Roadside Temple We Sheltered from Thunderstorms'. Scholar Yu had to help her with some of the characters, but one line struck her and she stopped to read it over and over – long after the others had stood up and set off.

'Quickly Little Flower!' her mother called out and Little Flower turned reluctantly away still trying to memorise the new characters, repeating the poem in her head, embedding it in memory.

> You ask me where is Flower Mountain,
> my heart tells me it's beyond the white clouds.

With each day they travelled along the capital road, the land became visibly richer. Here the peasants lived not in caves but in brick houses; Scholar Yu and his family passed ordered fields and well-maintained manor houses. Order here was well observed.

Sometimes the traffic of carts and wagons meant Scholar Yu and his family had to walk at the side of the road, where peasants had made paths of their own. Often they passed teams of conscripted workers, repairing the roads by ramming the fine earth flat and hard.

'When you find a good place, settle down,' Scholar Yu laughed, and his wife gave him a sharp look.

Better to light a dark place than cover a pagoda with lanterns, she thought. There was no shortage of scholars in the capital. Better to head south to the swampy fens. Better off taking culture to the Mongolians or Koreans. Set sail and head for the Eastern Islands, she muttered in her mind. Teach the monkeys how to read and write.

She kept repeating arguments to herself, winning each one. The scholar's dreams were foolish. It was a miracle Granny Pig and Uncle Jia had survived. She had imagined growing old in Diyi. She knew nothing of the capital, except that it was large and hungry and very far away.

The next day they reached the shores of the Chongbi Canal. The water was limpid and still; the banks were lined with willows and villages and bamboo groves that stretched rustling fingers high into the air. At the bends vast flocks of geese and ducks kept the capital fed; here and there folk from the city drifted in painted pleasure-boats, cormorant fishermen twirled their small paddles, turned their boats easily, their ranked birds taking turns to dive through the ripples, come up choking on carp and bream and whiskered catfish.

The Chongbi Canal connected Changan to the Yellow River. Boats could sail from there to the locks of the

Grand Canal at Luoyang. Scholar Yu had told Little Flower all about the Grand Canal. It had been built by the Second Sui Emperor to connect the major rivers, which all flowed east–west. Various branches connected major towns and cities with the Yangtze and Yellow Rivers. It was over three thousand li in length. It brought rice and silk and salt and taxes north. It took troops, culture, settlers and government south.

Uncle Jia had told her stories of how the Chongbi Canal was lined with palaces and gardens. He had said that coiffured beauties sprinkled the world with laughter and disdain, but on the second day the wind was cold and the rain steady. There were no pleasure boats adrift on the water. The rain doused the red leaves, left the world colourless and grey and ready for winter.

That day Scholar Yu and his family stopped at a canal village, found a thatched hut where they could shelter, paid the mule drivers in copper coins and then the landlady gave Scholar Yu an overcoat of straw and a conical hat, and he went back into the rain to call to passing barges.

The others sat on low bamboo stools and looked out through the dripping doorway. Granny Pig and Uncle Jia shivered, their hair wet, their joints creaking. Little Flower and Scholar Yu's wife steamed in the fireside warmth. They could see the cold raindrops splattering the puddles. The rain turned the fine loess soil to a thick yellow mud while the house owner carried on with her morning routines – washing pots and kneading dough.

Just before lunch a long trail of salt barges came round the corner drawing a long tail of gentle foam. There must have been over fifty barges, all tied together, two wide. The shouts of the goaders and the snorts and farts of the water buffaloes broke the stillness. As they came closer

Scholar Yu bargained and then came into the hut and ushered them all outside. Granny Pig winced as she stood up, too tired to carry her pole. Scholar Yu hurried back and forth, gathering his family and possessions, helping them all. They made a bedraggled huddle on the canal bank, waiting as the barges glided through the rain, fallen leaves chasing each other back and forth in the spreading wakes.

As they stood the rain lifted and a beam of sunlight appeared through the clouds, pointing north. Little Flower sat on a bag and stared at the puddle's reflection: through the trampled mud she could just make out the house they had stayed in. As she stood up and bent closer the reflection shifted. Looking down between her feet she no longer saw the thatched hut but Heaven, and imagined her mother in the stormy rainclouds peering back down at her.

> You ask me where is Flower Mountain,
> [she remembered still]
> my heart tells me it's beyond the white clouds.

AD 903

Minister Li and his party rose after dawn. Their faces were lined with red bites where the bugs had gathered: bites that were sore and addictively itchy. They ate a meal of steamed buns before the servants saddled the horses and they set off south. It was a long quiet morning; the minister rode at the back of the line, his eyes closed for much of the time, his beard wagging in sleep. Fang occasionally turned to look. The minister's horse was only being led by the horse tail in front of it.

'Take the reins,' he said, and a servant rode close to the minister's horse, and leant over in his saddle, took the reins from the minister's hands.

Minister Li jerked awake. He snatched back the reins.

'I'm not so old that I cannot ride a horse!' Minister Li spluttered – not to the servant, but to Fang.

They travelled in silence for most of the afternoon, past unkempt fields and stripped winter trees that were crooked and bent with age. About ten miles from the hostel they came upon the wake of the rebellion: unharvested fields;

ruined villages, still black and charred; the scent of decay foretelling disaster.

Late that afternoon they stopped at a village, paid for stabling, a roof and a meal of mutton noodles with half a brick of black tea, stamped with the Buddhist knot of infinity. The woman who served them wore a new set of hemp clothes, dyed blue. She had a green jade ring on her middle finger.

'Wa!' Minister Li said, in pointless disapproval. There were laws governing what peasants could wear: undyed hemp. Nothing more.

'Chilli?' she asked, as she served the noodles.

Fang nodded. Two of the servants shook their heads, till there was only Minister Li left.

'Chilli?' she asked him, as she set the other bowls on the table. 'Sir?'

Minister Li refused to look at her. 'Yes,' he grunted at last, and she gave him an extra large helping to wash his stomach clean.

When the peasant's husband walked into the room, Minister Li wiped his mouth and turned on his stool. 'Master peasant, women in the capital do not presume to dress in such clothes.'

The man looked at him, ran a hand over his bald scalp, tried to speak politely.

'We do not live in the capital,' he said. 'The capital has nothing to do with us. Our taxes don't go to the capital, and our sons don't get conscripted. We've had peace and quiet here for nearly ten years. Business is good.'

Minister Li refused to argue. He put his chopsticks down. He was no longer hungry.

It was another month of travel before they reached the

Li Family Manor. It had a forlorn look to it; the mistress accepted him back with her usual cold dignity.

'Greetings husband,' she said, and bowed as low as her joints would allow.

The minister walked past, through the crumbling old gateway.

Fang came next, leading the horses.

'Greetings mistress,' he said and bowed, but she was already walking away, trailed by a duckling crowd of maid-servants. One at the back was young and pretty. Fang caught her eyes for a moment too long. He smiled despite himself, Swallow blushed and turned, hurried after her mistress.

It took a week for Minister Li to recover from the long trip. When he found that his wife had put Fang in the servants' quarters he went and shook his bony old fist at her and told her that he was master of this household, not her.

Minister Li's wife accepted the reprimand without a word.

She had made her point.

AD 853

The prow of the barge met wind and rain and waves head on, ploughed through them. During the day they passed fields and villages. Little Flower lay on her front and watched the water buffaloes' tails flicking in time with the biting flies, sunken fish leaping for the dragon-flies. At night when the water buffaloes were rested, Little Flower lay on her back, stared up at the constellations and thought about the time before she had joined the Yu family. The details were not clear but she knew that life had not been good then: the days were unforgiving. She trailed her hand through the black water, leaves of water chestnuts snagging on her wrist, tempting the fish to nibble her fingers, the water cool but not cold. She wiped her hand dry, turned on her side and adjusted the bundle that served as her pillow. 'All roads lead to the capital,' the saying ran, but she had never thought she would go there.

The next morning Little Flower was full of questions for Scholar Yu. He told her that Changan was like a huge chessboard, measuring ten by twelve li. The criss-cross lines were vast avenues hundreds of feet wide. Each square was a ward with walls and gates and markets and streets of its own. The main avenue of Changan was called the Avenue of Heaven. It ran north–south, from the palace gate to the city gates; was three hundred paces from one side to the other. The palace was a town in itself, larger than Diyi; there was a huge screen with nine dragons coiled together, and when the Emperor slept the dragons guarded his bed. There were many parks of unrivalled tranquillity; red-skirted courtesans walked there, hopeful young men following them through the evenings like clouds of mosquitoes.

Little Flower listened wide-mouthed, didn't believe anywhere could be so graceful and serene and majestic until they arrived at the canal port to the south of the city and they joined the throngs and wagons and pushed through the great southern gates, red silk banners stiff in the breeze. The Avenue of Heaven was full of thousands of people jostling and pushing and shouting, more a four-mile marketplace than a road. Little Flower clung to Scholar Yu's hand, didn't let go, even when they were standing inside the calm of a hostel, which was even bigger than the yamen in Diyi. When Scholar Yu's wife went to find the cooking area, Little Flower followed, stood so close that her mother kept tripping over her. 'Stand over there,' Scholar Yu's wife said, and steered her daughter away.

Scholar Yu found a house in a ward to the west of the city, where the poor people were crammed in with drifters and transients and foreigners and beggars. The ward walls were tall and solid enough to keep thieves out at night; a moat surrounded it on three sides and the banks were lined with willows. By the gate there was an old apple tree, bent and twisted like an old crone, that hung on to its last few leaves like Granny Pig treasured her last few teeth.

With three halls on a central courtyard, the house was much like their home in Diyi, but smaller and less welcoming. Granny Pig and Uncle Jia took one of the side halls while Scholar Yu and his family took the one in the centre.

The rooms were cold but they were dry and solid. They were fine, they would do, Scholar Yu's wife told herself as they began to unpack, but there were too many changes for her to feel comfortable. Granny Pig was convinced that if she stepped outside the ward she would be swept away in the crowd of people and end up in Hindustan or paddling in the Eastern Sea, so she gripped Little Flower's hand and relied on the little girl to find the way back to the safety of their ward.

Little Flower laughed to see the old woman so frightened. 'Just look for the moat and the willows and the apple tree,' she said but Granny Pig didn't smile.

'You're young,' she told Little Flower when they went out to buy noodles in the night market, but the noodles came in so many different shapes and thicknesses that Granny Pig and Scholar Yu's wife didn't know what to ask for.

'We want Diyi noodles,' Granny Pig said stubbornly, but the noodle-seller's wife had never heard of Diyi.

'We have thick and thin, buckwheat, millet or egg noodles,' she said and shouted something to her husband over their heads.

'Three thick noodles.' Granny Pig was resolute. 'With smoked mutton.'

The noodle-seller's wife looked down. 'We don't have smoked mutton.'

'Do you have any mutton?'

The woman put her hand on her hip, shouted something to her husband again. 'Three thick mutton noodles?'

Scholar Yu's wife nodded.

'Chilli?'

'Yes,' Little Flower said.

Granny Pig hung her head. 'I feel foolish,' she said, and Scholar Yu's wife nodded. They all felt that the capital folk were laughing and pointing.

When they had been there a month Scholar Yu took Little Flower across the Avenue of Heaven to the eastern side of the capital. The ward walls were noticeably taller and more majestic. There were fewer vagrants and beggars, more men of standing and learning, courtesans and sedan chairs with beaded curtains. In one street Little Flower saw more government officials than she had ever seen before – put together! The colours of their clothes showed their rank. No one in Diyi had worn anything better than blue, but Scholar Yu stopped to stare at a man in the green robes of a second level official while Little Flower stopped as well and noticed a crab-apple seller, the red candied fruit raised high above the reach of passers-by.

The further north and east, the nearer they came to the imperial palace. Here the wards were taken up with palaces and temples and ministries of government. Scholar Yu and Little Flower passed one ward that was used as a polo field and another where horse archers were galloping up and down, feathering straw targets. They stopped outside one that seemed entirely filled with a palace called Pepper Tree Mansion, turned left and left and left again, walked round the ward's circumference, peered in at gracefully eaved roofs of yellow tiles.

Scholar Yu imagined a world of music and silk and leisure; Little Flower thought of playing all day and eating meat at every meal. High above the compound walls a brick pagoda peered down at them, the tinkle of wind-chimes drifting down to earth like softly falling leaves. Little Flower and

Scholar Yu stopped to stare and the scholar told himself that this was why he had come to the capital, so his family could live in such ease and style and Little Flower felt that she had tripped and fallen into Heaven.

When they had finished the circuit, they stopped outside the east gate of the mansion where long banners fluttered.

'What does that one say?' Scholar Yu asked.

'Honoured House of Vice Consul Wang, Third Grade Commissioner for the Salt and Iron Bureau,' Little Flower read and Scholar Yu rubbed her scalp affectionately. They stared for a little longer, neither speaking, then Scholar Yu picked up his daughter and they walked back towards the Avenue of Heaven, waited for a train of two-humped Bactrian camels loaded with bolts of silk to pass south, then hurried across to the western half, where the houses in the wards were pressed together like sheep in a pen and where the crowds rose and fell like tides of the Eastern Sea and made their way back to their ward, where the bent old apple tree welcomed them home by fluttering its few leaves.

When his family were settled, Scholar Yu followed all the advice the magistrate of Diyi had given him, walked all over town, looking for an introduction, found nothing.

'Father,' Little Flower asked, 'why not get a different job?'

Scholar Yu smiled. 'There is no other job for a gentleman,' he said, but his voice sounded tired.

'You could sell crab apples,' she suggested, and thought how good it would be to eat glazed crab apples day after day.

'If I sold crab apples I would be working for myself,' he told her. 'If I was working for the civil service I would be working for the country.'

Little Flower nodded, but didn't really understand.

'Why is it hard to find a job?' she asked, after a while.

'Because,' Scholar Yu's wife butted in, 'you need connections.'

'But I thought you passed the exams and that was that.'

So did we, Scholar Yu's wife thought, but said, 'Life is difficult sometimes.'

When the round of civil service interviews began Scholar Yu dressed and prayed and burnt a paper golden ingot in the local temple. The night before he was too nervous to sleep, turned and twisted and kept his wife awake, only knew that he had slept when he had woken up. He smelt cooking. Smelt a fire. Sat bolt upright.

'Go back to sleep,' his wife whispered. 'The drum hasn't sounded yet.'

Scholar Yu turned his back on his wife and pulled the blankets back over him. He shut his eyes, but his mind kept turning over things to say, all the possibilities that led from his interview, what would happen if he failed. He didn't think he slept, but the next thing he knew was his wife's hand on his shoulder, waking him gently.

'The drum has sounded,' she said and Scholar Yu rubbed his eyes and yawned. 'I've made some dumplings,' she said. 'They're almost ready.'

Little Flower was awake early. She watched Scholar Yu get dressed, and was excited that today was the special day her father was going to get a civil service job. Scholar Yu tried to eat heartily, but he was too nervous to sit down, too jittery to stand. Little Flower laughed and seemed immune to the tense air. She was animated as she ate her dumplings. She wanted to help comb Scholar Yu's hair, but Scholar Yu's wife told her to shush. 'Go and sit on the bed,' she said and Little Flower sat, swinging her legs back and forth, as Scholar Yu's wife combed her husband's hair, bound a black turban tightly round his head. When his turban was finished, she smoothed down the shoulders of his blue silk gown and bent to rub dried dirt from his felt boots.

They walked him through the streets to the edge of the ward, stopped by the apple tree and watched him walk almost out of sight, but Scholar Yu did not turn and wave, and when he was lost to view, Scholar Yu's wife and Little Flower felt somehow forgotten.

'Come on,' Scholar Yu's wife said, when he was gone, 'let's go home.'

But Little Flower pulled a face. 'Can I go play?' she asked, and her mother nodded and watched her daughter skip away. Care is wasted on things that are out of reach, the saying went. She looked back towards the gateway and hoped that the day would fulfil all her husband's expectations, then turned for home, wondering what she wanted so much that she would move the family three thousand li to an alien life in the capital.

When Scholar Yu arrived at the Temple of Sage Kung already there was a crowd of well-wishers, patrons and candidates like himself.

Scholar Yu pushed nervously past. 'Excuse me,' he said. 'Sorry, I have an interview, excuse me.'

In the courtyard there were rows of carved stone steles, like enormous headstones, each engraved with official records, imperial proclamations, learned essays from prominent ministers of long dead emperors. In the midst of all those centuries of learning and brilliance stood a nervous crowd of fresh hopefuls. They smiled and chatted in uncertain circles, waiting to hear their names called.

One by one they stepped into the inner courtyard, and when Scholar Yu's name was called, he wiped the sweat from his hands, straightened his straight gown one last time, walked through the gate into the main hall. The audience was brief and curt. Yes, he was from Diyi. Yes, he was now living in the capital. Yes, he had done very well in his exams. He hoped for a position in the Salt and Iron Bureau. At that the examiner gave a short laugh, and looked expectantly across the table.

'Is there anything else you want to tell me?'

Scholar Yu cleared his throat, held out both hands and presented the scroll of poetry. 'Just this,' he stammered.

'What's this?'

'It's a' – his voice squeaked and he coughed to clear his throat – 'a poem.'

'What's it for?'

Scholar Yu didn't know what to say. His face flushed imperial red, his voice clotted deep in his throat. 'It is a mark of respect,' he said at last.

'What's the title?' the examiner asked, the scroll balanced in his hand.

'"New Year's Day: Drunk I Watch the Geese Fly South".'

'Who wrote it?'

'I did.'

The examiner let the scroll drop with a tired sigh: so many poems and gifts and bribes and hopeful men whose dreams it was his responsibility to grant or deny. It was a hard morning: only three candidates had had the sense to commission verses from some noteworthy artist like Meng Jiao or Wen Tingyun.

'Next!' he shouted and Scholar Yu could hardly believe his chance was over.

'Next!' the man repeated – like a goad – and Scholar Yu hung his head and thought of his wife and family and his shame as the next man pushed eagerly in.

* * *

The Yu family had been in Changan for nearly three and a half months when their store of money began to thin. The threat of poverty stayed with them like a cold draught – unseen but palpable. No one talked about starvation, but when the cold weather arrived, Scholar Yu's wife cursed the price of charcoal, made pointed comments about how cheap life was in Diyi. The rest of the family listened, huddled together and waited for the fire to warm the kang.

Despite his setbacks, Scholar Yu tried to maintain an air of confidence. 'I will find a good job,' he assured, but weeks passed and hope could neither feed them nor keep them warm. In the morning Scholar Yu's wife had to break through the thin crust of ice in the bucket to get water to make the morning soup. When Little Flower got out of bed the shards had refrozen into overlapping dragon scales, like river ice. Soon they stopped heating the kang, slept fully dressed, their thin bones shivering inside their padded jackets and trousers. Scholar Yu's wife only lit the fire when she was cooking. They ate hot soup for breakfast, warm noodles for lunch, but when dinner came the coals had turned to cold grey ash and they ate cold buckwheat noodles mixed with raw garlic and sesame seeds and vinegar, then went to bed, listening to the sounds of their neighbours in their warm houses, drinking wine and talking, their laughter making Scholar Yu and his family shiver even more. No one could sleep at first, but no one told stories and no one talked about the cold, except Little Flower, who pressed close between her parents and rattled her teeth. Scholar Yu stopped drinking wine, and each morning his dusty cup and empty jar shamed him, made him quiet and thoughtful.

One day they woke to freezing rain, and no one wanted to get out of bed to buy vegetables. At last Scholar Yu took a few coins, went out, came back with spring onions and cabbage and a thin mouldy lotus root. His hair was wet and red blush showed through the tan of his skin. He went out again without speaking, came back with a pot of cheap sorghum wine and set it on the table.

'This'll keep us warm,' he joked, but Uncle Jia had fallen asleep again and no one smiled.

Scholar Yu's wife made thin soup while Scholar Yu rubbed his fingers and warmed the pot on the dying break-fast embers. As everyone else slurped soup, he poured himself a cup of gently steaming wine and drank it down. Spoons scraped the bowls clean as he drank, no one spoke as he drank cup after cup. Little Flower was thinking of the food the wine could have bought; Scholar Yu's wife was thinking of their life in Diyi; and Granny Pig wondered if she and her husband would starve or freeze to death. It seemed a shame to end a happy life this way, she thought, smacked her gums and counted her teeth, wondered how old age had come upon them so soon.

'I'm sorry,' Scholar Yu slurred at last. 'We should never have come here.'

There was a heavy silence. Little Flower fidgeted with the hem of her jacket.

'I am the one responsible for you all,' he said. 'I cannot let my family go cold and hungry.'

They were cold and hungry already, Granny Pig thought as the others nodded, kept her mouth shut.

It was decided that Scholar Yu would sell steamed buns. Each morning Granny Pig and Scholar Yu's wife got up and steamed the buns, sent Scholar Yu out with his trays.

'Steamed buns!' he would call. 'Steamed buns!'

When he had sold all his buns he came home and took another tray, went out again, whatever the weather. Some-times Little Flower would try to go with him, play in the streets. 'Little Flower!' her mother scolded. 'It's not safe!'

Her mother was always scolding her these days, and Little Flower sat down reluctantly to help Granny Pig grind wheat into flour. 'I've got a headache,' she said one day. 'I want to go to bed.'

'Finish grinding first,' her mother said.

Little Flower ground. 'Can we go back to Diyi?' she asked.

'Hush,' Scholar Yu's wife said and her face was hard. Little Flower turned the millstone as slowly as possible.

'Do it properly!' her mother scolded, but Little Flower pretended that she didn't know how to do it properly. She split grains and let the flour fall on to the floor, let the millstone slip so that grit and soil were mixed into the flour. When Scholar Yu's wife saw the wheat in the dirt she grabbed Little Flower's arm with one hand and hit her head with the other. 'I'll show you how to do it properly!' she told her. Little Flower tried to cover her head, but Scholar Yu's wife hit her again, then walked inside and slammed the door.

Neither Scholar Yu's wife nor Little Flower spoke to each other through the rest of that afternoon. When Granny Pig came out she found Little Flower on her own, grinding the wheat and sniffing back tears. She didn't like to ask what the argument had been about and Little Flower didn't say.

'Where's your mother?' Granny Pig asked after a long silence.

Little Flower shrugged.

'You haven't seen her?'

Little Flower shook her head.

That night Scholar Yu sat drinking warm water as his wife kneaded the dough for tomorrow's buns. 'I'm not going to shave her head any more,' Scholar Yu's wife said. 'It's time you looked for a husband for her.'

'Isn't she a bit young still?' Scholar Yu said, but his wife didn't look up, kept kneading the dough, stretching and pushing, over and round.

'She's nine,' she said, as if that explained everything. Scholar Yu put his feet on the table and stretched his arms out over his head. He watched his wife for a long time, waited for her to let the tired dough rest.

'Well, she'll have to grow her hair,' he said, not clear why his wife wanted to find Little Flower's husband so suddenly. 'There are a couple of years yet.'

Scholar Yu's wife put the cloth over the dough and let it settle for the night.

'There are,' she said and brushed past him and spilt the cup of water he was cradling. Scholar Yu dabbed away the water, frowned at his wife but she ignored him.

'Maybe she can marry another steamed bun seller,' Scholar Yu's wife said as she started repairing the soles of Little Flower's shoes. Scholar Yu refilled his cup: he couldn't talk to her when she was like this. The two of them sat alone, thoughts and arguments gathering like rainclouds. At last Scholar Yu cleared his throat and spoke: 'If I don't get a job by the summer we will go back to Diyi.'

Scholar Yu's wife said nothing, but plunged the needle with renewed vigour, began counting the days.

One day the neighbours came to complain that Little Flower was encouraging their children to run and jump over the open mouth of the well. Little Flower looked guilty and Scholar Yu's wife pulled her daughter into the yard and took off a shoe to beat her. When the neighbours kept shouting, Scholar Yu's wife gave them the shoe. 'Beat her yourself,' she told them, but they were frightened by her manner and hurried away.

'What will happen if you fall in?' Scholar Yu's wife demanded. 'Don't you know how dangerous it is?'

Little Flower tried to look as if she didn't care. Of course it was dangerous, she thought as she scratched the long stubble on her head. That was the fun, stupid.

'If you fall in, who will stop you drowning?' Scholar Yu's wife demanded, but Little Flower rubbed at an imaginary spot on her jacket.

'Can't you speak?' Scholar Yu's wife shouted and hit her daughter and despite all Little Flower's determination the tears came.

'Tears won't help you when you fall down the well,' Scholar Yu's wife said and went to tell Granny Pig what had happened. Granny Pig let out a screech of horror and came to the doorway to wag a finger at Little Flower, but Little Flower turned away, didn't care any more.

It wasn't long before Scholar Yu heard what had happened. He hurried home and apologised to the neighbours. When he had been to visit them all he shut the gate behind him and went inside.

'Well,' he said, 'what's this I hear?'

Little Flower wiped her nose on the back of her hand.

'If you die, who will look after us in our old age?'

Little Flower didn't care about their old age, but at last she mumbled, 'I won't do it again.'

'Promise?'

'I promise.'

'What?'

'I promise not to jump wells.'

'Never?'

'Never,' Little Flower said.

* * *

The last weeks of 853 passed in tense quiet. Everyone worked and kept their thoughts to themselves, even Little Flower, who tried to avoid her mother as much as possible. In the last days before Spring Festival everything was put away in its proper place: great care was taken so nothing should be broken that would bring another year's worth of bad luck.

Two days before the festival Scholar Yu and his wife counted their money and put aside a pile for the New Year celebrations. Granny Pig sent Little Flower out with her scissors to be sharpened, and Little Flower found the knife-sharpener, and watched while he scraped the blunted steel back into a blade, smoothed the grooves out with a metal plate, polished them with a leather strap. The metallic smell of steel fragments made her think of a man who beat iron all day. The memory niggled her because she couldn't picture it any more, just knew the smell.

'Here,' Little Flower said to the man, when he gave her the scissors, and waited for the change, ran to the ward gate and bought a crab-apple stick, the fruit encased in a shell of red sugar. The apple was tart, but the sugar with it made it tart and sweet in one mouthful. She finished the last one at the gate, spat the pips on to the dirt, went inside.

'Here!' she called. 'Here!'

'Where's the change?' Granny Pig asked, and Little Flower shook her head.

'No change?' Scholar Yu's wife said, and Little Flower shook her head again. 'Aya!' she said. 'You should have bargained!'

But Granny Pig took Little Flower's hand and led her to the table where she began to cut the folded sheets of red paper. 'Like this,' she said but Little Flower kept cutting too hard, turning flowers into petals, signs for double happiness into rubbish.

'Careful!' Scholar Yu's wife said. 'You're wasting it!' Little Flower put the scissors down and refused to try any more. Granny Pig gave up encouraging her and Scholar Yu took Little Flower outside to help him patch up the holes in the paper windows.

'She's spoilt,' Scholar Yu's wife told her husband later that night. Scholar Yu looked away. 'Don't you agree?' she said and he tried to answer with a 'hmm'. 'What does that mean?' Scholar Yu's wife asked.

'Yes,' he said at last. 'I agree.'

There were many things to see in Changan around the time of Spring Festival, and when the last night of the year arrived not even Scholar Yu's wife could maintain her glowering manner. Even unfriendly neighbours stopped to talk. When they sat down to eat their last meal of 853 everyone was loud and talkative, the troubles of the year put aside for a while. They ate dumplings and pickles and fish and meat and chicken, and Scholar Yu poured them all a cup of wine, Little Flower included, toasted the Kitchen God in his little niche and flattered him with ten thousand praises. It was important that when the Kitchen God made his secret report to the Magistrate of Heaven he gave good news. Their luck for the year ahead depended on what he said. Gods were invented by men: they were as susceptible to flattery as anyone else.

As the evening wore on Granny Pig reminisced, and when Uncle Jia heard what she had said he shouted out corrections, and Little Flower laughed the loudest. Although the food was simple there was three times more than they could possibly eat, and Scholar Yu's wife and Scholar Yu carried it to the side and covered the bowls with plates, and opened the doors and went outside.

The air was cold but it had a good fresh smell, scented with woodsmoke. There was a ragged thunder as people threw bamboo segments into their fires and watched them explode. A man was hawking crab apples: Little Flower heard his voice, almost sad in the winter dusk, shouting, 'Crab apples! Crab apples!' and jumped up and down with excitement.

Scholar Yu picked up his daughter and carried her to the front gate and they stood and watched the fires in the streets, showering sparks with each pop of bamboo. Little Flower put her arms round his neck as he showed her the new calligraphy he'd written for their gateposts.

> Wealth and honour are welcome,
> Each year brings a wealth of treasures.

'What is the character for "year"?' Scholar Yu asked, and Little Flower traced the character in the palm of her hand. 年. 'Nian.'

'What do you think it looks like?'

She frowned. 'A house?'

'It's the name of a *monster*,' he said, and she turned to look at him, eyes wide open, sensing a story.

'Long long ago, before the Yellow Emperor, there was a monster that had one leg and a huge mouth that could swallow people alive. He was called the Nian!'

Little Flower remembered Yang Guifei, thought of the Nian eating her up.

'On the last day of each year he came down and jumped around eating people! One day an old man came to the village and promised the people that he would get rid of this nightmare. He warned them that if the Nian should ever return they should put up red paper cuts on their windows and scare it away. When the Nian returned the old man jumped on his back, and they went round the world eating other animals.'

'Do you know the characters for "*Guo Nian*" – Happy New Year?'

Little Flower knew the character for '*nian*', but she didn't know '*guo*'. She tried a different character, and he watched her and waited till she had written all the strokes for it on her palm before he said no.

'This is "*guo*".'

過, He traced it in her palm; the skin tickled where he had written the strokes. '"*Guo*" here means "survive" as in Guoxiang. "*Guo Nian*" means "to survive the Nian". Each year we live we "Survive the Monster" – *Guo Nian*!'

Little Flower looked down the street and watched the crab-apple man come closer. 'So why do we pop the bamboo?' she asked.

'That's to scare the Nian away,' Scholar Yu said, 'in case he should ever come back.'

'Do you think he will come back?'

'I don't think so,' Scholar Yu said and shivered. 'At least, not tonight.'

Little Flower's attention drifted off as a fire flared high, and more bamboo exploded. Scholar Yu called the crab-apple man and let her pick a candied crab-apple stick. There were four apples on each stick, and she made the man turn his stick round so that she could choose the biggest.

'How much?'

'Four cash,' the man said.

Scholar Yu was about to argue, but he didn't want the Kitchen God telling Heaven that he was mean. 'Here,' he said, and gave the man five.

Little Flower ate slowly, then held up the stick. 'I've finished!' she said, and she felt the cold as well and blew on her hands. 'Can I have another?' she asked, but Scholar

Yu had no more money on him. He adjusted his grip and walked back inside. Little Flower looked over his shoulder back into the dark street, but it was empty. All she could hear, drifting from far away, was the sad slow call of 'Crab apples! Crab apples!'

––––––––––

The spring of 854 started badly for the empire with an outbreak of locust and then news of a rebellion in Lufu Prefecture, two hundred miles south-east of Taiyuanfu, along the Yellow River valley. Everyone was terrified of the Imperial Wrestlers, who marched into the morning, their thick thighs rubbing in the middle, their arms away from their sides, their hair tied back, their fat bellies full. They waddled through the streets of the capital and the surrounding villages like a flock of aggressive ducks, pulled out vagrants or young men without a job or profession and forced them into military service.

It was early summer, and when the conscript army was finally ready it marched out of the capital with great fanfare and ceremony: wagons rumbling, horses snorting and neighing, mothers and fathers and children running alongside to say their goodbyes.

There were many broken branches on the willows around their ward. Under the old apple tree was a peasant selling crickets. Scholar Yu bought one, woven into its own wicket cage. Its antennae felt the inside of its prison like Uncle Jia's blind fingers; every once in a while it shrilled and then stopped. Little Flower sat over it and tapped the cage, watched the cricket's antennae feeling the air, held her breath and waited for it to shrill; tapped the cage again. She kept the cricket for a week, at one moment giving it some grass to eat, then flicking its cage to make it shrill.

One day she was playing with her friends and they got bored of crickets altogether, decided to pull its legs off, took it in turns: you pull one leg and I pull one leg.

Your turn, my turn.

Your turn, my turn.

The cricket struggled, all writhing legs and antennae. Little Flower was afraid it might bite and dropped it. The cricket flew into the air and landed three steps away. It only had one leg left. Its wings flapped as they chased it behind the well and Little Flower's friend caught it under her hand.

'Let it go,' Little Flower said, ready to pounce. When her friend removed her hand Little Flower stamped on the cricket and felt the hard body crack. They prodded it and squeezed it so that its soft insides popped out; they watched curious as one of the thin legs flinched. What did it take to kill a locust they wondered, and only when they had stamped on it again and twisted their foot round to leave it a smear did it stop moving.

'That's what'll happen to you if you're bad,' Little Flower's friend said as they peered down at the mess. 'My mother says if I'm bad I'll come back as a locust.'

'If I came back as a locust, my mother would stamp on me!' Little Flower said and didn't laugh.

That summer Little Flower and her friends hunted all kinds of insects and killed them. They pulled wings off butterflies, turned daddy-long-legs into legless drones and even baited wasps and bees and ran screaming away from their stings. Scholar Yu still did not have a civil servant job, but even though they had the money for the return trip home, Uncle Jia became ill and no one mentioned returning to Diyi.

Scholar Yu's wife got up each morning to wash and feed the old man. By the end of the day she was worn out. She wished he would hurry up and die or get better, but kept her mouth shut as she spoon fed the old man chicken and seaweed soup.

As autumn came, most of the money for the return trip home had been spent on Uncle Jia's medicine. One night after supper Scholar Yu's wife sat down and started to weep. Everyone looked at each other and wondered what was wrong.

'My husband was an official in Diyi,' she said to no one in particular. 'We had name and cash and people looked at us with respect. Now we wear threadbare clothes. We do not eat meat. We'll all die in this wretched place!'

It was up to Little Flower to put her arms round her mother's shoulders. She had friends here now, didn't want to go back to little Diyi, where the world was smaller and colder and less colourful.

It was around this time that Scholar Yu was invited to a poetry lunch at the house of a man called Examiner Zhou. He was as nervous as the day he had taken the civil service interviews, but this time his wife refused to help him dress. Little Flower watched her father leave and decided to stay away from her mother until he came home, not long before sunset.

He was drunk and happy, like a man who has just fallen out of Heaven. Little Flower couldn't remember seeing her father so content, but Scholar Yu's wife almost smiled, and wondered how sick he would feel when he sobered up.

Autumn was a popular time to watch the frost melt and the leaves fall and celebrate all the sadnesses of life. Scholar Yu had made such an impression that he was invited out to a round of morning banquets where the scholars and officials took it in turns to compose poems, play drinking games and compete in learning.

Scholar Yu grew plump again. Sometimes there were pretty girls to sing for them, pour their wine and laugh at their jokes, and then he would stumble home full of excitement and fondle his wife by the chopping board.

'Hush!' she said to him. 'Not now – Little Flower might come home.'

Scholar Yu protested at first, but she slapped away his hands. 'I'll throw a bucket over you if you touch me!'

I didn't come all this way to be molested, she told herself, but after a little while she relented, and Little Flower slept with Granny Pig and Uncle Jia that night. Uncle Jia's health had improved, but he still wheezed and spluttered as he slept. Little Flower's hair was a long stubble by then, enough to keep her scalp warm, but their old bodies emitted no heat, and their bones and flesh sagged as if the strength and solidity had gone out of them, lives slowly fading away to ghosts. Little Flower pulled the quilt higher and tried to turn over but their bodies were heavy and refused to move. She tossed and turned and lay awake, sometimes with her eyes open but mostly with them closed, thinking just enough to know she was not dreaming.

When the dawn birds began to fight outside, Little Flower got up from the cold straw mattress and gently pushed the door open. Her parents were in bed, their breath misting in the air above them. She crept across the room, but there was no room between her parents so she lay on the edge nearest the stove, with her mother's arm draped over her.

In the tenth month Scholar Yu attended the interviews again, came home early and took the day's last tray of buns out to the street. When he had finished his wife gave him enough to go to the teahouse. She watched him get dressed and set out across the yard, and wondered if they would ever see Diyi again.

'Can I go?' Little Flower asked and Scholar Yu's wife smiled.

'Will you be good?'

Little Flower nodded.

'Alright,' her mother said, and Little Flower ran to catch Scholar Yu up.

Green powdered tea was the cheapest on offer, but still Scholar Yu reckoned it was about twenty cash a sip, so he drank it slowly, savouring every mouthful. 'Here,' he said to Little Flower, and let her try it. 'Like it?'

Little Flower shook her head and watched the table next to theirs eating dried plums. She wished her father would buy some of those.

'I don't have money for them,' Scholar Yu said. They sat for a while, then a few men came in that Scholar Yu knew, and they began to discuss the news from the market-place. Little Flower got bored and looked around. On the central wall of the teahouse there was a set of eight scrolls, written by Lu Yu himself, master of tea. The scrolls were yellow with age, curling at the edges. 'Tea is from a grand tree in the south,' the first scroll announced. 'There is nothing like tea: it has the health properties of ginseng,' the last scroll declared, in faded and yellowed calligraphy. 'It has the ability to cure bad bowels; lifts melancholy; refreshes the brain; eases sore eyes. Its liquor is like the sweetest dew of Heaven.'

Little Flower turned to ask her father what 'melancholy' was but he was deep in conversation with two other men, their beards wagging in time with each other. She folded her arms and stood by his chair and waited for him to say that it was time to go.

When they got back that afternoon Scholar Yu's wife and Granny Pig stood up in a great hurry and started talking all at once. The sudden noise was bewildering – Scholar Yu didn't know who to turn to or listen to.

'Husband!' Scholar Yu's wife shouted, and waved her hand to silence Granny Pig. 'We have news!'

'Another child?'

Scholar Yu's wife slapped him for being such a slow old brain. 'No!' she said. 'Here!'

Scholar Yu's wife handed him a letter.

He opened it and read the words. Went back and read them again.

'I have a job,' he said, in a voice barely above a whisper. 'I have a job.' Scholar Yu sat down, looked at his wife. 'I have a job.' His voice grew quieter and quieter, but Scholar Yu's wife's hands were gripped together with her excitement.

'Husband!' She started crying because he had a job and she would be an official's wife and they would no longer be poor. 'Husband!' she said, clapping her hands and Little Flower jumped up and down and giggled even though she had no idea why everyone was so happy.

––––––––

The next year went well for the Yu family. Each morning Scholar Yu dressed in his best silk robe and hat, brushed his red felt boots, and set out for another day as a ninth grade official. He was so happy with himself that he didn't touch the ground, but floated the whole way, like Daoist Immortals walking on winds and clouds, over the Avenue of Heaven to the eastern side of the city, past Pepper Tree Mansion, which he and Little Flower had seen when they had first arrived, and north a few more wards, so close to the palace he could see the green willows standing along the royal moat.

The ward he went into was taken up with offices and ministries. When he arrived at the appointed branch of the Department of Households he got off his cloud. The earth beneath his feet felt good and firm and lucky. The sound of Secretary Yen, his superior, dulled his sparkle a little, but his mood was so polished he inhaled the fine cool morning and smiled.

'Donkey's ass!' Secretary Yen's voice sounded in the front yard. 'Educated worm!'

'Ah – good. Come here, Yu,' Secretary Yen said. 'I've just had this letter from Eunuch Jian Long and I need you to read it to me.'

Scholar Yu took the letter and read it aloud. It was all about a family who had dug a well and accidentally hit the grave of a Sui Dynasty general. The locals had reported ghosts and bad luck. The whole ward was terrified. It seemed this ghost needed to be placated, the family punished.

'Sage Kung said, "Respect ghosts and spirits, but keep away from them,"' Scholar Yu began.

The secretary looked at him. 'And?'

When Scholar Yu had finished explaining a course of action that was in keeping with the traditions and rituals, Secretary Yen clapped him on the back. 'Good,' he said, and Scholar Yu followed him as the secretary walked out into the yard. 'Now go and sort that out. I have a game of polo.'

Scholar Yu bowed as Secretary Yen climbed into his sedan and waited till the gates were shut before he walked back inside. He adjusted his sleeves, ground the inkstone and added a little water. 'Right,' he said to one of the assistants. 'Pass me the seal.'

Secretary Yen spent his days playing polo and hunting, and each week Scholar Yu sent him a report of all that happened and Secretary Yen would invite Scholar Yu to his manor for banquets. At the end of 855 Scholar Yu was promoted to eighth grade official, and to celebrate he bought a duck from the market. It quacked nervously as it was put down in the yard, tried to waddle to safety, but Little Flower caught it and carried it with the wings crossed behind its back, as she had seen the men in the market do. Scholar Yu's wife scraped the knife on a stone and the duck's legs paddled frantically as it struggled to flap its wings, but Little Flower held its head and pulled its neck taut, her hand trapping its tongue between the upper and lower beak as Scholar Yu's wife finished sharpening the knife. Neither of them spoke as she stood over the duck, like a doctor inspecting a patient, put the blade to the throat and began to cut.

Death came with little more than a strangled squawk, the head came away from the body and the tongue protruded from the beak, and Little Flower wiped her hands on the dirt to get rid of the blood.

'Bring it here,' Scholar Yu's wife said and Little Flower dropped the duck's head into the bowl. She stood close to her mother's side to watch her cut out the innards, plucking long and short feathers together, white down sticking to her blood-smeared fingers.

'Take that inside,' Scholar Yu's wife said as she rinsed her hands. Little Flower carried the bowl inside to where her father was drinking some wine.

'Here!' he said and held out his cup.

Little Flower carefully slid the bowl on to the chopping board.

'A toast!' Scholar Yu said and Little Flower took the cup and drank the wine.

When she turned the empty cup upside-down and not a drop fell out, Scholar Yu laughed. 'You'll be out-drinking your father soon,' he told her, but Little Flower held out the cup again.

'Only when I'm promoted again.' Scholar Yu laughed and took the cup from her.

In time Scholar Yu's hard work and energy attracted the attention of men in neighbouring ministries. At the beginning of 856 he was promoted again, and was offered a job in the Ministry of Roads and Transport, where a hundred men worked together in one large palace, each man charged with different responsibilities:

- to supply 9200 runners (to carry exotic foodstuffs [lychees, fresh oysters, mangoes, horse-nipple grapes] to the Imperial Palace)
- to repair and maintain 27,000 li of road
- to supply each of the 1297 post stations with food and money for passing members of the Imperial Family/officials/officials' families/horses/innkeepers and runners
- to provision and pay twenty-one inn keepers and post horse riders

The work was harder, but Scholar Yu loved both the pay rise and the new responsibility. When he came home, exhausted, he fell asleep with a sense of achievement and worth. For too long his family had suffered at the hands of pawn-brokers; for too long they had worn old and faded clothes. His wife had counted out their last month's wages too many times; no longer would icy draughts wander freely through their house.

Despite their new clothes, the rich foods and the heaps of charcoal they burnt to keep the kang warm, Uncle Jia's illness returned and his lungs were too old and weak to cough the sickness clear. Scholar Yu bought two long roots

113

of ginseng and gave them to Granny Pig. She refused them at first, but he said, 'You're family,' and left the package on the table.

Granny Pig grumbled as she boiled the ginseng, but she gave the soup to her husband and in the space of half an hour his pulse had quickened. When Little Flower went into Granny Pig's house, Uncle Jia was sitting up in bed, his eyes shut, his chin propped on his chest, breathing slowly.

'Is Uncle Jia going to be alright?' she asked, but Scholar Yu's wife put her hand on Little Flower's arm.

'Go and play outside,' she said.

'I can go on to the streets?'

'Yes. As long as you're back when your father comes home.'

Little Flower left her books and walked round the ward for a couple of hours, stopped and kicked some pebbles around with her toe. When she looked up she saw a moon-faced boy watching her. He had large chapped hands and a rough leather jerkin like the blacksmiths wore. Little Flower turned her back on him, but a few minutes later the boy was still staring at her so she stuck out her tongue and made him blush.

When Uncle Jia failed to improve, Scholar Yu paid for the cousin of a man who worked in his office to visit. The cousin had graduated from the Imperial College of Medicine, was learned in acupuncture, herbs and medicinal massage. He gave the old man more ginseng and the cough receded, but when the effects of the medicine had worn off he was so frail he couldn't lift his cup to drink, spilt it down his front, lay back exhausted.

As a child Uncle Jia had seen his grandparents' dead bodies, seen the great people of his time, enjoyed countless nights of friends, family music and wine. He had suffered hunger and poverty and the ruin of war, the loneliness of blindness, the attrition of old age. 'I have had a full life,' he wheezed, each breath coming slowly, his voice little more than a whisper. Granny Pig stroked his hand. 'Don't be sad,' he told her, and he lay back to recover from the effort of talking. 'I have lived well,' he said, after a long while, and Granny Pig pretended she had something in her eye, tried to sniff silently, did not look up.

'I will wait for you at the Yellow Springs,' Uncle Jia said, and his chest heaved with the exertion. Granny Pig squeezed his hand to say that she was listening and that he had been a good husband, that she would burn money and clothes and the finest food for the afterlife. If they could have had one of their days when they were young again, just one, she thought, and squeezed his hand again to tell him all this.

'I always knew that I would die,' Uncle Jia said, after a while, 'but,' he coughed, then lay back and licked the spittle from his lips, 'I never thought I would feel so calm.' The rattle in his chest sounded like laughter, but Granny Pig didn't laugh. She kept rubbing her eyes and squeezing his hand and wishing that this day had not come today.

Uncle Jia slept the rest of that afternoon. Scholar Yu was at the ministry, his wife was sweeping ashes from the kang and Little Flower was reading the *Analects of Sage Kung* in the light from the window.

'Will Uncle Jia die?' Little Flower asked and Scholar Yu's wife sat back on her haunches.

'Maybe,' she said and sat down to steady herself, then let out a long sigh.

Little Flower looked back at her book, but she no longer understood the words she was reading. She remembered the nights in Diyi, when Uncle Jia had told the story of Yang Guifei and the Emperor Xuanzong. Who would tell them stories at night, she wondered. Who would correct Granny Pig?

The next morning Scholar Yu had just left for the ministry when a cat-screech wail made Little Flower bite her lip. Scholar Yu's wife had flour on her hands. 'Fetch me the cloth!' she snapped and Little Flower put down her book and stood up. 'Quickly!' Scholar Yu's wife said and Little Flower didn't know what she had done wrong. The wail came again. It sounded more like Granny Pig this time. 'Come on!' Scholar Yu's wife said, and then, when her hands were clean, she said, 'Here!' Little Flower took the cloth back and watched her mother dash outside.

Little Flower stood alone in the room, uncertain what to do. She listened for voices, but all there was was the terrible screeching. She didn't want to get into more trouble so she sat back at her desk and looked at the list of questions her father had left her to answer, but she couldn't concentrate and put it down again: kept her brush in her hand so that if her mother came in it would look like she was working.

The wailing continued and Little Flower heard the gate swing open. There were voices in the yard and one of the neighbours peered inside, but Little Flower pointed to the room where Granny Pig and Uncle Jia lived.

'It's Uncle Jia,' Little Flower said.

All the neighbours came to help: some went to fetch mourners, others stood and gossiped, or tried to stop Granny Pig tearing at her hair.

'Ssh!' they said. 'You'll make his ghost sad.'

Granny Pig didn't listen but wailed and moaned and pulled thin locks of dry grey hair on to the floor.

'Such was his fate.' They spoke less kindly now, frightened

that the ghost might linger. 'The Provost of Heaven makes no mistakes.'

When mourners came Granny Pig finally rested, and Little Flower sat next to her, let the old woman hug her as if she was her husband in the form of a child. Uncle Jia's cold body was cleaned and dressed, measured for his coffin of fine rosewood, laid out in the yard under the pear tree. It was unlucky to have it inside the house.

When dusk came Little Flower lingered in the yard, went to stand by the coffin, chest high on wooden trestles. After a long while she touched Uncle Jia's outstretched hand. This is death, she told herself, imagined writing the strokes of the character. A white page, black brushstrokes slowly forming the word, the wet sheen drying and the paper yellowing with years till it was torn and cracked like the books her father brought home from the office.

死

'There are two parts to the character,' Scholar Yu explained in the quiet, as they sat inside, one empty place on the kang. He drew on his hand to show Little Flower what they were. 歹 'Crushed bones,' he said, 'and an upside-down person.'

匕

The next day Little Flower drew the character on her palm, curious to see how broken bones and a person lying the wrong way meant death. She let out a long sigh and picked up a coin to play with. She wished her mother would come and talk to her as well, but her mother was with Granny Pig, keeping the cold body company.

Granny Pig looked ten years older: her hair was grey, her wrinkles deeper as her flesh sagged. Little Flower watched the neighbours come and go. Who were these people? Why did they have the right to go in there when her mother was always shooing her out?

In the end she slipped out of the gate, saw the moon-faced boy again, and this time she blushed. When she got to the corner she broke into a run and sprinted away giggling, stopped at the next corner and peered round to see if he was following. She was annoyed to see that he wasn't, but a few moments later he came round the corner and Little Flower stuck her tongue out again.

The loss of Uncle Jia struck Granny Pig, Scholar Yu's wife and Little Flower much harder than it did Scholar Yu. Their hours and minutes were left with the empty silhouette of a real person. Scholar Yu had a tear in the routine of his days, easily patched and forgotten. When he came home there was no other man to question his judgement; there was one less mouth for which he was responsible.

Scholar Yu questioned his daughter on her studies; gave her the poems of Wang Wei and Du Fu to learn by heart; looked at the food his wife cooked and wished she'd try some of the capital-style recipes, like pork broth noodles or dofu with hot oil.

Some days he seemed tired and irritable, and Scholar Yu's wife did not know where he got his airs from. When he left a string of two thousand cash on the chopping block she picked it up.

'What's this?'

'I wanted you to wear something less rustic,' Scholar Yu told her.

'We're from Diyi.' Scholar Yu's wife waved the cleaver she was holding, and her accent seemed stronger than usual. 'Of course we're rustic.'

Little Flower wished she could climb inside the book she was holding.

'Are you embarrassed of us?' Scholar Yu's wife said and Scholar Yu laughed.

'That's stupid,' he said. 'Why would I be embarrassed of my family?'

Scholar Yu's wife put her hands on Little Flower's shoulders. Neither of them answered him. No one wanted to list all the reasons.

After that it seemed to Little Flower that her parents were always arguing. When she forgot a word, Scholar Yu would speak to her in a stern, ministry voice, like the magistrate in Diyi had used when sentencing people to be beaten with the cane.

'She doesn't need to read and write,' Scholar Yu's wife said but Scholar Yu refused to listen.

'Fetch the cane,' he said as if his authority were being challenged. There was a heavy silence as Little Flower picked up his cane from its place next to the rubbing of Sage Kung, carried it across the room, her palms already sweating. She raised her hand without being told to, shut her eyes as the cane flicked down, pressed down on it to lessen the pain. That night she went to Scholar Yu's wife and sat on her lap. Her mother kissed her on the head, smoothed the hair from her face. Scholar Yu tried to ignore them. The only thing that Scholar Yu and his wife did not disagree about was the fact that Little Flower was no longer allowed outside to play.

'You're too old to play,' Scholar Yu's wife said.

'You need to study,' her father told her. 'You don't want to marry a peasant, do you?'

Little Flower thought of the moon-faced boy with the large hands and wondered what her father would say if he asked to marry her. Once she tried to sneak out and was caught. This time her mother hit her with the cane.

Little Flower screamed afterwards, but Scholar Yu's wife refused to listen.

'That's not as hard as your father hits you,' she said but Little Flower didn't care. When her mother hit her it hurt more.

'A girl must be taught the Three Submissions,' Granny Pig said to Little Flower, as her grandmother had said to her. 'When you are young you must submit to your parents. When you are married you must submit to your husband. And when you are widowed you must submit to your sons.'

'Why?' Little Flower asked, her palm still throbbing.

'These are the rules of propriety,' Granny Pig said.

'I don't want to submit to the rules of propriety,' she said, but the next morning her text was the story of Sage Meng's mother from *The Manual for Instructing Women*. At first Little Flower was interested because Sage Meng's father died and there were no male relatives alive, so that the mother was forced to look after the young sage herself. Little Flower hadn't known that Sage Meng was orphaned, like her, and she hunched over the page to read more closely. She felt more orphaned now; wanted to read how Sage Meng had coped.

'Sage Meng's mother moved to a house near the market-place in town. Sage Meng played games of buying and selling, so his mother said to herself, "This is no place to bring up my son." Sage Meng's mother moved to a grave-yard and there Sage Meng played games of burial and death. Sage Meng's mother said to herself, "This is no place to bring up my son."'

'I'm not interested in Sage Meng's mother!' Little Flower said. 'Sage Meng's mother is boring!'

Scholar Yu's wife looked over from the chopping board, looked back again, kept chopping.

'Your father will be back soon,' she cautioned.

Little Flower turned over to tomorrow's essay, and the day after that. 'You are his instrument for immortality. Industrious means . . . Obedience means . . . Fealty means . . . Continuing the Sacrifices means . . .' She flicked through the paragraphs. In another essay by Princess Li Hong Chen, Sage Meng's mother cropped up again: 'A woman's duties are to cook the five grains, heat the wine, look after her parents-in-law, make clothes and that is all . . . Sage Meng's mother moved to a house near the marketplace in town. "This is no place to bring up my son."'

Little Flower let out another sigh,

To be his.
To serve him.
To lie in his arms at night.
To fold his garments.
To bring him his food.
To pour his tea.
To heal his headaches.
To obey his command.
To obey the commands of his mother.
To test the flavour of a dish or the heat of the wine.
To care for him in his old age.
These will be your joys in life.

and shut the book with a tired flap of the pages. It was all silly. 'I'm going to the toilet,' she said, but instead she ran across the yard to the gateway, and was through before Scholar Yu's wife or Granny Pig could stop her.

AD 856

By the end of 856, Little Flower's hair had covered her ears. Throughout 857 it inched towards her shoulders. The longer her hair, the more strict her parents became. Little Flower was sure that the two facts were irrevocably linked. One morning her comb stuck in stubborn knots, she let out a long, exasperated sigh. 'I want to cut my hair,' she said and Scholar Yu's wife took the comb. 'Ow!' Little Flower said as her mother pulled the knots out on to the floor. 'That hurts.'

'That's nothing,' Scholar Yu's wife said, and thought of the day she had given birth to her son and the day she had buried him, and took another lock and pulled the knots free.

That summer Little Flower noticed that her nipples were beginning to swell. She tried to hide it from her mother, but when she started to bleed she didn't know what was wrong. It was Granny Pig who found her behind the toilet shed, desperately trying to wash the russet stain from her trousers.

'Please don't tell Mother,' Little Flower said but Granny

Pig took her hand and pulled her inside and made Scholar Yu's wife come and look. Little Flower wanted to cry, but her mother took her hand and pulled her across to the red lacquer armoire where the bedsheets were kept. She opened the door and pulled out a white sash.

'Each month you will bleed,' she said as she showed Little Flower how to put it on. 'When this one is done then tell me and I will give you another.'

Little Flower nodded and said nothing. She didn't know when 'done' was, but when it was uncomfortably wet she gave it back to her mother, who took it without comment.

'Well, you're a woman now,' Granny Pig said that night, and licked her gums with obvious relish. Little Flower didn't feel like a woman. Her insides ached and the cloth between her legs was bulky and uncomfortable.

'Granny Pig?' she said. 'Can I have a cinnamon stick?'

Granny Pig began to push herself off the kang but Scholar Yu's wife had overheard. 'You're too old for cinnamon sticks,' she said. 'Let Granny rest.'

At the end of the year an embassy arrived from Nippon, and Scholar Yu said he would take Little Flower to watch as it went to meet the Emperor. Little Flower combed her hair as usual, then her mother sat down with her and put something into her hand. Little Flower looked and saw it was a pot of powder.

'Thank you,' she said, but her mother shooed away the gratitude, wiped down the chopping block, wished that her daughter didn't have to grow up so quickly.

Little Flower dressed in her mother's maple red gown, looked at herself in the mirror and was pleased. She was still pleased as she stood in the cold with her father, waiting for the embassy to arrive. It felt like the first time she had been allowed out for months. She had hoped to see some of her friends, but none of the girls her age were allowed out any more either. There were only silly little children, who played silly little games.

'Little Flower, Little Flower,' they chanted when they saw Little Flower dressed and made up like a woman, her hair tied up in twin virgin knots. She hung her head and hurried along, taking three steps for each of Scholar Yu's two. The streets were different now. She was no longer a shaven headed urchin.

As they waited Scholar Yu became restless and Little Flower saw a handsome young man, in a scholar's gown, standing in the crowd on the other side of the street. There was no way for him to cross so she looked for a long time, then shyly lowered her eyes to her feet. When he stared back at her she averted her eyes again.

When the embassy arrived everyone stood on tiptoe, peered over, held their breath, but there were no tattooed archers, no giants or elephants or anything worth commenting on, just strange-looking barbarians riding mules, and more mules carrying packs covered with skins and furs.

Disappointment dispersed the crowd before the Nipponese had even finished passing. Stupid barbarians, Little Flower thought, as she followed her father through the tight mass, living stupid barbarian lives.

Scholar Yu was irritated, thinking about the work he had missed, and turned to speak to Little Flower. She was not there: she was a few steps behind, talking to two young men.

'Little Flower!' he snapped. 'Come away!'

Little Flower took quick steps to obey.

'What were you doing talking to those men?'

'I wasn't talking to them, Father,' she said. 'They were talking to me.'

'What did they say?'

'They asked me my name.'

'And did you tell them?'

'No, Father, certainly not!'

Scholar Yu debated whether to go back and reprimand the youths for their impertinence, but when he looked at the crowd all the young men seemed hostile and hungry for his daughter and he didn't know which ones to accost.

Even though she scowled and huffed when her father gave her more and harder books to study, Little Flower revelled in the things she learnt. Knowledge gave her purchase on the world of adults, gave her the currency she needed to win arguments and back up her wishes with quotations from the masters.

When her mother said that wealth and official position resulted from good birth, Little Flower quoted the *Classic of Filial Piety*. 'When a man follow the Sages' way then he makes his name famous in the future, and gives a good name to his parents.'

When her father was strict with her about her studies she quoted the *Book of Changes*: 'Position is the most precious thing for a Sage, and the way to hold on to position is through benevolence.'

Scholar Yu stopped then, looked at Little Flower and laughed. He ruffled her hair, remembered the sweet child who had had a tuft at the front. Little Flower wrinkled her nose. She didn't want to be treated like a child any more.

Sometimes Little Flower sat with her father and discussed affairs of state, the role of the Emperor, the influence of Buddhism on Daoist beliefs. At other times, when her mother asked to help sweep the yard she would shout and sulk and pick up her books.

'There's more to life than words,' her mother said, but Little Flower would rather read than sweep or chop or clean the toilet, but from now on the stories her mother told her became more serious and more real. They involved ruined girls, family feuds, shouldering sadness, childbirth, hard stepmothers.

'You're our daughter,' Scholar Yu's wife sighed, 'but it is a daughter's fate to leave her home and join her husband's. When you die you will be buried with his ancestors. You will not be buried with us.'

Little Flower promised herself that she would never grow up to be like her mother – who wasn't her real mother anyway, she reminded herself.

'Come here,' Scholar Yu's wife said. 'Is this ready?'

Little Flower pinched the dough, ate the little amount she had.

'Don't eat it!'

Little Flower shook her head. No, it was not ready.

'When a dog comes into the yard it brings good luck. A cat brings bad luck. One day a wild goose came into our yard. No one knew what that meant, but afterwards my elder brother fell sick and died.'

Little Flower wondered what moral she was supposed to draw from that story.

'So I should avoid geese,' she said and if she had been standing a little closer, Scholar Yu's wife would have hit her.

Little Flower listened to her mother as she kneaded the dough till it was thick and elastic, ready for pinching, then walked across the room, sat down, started tracing characters into the grain of the wood. 'My mother is stupid,' the words said, and she smiled because her mother would never know. 'Granny Pig is ugly.' Then she doodled for a while and wrote out the story of Sage Meng: 'Sage Meng's

126

mother moved next to the school house and Sage Meng then played games of ancestor sacrifices, and she said to herself, "At last, this is the right place for my son."'

'Dough?' her mother called.

Little Flower reached over, pinched the dough and it sprang back to its original shape. 'It's ready!'

At least on the eighth, eighteenth and twenty-eighth days of each month Little Flower was permitted to go to the public lectures at the local Daoist temple with all the other unmarried girls. They were segregated to the side, where they drew the attention of the men, both young and old. Little Flower listened intently to the priests and white-bearded sages, studied the other girls' clothes and hair-styles, wished she had hairpins as pretty as theirs. Occasionally she looked across the hall and saw the strain-ing faces of the young boys, but none seemed very hand-some. She kept herself amused by writing poems in her head with grown-up and literary introductions:

Last night the storm tossed and sighed; kept me from sleep. I lay and listened to mother and father's breath-ing and remembered the time my father took me to visit Chongzong Temple. The two main halls, which, it is said, people consider to be the finest in the capi-tal, were both open to public view. In the Sutra Hall were the statues of Sage Kung and Sage Meng; in the Hall of Prayer an old woman sat praying. I watched her for some time and thought how cruel it is that life slowly robs us all of beauty and spirit. She smiled at me and I smiled back and blushed, feeling that she could read my thoughts.

On the way home the willows looked very sad. I thought of a title my father had given me, which the candidates for the exams had been given: 'River Edge Willows', and I was moved to write these words:

> Green leaves paint the land,
> till mist rises beyond the pavilion
> and the shadows of autumn
> chill the river.

> Drifting petals fall on the fisherman's head.
> In the deep roots the fish hide,
> and under a low branch
> the traveller moors his boat.

> On a windy wet night
> I toss and turn,
> to find my loneliness again
> has grown.

The best times for Little Flower were when Scholar Yu brought friends to the house. There were so many festivals and dates and events that needed a banquet.

Spring was a time of great excitement. Invitations came in the form of poems, which Little Flower would carry to her father, sit with him as he opened the scroll and read the finely crafted words.

> Green beer freshly brewed,
> Red coals on the warm brazier.
> This morning my yard's filled with a fine
>   spring fragrance,
> why not come and share a cup of wine?

Sometimes men were so eager to catch spring that they threw banquets before the ice on the Serpentine Lake had even melted. Scholar Yu wrote back, teasing them for their impatience, but once a man replied in verse:

> Though the peach and plum have not yet blossomed
> buds and sprouts already fill their branches.

Double Third was a day to wash away last year's bad luck; Double Fifth was the day to commemorate the death of the famous Minister Chu Yuan. Scholar Yu usually went on his own, but one year he took Little Flower in a covered sedan to see the dragon-boat races down at the Serpentine Lake. She stood sequestered with the other young women, shyly ignoring all the young men's attention. On the Double Seventh Festival, the Herdsman crossed the Milky Way to be reunited with the Weaver Maid. That night Scholar Yu had friends to his house, lit lanterns with lily-scented oil, and scattered rose petals in the wine. Little Flower dressed in a pale summer robe embroidered with heavenly clouds, all swirling, sat under the pear tree and listened to the men's conversation. Their mood grew gradually loose and free; then banter and laughter abounded as they started composing.

At one moment the evening breeze made her scented sleeves billow, and it seemed such a happy thing to be a man and compose poems by moonlight, then she saw one of the men staring at her and looked away.

On the Double Ninth, Little Flower and Granny Pig and Scholar Yu's wife waved Scholar Yu off with his friends, on their way to climb the hill outside Changan and picnic in the autumn forests. When the winter sky threatened snow, Scholar Yu would put a pot of wine to warm and invite the neighbours round and they would sit and wait for the first tender snowflakes, wait for the wine to wash away inhibition, and then begin to compose. The snow was like joy:

beautiful, but brief. The morning dew lasted only a few hours, but each morning it returned, unlike dead friends. They toasted the full moon as if it were a guest at the table. When the geese flew north they wrote poems of the grasslands; when they flew south they wrote poems of the southlands, where the waters were full of moss and lotus, and the women were the most beautiful under Heaven.

Whenever friends came to banquet, Scholar Yu would go out to the market and buy fish and chicken or duck. Little Flower held the necks straight as her mother cut the heads off, helped remove all their feathered finery; the plucked bodies thin and cold and ugly. On a banquet day the kitchen was full of smells and flavours. Little Flower watched as her father took out his luminescent cups of Yuanyang jade, wiped them with a damp cloth; made the dark green stone shine.

Occasionally Scholar Yu would ask his daughter to stand by the table and compose. His guests listened and laughed and politely applauded. 'Clever girl,' they said, 'so clever for a girl.' When they left, Scholar Yu poured Little Flower a cup of wine and beckoned her to sit with him. 'You have grown into a talented young lady,' he said, without ruffling her hair. 'I am very proud of you.'

Little Flower put her hands to the pony-tails and smiled. She was proud of her too.

But Scholar Yu's wife shook her head. She didn't like her daughter being paraded like a brothel whore. Only courtesans entertained men with their intelligence; wives and pretty daughters were supposed to stay inside.

'She's not an adult yet,' Scholar Yu said, but from then on he stopped asking his daughter to come out.

In the seventh month of 858, Scholar Yu invited friends to a meal to celebrate his daughter's naming ceremony. As the full moon rose over the eaved roofs of the wards, his guests began to arrive. Chief among them was the poet Wen Tingyun. Scholar Yu clapped his hands with excitement.

'My wife and daughter are truly honoured,' he said, and pulled his guest inside.

Tingyun was a poet who could turn spring flowers into words, paint beautiful girls, and sum up a lifetime's sorrow in the turn of a sentence. Little Flower stuck her finger through the paper window to see him, but she was disappointed. He was balding and fat and he had the face of a toad. But with him was a young man in silken slippers and a tight-fitting jacket of the Turkish style; many jade and golden ornaments hung from his belt.

'My friend comes from Hedong as well,' Tingyun told Scholar Yu and Scholar Yu smiled.

'Oh – where?'

'My family's manor is near Taiyuanfu,' the young man said.

'My family is from Diyi.'

'Diyi?'

'North of Datong.'

'Ah,' the young man said. 'I've never been there.'

There was a moment's silence, then Tingyun laughed and slapped Scholar Yu's shoulder. 'His surname is Li,' Tingyun announced.

When they were ready to begin, Scholar Yu took the wine and offered it round. 'Young Li,' he said and Tingyun put his head back and laughed.

'Young Li! My dear scholar,' he corrected, 'this is not "Young" Li – this is the grandson of Emperor Xuanzong's Prime Minister!'

Scholar Yu blushed and Little Flower giggled.

'He is *Minister* Li,' Tingyun said and Scholar Yu didn't know where to pour the wine. He had never met a minister of the palace before, never met a man who was entitled to wear purple robes.

There was an embarrassed moment, then Scholar Yu stood to his feet. 'My home and family are honoured,' he said and filled all the cups at once. 'You both honour me and my family by coming here today,' he declared, raised his cup and gestured first to Tingyun, then to Minister Li and back to Tingyun, but throughout the meal Scholar Yu was like a man caught between mother and wife: he didn't know whose jokes to laugh loudest at, who to toast or who to give the choicest pieces of meat to.

'Tingyun,' he would smile as he refilled the cups.

'*Minister* Li,' he bobbed as he picked out a piece of Yellow River carp.

Minister Li and Tingyun played a private game, talking to the scholar at the same time to see which of them he turned to first. When they began to compose poetry, Scholar Yu bobbed and bowed and asked them to stop. 'If you honour my household thus,' he stammered, 'I must fetch brush and paper.'

'Little Flower!' he called. 'Bring brush and paper.'

Little Flower started to get the inkstone but her mother signalled her to sit on the bed.

'Stay here,' she insisted, and kept her hand on her daughter's shoulders.

Outside Tingyun was clamouring to see the scholar's daughter, and Scholar Yu was too impressed and too befuddled to refuse. He pushed himself up from his stool and wobbled his way towards the door.

'Daughter?' he called as he opened the door.

'Stop this!' his wife hissed, but Scholar Yu could not refuse his famous guests.

'Our guests want to see her,' he slurred. 'Come,' he said and took Little Flower's hand. 'Greet our honoured guests.'

Little Flower stepped out from behind the doorway and bowed. Tingyun laughed and clapped his hands. Minister Li sat forward: willow waist, cherry lips, jade-white skin, two virgin knots on her head. His heart seemed to stop beating, and then the scholar's wife bustled her daughter back inside. He took a sip of wine to steady himself.

Minister Li kept looking back to the doorway. After a few more cups of wine he turned his cup upside-down.

'Drink!' Scholar Yu said but Minister Li refused.

'I have had enough,' he said.

Scholar Yu laughed nervously. The tension made everyone quiet, but then Tingyun stood up and recited a poem entitled 'Mocking the Emperor'. That included a number of words that Little Flower knew she wasn't supposed to know.

'Your father is a fool,' Scholar Yu's wife said as they stood by the paper windows, listening, but Little Flower sat down, her hands folded demurely in her lap.

That night Little Flower's pony-tails were untied from the sides of her head in a private ceremony with Scholar Yu, his wife and a few female neighbours. Scholar Yu felt that the women were laughing at him; his wife was too angry to look at him.

Little Flower bit her lip as her virgin-knots were undone and the piles of hair fell to her shoulders like tumbling clouds. She was presented to the ancestors, and to mark her coming-of-age she was given adult names: a pen name for literary occasions and a personal name for intimates.

Her literary name was Yowei, which meant 'Young and Tender'.

Her personal name was Huilan, which meant 'Lily'.

She was Little Flower no longer. Now she was called Lily.

The same evening Tingyun and Minister Li sat with a pair of sing-song girls at a house in the South Hamlet. The girls were pretty and charming and interested, but Minister Li acted like a lovesick scholar, reciting poems in Scholar Yu's daughter's honour, comparing her to the Queen of Heaven. 'She's a fairie!' Minister Li lay on his back and shouted. 'A fox spirit in human form! A celestial beauty banished to the Earth!'

Tingyun got bored, put Minister Li into his sedan and sent him home, but when Minister Li said goodnight to the bearers and walked to his yard, the bright moonlight made his terrace seem unbearably lonely. He walked through the ward streets without knowing where he was going, ate and drank without knowing if he was full or not. The temple bells had struck midnight before he lay down in his bed, but as the night quiet deepened he still couldn't sleep. The next morning he woke early and stared out into a morning without colour. He tried scratching his scalp with the ends of his nails, splashing cold water on to his face, and breathing deep into his stomach, drawing his qi right down through the soles of his feet, but nothing he did could shake the conviction that the world he lived in had irrevocably changed.

Without the scholar's young daughter the earth was just a clod of soil – wide and empty and pointless.

AD 903

Minister Li did not sleep well now he was back in the manor. In the mornings his face was haunted and gaunt, his eyes detached and vague, as if he were not waking but returning to life. One time he ordered a meal of calf's liver and smoked duck tongues, but the flavour seemed to have gone from life and he sent them away, half eaten.

'The quiet life has many joys,' an arthritic poet had once written, 'something is achieved in just lingering on' – but Minister Li saw nothing clever in listening to the air wheeze in and out of his old body, each one counting ever downwards. He didn't summon his concubines to sing to him or to compose poetry; his wife was so uneasy that she summoned the local matchmaker and asked if there were any suitable girls who could be brought into the household.

'You mean for the minister?'

Minister Li's wife nodded. 'His concubines are old and fat. A young girl would suit him better.'

'Does he visit the flower house?'

'It is not right that a distinguished man should leave his house to eat a meal,' Minister Li's wife said. 'And besides, I want a virgin.'

The matchmaker seemed frustrated by the request. 'If you wanted a flower girl it would be easy but . . .'

Minister Li's wife gave her a small ingot of silver. 'That should help,' she said, patting the woman's hand, 'and for you, this.'

When Minister Li heard about the matchmaker's visit he took his stick and walked to his wife's courtyard, found her sitting in the thin sunlight.

'What is this I hear?'

'What?'

'You know.'

Minister Li's wife felt his anger turning upon her. 'I'm thinking of you,' she said.

'What do you mean you were thinking of me?'

'What do you mean you were thinking of me!' the old man shouted, spittle flying. He glared at her, then turned and slammed the door behind him. Minister Li's wife sent her maid away. Alone in the room, she tried to stop the tears brimming over. He would be dead soon, she told herself as she wiped her nose, and so would she, and then the only thing that would matter was that she had done her duty.

AD 858

A week after her naming ceremony, Lily joined her mother under the pear tree, doubling the silence. Her mother was mending holes in her old robes: gagging them shut with patches of silk. She thrust in the needle, pulled the thread through, gave the world a mistrustful glare. Lily watched her mother with mounting frustration; some days she felt that all she did was sit and watch her mother sew.

Lily felt the silence deepening around them. 'Are we expecting guests?' she asked at last.

'No. Why?'

'The yard's been swept,' Lily said.

Scholar Yu's wife held the needle between forefinger and thumb. 'Oh yes,' she said, 'friends of your father,' as if there were anyone else to come.

Lily sat back into the silence, watched as a butterfly sailed a draught over their wall, caught a pear blossom as it tumbled down into the yard, hung on long enough to taste the sweet liquid, fluttered on to the next. Lily followed from flower to flower. It stopped on a stone, wings open, imitating a red and white butterfly-shaped leaf. Lily was composing a poem, entitled 'I Sit and Watch Chuang Zi

Sitting in my Pear Tree, Sucking Blossoms', when there was a solid knock at the gate.

Scholar Yu's wife scowled. She bit through the thread and stuck the needle into the cloth on the floor. 'You'd better go inside,' she told Lily, who got up, lingered in the doorway. 'It's Tingyun and his friend.'

'Which friend?'

'How should I know?' Scholar Yu's wife said, but Lily waited by the door and caught a glimpse of the men – enough to make her skin blush – then ran inside and shut the door. Her heart was like a trapped moth. It couldn't be, she thought. Impossible! But when she put her eye to the hole in the window it was – it was *him*.

When Scholar Yu's wife came inside, Lily was lying on the bed.

'What's the matter with you?' her mother hissed as she went in and out, seeing to the guests. 'Get up and look after the fire!' But Lily did not get up.

'I don't feel well,' she said and Scholar Yu's wife shook her head.

Lily lay and heard the men's laughing and talking and the sound of her father coming home. Only when she heard her father telling them to go slowly did she turn over.

'Feeling better?'

Lily didn't answer.

'Come and help me clear up.'

'Have they gone?'

'Yes.'

'Where to?'

'How should I know?'

Lily helped her mother set the table, but that night she picked at her dinner, then went to lie on the bed where Granny Pig was snoozing. Scholar Yu went out to a wine shop with some friends and Scholar Yu's wife sat alone by candlelight. She poured herself a cup of wine and drank it down in one, poured herself another.

'Daughter?' Scholar Yu's wife called after a while.

'Umm.'

'Can I get you something?'

'No,' Lily said, feeling a little better. There was a long pause. 'Thank you,' she said.

No one seemed to know why Minister Li and Wen Tingyun had come to visit but the next day Scholar Yu's wife thought she heard a knock at the door. She listened and it came again, so she stood up, blinked in the doorway, the leaf shadows dark on the sunlit yard.

'Don't worry, Mother,' Lily called across from Granny Pig's room. 'I'm inside.'

Granny Pig stumped out to the gate licking her gums. 'Official Wen Tingyun is here,' she announced, as if the Emperor had arrived, then stumped back to the room where Lily sat on the edge of the bed, her stomach empty, her mouth dry.

Scholar Yu put down his book and raised his eyebrows as his wife dusted down their best lacquer tray.

'Official Wen!' Scholar Yu smiled. 'Again, you do my family great honour.'

Scholar Yu and Wen Tingyun sat down outside in the dark shade of the pear tree as Scholar Yu's wife served them tea. The men talked for a while on public matters: the state of the empire, gossip from the palace, the imminent rice harvest. Scholar Yu refilled their cups with fine green liquid and the tinkle of water sounded clear in the stillness. 'Your daughter is very pretty,' Tingyun said when the politeness was over. 'There must be many admirers.'

Scholar Yu laughed because he didn't know what to say.

'Actually, it was about your daughter that I'm here,' Tingyun said. He took a sip of tea, put the cup back on to the spot he had picked it up from and cleared his throat. 'I have a friend who I think would make the perfect husband for your daughter.'

Scholar Yu's wife was summoned. Wen Tingyun knew a young man for their daughter. Young, successful (had passed the Classical Masters Exam at the age of only twenty-two), of unimpeachable lineage (claiming a maternal link with the last emperors of the Southern Han as well as numerous ministers and prime ministers of the Tang), and a man of such character that any parent would be happy to attach their daughter's fate to his.

Scholar Yu's wife opened her mouth to speak but Tingyun talked over her.

'His uncle is governor of Shannan,' Tingyun said and Scholar Yu's wife forgot what she was going to say. 'His father was Prime Minister to Emperor Wuzong Shennan.'

'Well,' Scholar Yu grinned, 'I think we should meet the man.'

'Actually, you have met him. It is Minister Li.'

'Oh,' Scholar Yu said, imagining purple robes and brick pagodas and tranquil gardens. 'Minister Li! How wonderful!'

It was late that afternoon when Scholar Yu zigzagged home. He bumped the doorpost, struggled to shut the gate, wobbled for a moment, then staggered across the yard, clung to the privy door, pissed in the latrine's general direction.

Deep in the cesspit maggots squirmed and wriggled in the sudden warmth: Scholar Yu could see them, white and seething. A poem by one of the masters came to mind:

'8th Month, 9th Day, Getting Up in the Morning, I Go to
the Latrine and Find Crows Feeding on Maggots There'.

> Rat carcasses must be rare indeed
> For them to come peck at shit worms.

Scholar Yu hummed the tune as he shook away the
droplets. One landed on his hand and disappeared into the
swirling lines of his fingerprint. He clutched the doorway
till the world steadied itself, set off across the yard with a
determined expression, veered to the side and fell into the
swept dust. It took a few moments for Scholar Yu to push
himself off the ground. He fixed the doorway with a hard
look, staggered from side to side and a little forward,
grabbed the posts and pulled himself inside.

Scholar Yu's wife and Lily were both on the bed. The
bowls from their lunch were stacked awkwardly on the table.

'Ishall bin agreed,' Scholar Yu slurred.

Lily stopped fiddling and felt old and grown-up and
mature. Scholar Yu's wife clutched the shoes she was stitching, began to sniff.

'Ishall bin agreed,' Scholar Yu repeated. He took a step
towards them, fell flat on his beard, tried to push himself
up.

Lily helped her father steady himself on a three-legged
stool and listened seriously and intently to all he had to
say. 'Are you telling me,' Scholar Yu's wife said at the end
of the whole tale, 'that you have sold our daughter off as
a *concubine*?'

Scholar Yu opened his mouth. 'But,' he began, 'but, but,
but . . .' But there was no escaping the fact that was exactly
what he had done.

Scholar Yu's wife picked up the nearest cup and threw
it at him and missed, but Scholar Yu still ducked and the

movement was so sudden he fell forward on to the floor. Scholar Yu's wife didn't know what to say so she screamed, then fell to the floor and wailed. Granny Pig hurried to see what had happened and soon the neighbours were knocking on the gate, thinking that someone had died.

'Not a concubine!' Scholar Yu's wife wept, her mouth distorting the words, then she fell forward again and wailed.

'Didn't Sage Kung say it is better to scrub the shoes of a master than wear the boots of a fool?' Lily said. 'Maybe it is not my fate to be a first wife. If you think he is a good match for me, Father,' Scholar Yu pushed himself back to his feet as his daughter spoke, 'then I am happy.'

Scholar Yu's wife couldn't believe what her daughter had said. 'I'll kill myself first!' she declared and made a dash for the cleaver – but no one tried to stop her and she fell in a heap by the chopping board and wailed again. Lily watched her mother's theatrics with silent contempt. When I grow up, she told herself, I will never make empty threats.

Scholar Yu's wife's anger simmered as she banged and slammed her way through each day. Concubines are honoured for the hole between their legs. Is that what you want? she silently demanded of her daughter, as Lily sat under the pear tree writing in her diary.

What's so clever about being a rich man's whore? as she threw the bucket down the well.

What's clever about being the wife's servant? as she cut garlic for lunch. When she gutted the fish and cut off its head she looked at her daughter and told her: You'll wake up one day and know I am right.

Lily sat in front of the mirror, combed her hair over her shoulders and smiled back. At least I will never end up like my mother.

* * *

142

Geomancers were paid, a date was set, the sedan and musicians hired. Lily began to count the days. Thirty. Twenty-nine, still twenty-nine, she thought all the long afternoon and evening and night. Twenty-eight, she said to herself as she woke the next morning, and hated twenty-eight by the end of the day.

When there were only twenty-four more days there was news of an outbreak of smallpox in the west of the city. Granny Pig was convinced this was a curse on Little Flower's wedding and spent two thousand cash in incense and bribes that she burnt to the gods. Outside the temple was a thin old man leaning on his cane, selling certificates from the King of Heaven that exempted the bearer from the Heavenly life-tax. She bought three: one for herself, one for Uncle Jia and one for Little Flower. She was still Little Flower to Granny Pig.

Minister Li was kept busy at the Ministry of Good Works on the East Side of the City. He was put in charge of sending money to all the important temples to pay for prayers. He doubled the money once it was known that one of the Emperor's children was ill, but in the end the suffering was so commonplace that the Emperor took personal responsibility for the calamity, ate plain rice for a month, wore nothing but rough hemp clothing.

Lily lay in bed, turned her back on her mother and let out a long breath. Her new life was just nineteen days away. Nineteen days, she thought, as she fell asleep at night, woke up the next morning with eighteen days to wait, and wished the days would pass more quickly.

Seventeen – sixteen – fifteen.

'Now like Yang Guifei,' Scholar Yu's wife instructed as Lily practised dressing her hair. One day Yang Guifei had fallen from her horse and her hair felt loose on one side.

The Emperor had commented that it made her more beautiful so all the palace ladies had rushed to imitate her. The style was called 'Falling Off a Horse' and Lily struggled to get the mass of hair right: heaped on top and falling forward.

'No!' Scholar Yu's wife pulled the comb from her daughter's hand.

It took half an hour and seven hairpins to dress her hair. Her mother pulled all the strands together into one long glossy black lock that lay soft in her hand like a length of black silk, then tugged it one more time, a firm tug, began to arrange it in the Conch Style.

'There!' Scholar Yu's wife said.

Lily pretended to admire herself, but Scholar Yu's wife pulled the hairpins out, let the long hair fall to Lily's shoulder. 'Now you do it,' she said and Lily started to comb and pull, reached up behind her hair, combing the tresses and pulling them up, pinning them in place.

'No! Not like that!' Scholar Yu's wife snapped.

'No!' she snapped again. 'Here!' She pulled hard, yanking Lily's head back. 'Like this!'

Lily bit her lip. Fourteen days, she told herself.

'You're going to be a concubine, not a wife,' Scholar Yu's wife lectured and Lily nodded.

'Remember the Three Submissions?'

'Parents, husband, son.'

'You'll have Four Submissions now,' Scholar Yu's wife said. 'Parents, husband, husband's wife, son.'

Lily nodded. Eight days, Four Submissions.

'You'll belong to the Li Clan,' Scholar Yu's wife said. 'When you die your ghost will join their ancestors, not ours. You'll spend the afterlife with strangers!'

Lily nodded and Scholar Yu's wife burst out crying and

Lily watched without compassion. An afterlife without her mother seemed like Heaven.

When there were six days to go, Lily went to sit with Granny Pig.

'Do you miss Uncle Jia?' she asked after a while, and Granny Pig let out a long sigh. 'He was a good man,' she said.

'What is the difference between a concubine and a wife?' Lily asked.

Granny Pig smacked her gums together and felt her last two teeth. 'Respect,' she said. 'A wife is given respect. A concubine has to steal it.'

It didn't make much sense to Lily, but she nodded anyway, left Granny Pig and her teeth and her memories of Uncle Jia.

When she went back to her parents' room a book called *Canon of the Plain Maid* was lying by her bedside. It seemed to be a guide to marriage. Lily waited till her mother was washing the clothes in the yard, then took it out from under her pillow and began to study its advice.

I
(To be read together before bed.)
Heaven was created by the concentration of Yang, which is light; the earth was created by the concentration of Yin, which is dark. Yang stands for peace and serenity; Yin for change and confusion. Yang is destruction; Yin is conservation. The force of man is Yang; Yin is the force of woman.
Too much Yang will produce heat; too little results in chills.
Sex is the battle of Yin and Yang; good sex is a fragrant mix, which brings mutual satisfaction to both.

The coupled lovers move together, in mutual pleasure
till the moment of mist and rains, when they both
reach ultimate pleasure, and he discharges his seed
into her.

II
Do not copulate during menstruation: the children that
are conceived will be bad-tempered.
Do not copulate during the day: the children conceived
then will be prone to vomiting.
Do not copulate at midnight: the children of that union
will be deaf or dumb. Thunderstorm, insane; full
moon, bandits; drunk, they will suffer from ulcers;
indigestion, haemorrhoids. Do not do not do not.

III
Sexual intercourse is like fire and water, integral to life,
but taken in excess can bring harm.

IV
Do not do not do not. These will be your joys in life.

She shut the book and thought about what Granny Pig
had said. It was not going to be easy to be a concubine,
she decided. She would have to be diligent and respectful.
She would honour the wife, tend to her husband's wishes,
sing to him when he was troubled. She tried to remember
the man that day – so many ornaments around his belt
that they played random music, like wind chimes; in a
Turkish jacket of the very latest cut. Lily wished she had
listened to her mother when she had tried to teach her
recipes, but maybe he was so rich she'd never have to learn
them. It was too late now anyway. There was so much she
needed to know, and now it was all too late.

Lily remembered Yang Guifei. She was a concubine, she thought, and look what happened to her.

Five, four, three, two – one day to wait. The threat of pox lifted, the last morning arrived and Lily woke with a start. She wasn't ready to leave home, wasn't ready at all. She tried to hold on to her mother, slow the whole morning down, but ten years of routine were all upturned and washed away in the bath her mother gave her in the Eastern Hall.

Lily stepped into the brisk rub of the towel, as she had done so many years before, but there was no Eight Treasure Soup to follow it up: just quick commands and long periods when Lily felt forgotten and abandoned. Her mother was busy, Granny Pig was in her room, and there were neighbours coming into and out of the yard, like family, shouting and telling each other what to do.

Lily tried to find her father but he was outside in the yard meeting friends and chatting, and one of the neighbours told her that she should be dressed by now. Her mother clattered and banged and shouted at the world for forcing this fate on her and her daughter.

You'd think it was her being married as a concubine, Lily thought, as she sat at the dressing-table, too frightened to comb her hair. She could see the crowd through the blue silk windows, could hear the babble of excited voices. The mid-morning sunlight cast a faint blue light within the room.

'Being a minister's concubine is better than being a farmer's wife!' one of the neighbouring women reassured her, and took the comb from Lily's hand.

Lily nodded. She just wanted to get to the end of today and wake up tomorrow with it all over.

'Turn this way,' they told her, and she turned.

'Lift your face.'

'Smile.'

Lily sat forward as her face was powdered white, vermilion blushes dabbed on to each cheek, and a black crescent moon painted on to her forehead, a little to the left. They plucked her eyebrows in an inverted V, gave her face a sad appearance, sculpted her hair over two wire frames that were like the wings of a butterfly.

'Stop smiling!' the women told her as Lily looked into the mirror. Even though she wasn't smiling Lily tried to do whatever they said.

'You don't want to appear happy to leave home, do you?'

Lily shook her head and felt tears swell on her eyelids.

'Don't be a baby,' a woman told her, and Lily sniffed and blew her nose, wiped the offending droplets on her sleeves. When her mother came she took the make-up pots from the other women and dabbed a faint aura of yellow on to her daughter's forehead. A yellow halo was auspicious; so were the new set of red clothes. When Scholar Yu's wife was young the women wore tight bodices and ankle-length skirts, but now the fashion was for bright, loose gowns with high waists and full sleeves. Scholar Yu's wife watched her daughter dress, her disapproval apparent as she wrapped the white undergown round Lily's breasts.

'Tight?' she said as she strained to crush her daughter's ribs.

'A little,' Lily said.

Scholar Yu's wife pulled harder, held the red silk gown for Lily to step into. Lily stood rigid and uncomfortable as she stepped into her slippers; someone stepped close behind her and threaded green jade earrings into her lobes. She bit her lip when her maid asked if the waistband was too tight and shook her head.

'Good!' her mother said as her daughter winced. 'Good.'

Scholar Yu's wife gave her daughter a hairpin with a spray of kingfisher feathers.

'It will bring you good luck,' she said and Lily felt a tear well up.

'Thank you!' Lily said and smiled.

'I don't know why you're smiling,' her mother said. 'There's nothing so great about being second hole.'

The men of the carriage stood and sat around the yard like bored actors, but when Lily appeared, blinking in the sunlight, they stood up and the crowd went quiet. Lily paused for a moment, searched the crowd for faces she knew. She wanted to go back inside. She felt too old for marriage, too young to be leaving home.

Scholar Yu helped Lily into the sedan.

'Little Flower!' Lily heard her mother wail as she sat down and the curtains were shut around her. 'Don't take my daughter!'

Lily thought of the morning that Uncle Jia had died. She imagined his ghost in the crowd, shut her eyes and saw him sitting in the room where the bed used to be, playing his zither and singing in his old wavery voice, ballads from his youth.

I will not cry on my wedding day, Lily told herself. I will not bring bad luck on myself.

The sedan bearers marched three steps forward and two back: eagerness to be gone and the trepidation of leaving home for ever. Three steps forward and two back, round the yard and out of the gate, swaying and bouncing the girl inside, through the ward and behind the band, which was shrill and loud and brought everyone out into the street to see.

It was hot behind the curtains, and Lily felt sick as the procession continued, forward-back-forward, all the way out of the gates of the ward and into the busy stream of traffic, flowing north and south and east and west.

Onlookers stood in clumps at every doorway and chewed and spat and commented on the passing procession. Who's the father, who's she marrying, how much did he pay for her?

———

Minister Li had rented a manor for a wedding banquet as if Lily was to be his wife. She would have been his wife, he had explained to Scholar Yu, if it wasn't that he had a wife at home, in the care of his grandmother. Such was fate. The girl had been chosen for him by his father. He had had no choice in the matter. His heart had chosen Lily.

As Lily was taken to wait in the bedroom, the men of the two families sat around the tables in the front yard. Lily sat cross-legged on the bed and listened to shouts from the kitchens; the dull clatter of vegetables being shredded; a surprised squawk as a chicken was beheaded; another squawk; a disconnected swell of laughter.

Lily shut her eyes, felt sick.

The servant women gathered around.

'Don't cross your legs too tightly,' they laughed. 'There'll be a hot poker coming tonight.'

Lily was sweaty and uncomfortable in her robes. These were stupid women and she was hot and nervous and hungry. She thought of her new husband: he was down-stairs feasting and drinking and she was stuck up here with these idiots. She hummed a tune in her head, imagined Uncle Jia coming in and taking her hand and leading her knee-high spirit out for a walk in the street, as he used to. She kept her eyes shut, wished she could shut her ears as well, but through the babble of noise she strained to hear her father's voice, half hoped he would come up to see her, but the only person who came was a short boy with buck teeth who carried in a large bowl of noodles.

'Little Miss!' one of the women shouted across the room to the bed. 'You should eat!' She waved a bowl of noodles at the girl, and the boy dared a quick peek at the bride, but Lily shut her eyes again.

'You'll be needing your strength!' the woman called and the others snickered.

'Let her be,' one said, but she was laughing as well.

That is not kindness, Lily thought, and hated that woman more than the others for pretending to be kind. 'The man who speaks kindly but who behaves badly is twice as dangerous as the bad man who acts badly,' Sage Kung had said. She tried to think herself away from here. Granny Pig used to speak to her kindly. Her mother loved her. The neighbours were always considerate. One girl had stopped talking to Lily when she had learnt Lily was to be married as a concubine.

'It's not far,' Lily had told her. 'We'll still see each other.'

'My husband doesn't let me go outside the ward,' the girl had said.

'Oh well – I'll be just a concubine so I can come whenever I like,' Lily had said, even though she had no idea if it was true.

When Lily heard the tramp of feet on the stairs she began to sweat. The men sounded drunk and tears ran down her cheeks, not because she was sad but because she didn't know what else to do. As the voices grew louder, the light of lanterns glowing in the silk of the windows, she wiped her cheeks with the back of her hands.

'Come! Hush!' One of the servant women put her arm round her shoulder. Lily didn't trust that hand, that voice. 'Don't cry on your wedding day – it's a bad sign.'

Lily put her arms round the woman she didn't trust;

heard the door bolt being drawn back, the creak of the hinges; felt the woman press her face into her breast and stomach.

'Hush child, hush! The master is here. Come – greet your husband!' And Lily felt the woman pull away.

Minister Li stood in his fine embroidered silk robes, feet braced on the floor in red deerskin boots, grinning with wine. 'Where is my honoured bride?' he said. Lily tried to look up through her tears, and started to laugh.

'She was fine all this time,' the servant women explained, but Minister Li wasn't looking at them. 'She sat still and quiet all this time.'

Lily sniffed and wiped her nose, wiped her hand on her robe as Minister Li stepped up to the bed and put out his hand.

'Have you eaten?'

Lily shook her head, blinked him from a blur to a solid shape.

'I gave instructions she was to be fed,' Minister Li said, keeping hold of her hand. 'Didn't the cook send dishes here?'

The servant women shrank under his frown. Their attitude made him frown more. Lily could hear disapproval in his voice and she wiped her cheeks and smudged her make-up. He seemed so much larger and more grown-up than anyone else she knew.

'Why hasn't your mistress been fed?'

'We offered noodles,' one of the women said.

'You offered?' Minister Li roared. Everyone could hear his displeasure now, even the men outside in the yard. 'You offered her food? I said *feed* her not just *offer*!'

Minister Li picked up the bronze mirror from the dressing-table and began to swat the servant women out of the room, flapping and squawking out into the yard. Minister

Li laughed and the men in the yard laughed as well. He was still laughing as he swung the doors theatrically shut and threw the bolt closed, turned on his heel, his nostrils flaring with exertion. Lily half smiled, but her smile quickly faded as he strode back across the room, sat next to her on the bed, a hand's breadth between them.

'You should eat,' he said, picked up a plate of smoked duck tongues and brought them over to the bed, plate in one hand, a pair of bamboo chopsticks in the other. She could smell the wine on his breath, feel the nerves in her stomach.

'Here,' he said. 'Smoked duck tongue. This is my favourite dish. Maybe it will be your favourite dish too.'

Lily remembered the first duck she had held to be killed: how it had stuck its tongue out at death. She watched as Minister Li picked up a tongue, no longer than her fingernail, and lifted it to her mouth. Maybe it will be, Lily thought as he placed it carefully on her tongue, and she shut her mouth and chewed till there was nothing left but gristle.

'Spit it out.'

Lily leant forward, spat it on to the floor.

He held another.

'Good?'

Lily nodded.

'Did you try the calf's liver?'

Lily shook her head.

'You cannot sleep without trying the calf's liver.'

Lily blushed at any mention of sleep and wished she hadn't, which made her blush more. Minister Li's weight pressed the mattress down: Lily tilted towards him slightly.

'Another?' he said.

Lily nodded.

'You like it?'

'Yes,' she said, smiled briefly and lowered her eyes.

'You are more beautiful than I remembered,' Minister Li said as he knelt down in front of her, took her hands in his, kissed them.

Lily tried staring into his eyes and holding her breath and falling in love.

'Do you remember when you first saw me?' he asked, his voice hoarse.

'At my parents' house.'

'Yes, but when?'

His eyes were so wide Lily didn't know what to say.

'I remember the first moment you stepped through the door.' He spoke with a reverence Lily didn't understand. 'You were a goddess banished to the Earth.'

Lily bit her lower lip.

'I think we were fated to be together.'

'I think so too,' she said and held her breath again.

'You think so too!' Minister Li laughed, clasping her hands to his heart. He leant forward to kiss her and she shut her eyes and his lips felt warm and hard on hers – but then he tried to slip his tongue into her mouth and she jumped, kept her teeth closed and when they had separated she couldn't look him in the eye, but wiped the saliva on to the back of her hand, felt foolish.

'Come,' Minister Li said and lifted Lily from the bed. She held his left hand as he blew out the candle. When they were standing by the bed he reached for the silken sash around her waist that held her gown shut. Lily felt his hands move along the sash to the knot. He kissed her at the same time as he pulled at it, but it had been tied so tightly that he needed both hands. Lily concentrated very hard, willing it to come undone. She tried to help at one point, but then the knot loosened and his hands began to gently undress her, and she felt cool air on her chest and shoulders.

I love you, Lily told herself as her gown slipped to the floor and her undergown opened wide enough for his hand to slip inside. He touched her and she braced for a moment, but then his hands were pushing her back and down on to the bed. She lay back, heard him undress in the darkness in front of her, and kept her eyes shut. His hands stroked her stomach and thighs, gently opened her knees, and Lily felt him kneel on the mattress in front of her. The mattress moved again as he lowered himself over her.

'I love you,' he whispered.

I love you too, Lily said in her head and her eyebrows came together in concentration. He was pushing against her – she didn't think he would fit inside. He pushed so hard it hurt and she bit her lip to stop herself gasping. She bit down harder as he thrust deeper, thought of her mother and what she would think if she knew what Lily was doing. Dumb mother, can't read more than a few characters: her names, numbers, the name of the Emperor. Dumb mother, she thought, kept concentrating on keeping quiet until Minister Li started to thrust faster and deeper and she let out a few strangled sobs, then he moaned out loud and she squeezed her eyes shut and clenched her teeth. He pushed faster and faster and deeper and more painful – then fell on top of her, gasping like a chopping-board fish.

Lily didn't know what to do with her hands. She and her friends used to see who could hold their breath longest, she remembered, thought of a fish from the market: string hooked through its fins so you could carry it home. It flapped as you walked. It couldn't swim in air, which made it drown. After a while Lily put an arm round Minister Li and it felt odd to have her arm round a man. *My husband*, she thought. *He is my husband.* It made her giggle to herself. Only to herself, though. She didn't giggle aloud. There were things she guessed you did and didn't do in the bed chamber, just as there were rules for eating. She thought of the boy next door spitting watermelon seeds across the yard in summer, chasing her, spitting them at her. Now that the pain had gone she giggled to herself.

Minister Li propped himself up and looked down at her. 'Are you crying?'

Lily shook her head.

'Are you sure?'

Lily burst out laughing as if her mouth was full of melon seeds.

Minister Li spent the rest of that night and all of the next day in feverish attention to his new concubine. He gave her food and wine and massaged her delicate white feet, rubbed scented oil between her toes. He could not wait till evening when they would be unhampered by clothes and took her to bed half an hour after they had finished their lunch, lowered the bed curtains.

On the second day they lay naked except for a twisted silk bedsheet that coiled around them, like a rope. Lily stared at her husband's back and shoulders. The skin was smooth, muscles flexing and relaxing, a few black hairs on his chest, like an afterthought. She'd never had a body pressed so close to hers, marvelled at how well their bodies fit together.

'I think Heaven made us especially for each other,' she said, and Minister Li kissed her neck.

'I think so too,' he said, exhausted by the latest battle of yin and yang – wet and dry; weak and strong; male and female; hard giving way to soft.

Lily stroked her fingers over his shoulders and down his arms. 'You have a strong back,' she said. He poured another cup of wine. Lily's face was flushed, and he watched her drink the next cup, lowered his head to her small

156

breast, as if smelling a flower, began to lick and kiss.

Lily could feel him stirring against her leg. He moved to the other breast and she felt him stiffen. 'I love you, Lily,' he said and she lay back on the pillow, but when he tried to open her knees she resisted.

'Husband,' she said. 'I'm sore.'

Minister Li put his arms round her shoulders, his legs over hers, crushed her to him. 'It doesn't matter,' he said, but later on, after they had drunk a few cups of wine, he was unable to stop himself, made love to her anyway, and she buried her face in the pillow, stifled her gasps.

On the third day a man was paid to take Lily home to visit her parents, as tradition demanded. Minister Li walked his new concubine from the bedroom to the mule, lifted her up, then took the reins from the man and walked her through the gates, through the ward and into the avenue. When she saw how much attention she got Lily began to feel nervous. When the time came for Minister Li to let go of the reins she didn't want him to leave.

'Go slowly,' he called as she bit her lip.

'Goodbye.' Lily waved and Minister Li waved back till she was out of sight, and then he turned home with a sigh, wishing that she had called him 'love' or 'darling'.

Scholar Yu's wife was up early before breakfast, sat for three hours at the gate of the ward till her knees ached and she had pins and needles in her calves. Lily recognised the crouched figure and waved and the silhouette began to wave, stood up and limped towards her.

Lily had lunch and spent the afternoon at her parents' house. Her mother didn't know whether to treat Lily as child or guest, and Lily didn't know if she was daughter or concubine. By the end of the day they were all confused and weary. Granny Pig licked her lips and gave Lily a lucky charm that she had woven from red silk cord, but she did not get up to see Lily off.

'Granny Pig is getting old,' Scholar Yu's wife said, but Lily didn't feel any better. She didn't want Granny Pig to get old, didn't want her home to change at all.

As the man saddled the mule Lily's mother fussed around; Scholar Yu stood back, awkward.

'Goodbye,' she waved through the gathering gloom and the two figures waved back at her. The man led her out of the ward gates and across the broad Avenue of Heaven. When the drum tower signalled the closing of the gates for the night Lily let out a long dispirited sigh, wasn't sure why she felt that way.

When Lily got back to the manor house, there were a few servants but no husband. At last she wandered into the yard where the servant women stayed.

'I was looking for the master,' she said.

'Minister Li?'

Lily nodded.

'Anyone seen the master?'

There were muffled answers inside. Another woman joined the first. 'Isn't he in the yard?' they asked.

Lily shook her head.

'Why don't you come inside?'

'It's nice and warm. We're just having dinner,' another woman said.

Lily didn't want to go inside. She tried to smile. 'I'm sure he'll be back by now,' she said, and turned to go.

Lily wandered through the rented manor, looking at the empty buildings, flapping paper in the torn windows, breathing in and out. Each empty building made her feel more alone. The evening windows were dark and silent, brass chains rattled against wooden doors. At the end of the path Lily came to an overgrown garden, wild flowers and weeds slowly smothering the paving stones, a thick green algae soaking up the pool like a sponge. In the twisted tendrils of green were gobbets of frog spawn. Lily peered in, trailed her fingers in the water, looked back on her three days of marriage as if they were a dream.

A door opened and footsteps followed, but it was just one of the women fetching water. Lily watched her go down to the well and then walk back. An ornamental fish rose from the green depths, fanned itself on the green algae surface. It was blotched with white and orange, bulbous eyes peering out to either side.

'Any news?' Lily asked, but the fish said nothing.

She splashed some water at it and it disappeared.

Go away, then.

I asked the fish for news, but they did not know where you were. In our bedroom the imprints of our bodies were still on the sheets, but when I put out my hand to feel you, the sheets were cold. I thought of the women whose husbands have travelled to the ends of the empire, and remembered Du Fu's line: 'A letter from home is worth ten thousand ounces of gold.'

How true it is, I thought, and wrote a poem to express my sadness. I called it 'Boudoir Resentment'.

The dry white paper sucked the brush dry. She dipped it into the ink, wrote another gleaming wet word, dipped the brush again, wiped away the excess. When she had finished she shut the words inside, put the book back into her chest, picked up the three-inch stick of lip rouge, wandered to her dressing-table, hummed to keep herself company.

When Minister Li came home he saw the mule, unsaddled and brushed, and hurried across the yard, pushed the door open, saw Lily at her dressing-table, looking into her mirror.

'Where have you been?' the face in the mirror asked.

'I went out.'

'Where did you go?'

Minister Li laughed.

'I went out with some friends.'

'You didn't leave a message. I didn't know where you were. I thought something had happened to you.'

Lily turned to face him. 'I was worried,' she said. 'I thought you'd been killed. I was going to send one of the women to the magistrate's yamen to see if you had been conscripted.'

Minister Li couldn't stop himself laughing. 'I'm back now,' he said. 'No need to worry.'

Minister Li tried to hug her, but Lily did not feel like being held. 'I was worried,' she told him.

Minister Li knelt in front of her, took her hands in his, kissed them.

'I missed my beauty.'

'What beauty?'

'You,' he said and smiled.

Lily looked into her reflection.

'I missed you,' she said.

'I'm sorry.'

'Are you?'

'Yes!' he said. 'Very, very sorry.'

Lily looked into his reflection's eyes.

'I didn't think you'd be back so soon,' he said.

Lily's expression softened.

'The moon is very bright tonight,' Minister Li said. 'Shall we go see it?'

At last she got up, let him kiss her. He blew out the candles. They stepped through the beaded hangings into the cool night air. The strands of beads knocked and jostled and eventually hung still.

Lily remembered the poem she had written.

> Clutching a handful of herbs
> she cries at sunset,
> hearing the neighbour's husband
> had returned.

And Minister Li stared at the high clouds, racing across the moon.

> The day her husband left
> the south-flying geese turned north.
> Today the north-flying geese
> turned south.

He took in a deep breath as if he could inhale the beauty of the marble-white moon on a sheet of night black silk.

> Spring comes, autumn goes,
> her feelings remain.
> Years come, then go –
> his messages dwindle.

Lily let go of his hand and raised her hand to the moon, her long silk sleeves hanging down from her arm, and spoke the last stanza aloud:

Unbolting her red door each night,
she waits for no one to visit,
listens through the curtains
to the sound of washing clothes.

She held the final note, then she dropped her hand, and they both started laughing.

'You are beautiful and talented!' he said to her as they lay in bed. When they made love Lily's body shivered. Afterwards she wanted to ask what he had liked about her poem, but now they had made love words didn't seem to matter. That night she held onto his hand; watched the white moon rise in the silk window-frame. The moon in her parents' yard looked bored and lonely, but as it rose through the straight bamboo stalks she saw that this one was full of youth and excitement as she took the first tentative steps of love.

Each morning Minister Li dressed and ate a meal of soup noodles, rinsed his mouth out with green tea, spat it into the yard. When he had dressed in his purple robes, Lily adjusted his sash and hat; the beads dangling in front of his face gave him an imperious air that her father had never had. Lily insisted on walking him to the gate; as always, she snapped a branch from the willow tree.

'There are not many branches left,' Minister Li said one morning, but Lily tore off another regardless, stood and waved as if her husband had been sent to the furthest frontier of the empire.

'Go slowly!' she called as he turned the corner. 'Go slowly!'

When Minister Li was at work Lily tried to fill her mornings reading books and poems, but there was no one to test her and no one to make her recite them at night. She read her way through the dynasties before her, anecdotes, parables and profound jokes that inspired silent revelation, not laughter. When she tried to discuss them with her husband he kissed her and poured himself another cup of wine.

'Why don't you sing to me,' he said and picked up a fat brown date, began to chew.

The next day Lily read Tao Qian's *Account of Peach Blossom Spring*, where a perfect community had lived in a sheltered valley, cut off from government and the cares of the world since the fall of the Qin Dynasty. Good fields, neatly arranged cottages, greybeards and children – all harmonious.

That afternoon she walked through her garden, imagined that this garden was in that sheltered valley, that she lived without a care in the world, except how best to please her master; unaware of the rise and fall of the Han, the Wei or the Jin dynasties – unaware of the ruin of Yang Guifei and Lu Anshan. She hummed tunes to the bees as she wiped dew from the leaves, dabbed it on to her cheeks, sat by the pool and watched the still water, the reflection of the world rippling slightly in a breath of air; paused to eat a lunch of steaming pork dumplings that she dipped into slippery vinegar. When the sun began to silhouette the Small Goose Pagoda, she returned to the overgrown garden, assumed a whimsical air, reading or writing calligraphy or plucking music from her zither.

She imagined Minister Li coming home, hurrying to their yard and finding it empty, except for the distant call of music, carrying from the garden like the scent of evening jasmine. She imagined him calling her name out, picking his way down the narrow garden paths, hearing the music playing over and over again, knowing she was somewhere by the pool.

* * *

163

Every ten days, officials were given one day's holiday, and on each ninth afternoon Lily was full of excited expectation. She went to the market with the maids, haggled for aubergine, salted fish, deep-fried dofu, listened to the vigorous chopping and imagined the steaming dishes she would eat with her husband.

'Welcome home, dear husband!' Lily would call down the street. 'I have a delicious dinner prepared.'

After dinner they sat by the pool, poured cool grape wine.

'Husband,' Lily said after a while, 'I have something to tell you.'

She seemed so earnest that Minister Li put his chopsticks down, watched her take a book from under her and pass it to him, still warm.

'What's this?'

'Look,' she said.

He opened a random page. It looked like a journal. There were poems and essays and sections of text that had been copied out. Minister Li laughed but Lily was sitting on the edge of her seat, concern tugging her pretty face out of shape. When he saw her furrowed forehead he laughed again. Her handwriting was very fine: it showed neatness and loyalty and respect for her husband.

'I have not shown anyone else,' she said and he chuckled again and leant forward to kiss her.

'It is very fine,' he told her.

'Can I read you something?'

'Of course.'

Lily read an essay she had written, and he complimented her.

'You're very clever,' he told her, but he was not in the mood for philosophical discussions. He poured more wine, and around them the night darkness deepened, the city grew still. They watched the moon rise in their wine cups, the cool night air made Lily shiver for a moment, take Minister Li's hand, warm and firm and strong.

'Do you think there are any other couples so in love as us tonight?' Lily asked.

Minister Li laughed and finished his cup, stood up to lead her to bed.

'Impossible,' he said.

In the sixth month, Minister Li was assigned to magisterial duty in Mount Li Prefecture, not far from the Hua Qing Palace, where Yang Guifei and Emperor Xuanzong had spent so many days enjoying each other and the hot springs there. It was two days' wagon ride from the capital gates, and Lily moved to an empty wing of a Buddhist monastery, in hills ten miles from the city, to be near him. She clapped her hands with excitement when she saw the empty courtyard. 'This will be our bedroom,' she said, pointing to the three rooms in turn, 'this the kitchen, and this the room where we entertain our friends.'

The servants set to work, moving chests and painted armoires from one side of the central hall to the other; back into the corner again.

'Good!' Lily said, and began to hang scrolls: a Heavenly horse went opposite the door, his father's calligraphy over the lintel; the panels of a silk screen, painted with a mountain and river, zigzagged across the corner of the room. On the end panel there was a boat adrift on a stormy sea, waves rising to a cliff, the cliff to a mountain, and in a narrow crook of hillside a simple thatched hut where a hermit sat with his concubine, a pot of wine between them, undisturbed by the world.

Lily smiled and adjusted the angle of the panels so that the painted figures had a view across the room. She unfolded the quilt and laid it flat on the bed, went outside to the garden to wait for Minister Li, leaving the hermit and his concubine alone for a while, sitting with their half-finished pot of wine; always in love; always young.

Minister Li had been assigned to check on the governors of the prefecture, and his work meant he was away for days at a time, leaving Lily alone in the monastery.

On the hottest afternoons she walked along the hillside to the stream, felt the strength of the current, then walked in barefoot, stepping on the stones, the breeze catching her clothes for a moment. When she had finished Lily spread a cloth on the grass and looked out over the vale of Changan, layer upon layer of green hills, and in the foreground the serpent of the Wei River as it coiled and twisted through the millet fields and wondered why, now she was in love, the simplest joys came so often and so easily.

Last night there was still no news. I tried to sleep, just me and my pillow. I walked through the monastery grounds, saw two shooting stars and wished that dear Zian was here with me, then opened the door and shutters, lay awake and thought of my husband and could not sleep even with the cool night breeze.

In the morning Lily wrote a poem for Minister Li, imagined it finding him, out there in the countryside, where he sat to administer justice and order.

Recently I laid your beautiful mat
on my bed in this emerald house,
and lay watching the river's deep green currents
directing the flowing rafts.

Lily could picture him sitting alone with a cup of wine, enjoying her poem and feeling her close to him. That evening she danced alone in their courtyard, whirling gently as an autumn leaf, humming her own tune.

> Only a fan of clouds and soft breeze
> could match your gift.
> I turned to my silver bed
> and wished that autumn would wait.

She lay in bed that night and imagined kissing him, lying down next to him, slipped peacefully to sleep, imagined for a moment she could hear the ram's hide drums of the capital being beaten at the end of another day.

Every few days Minister Li came back to the monastery and Lily paid the monks to prepare a welcome feast. While he wanted to stay and rest she had planned excursions for them.

On the second day of the second month we set out to Hua Qing Palace, and stopped at a Buddhist monastery in the hills called Temple of Divine Brilliance. The temple was founded in 698, by a monk called the Great Bald Master, who returned from India with scriptures. The present abbot was the thirty-sixth since the founding of the temple.

There were hot springs nearby, which were said to be more fragrant than those of Hua Qing Palace, and Zian became very excited. The monks charge a string of cash to go and bathe. Afterwards we went to the temple and requested tea and admired the prayer halls. The temple has been rebuilt twice, we were told, with donations from the First Sui Emperor and also by Tang Emperor Xuanzong. It was said that he came

here with Yang Guifei to admire the yellow glaze roof
tiles he had commissioned. The monks took us to a
spot a little way off where they said the Emperor and
his consort ate lunch. We sat there in silence, 'at one
with the wind and the clouds', and thought of all the
trouble their love had brought.

'When statesmen fall in love, even they lose ambition,' my husband said.

'You must never lose your ambition,' I told him,
very sternly, and he laughed.

The next time they went north to the Huan Forest, which
was said to be an abode of sages and hermits and Daoist
Immortals disguised as grey-bearded old men, who rode
cranes through the clouds, bestowed strange gifts on
random travellers.

We reached Cun Village the next day, and found an
old stone lantern by the side of the path. There was
an inscription, which read 'Donated by Magistrate Ai
Shan in the third year of the Empress Wu Zetian'.

We talked about Empress Wu, who is the only
woman ever to have ruled the Middle Kingdom in
her own name. Not only was she the Seventh Ruler
of the Tang, but she was also the Fifth. We tried to
work it out but were confused and not even our recol-
lection of dear Sima Qian helped us out.

The next two days we went to see all the places
made famous by poetry.

One day they were sitting in the garden when Minister
Li compared Lily to Yang Guifei, who was given an entire
garden of peonies, the Queen of Flowers.

'What about the lily?' she asked.

'The lily is the fairie of flowers. It is rarer, more precious and more magical than queens. Queens grow old and wrinkled; their teeth fall out.'

'And fairies?'

'Fairies never grow old.'

'I want to grow old,' Lily told him. 'I want us to grow old together.'

Minister Li laughed at her expression, but Lily was serious.

'Will you still love me when I am old?'

'I will love you more.'

'Why more?'

Minister Li didn't answer at first, but Lily's eyes were full of disappointment, so he thought. 'Because when I am old I will look back and think of all the days and times and moments with you and—' He looked for a way to end this thought and couldn't.

Lily laughed at him, but that night she wanted to know what he had been going to say.

'I don't remember,' Minister Li said, yawned into his pillow.

The next time Minister Li went on a tour of duty, Lily went with him, sat behind a screen and listened as he judged a case against the local magistrate, brought by the farmers of Bamboo Shoot Village. Lily laughed as Minister Li questioned the villagers, who spoke simply in their thick country accents. The magistrate had failed to protect them from yearly floods, had failed to carry out the proper sacrifices, had not put policies in place to improve their lot. Each year the wooden bridge was washed away and they had no means of getting to market except by ferry at Dukou. The ferry was too expensive. They were unable to pay their taxes. It was the magistrate's fault, they summarised in their thick

169

country accents, for refusing to cut the tendons of poverty.

Lily caught a brief glimpse of the local magistrate. He was a thin man with a scraggy beard that clung in patches to his cheeks. He called the villagers robbers and thieves, denied their accusations of inactivity. But Minister Li found in the villagers' favour, ordered the dykes along the river to be raised, commissioned a pontoon bridge to be built that would survive flooding, wrote a petition to the governor asking him to grant the affected villages five years' tax-free status.

When the morning session was over Lily could barely wait for all the people to leave. 'I'm so glad you found in their favour,' she said as they walked back to his room. Minister Li was tired, but he smiled and took her hand. 'I think we agree on everything, don't you?' she continued.

'Yes,' he said simply, but was too tired to talk much more. When she tried to talk through his judgements he changed the subject; when she quoted the *Analects of Sage Kung* he put his hands to his temples and shut his eyes.

'Please,' he said, 'I have a headache.'

After lunch Minister Li went back to the yamen to hear more cases and Lily stayed in the room, not sure why she felt so unhappy. She lay reading a book called *Discourses of the Domains* – the king in the story was cruel and harsh, punished anyone who criticised his rule. When he claimed to have removed all dissent, the Duke of Shou contradicted him. 'You have not removed dissent, just stopped anyone talking about it. Trying to stop up people's mouths is like trying to dam a river. The waters will break through and flood the land.'

Lily lay on her back and remembered the cold days she had spent with her mother, her real mother. Sadness seemed to fill the room, she shut the book without waiting to see if the cruel king survived, wished she didn't have to read silly books when she could be sitting in moonlight. She lay and thought of all the people who had come to see Minister Li, thought of the painted screen in their room in the monastery, where the hermit and his concubine sat, always drinking and laughing and being in love.

That night Lily rested her head on Minister Li's chest, listened to the steady drumroll of his heart.

'Husband,' she began, 'promise me that you will not be angry with me.'

'Why should I be angry?'

'I have a question.'

'Hmm.'

'First promise.'

'I promise.'

'What?'

'Not to be angry.'

There was another long pause.

'Who do you love more – your wife or me?'

'Where am I?' Minister Li asked.

'You are here.'

'Exactly.'

'But what if *she* wanted to come?'

'I would not let her.'

'You do not love her?'

'No.'

'Do you love me?'

'Of course.'

'Promise.'

'I promise.'

Spring brought sun, warmth and green back into the world. There was a festival at Narcissus Temple on the Double Third Dan where the monks there built a Ten Thousand

Candle Tree. Women were forbidden so Minister Li went with his colleagues, came back drunk.

Lily had spent the evening playing on her zither, but the tunes seemed listless; the spring night's shower fell as cold as winter tears. When Minister Li climbed into bed with her she shrugged off his hug, was unresponsive.

'It is no good being a woman,' Lily said after a while, but Minister Li said nothing.

'Did you see anyone there?' she asked after a long pause.

'Yes,' he said, 'lots of people.'

'Any banished goddesses?'

'No,' he laughed at her worries. 'There were no women allowed.'

But women and goddesses didn't seem to be the problem.

'I thought of you the whole time!' he said and she almost laughed at herself.

'I love you,' she said, let him kiss her, but the next morning tattered clouds scattered showers through the morning, and Lily tried to shake off the chill. She looked at all the books she had read and couldn't face reading any of them again. She was quiet that evening when Minister Li came home and they sat across from each other, a wide bowl of dumplings steaming between them.

'Are you angry with me?' Minister Li asked, between mouthfuls.

'No.'

'Are you sure?'

'Why should I be angry with you?'

Minister Li lay in the darkness and said nothing.

'Exactly,' she said. 'You have done nothing wrong.'

After our visit to the Hua Qing Palace we came back via Dongkoufu, to see a Buddhist temple that Wang

Wei recommended for the beauty of the gold-leaf statue there and the purity of the silence in the evening. When we got there we saw that the place had long since fallen into ruin: the gold-leaf pillars decayed by frost and rain; the doors blown open by the wind; the hall itself a pile of rubble in an empty field of grass. All that was left were the two tall cypress trees he mentioned by the front door.

The villagers there told us that the place had been burnt by Lu Anshan's army. All beauty fades; even great men grow old and die. I recited Du Fu's poem:

> Over the castle ruins, in spring,
> The grass grows green again.

That night we stayed at an inn with an upper storey and a balcony facing the mountains and got very drunk, chanted poems to each other under the stars. The next day we took a shortcut to a village we could see over the fields, but it seemed the path was not used by anyone but hunters and woodcutters and before we could reach it the rain came on. We found shelter at a poor shrine, and marvelled at how many travellers had written their thanks for the temple's shelter. I scratched this poem for Hermit Ren, who founded the Zi Fu Temple.

> In this secluded spot
> you created an ideal place
> for tourists and travellers to stop
> and rest awhile.

Lily sat and read her diary to cheer herself up on nights when summer had already passed.

The whitewashed walls
hoard their passing praise.
In the lotus palace their fame
has no value.

They had made love in the temple courtyard, she remembered. A bulging-eyed monk had disturbed them, they'd sniggered as they tied their sashes again; the old fool had spluttered something about old paintings he could show them. For a few coins they had followed the paper lantern, crawled through the generations of hangings and scrolls and mouse droppings, and at the back of the temple, low down on the wall, they'd found a painting of Buddha in the style of the Wei Dynasty.

Minister Li had been unimpressed. 'There are finer paintings in the palace,' he'd said and the fact he had not been stolen by the same thrill and excitement that she had, made Lily feel alone.

When the rain eased we left our words and set off home, leaving the monks to their seclusion from the world.

When happy the nights are short; when lonely they're long.

It is a good thing to be in love, I think. The sun is brighter, the days more peaceful; it is worth the sadness of parting.

After Minister Li's work had finished in Mount Li Prefecture, Lily stayed at the monastery while he looked for a suitable manor in the capital. He enquired about the one he had rented for the wedding, and heard that the family who owned it had grown heavily indebted to a family of salt merchants. He offered them four gold ingots, and they settled at five. The next day Minister Li strolled through the empty courtyards. The walls of the central hall needed repairs, but the tiled roof was square and solid, the cedar pillars strong. When he cut back the thickets of gorse and dried grass, he found the remains of a garden, landscaped in the time of Yang Guifei. That night he wrote to Lily, asking her to come.

Three days later Lily arrived with a train of camels and belongings. When she realised which house he had bought her eyes brimmed with joyful tears.

'Don't you like it?' Minister Li said, but she pummelled his chest.

'Of course I like it!' she said, and while the servants hurried back and forth, he took her hand and led her from courtyard to courtyard, through the gardens and down to the thatched stables, and they talked about how they would paint each room, imagined their lives ahead of them – children, love, promotion, the slow winding in of the years.

'What shall we call it?' Minister Li said that night as they sat in the overgrown garden.

Lily thought of the mountain valley that history had left unmolested. 'Peach Blossom Palace,' she said – and the next day artisans were summoned to carve wooden signs to hang on the gateposts.

Minister Li Zian, son of Prime Minister Li Zifu, to the left.

Peach Blossom Palace, to the right.

———————

Minister Li was commended for his work in the prefecture, but official pay did not cover all the expenses of life so he wrote to his grandmother. The letter was stamped with his personal seal, Zian, and added to the official correspondence. Every ten li a horse was set galloping – it took less than a week to arrive at her house; another week for her reply to arrive. Minister Li did not bother to read it but took out a note, with the stamp of the Organisation of Rice Traders in Taiyuanfu, redeemable at their offices in the Western Market for the said amount of money.

Minister Li looked at the quantity, eight ingots of gold, and thanked Heaven that his grandmother was stingy in all things except family appearance. Lily clapped her hands: eight ingots of gold seemed wealth beyond her imagination.

Lily instructed the laying out of the furniture. When Minister Li came home he instructed the gardeners: apricot blossom in spring, a grotto stone set up like a miniature mountain in the middle of the pool, lotus fronds clotting the clear water. They repainted the pavilion, Lily's fluid hand writing the name above the door, Moonlight Pavilion.

'I think we will live here many years,' Minister Li said, and he and Lily watched a cloud grow across the moon like mould, darken the pavilion and thought their separate thoughts.

'I hope so,' she said.

One morning Minister Li and Lily woke to a strange still-ness, opened the doors and saw snow in the yard, falling thick as feathers. They summoned the servants, ordered wine to be warmed, sat with thick quilts over their knees, a few cold dishes to go with the wine.

Lily marked some lines on paper, and they played chess for a while, stopped and drank a little more wine, which made their cheeks glow.

'My mother used to make Eight Treasure Soup when it snowed,' Lily said.

'I remember walking to my classroom through the cold,' Minister Li said. 'Snow makes me think of my tutor. I hated my tutor.'

Lily poured him more wine. She wished she could go back to the minister's childhood and make all his memories glow like hot coals, to warm him in his old age.

'I remember the day my father died,' she said. 'It snowed that day.'

'Your real father?'

Lily nodded, thought of black crows in pine trees and a large fat laughing Buddha.

'What was he like?'

'I don't remember,' she said, and they sat in silence. She remembered playing on a hillside, pine trees, bleak steppe winds, ten thousand miles of flat grasslands – but the real events had long since reorganised themselves into memories, vivid and unreliable.

'I was too young,' she said at last.

In the last weeks of 859, Scholar Yu and his wife were sitting inside, their legs muffled under a thick blanket. He was reading Lu Yu's *Classic of Tea*, she was stitching shoes.

'You don't need to stitch shoes.'

'I like to,' she said, and he returned to his book. His wife didn't need to do anything now that their daughter was the concubine of Minister Li.

Granny Pig licked her gums, prayer beads rattling in her bony old hand. When they heard the gate hinges squeak Scholar Yu and his wife looked at each other. Scholar Yu thought it might be one of his friends from the ministry; his wife thought it might be one of the neighbours. Granny Pig prayed to the Buddha: Bring me back as a good person, not as an animal. Bring me back with Uncle Jia. Let us be fated to meet again.

There was the crunch of snow: Small Pan, a local scholar, usually shouted hello by now, so Scholar Yu thought it must be one of his wife's friends. He looked back to his book, decided he'd go out to the teahouse.

The person stamped their feet. The door swung open. Scholar Yu's wife saw a rich young girl and tried to match the clothes to the girls who lived round about, but her husband recognised Lily, threw the blanket off his legs, clapped his hands.

'Daughter!' he said and Scholar Yu's wife dropped the shoes, the needle and thread, all tangled together. She pulled Lily inside, shut the door, bolted it shut, and such was the fuss and excitement that even Granny Pig put her prayer beads down.

'Little Flower!' she said, felt the impulse to reach for a cinnamon stick, smacking her lips as she shuffled forward, made as if to come down from the kang.

'Granny Pig,' Lily said, and tried to hold her still, but the old woman would have none of it.

'Little Flower!' she said, stood up, took Lily by the cheeks and shook her affectionately.

'Sit down!' Scholar Yu's wife pushed the old woman back on to the bed. 'Stoke the fire!' she fussed. 'Come and sit here,' she said and took Lily to the warmest part of the kang. Lily noticed that they no longer fed the fire cheap wood but the best split cedar. The flames fed quickly, the cedar blocks turned ruby red, split into embers with a sound like crystal breaking. Soon the room was so warm that condensation began to drip down the silk-screen windows. Lily took off her coat and hat; her hair looked dishevelled, her nose began to run in the warmth.

'Well, we stayed at the rented manor for a month . . .' She told them all about her trips and adventures and picnics in the countryside, all the famous men she had met. She felt like a guest: she spoke louder than normal, laughed and smiled in a way that made her mother feel like a stranger. Lily told them about their new house as her mother waited on her, the formality uncomfortable.

'It sounds very grand,' Scholar Yu's wife said, and Scholar Yu nodded enthusiastically.

When Lily asked her parents what they had been doing they didn't have much to say: their world seemed to have shrunk as hers had grown. Even Granny Pig seemed smaller and more toothless than before.

'You can stay here,' Scholar Yu's wife said when the sky started to darken.

'I'd better get back,' Lily said, and her father and mother stood up, awkward and eager. They walked Lily out of the gate and down the street to the edge of the ward, stopped to wave.

'Go slowly!' they called and Lily waved, but as she mounted the mule she slipped on the trampled snow, felt foolish, and even though she was leaving them behind, there was something about the afternoon that made her feel as if she had been abandoned. She turned for home, but was unable to dismiss the image of Scholar Yu and his wife standing at their gateway, calling to her, their winter silhouettes seeming small and remote.

AD 906

Minister Li spent the morning in the ancestral tomb, sacrificing to the generations before him – meat and wine heaped like mountains: grandmother buns, spring rice wine, sweet date lotus root and crusty chunks of sugar-fried pork. The dishes were laid out in a circle like a huge banquet, cups of spring wine spilling over the brim, ivory chopsticks perched on bronze rests. The mice would eat well, Minister Li thought as he shut the vermilion doors, wandered back through his manor, left the hungry ghosts behind.

Minister Li picked up his walking-stick from its stand and trudged over Zigzag Bridge: a three-legged man walking painfully along. He paused for breath, then turned off the path to the Spring Garden Pavilion, which his father had built to view the peach blossoms. There was a contorted rock that the minister had set up when he was a young man. It had aged with him and now trailed moss like a beard. From the top a pine bonsai grew – trained from youth to appear a thousand years old. Minister Li liked to sip spring rice wine and contemplate them both from his pavilion, but this morning he felt too old and stiff and futile.

It would have been better to be asleep, he thought as he slowly lowered himself on to his chair. In his dreams he visited a world of summer gardens, ponds and pavilions and music; there was no decline of government, no sour taste of regret.

As stormclouds gathered the earth and sky grew dark; the colours of the garden went dull. Minister Li closed his eyes and after a while his head fell forward and the noises of the twirling wind faded. He took stick and coat and wandered back into the past, looking for good memories. As always he kept to the well-worn roads, safe paths for an old man to visit.

When Fang found the minister he stood for a moment before clearing his throat. The second time Minister Li's eyes opened: pale and dreamy like a baby's.

'Shall I bring lunch here?' Fang asked, too loud and sudden. Minister Li wiped a thread of dribble from his beard and looked confused.

'Lunch?' Fang reminded him.

'Ah yes,' Minister Li said, sitting up. 'In my courtyard. You can read me poetry.'

Fang nodded, but when he was long out of earshot he cursed: 'Turtle!'

Minister Li chewed slowly. '"Selling Tattered Peonies",' he called, when one poem was finished, picked up another piece of cucumber from the plate. Fang recited:

> Facing the wind I sigh,
> as the petals keep falling,
> their perfume fading
> with the passing spring.

Flowers like these should command
a high price, but there's no one to buy them.
Their perfume is so rich
it even scares the butterflies.

Minister Li picked out a piece of winter melon from
his soup and sucked it till it was ready to swallow. He shut
his eyes and cast himself back to a far-off spring day when
they had sat together. His mind re-created the scene before
him: black ink moat rippling with sunlight, steep stone wall
rising from the water, dragonflies glittering like sparks.

These exquisite buds
will only open in the palace.
Green foliage like theirs
would be ruined by the dusty roads.

. . . and his wonder as Lily recited this poem . . .

but noble lords, if you wait for these flowers
to be transplanted to the Imperial Gardens
even you will come to regret
that you have no way to buy them.

Minister Li opened his eyes, but instead of her smile
was the face of Fang – blank like a monastery wall.
'Another?'
Minister Li put his hand to his face. 'Enough for today,'
he said, opened his fist slowly, like a flower. Memories were
like rebellions: they needed to be crushed.

Fang rushed through the lanes and courtyards of the Li
Family Manor, racing the thinning daylight. He paused
outside the gateway of the minister's wife, long enough to

judge that she was not there, then scurried past. He was almost round the corner when he heard Swallow's voice, coy and teasing.

'Manservant!' she simpered. 'The mistress wants to see you!'

Swallow's voice had a taunting lilt, as if she was daring him to run. She watched him approach with something like a smile, fish lure earrings flashing.

'So who told her I was passing?'

Fang had a knack of turning cowardice into charm. 'Not me,' Swallow grinned. 'You're just too clumsy and loud.'

Fang followed her inside, watched her hips sway like a willow branch, waist fragile as a flower stem.

Minister Li's wife sat in a black lacquer chair, silk shoes embroidered with butterflies, sipping bitter green tea. She put her cup down when Fang entered, folded her hands on her lap.

'Mistress?' Fang said and his tone made her jaw stiffen. The years had left her thin, miserable and infirm: deep wrinkles ploughed into every expression.

'I hear that you have been down into town again,' Minister Li's wife said.

Fang did not try to argue. She had seen him riding home. They both knew it.

'I forbid it!' she told him, yellow and black teeth between thin lips.

Fang folded his long sleeves back over his arms. 'Why?' he asked.

On the black sheen of her chair the old woman's knuckles tensed white. 'You are to attend to the minister at all times,' the Mistress said, her intonation high and frantic like a trapped wasp. 'Day *and* night!'

Fang thought of continuing the game, but held her dark

betel-nut eyes for a long moment and then bowed. The mistress looked away, pretended she did not see him return Swallow's smile. 'Be careful of him,' the mistress said when Swallow had shown him to the door. 'The crane does not hatch snakes.'

A stagnant hush returned to the Li Family Manor after sunset. Only black crows disturbed the stillness, flapping through the gloom on homeward wings. Fang's small courtyard was hidden behind the trees of Lacquer Tree Garden. The scent of the plum blossoms faded at sunset, but he could still hear the jostling bamboo as he cooked himself a meal of bean curd and spring onions, shovelled it down, washed his mouth out with cold green tea.

'Don't fret about things that can't be changed,' a poet once wrote, 'drink a cup of wine instead.' It seemed good advice as he poured himself another cup of Forget Your Cares wine, emptied it in one long mouthful. A few more cups and he would head down to town, he told himself, tipped the wine pot again, drank the next cup. He was on his fifth when he heard a scratch at the door, found the watchman's face blinking in the candlelight.

'The master is sick,' the short man stammered.

'We're all sick.'

'He is calling for you,' he said but Fang kicked the door shut.

He's always calling for me.

The man scratched again and Fang drew the bolt shut. 'Tell them I'm in town!' he shouted and stared around this tomb. His bed stood on one wall and a table against the other, a few worn books leant together for support: but all Fang saw were four mud walls, hemming him in. He thought of the town with the night streets aglow with lanterns – oil lamps in the night market glimmering like fireflies, spiced mutton kebabs, shining lard soup; fragrant bordellos where a man could buy intelligent company, drink wine, write poems, drift through life, a wandering white cloud.

Fang pulled off his robe and hung it on its peg and lay down, heard the wind rattle the door as he put his head down to sleep. Now he felt too tired for that. Maybe tomorrow, he told himself as he listened for the night watchman's rounds, thought briefly of Swallow's willow waist caught in the breeze and then blew out the candle.

AD 860

In the capital Lily and Minister Li were busy attending banquets with friends and colleagues and with the aristo- cratic relatives of Minister Li. Minister Li loved to show off Lily, bought her the finest gowns, gave her gifts of extravagant hairpins, earrings and bracelets of pure white alabaster and jade. Lily laughed at all her husband's jokes. She felt like the Queen of Heaven.

After the Double Third festival a letter came from the Li Family Manor. Lily watched it suspiciously as it lay on her husband's tea table, one corner tucked under the orna- mental bonsai. She considered opening it, but went out into the spring garden instead, and diverted her attention by trying to compose peach-blossom poetry – but each time she tried to think of a line her mind went back to the folded paper lying on the tea table, unopened like a strange and sinister flower bud.

When Minister Li came home Lily rushed to meet him and take his coat, sat him down and gave him the letter, expectant as a puppy.

Minister Li put it down again to ask her about her day, but Lily was too impatient.

'Open it!' she said.

'Later.'

'Now!' she said and blushed, but Minister Li picked open the seal, unfolded the letter.

Lily tried to read his face.

'What is it?' she asked.

Minister Li poured himself a cup of wine.

'What is it?' she asked, but he did not look up. 'Husband?'

'My grandmother says my mother is sick,' he said.

Lily felt that she didn't know anything about parents dying.

'We should go and see her,' she said.

'Hmm,' Minister Li said and put the letter down. 'You don't know my grandmother.'

Minister Li was quiet all through dinner; when they talked of other matters neither of them was interested.

'I feel like going to Moonlight Pavilion,' Minister Li said and the servants were summoned to get the place ready with lanterns and wine.

Before they went Lily took his hands. 'What if she is sick?'

'She was well enough when I last saw her,' he said, even though it made no sense.

That night Lily woke and found that Minister Li was not in bed. She saw his silhouette sitting on a chair, staring at the shadows of the bamboos outside, waving in the night breeze.

'Zian?'

Minister Li didn't turn.

Lily pushed back the furs, put her arms around him. 'You will see your mother again,' Lily whispered into his hair. 'I promise you that.' There was a long pause. Lily stroked the hair back from his face, kissed his head. 'You have nothing to fear,' she assured him. 'We will go there, see your mother, then come home. I promise you.'

Minister Li came back to bed, but the next morning, as Lily organised the servants in packing for the trip, he sat with a pot of cold wine and stared out into the chill morning. There was a heavy dew in the air, the new spring leaves hung dejected in the misty drizzle; birds swooped low through the gloom, but none of them landed, none of them sang.

It did not take long to organise their departure and on the appointed day Minister Li and Lily set off from the capital by barge. Friends came out with them on the first day, gave them a farewell banquet the next morning: sent them on their way with bellies full of food and wine and good memories. The willows along the banks had many broken branches.

My husband was eager to set out so we finished our meal and ordered the barge master to push off. Our friends stood and watched us pull away and called out to us many times with good wishes. Even the willows hung their heads; we wet our sleeves with our tears, promised to return soon. Our friends broke off willow branches, and held them as a mark of sadness.

> Tears wet the flowering branches
> day after day.
> The stripped willow blows
> in the windblown drizzle.
>
> I wish the rain fell
> on treeless slopes,
> saving us all the grief
> of leaving.

In the evenings Minister Li and Lily drank wine and competed with poems. When they composed poems on the theme of the grasslands Minister Li eventually held his hands up in defeat.

'I'm tired,' he said.

During the day, they sat in the barge and watched mile after mile of fields, river hamlets, flapping tavern signs, all reflected in the wind-ruffled water. The agricultural year was already under way. There were men hitching cattle, ploughing the fields, cattle and sheep returning through narrow lanes, an old man leaning on his staff at a village gate, waiting for an unseen shepherd boy over the rise of the hill. Well fed and clothed, to Lily it seemed that the peasants' simple lives were untroubled by history or learning or poems. She remembered the story of Peach Blossom Spring, looked towards the mountain valleys, filled with morning mist, and wondered if there were villagers deep in the hills who had not heard of Changan or the Tang emperors.

They went by barge as far as Luoyang, garden city and second capital of the empire, paused to visit the Buddhist grottos there, ate many fine lunches with men who had passed the exams the same year as Minister Li. They were young and enthusiastic. The empire still stood, they thought, as strong and defiant as the mountain peaks.

'I wish I'd been posted to Luoyang,' Minister Li said as they lay in bed that night and the many temple bells that sounded the passing hours entered their different dreams.

'When we get back we will find you another job.'

Minister Li laughed.

'Where?'

'Here.'

Minister Li laughed again.

'How about Hangzhou?' he asked. 'Or Suzhou?'

Lily thought of the emperors who had fled from barbarians and civil war, founded the brilliant southern dynasties where, for a short while, the exquisite gardens, painters, poets, musicians and courtesans had all survived a precarious existence, until war swept them away, leaving nothing to brighten a land devastated by suffering, except memory.

'I always wanted to see the southlands.'

'Did you ever think of going back north?' Minister Li said, his tone suggesting he hadn't listened.

Lily stopped for a moment, imagined herself out in the grasslands, horizon to horizon to horizon – each way you turned – not a tree in sight: just grass and hills and the great expanse of lifetime still ahead of her. Even though life was good and she was happy, there were times when she felt sad and she didn't know why. In the long hours of waiting she wished that she had never left the grasslands, was still a child with her real mother and father, had never been constrained by the slow twisting of the years. There were times when Lily felt restless and sad, and the world seemed nothing but books, hairpins, new gowns and her husband – her learning no more use than the vase on the table, dusted and polished and occasionally taken out to amuse their friends.

'I'm sorry,' Lily said after a long pause, 'what was the question?'

Lily and Minister Li set off from Luoyang, going north through Dongshan Province. The weather was colder here, and while around Changan they were sowing wheat, here they were still ploughing the thin yellow soil. Lily watched a young girl, gaunt after winter, carry steamed bread wrapped in a cloth and a gourd of water to her father and brothers in the fields. The men were small against the backdrop of mountains as they sat to eat. Lily watched the girl return to the thatched hut under the bamboo grove, looked back at the mountains.

It seemed so strange that the little girl who had looked out from the battlements at the Last Fort Under Heaven had grown into Lily: here, now, married to Minister Li. When she thought of her real mother and father, Lily drew in a long breath. After a while she turned in her saddle.

'I love you,' she said to Minister Li.

'I love you,' he told her.

Lily and Minister Li stayed at government hostels, fed their ponies on broken rice, the rich smell of horse going to bed with them, on their hands, their clothes, in their hair, waiting for them the next morning.

Lily imbued the hostels with artistic charm, blotted out the discomforts of travel – bugs, rats and leaking roofs. She tried to lighten the weight of worry by honouring nameless hills with lines of poetry daubed on walls or stones, or scratched into the green polish of bamboo stalks; and sometimes Minister Li brightened up, but sometimes he wasn't in the mood for poems.

His face was overcast and solemn; she could not read his thoughts.

As they travelled north they saw evidence of an uprising that had been suppressed ten years earlier. Lily vaguely remembered it as a place name and unrest, but still the land was desolate and deserted, crumbling ruins memorials to long-dead villages.

But there was also beauty in the ruins, as if the melancholy ghosts still lingered. Occasionally they stopped and wished for a pot of wine to savour the moment. All lives were brief, all beauty faded; all that is loved fades and dies and is forgotten. There was nothing to do but drink a cup of wine and celebrate the moment. Young, in love and beautiful.

Sometimes they made love; sometimes they held hands; sometimes they kissed and held each other against the coming of the night.

After a few days' walking they returned to inhabited areas, stopped that night at a village where the chickens squawked frantically at their arrival, and a middle-aged peasant woman came out of her hut, drying her hands on her apron.

The next morning they paid a few cash and watched as one of the backyard chickens was picked out and slaughtered, its guts washed away in the playful stream water, spring rice wine keeping them company while the chicken was fried with shallots and ginger and cloves of garlic.

We stayed at the house of a magistrate, whose surname was Fen, and whose literary name was White Cloud. Although he was a rich man he was not coarse or vulgar. He insisted that we stay and rest from the journey and showed us all manner of hospitality. He took us to see the ruins of Sweet Brook Haven, where the Han Dynasty poet, Su Han, died. There was nothing now except empty fields and a melon patch, but there is still a hill there called Golden Pheasant Hill, where it was said he would sit to watch the moon rise.

Magistrate Liu said there was a ruined town a few miles north. After a heavy rainfall, he said, the local villagers would go and look for uncovered treasures. We were very interested, and he showed us a coin that dated from the Qin Dynasty.

He invited us to go and see the ruins, but my husband told him we had pressing business at home.

When he questioned us we told him that filial duty meant we had to refuse his hospitality. He did not question us after that. The last night we drank ten cups of wine and I played the zither and we each recited our favourite poems.

Each day Minister Li became quieter and quieter. His moods were harder to shake off; he and Lily talked less and less.

'Let's go back to the capital,' he said one night, and forced a smile. Lily reached out to hold him, wished she could take the sadness from his eyes.

'We will go back tomorrow,' she said, kissed his forehead.

Minister Li imagined the return journey and smiled. 'We can stop off at all those scenic spots,' he laughed and they toasted the return of their carefree life with imaginary cups. But in the morning Minister Li turned his pony to the north, and Lily followed slowly behind, dreading their arrival.

On the last night of the trip Minister Li and Lily stayed at a private hostel. It had once been a monastery, and was now run by a gruff man and his short fat wife. The old prayer hall was weatherbeaten – grass grew between the tiles, and the front step overgrown with weeds – but the couple kept the rooms and stables immaculately clean; the crisp sheets smelt of good lard soap. They gave the travellers vegetables and vinegar; Lily used the rice they had brought with them to make a simple dinner. She hummed to keep herself calm, fried onions with salt pork slices, garnished the rice with yellow millet, served it on a white earthenware dish, sprinkled with spring onions, cut fresh after an evening shower.

'Is your wife pretty?' Lily said when her meal was finished.

'No, she's not.'

Lily nodded, they sat in silence, and after a long time thinking, Lily poured them both another cup of wine.

> Wandering along, we stop,
> listen to the birds, my heart soaring,
> watch the crane flapping free from the open cage.

> At night in the temple hall
> Under the high rafters I sleep deeply,
> while outside the dusk rains
> build to a downpour.

The last day was warm and summery. At the end of a short day's walk, Lily and Minister Li arrived at the Li Family Manor, the rammed earth walls stark against the afternoon sky. They were thirsty and dusty. Lily took off her wide straw hat, wiped the sweat and dust from her face, waited for the gates to open. Minister Li knocked and knocked and nothing happened.

'Ho there!' he shouted, and after a few moments a peephole opened and an eye appeared: peering first at one then round to the other.

'Yes?'

'Open up!' Minister Li shouted, and there was no mistaking his voice.

'Master,' the gateman apologised, 'we did not know you were coming.'

But Minister Li was not interested. He dismounted and led their ponies through the door, helped Lily down as a handful of servants arrived and stood a little way off, staring. They seemed to be afraid that Minister Li might speak to them, began to take packs and bags and hurry away.

'No, not that way,' Minister Li told them and they stopped and looked nervous.

Minister Li turned to the steward. 'Who is living in the Western Chamber?'

'No one, sir.'

'Then clean it out, I will stay there with my concubine.'

Lily couldn't tell why, but it was a different Minister Li who gave orders – not the man she had married.

'Her name is Yu,' Minister Li finished. 'You will call her Mistress Yu.'

The steward nodded. The information was whispered through the manor from servant to servant. Pretty, they said, pretty and young. Her family name is Yu. She is not tall. Yellow skin; large eyes; a Changan accent. You will call her Mistress Yu.

When everything had been prepared, Minister Li led Lily through the narrow lanes to the Western Courtyard.

'This way is Lacquer Tree Garden,' he said. 'We can sit and drink there. That way is my old classroom. I'll show you that tomorrow. The hunting here is very good – maybe we will take the ponies out. What do you think?'

He turned to smile to her and Lily smiled back, but when he looked away she walked behind him and felt as if he was a stranger – and that nothing he was telling her would ever happen.

Minister Li left Lily to wash and change, then went to pay his respects to his grandmother.

Lily sat alone with the packed bags, wished that they were still travelling. After a long while she picked herself up and tried to arrange the room as prettily as possible. She went to the garden and cut some peonies, arranged them in front of the silk-screen windows; sprinkled the yard dust with water; wiped the furniture, made the red lacquer shine.

When a servant came she let out a squawk and took the rag from Lily's hands. 'Please Mistress Yu,' she chastised and Lily watched the servants do everything she had done, including move the flowers from the window to the dressing-table. Lily wanted to say something but decided to wait till they left – but they were still there when Minister Li came back.

'Enough,' he said in a tone that alarmed Lily. The women stopped abruptly, bowed and hurried out, shut the doors behind them and Minister Li sat down.

'Mother's dead,' he said simply. 'She was dead before we left.'

Lily looked at him but his eyes seemed closed. When she came to sit next to him he took a deep breath, put his hands up to cover his face. Now he would have to resign his government job, she thought, as if that was the worst thing that would happen.

It was a few hours later that Lily was taken to pay her respects to Grandmother Li. She stood nervously as the old woman stared down at her.

'My husband had a concubine once,' Grandmother Li declared, her beetle-black eyes sparkling malevolently, prayer beads steadily crawling through her palm, 'but she only brought disruption and deceit. In the end I had her banished from my household.'

Lily bowed and didn't know what to say.

'From my experience concubines only bring trouble.'

'I do not want to bring trouble, Honoured Grandmother,' Lily said.

'Do you not?'

'No,' Lily said.

'What is wrong with the wife I chose for my grandson?'

'I don't know.'

'You don't know?' Grandmother Li repeated. 'Why don't you know?'

Lily blushed and was about to speak when Grandmother Li indicated a spot on the bed next to her. 'Come and sit here,' she said, and her frown almost turned into a smile when Lily tried to climb up and slipped back down again, and had to jump up a second time. 'You are short,' she commented.

When Lily was seated next to her, Grandmother Li took the flower cup from her lap, held it out. 'This cup was given to my husband by Emperor Wuzong,' she said, face and tone severe. 'Look at it!'

Lily took the cup. Each petal depicted noble scenes: four of men shooting, hunting, fighting and riding on horseback; four of women relaxing in a garden, grooming themselves, combing their hair and looking after babies.

'My husband served Emperor Wuzong. His grandfather served Emperor Xuanzong; his great-grandfather was a minister in the time of the Sui Dynasty.'

Lily didn't understand.

'How old are you?'

'Sixteen.'

'Sixteen.' Grandmother Li tasted the word for a moment. 'That would mean you were born in the Year of the Pig.'

Lily nodded.

'I was born in the Year of the Snake,' Grandmother Li said. 'That means we will be friends, you and I.' Grandmother Li smiled neat brown teeth, put out a liver-spotted hand, patted the back of Lily's hand. 'What I mean,' she said, 'is that the men of this family are bred for office. Do not disrupt that noble calling.'

I was invited to meet the minister's wife and son. I was very nervous at first and wanted to make a good impression, but she greeted me and called me 'Little Sister' and thanked me for taking such good care of her husband while he was in the city.

This afternoon I went for a walk in the gardens and realised how sad everyone in the Li family is; even the faces of the servants seem dour. I thought of my parents as I watched the bamboos tremble before the wind.

That night Lily sat alone as ten shaven-headed monks arrived and Minister Li went with them to pay respects to his mother's ghost. The noise of their chanting rose and fell like the sound of wind on the mountainside. She picked up a twig, bent and snapped it into two, then three, then six small pieces that she tossed to the floor.

As the sun set the monks were still chanting sutras. Lily took out her book, but didn't feel like writing. As daylight failed, the world around her shrank to the circle of candle-light. She lay back and listened to the insects, distant bull-frogs croaking, and imagined Changan: the ward gates closed, the streets dancing with lanterns and street markets full of the scents of perfume and oil and frying noodles. The cicadas went quiet for a moment, and only then did Lily notice how loud they'd been before – then the noise rose again, and she stopped hearing it. All she heard was the monks going to bed. She expected Minister Li to come back to her room, but she waited an hour, then two, and the only sounds she heard were the bullfrogs and the cicadas.

When Minister Li came back Lily tried to soothe him but he was tired and frustrated and irritable.

Dreams drip
through the cold wet nights.
No one wants to talk
of the lonely
hours of loss.

Lily didn't know what to do. When she tried to touch him
he pushed her hands away. She didn't try any more. She didn't
want to be here. They lay back to back, unable to sleep.

Behind the western mountains,
sunset,
Behind the eastern mountains,
moonrise
Recollections of her
keep rising.

The next morning Minister Li had family business to
attend to. Lily sat alone, missing the capital, missing her
parents, missing the day before yesterday, before they'd
come to this horrible place. Minister Li's wife sent her an
invitation to visit, addressed her affectionately, but still Lily
didn't feel like company.

'Please thank the minister's wife,' she told the maidservant, 'but tell her that I am not feeling well today.'

The maidservant hurried away and Lily walked around
the manor. There were alleys and gardens and courtyards
– high walls, derelict stables, thatched huts with roofs that
leaked, doors that had rotted on their rope hinges. In the
parts that the family still used, the halls were covered with
blue-glazed tiles, the ancestral temple was tiled with green.
Lily stopped outside it and listened to the monks chanting. At one point a monk coughed and cleared his throat,
but after a long pause Lily decided not to go in.

She found a round moon gate and stepped through it into a walled bamboo-and-water garden. The paths were weeded, but the place felt as if the gardeners were slowly losing the battle against nature. For the first time since arriving, the world seemed almost happy. When Lily found a basket of freshly cut bamboo shoots set on the ground, but no sign of anyone, she felt a thrill of anticipation, as if she had disturbed the Immortals – but then a kitchen girl came bustling into the garden, singing a crude country song, till she saw Lily and yelped with surprise and then embarrassment.

'Mistress Yu!' she stammered, gathered up her basket and hurried away.

All day with no one here, Lily thought, I watched light rain. A master had written a poem about that, but all that afternoon the flat grey clouds passed overhead, too preoccupied to shower, and Lily was unable to summon the literary mood. She eventually went inside and lay down, was woken by a maid bringing a fresh bucket of water to the room.

'Sorry Mistress Yu,' the maid said and clumped around the room. 'Oh Mistress,' the girl said as an afterthought, 'there is a meal tonight in Grandmother Li's courtyard, which you have been asked to attend.'

Lily sat up and nodded, but she still felt like a fallen flower, bobbing in the wake of passing boats.

Lily was nervous as she dressed in her best gown, woven with kingfisher feathers, dressed her hair in the latest style – but no one came and she wished she had brought other gowns with her, wished she was going out to the Serpentine Park rather than to Grandmother's courtyard to eat with Grandmother Li and Minister Li's wife and son.

When the cicadas were shrilling a man with a lantern

came to light her way, and she stepped softly, imagining herself an Immortal who had tripped and fallen down to earth. When they reached Grandmother Li's courtyard the gates stood open and a side hall was lit with rows of candles. The dishes were laid out and when Grandmother Li was seated the others took their places, according to rank.

First Minister Li, then his wife and son.

Lily smiled as she waited, even helped Minister Li's son on to his stool.

'We have servants for that,' Grandmother Li said and Lily stood back and blushed.

The last stool, shorter and less ornate than the others, was for her. She sat and lowered her eyes, could feel the candlelight shimmering off her gown, her cheeks suffused with blood. Across the table she could feel Minister Li's wife watching her. She seemed the kind of woman a grandmother would choose for her grandson: solid and plain and a little stupid. She looked a few years older than Minister Li, which made Lily curious. She caught Minister Li's wife's eyes and the older woman looked away.

She is afraid of me, Lily thought, and felt sorry for her.

'Little Sister, you should try the carp,' Minister Li's wife said.

'Thank you,' Lily said, reached with her chopsticks.

'You're my father's concubine,' Minister Li's son said. He spoke like Grandmother Li, his young voice hard and censorious.

'I am,' Lily said.

'When I am old I will have many concubines as pretty as you.'

All the family laughed then, even Minister Li, but Lily blushed.

'I hope you have one as good as Mistress Yu,' Minister Li said, but still Lily could not shake off the feeling of

201

inferiority. 'Second hole', as her mother had put it. But there was no limit to the number of concubines a man could take. She might end up third, fourth or fifth hole, Lily thought and took a deep breath and forced a smile.

'Where are you from?' the little boy asked.

'My mother was a concubine and my father was a marshal in the Army of Divine Strategy.'

'I want to be a soldier,' the little boy said, his eyes wide, chewing as he spoke, 'and kill many barbarians!'

'Did you see the grasslands?' he asked later in the meal. 'And were they frightening?'

Lily smiled. 'No,' she said. 'I used to play there when I was your age.'

The little boy's eyes opened even wider – he seemed to be wondering how a girl had survived there.

'I did see a few barbarians,' Lily said. 'Their sheep were like ants on the grasslands.'

Grandmother Li cleared her throat and spat a gobbet on to the floor.

'Eat,' she told her great-grandson, and he stopped questioning.

'Eat,' she told Lily, and Lily bowed her head and picked out a few vegetables to mix with her rice.

'Eat!' she told her grandson, and even he bowed his head to his bowl.

When the meal was over, they stood up in order; Lily left her stool last of all, watched Minister Li take his grand-mother to her chambers. She said goodnight to Minister Li's wife and son.

'Another time Aunty Yu will tell you all about the grass-lands,' Minister Li's wife said, but she didn't quite look Lily in the eye.

'Goodnight,' Lily said.

When she got to her yard, she took off her gown, the kingfisher feathers shimmering an oily blue and green and turquoise, let out a long sigh and sat down at the dressing-table. She turned up the lamp wick and the flame grew as long as her hand, rubbed the bronze mirror to a shine. Tears started quite gently, red cheek powder running in tears down the candlelit mirror. She thought of a line of poetry that described tears falling like winter rain – but hers were hot and stuffy and made her nose run and her cheeks burn. She sniffed and wiped them away, left smears of white and red across her face – and then she blew her nose on her sleeve and finally laughed at herself.

I have been picked by my husband, as she wiped both make-up and tears away and stood up to go to bed. That is a much stronger bond.

It was very late when the door opened. Minister Li blew out the candles, undressed in the darkness and climbed into bed. Lily was not asleep, but she didn't speak. When he turned his back on her she gently touched him.

'Husband?'

'Mmm.'

'Will you put your arm around me?'

Minister Li turned over, stretched out his arm and pillowed her head.

'Where have you been?' she asked after a while.

'I went to see my wife.'

They lay for a long time, as close as they had always lain, but Lily felt separate. She didn't know if she should ask her question, but she thought she couldn't sleep unless she did.

'Husband.'

'What?'

'Did you sleep with your wife?'

'No.'

'Promise?'

'Promise,' he lied, stretched out to sleep.

When a parent died, officials were obliged to resign their positions to fulfil the necessary mourning duties proscribed in both law and custom. Minister Li sent a letter to the local magistrate stating that his mother had died and that he would be spending the six-month mourning period at the Li Family Manor. Filial laws also required that a grieving son should refrain from sexual relations. Lily did not want to bring the subject up. They slept as close as ever before, but she missed the lovemaking, missed the feeling of being loved.

Day after day Minister Li spent in the Ancestral Temple, his days passing to the tune of chanting monks. Lily came with him at first, both of them dressed in white robes with white headbands wrapped round their heads, but after a week Grandmother Li forbade it.

'It is not proper,' she said, 'for a concubine to be honouring your respected mother.'

Lily sat in her yard and read poems of the Southern Dynasties. Living in the country reminded her of Wang Family Village, when each day seemed to have been taken up with labours. She stood and watched the servants carrying armfuls of mulberry branches, and the smell of the thick glossy leaves took her back to the slopes of her childhood, when she was small and frightened and set to become Number One Son's wife. The thought made Lily laugh, and she turned for home, waited for Minister Li to return.

Some days Minister Li's wife invited Lily to the courtyard she shared with her son. She had a rosewood chessboard, and she and Lily sat moving the pieces, trying to trap the other's king.

'I was born in Taiyuanfu,' Minister Li's wife told Lily. 'I remember there were so many things to do and see there.'

'Have you been back?' Lily asked as she moved her castle forward.

'No,' Minister Li's wife said. 'I stay here with my child. We have all that we could want. The gardens are very beautiful in autumn. It is a little cold in winter, but then Taiyuanfu was cold too.'

Lily nodded, but the woman's wistful tone made it sound like each year was four seasons of sorrow.

When he wanted attention Minister Li's son would jump up on Lily's lap. 'Aunty Yu!' he would shout, stab her in the ribs as if she were one of the many barbarians he wanted to kill.

'Leave Aunty Yu alone!' Minister Li's wife said, but she did nothing to stop the boy. Lily tried to laugh at first, but then the blows started to hurt.

'Leave Aunty Yu!' Minister Li's wife said, but the boy's imaginary knife plunged in again and again, and Lily had to push him off and he fell awkwardly on his wrist, began to wail and Minister Li's wife hurried to pick him up, cooed over him like a hen. Lily straightened her hair, adjusted her clothes, but Minister Li's wife didn't seem to care that he'd torn the corner of her gown.

'Is he alright?' Lily asked and Minister Li's wife gave her a tight smile.

'I think so,' she said and resumed cooing.

Lily stopped visiting Minister Li's wife so often, got invites less often too. She didn't tell her stories of the grasslands, and as she lay on her own all the anecdotes began to percolate through the intervening years.

The day at White Water Monastery.

205

A day her father had brought a bag of lychees to the fort.

The day her father had marched out of the gates of the Last Fort Under Heaven, and they had stood on the walls, watched the yellow banners stiff in the wind, had seen him turn to wave, her mother holding her close.

The long hair on Old Fart's mole.

One day Grandmother Li sent a message through the manor that Lily was to come and keep her company. Lily dressed in a simple blue gown, only used a few modest hairpins, did not perfume her sleeves.

It was a long walk from the Western Courtyard to Grandmother Li's yard, next to Lacquer Tree Garden. Her courtyard was peaceful, her chambers spacious, each hall hung with curtains of blue and yellow and green silk.

Grandmother Li sat in the shade, the green light of the window gauze giving her skin a sickly hue. Her eyes glittered, she licked her thin lips, folded her small hands on her lap. Her legs were too short for the chair, her two embroidered shoes were supported by a lacquered stool.

'Concubine Yu,' Grandmother Li said, and Lily bowed. 'Come, sit.'

As she walked across the room Lily felt stiff and awkward; blushed as if she had done something stupid. She thought of Granny Pig, and wished that she was Minister Li's grandmother.

'How do you like the Li Family Manor?' Grandmother Li said.

'It's very fine,' Lily said, and stopped.

'I suppose it compares unfavourably with Changan.'

'No, madam.'

Grandmother Li gave her a hard stare and Lily didn't know whether it was the 'no' or the 'madam' that had offended her.

One of the servants coughed.

'Oh, bring it here,' Grandmother Li said, and a table was carried to the spot she indicated, set with Turkish pastries and a pot for tea, two cups.

'Changan is full of amusements,' Lily said as Grandmother Li signalled that the tea should be poured, 'but this place has the intimacy of family.'

Grandmother Li raised an eyebrow, waited till Lily had taken her tea, then took her own cup, held it in her lap then slurped.

'I had a man sent from the capital to make these pastries,' she said.

Lily took the one nearest to her and complimented it before she had even taken a bite.

'I think if I were you I would prefer Changan.'

Lily swallowed her mouthful. 'Why?' she said and, remembering the look she got earlier, added, 'If I may be so bold.'

'"The phoenix lives on nuggets of cinnabar,"' Grandmother Li quoted a local saying.

Lily didn't understand.

'Look at you,' Grandmother Li said. 'You do not fit here. We do not educate our women. We do not waste money on frivolities. I never wrote a poem in my life.' Grandmother Li snorted at the very idea, and Lily took another bite of pastry because she didn't know what to say.

'I hear your parents were from Hedong Province,' Grandmother Li said after a while.

'Yes,' Lily said. 'My adopted parents were from Diyi.'

'Adopted?'

'I was an orphan,' Lily said. 'My father was a marshal in the Army of Divine Strategy. My mother was a concubine.'

The more Grandmother Li heard the less she liked Lily. She signalled that the servants should pour Lily more tea, offered the plate of pastries again, let the young girl keep talking.

'I think we should have more conversations,' Grandmother Li said as 'goodbye', but she didn't invite Lily back to her courtyard and they only met at family meals, when Lily was never addressed, never called upon to give her opinion. Lily was not even allowed to pour Minister Li's wine or serve him food – those were the tasks of a wife.

Lily began to plan a return to the capital. 'Maybe it would be better if I left before the summer heat,' Lily said one day, but Minister Li kissed her and tried to cheer her up.

'I'm serious,' she said. 'I could go back to live at our manor.'

'What would you do in the capital?' he said.

'I don't know,' she said and thought how quiet the Plum Blossom Palace would be without him. Then she thought of moving back to her parents' house. But people would think she'd disgraced herself.

'It's better you stay here,' Minister Li said, and so it was agreed.

Summer came with bright days and sharp dark shadows. Lily rose early and wandered through Lacquer Tree Garden with her fan, dressed only in a simple light gown. The air was still and cool; she listened to the birds wake and sing.

Lily was sitting by an old apple tree when she heard Grandmother Li enter with her train of servants. She stood up and hurried away before she could be seen or spoken to. Each day it seemed she was running away – from Grandmother Li, Minister Li's wife, even herself.

In the summer afternoons Lily lay down and tried not to move, her armpits slick with sweat.

'All you do is sleep,' Minister Li told her that evening, when he had returned from inspecting the estate. Lily was bleary-eyed. She sat up and tried to look fully awake, but Minister Li went outside and waited for her to splash water on her face, come out and join him in the shade.

That evening, as they sat in the garden eating slices of honeydew melon, slapping mosquitoes, they watched the evening star fade into the horizon.

'Aren't you tired?' Lily asked.

'No.'

'I am.'

'It must be the heat,' Minister Li said.

'It's not as hot as Changan.'

'Isn't it?'

'No,' she said. 'You know it isn't.'

Minister Li didn't know why he had to know it wasn't. They sat in silence for a long while. Lily yawned again.

'I'm going to bed,' she said.

Minister Li did not move.

'Are you coming?'

'No,' he said, in that tone he had. She watched him look up at the stars, pretend he was interested.

Lily undressed and stretched out on the bamboo mat, too angry to sleep. It was at times like these that she hated him.

It was a few weeks after the summer heat had passed that Lily's maid came to clear the breakfast bowls away, then stood and cleared her throat.

'Mistress Yu,' the servant said.

Lily smiled.

'I think you're pregnant.'

Lily blushed. 'Impossible,' she said, but the woman was positive.

When she had left, Lily sat down and poured herself a cup of wine, remembered Minister Li's wife saying, 'It will be so nice when my son gets a brother or a sister.'

Lily poured herself another cup of wine and promised herself that she would keep the child as her own. She did not know what Grandmother Li would say when she heard the news. They had broken the Filial Laws. There was nothing she could do.

When a maid came to summon Lily to Grandmother Li's courtyard, she dressed simply and dressed her hair modestly, but Grandmother Li did not seem angry.

'Rules of conduct are not as strictly enforced as when I was young,' she commented. She dictated a strict diet of eggs, fish and vegetables to Lily's maid.

The next day Lily asked for sweet and sour lotus root, but the maid refused.

'Sorry, Mistress Yu,' the girl said, 'that dish is not allowed.'

Minister Li's wife came to offer Lily her congratulations, gave her a pair of embroidered baby shoes.

'I made them myself,' she said.

'Thank you,' Lily said. 'I am lucky to have such a kind elder sister.'

Minister Li's son didn't like Aunty Yu very much. He stayed behind his mother's leg and stared up.

'Well,' Minister Li's wife said with a smile, 'I should be letting you rest.'

Rest was very important – Grandmother Li had said so, and if ever she heard that Lily had been out for long walks she sent word to the steward that the minister's concubine should stay in bed more. The old woman was so severe that when Lily tried to go out, her maid ran to stop her.

'Mistress Yu!' she called. 'You are not allowed out.'

Lily laughed at first, but then she stamped her foot.

'Speak to her!' she hissed to Minister Li that night, but he refused to get involved.

'How can I argue?' he said. 'She's thinking of the best for you and the baby.'

'Yes – the baby!' Lily said, and hated her pregnancy for the rest of the day. Minister Li brought her scrolls to read, but she was tired of reading and tired of being unable to take walks through the garden. Minister Li tried to cheer her up by asking some of the local officials round for a banquet, but when Grandmother Li heard that he was banqueting while in mourning for his mother she summoned him and wagged a bony finger in disapproval.

'I think we should wait,' Minister Li said but Lily threw a vase against the wall, watched the pieces scatter across the floor.

Minister Li promised Lily that he was merely postponing the banquet and each day she brought the matter back up, refused to let it be forgotten.

Eventually Minister Li set a date, apologised to the coffin of his mother, kowtowed to his grandmother, who tapped her black fingernail on the arm of her chair.

'It will bring bad luck,' she said. 'Your mother's ghost must be assuaged.'

Minister Li personally organised a sacrifice to his mother's memory, burnt heaps of golden paper ingots, left heaps of her favourite foods, jugs of wine, even a box of paper cosmetics – face powder, cheek-red and lip-rouge.

But all Grandmother Li's warning seemed to be coming true when on the morning of the banquet Lily complained of trapped wind. It was so painful that she ate breakfast in bed, but after a while she sat up to go to the latrine, saw a russet smear of blood on her thighs.

Minister Li was instructing the steward in the arrangement of the torches, the tables and chairs when Lily called out. He saw the blood on her hands and ran out in a fluster, called the maids, who came flapping and fussing and calling to one another, tumbling through the manor grounds like windblown leaves. They tucked Lily into bed, fetched eggs from the chicken hutch, sent them to the kitchen to be boiled.

'Rest, dear,' they fussed as they scurried in circles. 'Rest. Don't move. Rest, dear, rest.'

Lily didn't want to move, but different positions made the pain easier. She kept trying to roll on to her side and they kept rolling her on to her back.

'You've got to keep the baby inside,' they told her, kept her legs together, wrapped in blankets. When the hard-boiled eggs were ready, they were brought to Lily, and the maids insisted she eat them. By the fourth Lily felt nauseous. As she cracked open the fifth she retched, closed her eyes and concentrated on not vomiting.

'Eat!' they told her. 'Eat!' Lily shut her eyes, smelt cooling egg white, and bit into the still-warm egg.

Minister Li almost cancelled the banquet, but the bleeding stopped that afternoon, and the maids seemed hopeful, kept fussing. You must not move, they told Lily. You must not lose the baby. It is the minister's child. She can't lose the minister's child, they said to each other.

Even so, it was only when Lily said how much she was looking forward to intelligent conversation that he decided to go ahead.

'I warned you that Heaven is against this meal,' Grandmother Li told him and Minister Li bowed.

'It is a very small affair,' he said. 'The gods will not punish us for something so small.'

Grandmother Li did not seem convinced. Even Lily

began to doubt the propriety of the banquet, and a gloom seemed to gather throughout the afternoon.

One of the maids sat next to the bed to keep her company. She smiled, but Lily didn't feel like smiling back.

'Cheer up, dear,' the woman said. 'You'll be fine.'

Lily nodded.

'You're still young,' the woman told her, then stood up to tuck Lily in. 'You know, I once lost a baby. It had to come out,' she said, raising her eyebrows. 'I had to give birth to it anyway. I was in agony for a day and then it came out, quite still. No bigger than my hand. My husband picked it up,' the woman said as she sat back down and smoothed out her clothes. 'He wanted to see if it was a girl or a boy. Do you know what it was?'

Lily shook her head.

'It was neither,' the woman stated, then she leant in closer and whispered, 'it was a frog.'

Lily didn't want to know any more. She didn't want to know anything about giving birth to frogs.

'Well, I say it was a frog,' the woman laughed at herself, 'but we called the doctor to the house. He had studied in the capital, at the Imperial College of Medicine. He was the seventh generation of doctor in his family. He said they all looked like that. He offered us five strings of cash.' She raised her eyebrows again in horror. 'Five strings of cash for a frog! We said no. The minute he'd gone I ordered my husband to take it down to the canal and throw it away. He wanted to bury it in the family graveyard, but I refused. We don't want frogs there. What would our ancestors think? I made him take it down to the canal and throw it away. Then when I was better I went to see an oracle. He said that we must have eaten lizards before we conceived. I said I never ate a lizard in my life!'

I've never eaten lizards either, Lily thought, then

wondered what she *had* eaten, rubbed her temples and let out a long sigh. The longer they stayed at the Li Family Manor, the further away their return seemed, the less real the rest of the world seemed.

When Minister Li's friends arrived they were shown to Lily's courtyard. 'My friends have come to greet you,' Minister Li said, and his eagerness reminded Lily of their time in the capital when he had seemed so proud of her. She wanted to know where he had been all day, and glared at him; glared at the men who came and stood in a semi-circle, folding back their sleeves, bowing before her.

'Thank you.' Lily's face was set as they presented her with gifts: silk and make-up, a stick of lip-rouge, a silver hairpin. 'Thank you,' she said to the last – a young man with a thin beard dangling from his chin – and almost smiled.

When they had all gone Lily sat for a while looking at the two ridges her legs made down the bed, then threw back the sheets, shuffled to the edge of the bed, swung her feet to the floor.

'No, mistress!' Frog Woman sat up in her seat, but Lily took no notice.

'Mistress, no!' she said again and tried to swing Lily's legs back on to the bed. They struggled for a moment, then Lily gave in. 'Rest – rest. It is good for you,' Frog Woman insisted.

The banquet was short: each man made his apologies and went home before sunset. Minister Li showed them to the gates. Lily waited for his footsteps to return, but the sun slipped to the ocean floor and the stars were bright before he came back to Lily's yard.

'I hear that you tried to get up,' he said.

Lily nodded.

'You should rest.'

'You rest!'

Minister Li sat on the bed and stroked her cheek. 'It is only for a few days.'

'Nine!'

'So, only another eight,' he encouraged but it was hard to shift her gloomy mood.

'Good,' he said, when she managed a smile, and he seemed to think that was that, but Lily started glaring again, forced herself to look away, her fingers under the bedsheets touching her stomach thinking of the frog inside her: red and slippery and no bigger than her hand.

'I will sleep here tonight,' Minister Li said and lay on the bed. He looked up at Lily.

'When will we go back?' she asked and he put his hands behind his head.

'We cannot leave until my mother is buried.'

'And when will that be?'

'Winter,' he said.

After a long time Lily asked the question that had been tormenting her.

'Did you go to see your wife today?'

'No,' he said. 'My grandmother summoned me.'

Oh, Lily thought, but when they lay down to sleep she smelt his nape just in case.

I had a letter today from my father. There were so many names of places and people I know so well, and I thought how strange that their lives continue when they are so far away from me. I wrote this poem for him, matching his style.

He asked me how it was here in the north, and I sat and thought for a long time. I do not know how it is in the north. I know how it is to be here, in this courtyard, day after day, waiting.

The next night Lily blew out the candle and lay down in darkness, left the door ajar, wondered if Minister Li would come to her tonight, but only the moonlight visited her room, casting long shadows across the floor.

When we get back things will be better, Lily told herself the next day. We will have a child, and I will be a mother, and we will be a family. She put her hand to her stomach and felt the baby pressing down on her spine, rolled on to her side, imagined their life in the future: a thatched hut, a stream, bamboo, lots of tuft-haired children and laughed at herself – it was like a Du Fu poem. But Minister Li spent the next night with his wife, did not even visit Lily, but went for a long ride through the fields.

When he came back Lily was tired and restless.

'I wish we were back in the capital,' she said.

'Hmm,' he said, pulled off a boot.

'I want to give birth in the capital,' Lily told him.

'Hmm,' he said again, tugged at the other.

'Have the geomancers set a date?'

'Soon,' Minister Li said and sat down with his back to her. When he had eaten a few pieces of chicken he turned to say something and saw that Lily's hands were covering her face, her body was shaking.

'Lily?'

She didn't answer.

'Are you sick?'

Minister Li touched her shoulders but her body kept shaking and she shrugged away his affection. 'Go away!' she repeated, even though she wanted him to touch her and hold her more than anything.

'Mistress Lily is upset,' Minister Li told her servant. 'Make sure she has all the food she needs. Her favourites, you understand. I will make sure the cook knows.'

The servant nodded.

Minister Li could still hear the sobbing from inside. 'Well – go on!' he said and the servant hurried away.

Lily grew tired and restless as summer turned to autumn and the servants pruned the mulberry trees with axes, burnt the branches to boil sorghum, set the pungent must to ferment. For a while she stood watching, but after a few days she had worn out the memories they provoked. Idleness was the father of boredom and sadness, but Lily found so little there to entertain her. Changan was full of amusements; the Li Family Manor had narrow horizons, the weather was cold and lonely. Lily looked wistfully towards the Ancestral Temple, where Minister Li's mother's coffin still waited for the auspicious date set by the geomancers. She wished the woman was still alive and that she and her husband were back in the capital.

When Minister Li came to her Lily had to remind herself that it was natural for a husband to sleep with both wife and concubine, but still she did not want him to touch her.

'Wash first,' she said, pointing at his groin.

In autumn the leaves fell; the north windows were sealed with felt; the bottom of each door was fitted with a padded cloth. Each day the manor was busy bringing in wheat and millet, hemp and beans, grass for ropes, reeds for rain-coats, but Lily had nothing to do except wait. Her sleep was fitful, she sat on the steps of her courtyard and flipped a coin, won the toss a few times.

When the harvest was finished the tenant farmers were gathered into bands to repair roads, dig ditches and ponds for fish. She had a few days with Minister Li, and for a

while they re-created the carefree atmosphere of Changan
– laughed and joked and forgot the walls that hemmed them
in. But in the first weeks of winter Minister Li was busy
meeting the tax collectors, who left with their due two-tenths
of produce. When they had gone the snow fell, the pools
froze, and Minister Li went out in the morning to hunt badg-
ers, brought one home, black and white and bloodied red.

Lily refused to have it dripping in her room.

'It's bad luck!' she told him, touched her womb protec-
tively. 'Haven't you heard the tale of Headman Song and
the badger spirit?'

Minister Li shook the badger's head.

'That's not funny,' she said, turned her back on him.

As the weeks passed, winter deepened. The door shivered
in its frame, the servants' faces grew pinched; she seemed
to see Minister Li less and less.

Five times a day the servants brought Lily meals, watched
her grow steadily fatter. Lily walked each day to relieve her
boredom, summoned her maid to come and rub her back.

One day Lily stood to watch men bring cut ice from the
river and carry it down to the cool-house. Before she turned
for home again her breath steamed in front of her face and
she looked up at the white sky, wondering if it would snow.
That night she put her hand to the bulge and felt the child
growing inside her. She hoped it would be a girl. Minister
Li's wife would raise any boys; if she had a girl, she thought
that she might be allowed to raise it herself.

On the nights she was not summoned to Grandmother
Li's room to sing and talk, Lily sat in her chambers, a pot
of wine on the brazier, drinking till she was tipsy and then
going to the toilet and then to bed, wondering what her
husband was doing.

Sometimes she went to bed and waited; at others she called her servant to her.

'See if the minister is in his wife's courtyard,' she said, waited impatiently in her doorway.

When Minister Li did come Lily pulled him inside, put more charcoal on the brazier, poured him some wine.

'I hate it when you go to her courtyard,' she said.

'What can I do? She is my wife.'

'I know,' Lily said, but knowing made it no easier.

The Li family had so many traditions and customs they seemed to consume all her husband's time and energy. No sooner was the badger-hunting season over than the date set by the geomancers was looming, and Minister Li was busy making preparations for the long journey to the Li Clan's hometown, Lingfen, where all their bodies rested.

Lily decided to keep herself busy. She wrote letters to her father, wished she could sit at home being spoilt by her mother – but the courtyard was empty except for the whistling wind and the overcast sky. Each night Lily lowered her bed curtains and hoped that her husband would visit, but each evening she walked alone through the garden, with twilight crows watching her pass.

Each night Minister Li did not come she lay and swore at her father for damning her to the fate of a concubine.

Then, quite suddenly, the date set by the geomancers for Minister Li's mother's funeral arrived.

It would not have been fitting for Minister Li to spend his last night in the Li Family Manor with a concubine, but still Lily lay and waited for him to visit, then wept into her pillow, cursed the day she had fallen in love with him.

The next morning she dressed in a fox-fur coat and powdered her face, waited for the servants to tell her that the procession was ready. She made her way through to the front courtyard, where the wind clutched at the white banners, pulled a strand of hair loose from her head, whipping it across her face. There were six guards to either side of the hearse, six banner-bearers, six bell-ringers and six nuns, who had been hired from the Monastery of Universal Salvation, and her husband, dressed in white silk, on a black yearling.

The coffin was carried out of the Ancestral Temple. Minister Li dismounted to pay his respects to his grandmother and wife, and finally to Lily, but she stared fixedly at the coffin in front of her.

'Farewell, dear concubine,' Minister Li said, but she could not bring herself to look at him.

'Go slowly,' she mumbled.

After the procession had left, Lily pushed the hair off her face, watched the gates of the manor shut, and its walls seemed to rise up around her.

That night she lay in bed, heard urgent knocking drift from a distant courtyard, felt twice as lonely.

Don't listen to plain songs or drink strong spring wine,
Forget evenings spent with losers, addicted to games
   of chess.

We're like the pine and crag that endure many winters
   together,
two migrating birds, we'll be reunited.

I hate this lonely winter walking through cold days.
The day will come, we'll meet again, and the moon will
   be full.

So far away, what can I give you to remember me by?
Just melting winter tears, and this poem.

The only excitement in the Li family household was when a letter arrived from Minister Li. In the first he said that he had been forced to stop at Xinjiang because a local festival meant there were no ferries for three days. He had gone travelling with an official there called Liu, and they had visited the home of a famous beauty – but had found the place overrun with tourists and knick-knack sellers.

Now he was travelling again and he was thinking of them all and he was looking forward to making his way back to the capital in the spring.

'It is so good to hear news,' Minister Li's wife said as she poured them both tea.

Lily nodded and tried to smile. 'We all miss him so,' she said, and hated having to share his letters with anyone.

Lily and Minister Li's wife sat together to write their replies. His wife dictated and Lily turned her words into characters, sealed them into a large scroll case, sometimes including a letter to him, written in poem form.

'Join me for dinner,' Minister Li's wife said.

'I'm tired,' Lily said, went back to her room, shut her tomb door.

She sat at her dressing-table and imagined the scroll being carried all the way south, loaded on to a boat and carried downriver to the hand of Minister Li. She counted the days for his reply to arrive, guessed how long it would take for the journey one way and the return. The appointed day arrived and passed, much like all the others: no news; cold weather; nothing to do.

The well beside the tree echoes with autumn rain
under the window ledge
dawn blows softly in

From the long miles I wait for a letter
spend all day fishing, waiting for news
but the green river is empty.

Occasionally Grandmother Li would summon Lily for
breakfast. When she came back to her courtyard Lily took
out her diary and flicked through the accounts of their
adventures near the capital – cheered herself up with the
account of Huan Forest or Hua Qing Palace. When
lunchtime came she ate a light meal, then drank a few cups
of wine to savour the sunlight – but now the wine gave
her a headache and she called her maid and asked her to
bring tea.

Three weeks after Minister Li had left, Lily's headaches
got worse and she lay down, but even though she turned
to left and right, still she could not sleep. Later that afternoon she went to the latrine, bergamot berries stuffed into
her nose and sat uncomfortably as her bowels emptied in
a pungent stream of brown liquid. The diarrhoea was so
forceful that it splattered her shoes and stockings and she
stripped them off and gave them to the servants.

'I'm sorry,' she whispered, but the maids stroked her
head, wiped her cheeks with warm cloths.

'Lie down and rest,' they soothed, sent herbs to the
kitchen to boil into medicine. Around midnight Lily's
bowels were still heaving, even though she was passing
nothing now but strings of mucus. In the early hours she
began to bleed and there was an awful pain in her stomach.

Grandmother Li was woken and she recited the health
sutra a hundred times, ordered that sacrifices be made to
the gods to restore Lily's health and bring her better luck.
A special sacrifice was made to the ghost of Minister Li's
mother, for the breaking of the Filial Law on celibacy.

But while the maids had originally worried that Lily might lose the baby, they were worrying that they might lose the concubine too. Her blood came in bright red rivulets. They wiped it away, reassured Lily, 'Don't worry, you'll be fine,' but none of their assurances stopped the blood from flowing.

'Don't worry, you'll be fine,' because there was nothing else to do.

Lily went into labour after midnight, contractions pushing her child out in a torrent of pain and blood and wordless groans. Her baby was covered with a white waxy substance. It was fully formed, but not much longer than Lily's hand. The woman cleaned it and looked for a breath, but the baby never wept or screamed or even opened its eyes. The maids cut it loose from the umbilical cord, hurried it away to feed it to the dogs, as Grandmother Li had ordered. Sometimes the ghosts of babies didn't know they were dead, but wandered the courtyards looking for their mothers. This whole pregnancy had seemed unlucky.

Lily could hear the dogs barking as she went into labour again, passed the afterbirth, which left her too exhausted to even cry.

When Minister Li heard the news of Lily's miscarriage he sent word that he was hurrying home. It was nearly two weeks later that a servant knocked and told her that the minister had returned. He had lost a little weight, but he was still tall and handsome and broad-shouldered. He ran to greet her and kissed the top of Lily's head as she held him. Neither of them spoke of the dead child, she was too happy just to be held.

We can go home now, Lily thought, back to the capital,

but a day passed, then two, and Minister Li did not mention their return.

'When are we leaving?' Lily asked one morning.

'Leaving for where?'

'Changan.'

'My grandmother wants me to stay,' he said.

Lily propped herself up on her elbow. 'Of course she wants you to stay! She *never* wants you to leave!'

'There are problems,' Minister Li said.

'What problems?'

'You wouldn't understand.'

Lily folded her arms, refused to accept that she couldn't understand.

'The estates are in trouble,' Minister Li told her. 'I need to arrange the sale of some land.'

Lily didn't know what to say.

'Can I help?' she asked but Minister Li shook his head.

'Let's talk about something else,' he said and kissed her, but when he tried to make love to her she cried for the child she had lost.

It was that week that Lily's maid came to tell her that Minister Li's wife was pregnant with her second child.

'Are you sure?' Lily demanded.

'I was there when Minister Li told his grandmother,' the maid said.

'Minister Li?'

The woman nodded.

'He told his grandmother?'

There was a warning note in Lily's voice but the maid nodded.

'Is it true?' Lily asked as soon as Minister Li stepped over the threshold.

'What?'

'You know.'

Minister Li hesitated for a moment but Lily lifted the wine pot and threw it at his head; she watched it hit and shower the wall with rice wine.

He tried to talk to her but she screamed and cursed and then fell down among the shards and wept. The next night Lily refused to unlock the door.

'I can smell her on you!' she shouted.

'Who?'

'You know who!'

He stood waiting, and then he banged on the door.

She listened but did nothing. She heard his footsteps on the porch.

'Jealous bitch!' he muttered, and she walked across the room to the door.

'I am not jealous of your whore!' she screamed. 'Why would I be jealous of your old whore?'

'She's my *wife*!'

Lily didn't know why she had to be there, talking through a door.

'Why bother me? Go and sleep with that bitch!' she shouted.

She could hear him pace up and down.

'I can smell that old dog from here,' she told him. 'Go and wash that pig's filth off you, then come back and see me.'

The next night and the next Lily sent Minister Li away. After a week Minister Li could feel the servants laughing at him, knew why his grandmother gave him sharp looks, only had his wife to comfort him at night.

'You spoil her,' Minister Li's wife said. 'She thinks she is wife and mother and grandmother all in one.'

Minister Li refused to listen, but when he pushed his way into Lily's room she tried to scratch his face and he slapped her once – hard and sharp.

'Who is the master of his house?' Minister Li demanded. 'Where does it say in any of the classics that a man needs to ask a concubine's permission to sleep with his wife?'

Lily knew the classics as well as he did. 'I don't care about the classics!' she screamed as she threw the pillow across the room at him. 'I don't care about you or your whore or your fucking children!' Then she collapsed on to the floor and sobbed.

Arguments filled that month. In the Lacquer Tree Garden the plum trees budded; the peasants were back in the fields, ploughing and sowing the new year's crop. After each shouting match Lily lay on her bed, hair dishevelled, spirit crushed, sobbing – waiting for Minister Li to come back to her.

'Why are you doing this to me?' Lily asked him one night.

Minister Li just kissed and held her.

'Why did you have to get her pregnant?' Lily said and stroked the hair from his face, kissed him. 'Why did you have to get her pregnant?'

Grandmother Li watched the disharmony develop between the Minister and Lily with curious pleasure. One sunny day she summoned Minister Li to her yard and told him he had to go to the provincial capital to supervise the selling of some family property. The next day she summoned Lily and asked how the servants were treating her.

'They are good,' Lily said.

'Does my grandson treat you well?'

'Yes. Very well,' Lily told her.

Grandmother Li pursed her lips. 'He is to go to the provincial capital on business. I would like you to stay here.'

Lily opened her mouth to argue but Grandmother Li put up her hand. 'I have decided,' she said. 'You and his wife will stay here and keep me company.'

The day Minister Li left he came to visit Lily, but she would not come out.

'Lily?' he called but she sat on her bed and hugged her knees. 'I'm leaving.'

'I'm not feeling well,' she said, but Minister Li came in to see her. She was wearing everyday clothes, her hair was dishevelled, she stared into the corner, as if she couldn't bear to see him leave.

'I'm leaving,' he said again, footsteps bringing him close to her.

Lily nodded but did not turn towards him. He knelt on the floor next to her, leant his head against hers.

Go! she thought, but he took her hand and kissed it. She pursed her lips as he pressed her hand to his cheek, then he stood up and she forced herself to keep staring into the corner as his footsteps left her behind. She wished he would stay, even if it was only to argue with her.

AD 907

All the places Minister Li could call home were moments in the past – with certain people, at moments in his life when the world was good. Old age stripped him of friends and lovers and his sense of belonging; with each year his ability to recognise happiness diminished. Only poems soothed him, and on days when he swore and cursed, the servants begged Fang to go and recite some verses, but he was sick of pandering to the old man, and stayed in his courtyard.

Eventually the mistress summoned Fang and he put on his gown and walked through the gardens to her courtyard, walked into her hall. She sat on her chair and her lip curled with distaste: her hands gripped the arms of her chair, knuckles standing out like knots on a branch; her face screwed up into ten thousand wrinkles. 'Even you have to earn your keep!' she told him and when she had finished her speech he nodded silently, looked as always towards Swallow – but this time her eyes were lowered.

Stormclouds were darkening the blue sky when Fang walked to Minister Li's courtyard. An hour later Minister Li was becalmed: his breathing slowed, his anger burst like a virulent boil. He sat watching rain drip, drip, drip from the eaves: a puddle on the ground, remembering a day when he was a boy and he had stood with his bow and shot arrows across that same courtyard. 'Do not aim,' his martial teacher had told him, 'assume the correct posture, perform the right steps. With the correct state of mind the arrow will do the rest.' He could not remember if he had hit: all he remembered was the dripping of rain and the effort required to stop the bow snapping straight.

'Enough,' he said without warning and Fang's sentence ended on a rhyme, hung in the air while the young man turned.

'Enough. I've had enough,' Minister Li said and held open his hands like a defeated man. 'Go on,' he snapped. 'Go fuck your whores!'

Fang hesitated for a moment and Minister Li's face reddened.

'Go!' he shouted, spittle flying.

The next morning Fang was in town, enjoying a literary breakfast with a few friends when a messenger arrived at the town gates. A clamour soon arose from the market-sellers and shoppers and even respectable women came out to shout and listen. Fang and his friends tried to continue their meal but despite their best efforts the news came to them as well: a warlord's army had invaded, its war wagons trundling south, soldiers singing Mongol songs in burning marketplaces, their swords and arrows black with Chinese blood.

> Sheep and yak now graze on millet and wheat,
> Chinese children dress in cloaks of felt,
> learn to speak the Mongolian tongue.

When Fang got up to leave and his friends battered his concerns down with their laughter. 'That old bastard won't miss you,' they told him, but he wouldn't listen.

'I need to warn them,' he said, even though he was sure they'd have found out by now. His friends laughed again, their camaraderie stronger than the threat of invasion. 'The barbarians are always fighting,' they insisted. 'Drink more wine – have a banquet, let's celebrate the morning.'

Fang strapped on his sandals to his friends' open-mouthed laughter.

'What can I do?' he asked, and they insisted on giving him more than a hundred answers; he stood in the door, hearing them out, then laughed and turned to go.

'I have to,' he said.

News of the fighting kept the household busy for a week. Heirlooms were buried; the Ancestral Temple – which held all the annals of the Li Clan, all the portraits of Minister Li's many and illustrious forebears – was carefully sealed; stores of rice and grain were hidden in the stables and in the garden pavilions. Most of the servants took refuge in the hills and forests, honest men hiding like the bandits of old.

Minister Li still swore and cursed but there was no one left to hear him. Only Fang went to see him; was sent away regardless. Not even poems could help the old man now. He kept himself busy writing letters to men he no longer knew, imploring them to remember their oaths to the Son of Heaven and protect the people from this ruinous violence. The opportunity to do something other than dwell on the past seemed to invigorate the old man. Everyone noticed it and they were all afraid – none more so than his wife, who begged him to stay in bed and rest.

'"The kingdom is gone",' Fang quoted from Du Fu, '"but the hills and rivers remain".'

Minister Li laughed. 'She sent you, did she?'

Fang blushed. 'The mistress wants you to rest.'

'Oh,' Minister Li laughed, 'she always wanted me to rest.'

The rebel foragers missed the Li Family Manor, turning west towards town. Like a lamp-flame, Minister Li's enthusiasm, which had burnt bright for three full days, began to consume itself. On the third evening he looked at all the unsent letters and lay down, too tired to stand. Sleep brought welcome relief, but as always the morning waited: cold and clear and cloudless. Minister Li was too tired to rise, unable to face another day, dripping past like cold wet rain. But the next morning the old man woke from a dream where she had come to him and they had eaten in Serpentine Park, in the shade of the Small Goose Pagoda. Minister Li threw the sheets back, felt the air on his body, cool like tomb breath, sat breathing heavily. For a moment he thought he could hear singing, a woman's voice and hobbled across to the door, clutching the wooden door-frame for support, and stared into the courtyard.

It was empty.

The singing played in his head, but the courtyard was empty. He rubbed his eyes and looked again, but there was nothing – just a red-brick courtyard and hopeful flecks of snow drifting down from a hammered grey sky.

Minister Li spent the morning in Lacquer Tree Garden. He was enjoying a cup of green tea his mind rambling through the possibilities that the warm weather offered, when he looked up and saw Fang come running into his courtyard.

The young man stopped in a cloud of hot misty breath, panted for air.

'There are soldiers,' he said between breaths. 'Marching north. Loyal soldiers.'

'Are you sure?' Minister Li said and Fang nodded.

'I read their banners,' he said.

Minister Li put the bamboo whisk down, and stood up as the froth began to dissipate to the edges of the cup. He set his lips in a determined grimace and gripped the carved window frame and pulled himself upright. His left knee twinged, and his face twitched with the pain. Fang was afraid that the old man's legs might give way, or that he might unbalance himself, but Minister Li cleared his throat and in a clear slow voice he said, 'Fetch my robes!'

'Your robes?'

Minister Li's face was set. He did not speak.

'Your robes of state?'

Minister Li stared at the man as if he were an idiot. 'Yes, my robes of state!' he said at last. 'Have them brought to the front gate.'

Fang bowed and turned to go.

Minister Li stared after him and shook his head. Idiot, he thought.

Minister Li thought about going to his rooms to comb his hair but decided to go straight to the main gate of the compound. He looked down at the ground, to avoid pitfalls, and stared at his feet as he walked, making sure they moved where he wanted them to.

He stopped at the corner, where the path ran down to the pavilion, and saw a young woman running along the path in front of him: she was wearing a long red silk gown, and in her hand she held a painted fan. It seemed strange that anyone should carry a fan in wintertime. He screwed up his face and stared again, but the woman turned off the path behind the standing cypress. Smoke still rose in the north, a blue smudge against the sky, but Minister Li kept walking, staring at his feet to make sure they went where he wanted them to.

When Minister Li reached the main gate, the servants had not arrived yet, so he waited in the gateman's room, warming his fingers over a brazier of coals and pushing the thin grey hair back from his face. When the robes did come, it took four men to carry them. There were over- and undergowns, sash, hat and shoes of state. He let them take off his fur-lined gown, stood shivering till Fang wrapped the undergown over his shoulders, then unfolded the outer robe, with the help of two others. It was made of thick blue silk, and shimmered with embroidered 'Spring Clouds on Holy Mountain' as the servants lifted it on to his shoulders. They tied the red sash of office round his waist, pinning the sides of the gown and squeezing his ribs, and hung the ceremonial sword from it. The jade fittings on the scabbard jingled as they did when he walked the courtyards of the palace. The sound made him feel young again, made his legs feel strong.

When the red silk seal pouches had been slung from his belt and weighted with small stones, Fang gently loosened Minister Li's fur cap from his grey hair and placed his hat of state on his head. Strings of pearls dangled in front of his eyes; the toes of his silk slippers peeped out from beneath the robes; his voluminous sleeves hung down below his waist. There was a murmur of surprise from the younger servants. They'd never seen Minister Li in his official robes before: there was so much silk and finery that many of them were speechless – enough silk to keep a mulberry forest of worms.

When the robes were hanging properly, Fang helped him fold his sleeves back over his hands.

'I need something to hold,' Minister Li snapped imperiously.

Fang clicked his fingers at one of the servants: 'A scroll,' he snapped. 'Go get a scroll.'

They all watched the man run off. Long moments followed, and the servants could hear the dull pound of blood in their heads, heard someone clear his throat, spit the phlegm on to the floor.

When the boy came running back Fang put the scroll into his master's hands; now he looked like a minister with a petition for the Emperor.

'Open the gates!' Fang commanded, and the doorman rushed to work, his straw-sandalled feet and bronze keys flapping and jangling, then the long slow squeak of the hinges as the heavy ash doors peeled left and right. Minister Li stepped outside the Li Family Manor, heart pounding, heard her laughter behind him, remembered the girl in the red robes. Damn you! he thought, his shallow breaths straining against the weight of his robes, took one step forward, then another, marched down the lane to where the soldiers were passing. Damn, damn, damn, with each single step.

She laughed at him the whole way. The closer he got the more ridiculous he began to feel. The soldiers turned and looked curiously on. Harness jingled as their starved ponies tripped on potholes; the rammed earth road was in need of repair. Twenty feet away he could smell butter and horses, the cold stink of oiled blades. Minister Li could feel his breath condensing on his beard and brow. The robes were heavy, too heavy for such a tired old man. He swayed on his feet as he marched the last steps, concentrated on perfecting the correct air of dignity and state.

Ten paces away Minister Li cleared his throat and began his speech in classical Chinese: 'Soldiers of the Tang Emperor! You are marching to defend our country from the barbaric invaders!' Each deep breath felt cold in his lungs. 'Your ancestors will watch your every blow! Your emperor will count every criminal you cut down! Defend the state! Defend the Son of Heaven!'

The long file of soldiers kept riding past. Their faces were foreign: pale skin and wavy black hair, deep-set eyes, high cheekbones. They were Turks employed from the west of the Empire. No more Chinese than the men they were going to fight. Use barbarians to fight barbarians was a policy that had protected the empire for nearly two hundred years, but not any more. Use barbarians to conquer the Chinese was much more apt.

Behind the soldiers trailed a few Chinese peasants, leading a line of donkeys hung with wine jugs and leather packs of arrows and hard smoked mutton. None stopped to listen or cheer. Dust rose in their wake, the noise of their harnesses began to quietly fade, grew dimmer and dimmer till Minister Li felt her laughter rising like floodwater and his speech fell away to a mumble.

Fang watched from the gateway, saw Minister Li sway and stumble, heard the dull thud of head on earth, saw the hat of state spill free. He called to the servants in the doorway, and three came out, scampered down the lane, still disturbed by the sight of so many foreign warriors.

Minister Li moaned as they picked him up, blood trickled from his nostrils, bright silk red. It dripped as they carried him, leaving a trail of brown splatters, clotted the grey threads of his moustache together. A few more servants were waiting at the gates: they all pushed and shoved to get a hand on the minister. Fang was squeezed and crushed by them all and shouted for someone to close the gates. He didn't look back, didn't know if it was done, was carried all the way to the minister's room where many hands rolled the old man on to his bed. Fang stood on a chest and issued orders: bronze braziers to heat the room, extra charcoal, food, a cloth and some water, and then he thought of the commotion and sent a servant to tell the mistress what had happened. When the room was empty he went to the bedside to check the minister's breathing. It was slow and erratic.

'Sorry,' the minister whispered, almost too faint to make out as Fang stood up straight. 'I'm sorry,' the old man tried to explain, but no one was listening. 'Please,' Fang heard as he walked across the room. 'Please,' the voice came weaker this time, then incoherent mumbles and moaning.

The soldiers kept riding north, village after village in abandoned ruin. At the Fen River the waters were choked with the charred timbers of a collapsed bridge; bloated bodies were floating to the sea. They forded the dark currents, halted to rest around their fires, their cold bodies wrapped in blankets of felt. The young men chewed their meat, ladled sips from the river, and told a few jokes to bolster their courage. A few thought about the old Chinese man dressed in imperial robes, and when they talked about it, it made them wonder what he had been saying, made them all laugh for a while.

By midnight the whole camp was still, except for the sleepless guards who talked together in hushed voices, thinking Turkish thoughts of their Turkish home, far away in the western steppes. A soldier's fate is to leave the world young. They hoped it was not true as, one by one, they stretched out their legs, shut their eyes to tomorrow.

In the Li Family Manor, ghosts bent in close over the minister's bed, listening to his ramblings. In her room the mistress sat by a pile of money for her husband to spend in the afterlife, that grew smaller and smaller as she fed it by wads into the fire, praying aloud that Heaven's bureaucrats would not collect her husband so soon. The few remaining servants hid in their huts and hoped for the best. In the quiet moments they thought of their own deaths, waiting somewhere ahead – wondered if it would be like this, or not.

Swallow took advantage of the chaos to knock very quietly on Fang's door and slip inside. When the door was shut and the bolt drawn they stood face to face, and Swallow felt uncertain of what to do next. She smiled and swallowed as he touched her cheek, whispered restraint as his hands travelled lower, touching her breasts and loosening her sash, and as the sun set again he laid her down on the bed, took her virginity, a red flower smudge forgotten among the furs.

When darkness came and the moon rose through the willow branches Swallow got up to leave, but Fang took her hand and held her down. They lay in silence, thinking of the soldiers and the rebels.

'Do you think it'll be quick?' Swallow asked.

'What?'

'Death,' she said.

Fang pursed his lips.

'It'll be like falling asleep,' he said, gave her body a silent squeeze, kissed her forehead. After a pause they made love a second time, lay still together, warm and breathless and alive.

AD 862

This time Lily waited but there were no letters from Minister Li. Spring passed; the summer weather was hot and humid. When the sun shone Lily stayed inside; when it rained she imagined going out and splashing through the puddles. Sometimes she read and others she drank, flavouring her wine with fresh raspberries. In the evenings the air was thick with insects. Lily sat watching the colour drain from the sky and tried to remember the capital. When darkness fell she trimmed the candle wick, sat in its light and wrote letters to friends and family.

Tomorrow I will visit Grandmother Li, she told herself, and sometimes she did.

Lily kowtowed and the old woman patted the space next to her, told her stories of the Li family, long dead, soon to be forgotten. When the appropriate moment came Lily enquired after Minister Li.

'No news,' Grandmother Li said, and Lily nodded. After a little while she excused herself and went back to her courtyard.

'If he should write, tell him I send him my love,' Lily said on one visit, and Grandmother Li nodded, but autumn

238

brought cold back into the world, and with the cold came grey skies and the dull splatter of days of rain, and there was still no news.

Her husband was a man of both feeling and talent, Lily told herself. It was not like him to forget – but her imagination began to torment her. He was dead. He had fallen in with gamblers and drunkards. He had lost his way, been seduced by wine, women and misty landscapes. If she were with him, she could cure his waywardness. Maybe she should set out to find him. They would meet in some desolate spot where the peasants were still talking about the fall of the Han Dynasty, would retire to some mountain hut and watch mist rise over the river, mating ducks, necks entwined, circling round and round on the clear water. But then reality closed in like high earthen walls and all she thought about was his absence and her loneliness – felt like the songbird, wings clipped and caged, forced to stare through the bars and watch the common birds fly.

> Caring and affection
> are sorrow enough,

Each day seemed less vivid, less real. Lily poured herself another cup of wine. The beautiful scenes of poetry were more true than the world around her. Sometimes, when men came with rushes to rethatch the barn or when the serving girls came to collect the laundry, Lily wished that they would pause in her courtyard and she could listen to their conversation – but they passed by, left her alone again.

> even more when autumn
> moonlight fills the yard

He does love me, Lily thought. Between me and his wife he loves me most because I am young and beautiful. She pushed herself up on to her elbow, reached for the pot and poured herself more wine. Lifting the wine cup was easy. It was a good feeling to know you were loved.

> and the bridal chamber
> echoes with chance voices
> of passing watchmen;

A cricket chirped in the corner of the room. Lily threw her brush and the incessant shrill abated.

> every night
> watching by lamplight
> waiting for frost
> to whiten my head.

———————

It was the fifteenth day of the tenth month when Lily's maid came to her to tell her that she had overheard Grandmother Li talking about Minister Li's return. Lily looked through the doorway, watched dry leaves rattle in the breeze. Some days they blew into the east corner; others they blew into the west.

The moon that night was very bright, but even so Lily lay on her bed. She did not leave her courtyard for the next week, but sat inside as if the world had become too large and frightening.

Her maid became concerned, made sure Lily ate her meals of dumplings and lotus root, Five Spice Rabbit or pigeon soup. She hid pots of wine, assured herself that Lily was half sober, ignored the fact that she was half drunk too.

'Mistress, Minister Li is due back tomorrow,' the maid said, but Lily did not look up. 'Mistress,' the maid tried again and Lily turned to her for the briefest moment; the look in her eyes showed that she had heard, and understood.

That evening Lily walked through the Lacquer Tree Garden and thought of the southlands, how the autumn there would just be beginning. She imagined the paintings of misty rivers and limestone hills brought to life; the evening sun sending the fishing-boat back home; high peaks where sages lived far from the troubles of the world, or love, or lovelessness.

That night her courtyard seemed unchanged: the moon still rose over her wall, the cold pear twigs were still black and tangled. A concubine and a pillow – waiting.

The servants were piling dried firewood in Lily's courtyard when the message came that the minister had arrived at the front gate, had been taken to wash and pay his respects to his grandmother. Lily jumped up as if he had just returned from a day's ride.

'Hot water!' she laughed and her maid hurried off, came back rolling the wooden tub.

Lily clapped her hands, and her sudden excitement made the maid uneasy. She watched her mistress undress, folded the clothes and stacked them on the bed.

'Anything else?' she called, but Lily was humming to herself. Now we can go back to the capital, the tune seemed to say, conjured up the lights and amusements of Changan. Lily lay back and remembered the winding lanes of the pleasure quarter, where Persian girls danced the whirl. I'm sorry, of course I'm sorry, she hummed. I missed you too much. I never want to be away from you for so long again, she thought, decided to wear the blossom blue gown with the yellow and white clouds swirling round the hem; decided to dress her hair in the Fluttering Butterfly, just like on her wedding day.

'Anything else, Mistress?' her maid said and Lily opened her eyes and sat up.

'Oh – no – thank you,' she said.

Lily hung the gown on a peg, let the folds fall out to the floor. She kept humming as she dried herself, summoned the maid.

'The minister might want to eat dinner here,' she said and her maid took out the square paper lanterns, dusted them down, lit the candles with a long taper, used bamboo poles to hang them from the eaves. As she worked, Lily dabbed fragrant rosewater on her breasts and around her genitals, sprinkled some on her feet and also on the gown she was going to wear. Extravagant hairpins hung with pearls and jade and kingfisher feathers, cherry lips, red cheeks, white-powdered skin. She leant forward far enough that her eyebrows were reflected in the mirror's brazen surface, plucked them, the skin lifting with each hair then springing back against the bone. Just the thought of being held by him excited her. When she had finished she gave herself an alluring smile and then burst out laughing, clapped her hands with excitement.

Lily was still sitting at the mirror when her maidservant knocked to say that the minister had gone to pay his respects to his wife. She nodded, dabbed powder on her cheeks, refreshed the red of her lips.

'He has a guest,' the girl said. 'Official Liu.'

Lily kept nodding as if everything was expected, but no word came and when she had heard that torches were being taken to the pavilion in Lacquer Tree Garden, she stood up and paced up and down, picked up the pot of wine. Her hand shook as she poured, she sat and waited, kept turning to the empty gateway – each time she heard footsteps her heart began to flutter as violently as a trapped bird.

When her maid reported that Minister Li was sitting in the gardens, with his guest, Lily took a deep breath and stood up. It would have been better if he had come to her.

The servants watched Lily leave the courtyard, proud and beautiful, a blue-robed fairy with a powdered face, trailing the scent of roses, hair poised high above her head, two butterfly wings in flight. She glided past two manservants carrying sacks of rice on shoulder poles: they stopped to let her pass, their eyes lowered to her dainty red silk slippers. The minister's empty sedan was sitting in the front yard. The bearers wore uniforms with the character 'Li' stitched in black. They looked up when she arrived but she ignored them, except for a slight glance with her painted eyes: shy and demure.

Lily passed silently through the gateway to Lacquer Tree Garden. There was candlelight through the tangle of leafless twigs, laughter and conversation drifting through the still evening air. She concentrated on each step, still meek and demure, the conversation faltered and there was a murmur of appreciation as Lily entered the ring of light. Official Liu raised his cup and Lily nodded to him, then to his concubine – plunging neckline and snow white breasts – and lastly she looked at Minister Li, not sure whether to smile or glare or cry. Their eyes held for a long moment, then Lily braved an optimistic curl of her lips and Minister Li smiled back.

'Welcome home,' she said in a voice that almost betrayed her, 'beloved husband.'

There was silence.

'Thank you, dear Lily.'

Lily bowed, still concentrating on meek and demure.

'Lily,' Minister Li said, 'I would like you to meet your little sister, Aroma.' He signalled to the girl sitting between him and Official Liu.

The girl's hairpins sparkled as she turned her head. 'I have heard so many good things about you,' she said, snowy breasts rising and falling as she spoke. 'I look forward to getting to know you much better.'

Lily looked confused.

'Aroma is to be your little sister,' Minister Li explained.

'Sister?' Lily said, forgetting that Official Liu was there. 'What do you mean, "sister"?'

'I have joined the family as well,' Aroma said. 'I look forward to getting to know you better. I have heard so much about you.'

'Aroma is my new concubine,' Minister Li said, as if he were giving instructions to the servants. His tone was hard and final, and even the bullfrogs stopped to listen.

It seemed Lily had lost the power of speech.

'Come sit!' Official Liu said, but Lily looked at him as if she could not understand. Aroma smiled, and that smile hurt more than anything. Lily felt her face go red; the blood in her fingertips throbbed. She took a deep breath and shook her head, said nothing as she turned and walked back into the shadows, her departing candle flickering as she made her way back through the bamboo.

News spread quickly, servant to servant, across the Li Family Manor and out into the villages that lay on the estates: Minister Li had taken a new concubine. Mistress Yu had retired to her courtyard. The master was still banqueting in Lacquer Tree Garden. As soon as Minister Li's wife heard she hurried across the manor, banged on Lily's gate till the maid opened it.

'Where is she?'

The courtyard was still lit with square lanterns, the maid pointed to the central hall, where the windows were dark, except for the flicker of a single candle. Lily's face was powdered white, her lips were cherry red; a yellow halo was powdered on to her forehead.

'Sister!' Minister Li's wife gasped. 'I did not know!'

Lily waved her hand and made a noise between laughter and tears.

Minister Li's wife took both Lily's hands and brought her to the bed, made her sit down, put her hand to Lily's cheek as if she were taking her temperature.

'This is women's fate,' she said. 'Our beauty fades so fast.' There was desperation in her voice, in the way she wrung her hands and hugged Lily, and tried to get her to speak, but Lily stared at her room, strewn with discarded clothes and smashed make-up bottles and their lurid contents, half visible in the candlelight and it all seemed unreal – even the hand on her cheek and the words that Minister Li's wife was saying.

'Please don't do anything,' Minister Li's wife was begging. 'My son enjoys your company so much, don't rob him of that.'

Lily nodded slowly. 'I'm fine,' she said, and forced a smile. 'I'm fine,' she repeated. 'Trust me,' she smiled and put her hand out to calm Minister Li's wife. 'Don't concern yourself.'

Minister Li's wife left Lily in the care of her maid, but Lily sent her away, walked through her dark courtyard, waiting for the moon to rise.

At one point her maid opened the door.

'I should take the lanterns down,' she said.

'Let them burn themselves out,' Lily told her, and she went back inside. She did not seem like she would try to kill herself, the maid thought, but even so she stuck her window through the paper window – peered out – just in case.

About an hour after everyone had gone to bed a scream pierced the night, made the servants' skin shiver.

Minister Li's wife sat up. Her son wailed.

Aroma and Minister Li were lying in bed. Neither talked about the noise but when she slid her hand down his stomach he pulled it away.

'What's wrong?'

'Nothing,' Minister Li said, stroked her cheek.

'Blow the candle out,' she told him, but the screams kept coming, as sinister as a screeching owl; made both sleep and sex impossible. At length Minister Li, pushed his concubine's feet away, threw a robe over his shoulders.

'Where are you going?' Aroma called, but he marched out into the night, left the question unanswered.

Lily was wearing her under-robe, white in the night, hair dishevelled, face streaked with red and dried tears of eyeblack. A breeze made the lanterns swing back and forth. They cast lunatic shadows as Lily rocked with them, screaming at odd moments, continued rocking. She did not look up as Minister Li kicked her gate open. She did not turn even when he took her by the hair and pulled her to her feet.

'Get up!' he shouted, but each time he let go she fell to the floor and writhed. 'Get up!' He yanked again, but a knot of hair came out, and he shook it off his hand in disgust.

'Get up,' he said, more softly, but she fell to the side and he paced up and down as she clawed at the dirt. For a moment it looked like she was trying to dig her own grave and he looked away in disgust.

246

'Why do you hate me?' Lily moaned at last.

'Go to bed.'

'Why do you hate me?' she said, her mouth and words all distorted.

'You look ridiculous,' he told her, walked into her room to wash his hands. When he came out Lily pushed herself up and ran at him. He caught her wrists and pushed her across the courtyard. When they were in her room she tried to scratch and punch and realised the hopelessness of the situation. 'Why do you hate me?' The words were weak and barely audible. 'Why do you hate me?' she asked over and over, even after he had walked back to his courtyard.

The Li Family Manor might have been expansive, but it was not so large that Lily could live there without hearing of Minister Li or Aroma, or stumble upon evidence of their passing. Whenever she saw them in the distance Lily turned and hurried back to her courtyard, ordered her maid to shut the gates, poured herself a cup of wine or sat with a book and tried to concentrate on the words in front of her.

If the minister ever dared call, Lily shut herself into her hall.

'I'm sick,' she said to the maid, but at the same time she composed herself – just in case he should come in.

If he was sick I would go in to see him, Lily thought, even though he had treated her so badly. If he loved her, he would come in, she told herself, but then she heard his footsteps leaving, the gates shutting behind him, and her deep loneliness returned.

Grandmother Li took perverse pleasure in Lily's distress, told everyone who came to see her – including Lily – how concubines only brought disharmony into a household.

'And now there are two of you!' she said to Lily, black eyes sparkling and reached for another pastry.

One day Grandmother Li invited each family member to a meal. Lily promised to attend, but when the moment arrived she did not have the courage. If he comes for me I will go, she thought to herself, stayed waiting: dressed, and powdered and abandoned.

In the end Grandmother Li sent her maid to see how Lily was feeling. She came back with the news that Mistress Yu was not well.

'She was eating well yesterday,' Grandmother Li said to Minister Li. 'I wonder what can have come over her so quickly.'

'I do not know,' he said, steered the conversation to other matters.

'I do like Lily,' Grandmother Li said, turned back to Minister Li. 'You two don't seem to spend much time together any more. Why don't you go for a trip together? You could visit Tall Turret Garden and go boating.'

Aroma cleared her throat but Minister Li didn't know whether his grandmother was being deliberately obtuse.

'Take Aroma with you,' Grandmother Li said, as she picked up her prayer beads. 'And your wife. I will organise it.' She clapped her hands to get the steward's attention. 'My grandson is going to take a trip to Tall Turret Garden—' she began, but Minister Li cut her off.

'I'm not sure the weather is so good for a trip.'

'No?'

'No,' he said.

'Oh well,' Grandmother Li sighed. 'Another time.'

Grandmother Li insisted on inviting Lily to her courtyard at the same time as Minister Li – as if she had the power to cure the household of its sickness. But whenever Lily saw her husband arrive at the yard she stood up and made her excuses.

'She doesn't seem well,' Grandmother Li said as they watched Lily hurry away.

Minister Li said nothing.

'It seems you should take better care of her,' Grandmother Li said. 'Why bring a young girl inside these walls to grow old?'

Minister Li said nothing and bowed, blamed Lily for upsetting his grandmother.

She is manipulating the old woman, he thought, through the whole afternoon. She is like slow-working poison, turning my family against me.

'How is Aroma?' Grandmother Li asked.

'She is well,' he said.

'She does not like me,' Grandmother Li said. 'She is possessive of you.'

Minister Li wished he could leave all the women behind and go back to the capital.

'We're possessive of you,' Grandmother Li said and put her prayer beads down.

Minister Li looked at her, did not know what to say.

Later that afternoon Minister Li pushed past Lily's maid, walked into her room.

'This cannot continue,' he said and Lily turned to stare at him.

'What?'

'This,' he said and waved his arm at her and the room.

'I don't know what you mean,' Lily said, and turned her back on him.

'Your maid said you were ill,' he said.

'I was.'

He stood over her, glared down. 'What was wrong?'

'Nothing,' she said, her cheeks red as she stared back – and despite all the arguments he had rehearsed inside his head, he did not know what to say.

'Pah!' he shouted, and stormed out of the room, left her feeling that she had won.

On the first day of the eleventh month Grandmother Li paid for some shadow puppeteers to come to the manor. She spent the day at the pavilion in Lacquer Tree Garden while the servants set up a stage in her courtyard. The movement affected the manor like an illness: there was heat and blockages, the paths to the garden were unusually busy, lunch was delivered late; the paths to Grandmother Li's courtyard were unnaturally quiet.

Lily put on a long red gown and wandered down unfamiliar paths, avoiding the bustle, hurrying away if she saw Grandmother Li, Minister Li, his wife or Aroma.

'I want Concubine Lily to come,' Grandmother Li told her grandson when he came to the garden. 'What's her favourite story?'

'Yang Guifei and Emperor Xuanzong,' he said.

'I will ask them to play that. I want you to make sure she comes.'

The fact that his grandmother was making this special effort made Minister Li feel somehow closer to Lily. Instead of sending his servant to Lily's courtyard he went personally, for the first time in more than ten days.

'If *you* want me to come,' Lily said, 'then of course!'

Despite her smile, her tone was hostile.

'It was my grandmother who wanted to see you,' Minister Li said. 'Not me.'

'Thank you,' Lily said. 'How very kind.'

She turned her back and waited till she heard the door close, then threw her book across the bed. She hated him, she told herself – hated, not loved.

The shadow puppets danced before a white silk screen; two men sat with zither and drum, punctuating the scenes. When one was beating the drum, the other struck the gong. When one was playing the zither, the other picked up the reed flute and as he played the shadows danced: Yang Guifei whirling around Emperor Xuanzong, turning night to day, Heaven into Earth.

'And so Emperor Xuanzong saw her rise from her bath and his heart was stolen!' The shadow puppets moved along the screen. Lily yawned and glanced at Aroma, who sat next to the minister, fat and content, like a well-stuffed pig.

Growing rich, many jade pins adorn her glossy hair.
Growing plump, the silver bracelet on her arm is tight.

'That didn't happen until after he had married her!' Lily corrected, and the shadow puppets faltered and the two musicians looked up in confusion, gong and drum waiting to be beaten.

'Continue!' Minister Li called out and the two musicians hurried through the life and death of Yang Guifei, reproduced her screams with the zither, made the shadows shiver.

Lily watched as the rattle of Yang Guifei's last breath sounded on the drum with a strange fascination. Then the shadows quivered, then descended from the stage, the lanterns were extinguished and the cloth-screen stage refilled with shade.

'Very good,' Grandmother Li pronounced, and no one disagreed.

'How did you find it?' she asked Lily.

'Good,' Lily said. 'Though my favourite part happens after Yang Guifei is killed.'

Grandmother Li nodded. 'Do you think they had a true love?' she asked no one in particular.

'He devoted himself to her and she to him,' Lily said, as a student might speak of matters beyond their understanding. 'That must be love.'

Grandmother Li seemed satisfied. True or not, love was doomed, of that she was sure.

They talked for a few formal minutes, then each got up and left, according to rank.

When it was her turn to leave, Lily waited to let Minister Li and Aroma go ahead of her, then she went in the opposite direction, made her way back through Lacquer Tree Garden. The garden paths were dark but Lily knew them so well she only occasionally stretched out her hands, felt her way round the overhanging plants.

She sat by the pool for a little while, trailed her fingers in the water. There was no moon that night, just a few clear stars in the breaks in the clouds, casting just enough light to make the ripples shimmer. Eventually she made her way out of the garden, down the path that led to her courtyard. She stopped at each corner, checked that there was no one to see, then hurried past. At one moment she saw Aroma's maid hurrying with a basket and stepped back into the shadows and held her breath and wondered what the basket contained – almost giggled as she flitted on again, insubstantial as the shadows that had entertained them that evening.

When Lily peered into her courtyard she saw that her maid had lit lanterns in her room. She shut the gate as quietly as possible, and scampered across the yard, up the steps into the house and shut the door behind her.

'I've been waiting,' Minister Li said and Lily almost shrieked.

He moved towards her, but Lily kept him at more than two arm lengths.

'What do you want?' she asked and for a moment she thought he was going to hit her and shrank back but instead he grabbed her hair.

'I'm sick of this!' he kept saying, as he swung her round by the hair. 'I'm sick of you insulting me and my grandmother!' Minister Li stood over her but Lily refused to get up. 'What has my family done to deserve this treatment?' His grip was slipping so he took another handful, dragged her to the bed and threw her across it. As she tried to get up he pushed her down again. 'Where did you learn this disrespect? Where do the classics talk of this?' Minister Li was so angry that he didn't know how to finish his sentences, and when she shouted he took her by the shoulders and shook her so violently her eyes throbbed. 'You are my concubine!' he roared, and as if to emphasise the fact he pushed her back on the bed and yanked her sash open. Lily kicked and fought but he was stronger.

'Please,' Lily said, 'no' – but he did not seem to hear her, took her legs, pulled her to the edge of the bed, gripped her ankles and held them firm. 'Please no, please,' Lily said, and shut her eyes and ears, kept her senses shut until he had finished – but instead of holding him she pushed him off, his body less rigid now the violence had gone out of him.

'Get out,' she said as she pulled the edges of her gown together.

Minister Li tried to kiss her but she fended him away.

'Get off me!'

253

'Lily,' he said, but she scrabbled away from him, grasped the first thing to hand and threw it at him.

'Get off me,' Lily screamed, even though he was two arm lengths away. 'Get off me!'

Minister Li could hear the maid calling outside. He tried to catch Lily's wrists but she pushed and kicked at him.

'Get off me!' she screamed and threw a hairpin at him, then lay back on the bed and tore at the sheets.

The next morning Lily refused to eat or drink or get up – but that afternoon she tore the paintings from her walls, heaped them up in the courtyard, threw on the books that Minister Li had given her, or which reminded her of him, set light to one edge, stood a little way off, watching the flames consume the lot.

That afternoon she walked out of the manor, set off north, through millet fields where the peasants worked. It was better to be a concubine than a peasant, she thought, determined that she would take revenge upon her husband. She would poison his wife and child and concubine; burn the Ancestral Temple to the ground; throw herself down the well; return as a vengeful ghost to haunt his failing years. The longer she walked, the more elaborate her plans became, and when she came home that evening and found a poem from her husband she put it to the candle flame, then dropped it to the floor, unread.

Her walk had exhausted her, and Lily slept soundly that night, woke early the next morning and remembered a time she had climbed down the well in Changan. It was after Uncle Jia had died, when she felt alone. Lily laughed at herself: she had had family and friends then; had no idea what loneliness meant.

Now she did, she told herself: Li Family Manor was loneliness.

These four walls.

All day – this courtyard.

As each day went by it seemed less and less likely that that night had happened as she had remembered. Her husband would not do that, a voice in Lily's head kept telling her. He loved her. *That* was not love.

Each day Minister Li sent food or wine or poems, and each day she received them with a curious interest, as if they were leading her back to the days when they were together and happy and ten thousand li away from here.

After three days Minister Li came to Lily's courtyard and smiled. In his arms he held a spotted puppy, a ribbon tied behind its white ears. Lily looked at the animal, clumsily balanced between contempt and affection. Minister Li set it on the floor and waited in the doorway.

'Can I come in?' he asked.

'No,' she said, as the puppy worked its clumsy charm. 'Stay there.'

Minister Li leant against the doorpost, half smiled. He was dressed in a casual gown. He removed his headband, let his long hair fall down to his shoulders.

Lily played with the puppy, pretended she had forgotten him.

'Lily,' he said after a while, 'why are we doing this?'

Lily picked the puppy up, cradled it in her arms.

'Doing what?'

He lay across her threshold, stretched out his legs.

'Do you remember the time you wrote a poem for Hermit Ren?'

'No.'

'I wish I had that girl back.'

'I wish I had that boy,' Lily said, rubbing behind the puppy's ears.

Minister Li gave a short laugh.

255

'What must I do to stop this?'

'Get rid of Aroma,' Lily told him as if she ruled the family, the puppy licking her face.

It was a week later Lily found out that Minister Li was going to Taiyuanfu.

'Is he taking Aroma?' she asked her maid, as if it were a matter of only passing interest.

'Yes, Mistress Yu,' the girl said.

When he came to her yard again she would be ill, Lily told herself. If ever he made love to her again she would not be in that body. If he ever told her that he loved her, she would never believe it.

On the day he was to leave, the family and servants were assembled. Lily watched him leave and wished that he would never come back.

She walked back to her courtyard as snow began to fall: hard small flakes, white on the stones and trees and on the walls and the grey roof tiles. How could a year pass so slowly and with so much misery, she wondered, thought that the next year would have to be better.

Lily flitted through the succession of days, haunting the places she had once lived and loved and hated in. Grandmother Li indulged herself in Buddhist prayers, and Minister Li's wife gave birth to another boy.

Lily heard the baby at times, hurried away from the sound before it made her feel too sad. The only company she had was her puppy, which she called Aroma.

Lily fed Aroma scraps of her dinner, combed her hair and ruffled the skin under her chin. One afternoon she took the puppy for a walk through the garden, the coral trees black against the cold winter sunset. She could imagine her mother telling her, 'Misfortune's an avalanche when it starts to roll,' and now it seemed the avalanche had buried her so deep that there was no way out. Aroma sniffed around the early spring flowers, pissed on one, then came back wagging her tail.

'Come here!' Lily called, but Aroma sat down and started to lick her rear end.

'You dirty little slut!' Lily laughed. 'No wonder he likes you so much!'

For Spring Festival Minister Li's wife and Grandmother Li invited Lily to play chess and mah-jong – but nothing cheered Lily up. She watched Minister Li's wife lose another game and tried to enthuse at another win for Grandmother Li.

'Let's play pitch pot!' Minister Li's wife said, and Grandmother Li made Lily join in – tossing chopsticks at the neck of a jug. The sticks Lily threw fell flat, slid off the side, bounced off, refused to slide down the jug's gullet. At last Lily put her chopsticks down.

'I'm tired,' she said, left Minister Li's wife to play on her own – but after Lily had gone there didn't seem much point and she asked the servants to take chopsticks and jug away.

Lily came back the next morning but the women's conversations went round and round like whirlpools. She knew everything they had to say, how they thought, how they would respond to anything the other said. Each day was the same as the last, over and over and over again.

'Are you alright?' Minister Li's wife asked after lunch.

'I'm well.'

'My dear, what is wrong?' Grandmother Li asked.

'Nothing.' Lily felt like screaming. 'Nothing at all.'

That afternoon Lily beat Grandmother Li at chess.

'Oh dear,' Minister Li's wife said, as if Lily had just insulted the old woman and Grandmother Li's jaw tensed.

'Another game?' Lily asked, but no one wanted to play her.

'I'll go and see what my son is doing,' Minister Li's wife said.

'And I will go to the temple,' Grandmother Li said, as if her company was a pleasure she had decided to remove from the world.

A week after Spring Festival was the lantern festival. Each yard was hung with coloured paper lanterns, circles, squares, even a set of lanterns painted with the heroes of 'Journey to the West' – Monkey, Tripitaka, Pigsy and Sandy.

Lily walked behind Minister Li's wife and Grandmother Li, admiring the work of the servants. When it was time to visit her courtyard she felt foolish. Her lantern had four panels, each painted with a poem she had written, but which neither Minister Li's wife nor Grandmother Li could read.

'What does that say?' they asked.

'It's an essay by Han Yu on the corrupting influence of Buddhism on society,' Lily lied, and Minister Li's wife looked at her as if she were mildly deranged.

'How peculiar,' Grandmother Li said, and turned to go to the next courtyard.

The next morning the servants were steaming bread when the buns blew up and burst – spread open like pomegranates. The servants whispered that the household's fortune for the year ahead had burst as well. When she heard Lily laughed: she had no fortune left to lose.

'No fortune left to lose, Aroma?'

Aroma opened one eye and looked up from doggy dreams.

'You ugly little bitch!' Lily scolded, slapped Aroma's nose.

AD 907

The mist was already rising when the half-moon broke the horizon, began to highlight the Li Family Manor with pale white light, weeds sprouting from the compound's eaves, rammed earth walls eroded into irregular teeth, loss and decay like pervasive odours. Fang could taste them as he stroked a lock of Swallow's hair from her jade white cheek, chilled in the moon's clear light, falling like frost on to the bedroom floor. Her cheekbone was hard; beneath the skin a skull waited.

The world was old and dying, except for the two of them, here tonight, as Fang kissed her moon-chilled cheek, still warm to his lips.

In his room Minister Li did not lie quiet. The fall had cut the thin skin of his scalp, the young scab leaked blood; dreams and memories mingled.

White. The day his father had died: the funeral cortège pulling away from the gateway, white flags flapping; the soft fall of snow; being held close in bed on a winter's night.

Red. His mother stayed with him as a kiss and an

embrace, a soft voice talking to him. Walking in the gardens: red peonies like splashes of blood, standing by a fish pool. His mother served him food: he chewed and swallowed and opened his mouth for more.

'Ma,' Minister Li repeated in his dreams, talking in a child's voice, 'I love you.'

Sparkling yellow. Lily appeared in a place she had never been, laughing, loving and happy. He tried to reach out to hold her spirit down but then he was a child again, locked in a room, pushing and banging and kicking angrily, shouting; alone, alone for too long to keep crying.

'Your mother is in the family shrine,' a passing servant said as he was suddenly five years old – looking out into a cold winter yard.

'Your mother is praying,' the servants said and ran to head him off. He had his arms out wide, giggling, a fun game, then angry and determined, and when they caught him and lifted him off the ground he stopped giggling and kicked, but they wrapped him in silent and unloving hands, hurried him away.

Black. Blank eye-sockets; a well spinning him down and down then he was lying on the road with a cut on his head and a memory of soldiers that blurred again, and he was young and small, like a sparrow, and his mother was teaching him the pronunciation of a character.

'Oh dear,' she blushed, 'you're so clever!' She kissed him, pushed the date bowl over to him.

Brown. The shiny date was long as his finger; he put it into his mouth, started to chew round and round in circles. On the wall the scroll of the family genealogy: in the foreground sat his great-grandfather and his wife, and set behind them in a widening pyramid of lives, great-great-grandparents, great-great-great-grandparents, and their great-grandparents, right to the small figures sitting on the back row, peering down at him from a dynasty so distant even its name was forgotten.

'We start each morning by bowing to the ancestors,' his tutor intoned, his brown-robed sleeve ending in a cane, tapping on the brown desk.

'Not respecting the ancestors is the mark of an animal or a barbarian.'

Blue. A cold spring day: leaf buds showing green and songbirds – so long absent – twittering in the trees. Minister Li's mother standing in the yard.

'I have employed another tutor for my grandson.' His grandmother spoke from the heights of her bed, silk cushions jostling together to keep her upright. Beetle black eyes twinkled as she talked. 'Your services are no longer needed.'

Waiting for his mother to come; Tutor An putting him to bed instead. A yellow and blue candle flame flickering unsteadily, burning itself out to black.

Minister Li's wife sat, furs pulled over her knees, mumbling prayers to the Lord Buddha. Have compassion, he was a good man, she told him. Understand that, Lord Buddha, understand that he is a good man, understand that I love him and I do not want you to take him yet. Understand that this world would be shallow without him here, she thought, don't leave me paddling in a shallow pool. Have compassion, Lord Buddha.

Minister Li's wife kept praying with each bead, the necklace taking her round and round in a circle of devotion. That evening Minister Li woke for a moment, moaned through his delirium.

At one point his eyes flickered open and he mouthed silent words.

'Husband,' Minister Li's wife held his head, 'I am here.'

'I fell,' he mumbled after a few moments.

'I know.'

'I was exhorting the soldiers.'

'I know,' she said, and then his eyes flickered, closed again, and she rearranged the furs so that they covered his body to his neck.

'I'm sorry,' he said. 'I'm sorry,' he said again, his voice growing fainter. 'I fell.' He slipped another moment closer to death.

AD 863

The spring of 863 arrived with green leaves and birdsong, but there was still no word from Minister Li.

Sometimes Lily carried Aroma through the manor and the gardens, sat by the pool and floated wine cups on the water; she talked to herself as if she was sitting with friends. At other times she played her zither, chanted poems to the bamboo, remembered the songs Uncle Jia had sung to them on winter nights in Diyi and Changan. She became so intense that the servants began to whisper. Gossip spread: Mistress Yu was possessed.

When she saw Lily – hair uncombed, dressed in her under-gown – Minister Li's wife believed everything the servants were saying, hurried home to forbid her son from visiting Aunty Yu.

'I want to see Aroma!' the boy said and his mother scolded him.

'Don't call her that!'

'That's her name.'

'I don't care. Anyway, you're not to go.'

'Why not?'

'Because Aunty Yu is very sad,' Minister Li's wife told him. 'She wants to be alone.'

In early summer Aroma came on heat.

'You dirty little slut!' she teased Aroma, tossing food from her plate into the dirt. 'You dirty, dirty little slut!'

Lily lifted a piece of pork high in the air and Aroma whimpered, wagging her tail and drooling. When Lily dropped the pork Aroma caught it and swallowed.

'If you weren't such a slut,' Lily said, picking out another piece of battered pork, 'I could have you inside.'

Aroma wagged her tail, but it wasn't food that interested her in the middle of the night when the stray dogs barked outside.

'Quiet!' Lily shouted, but Aroma was running around in excited circles. In the end Lily locked her dog into a side hall, had her maid chase the dogs away.

Each night was the same. On the fourth Lily sat down at her dressing-table, moved the bottles and pots of make-up and powder to the side, laid a piece of paper flat on the table. It took a while for her to grind the ink into the right consistency, then she took out her brush and dipped it into the ink, wiped away the excess.

Her hand began to shake as she wrote the first characters, once so familiar. 'To my darling Zian,' she said, and dipped the brush again. After the usual formalities she told him about Aroma. 'If I let her she would sleep with every dog within ten miles. She eats too much. She is fat – but I am very strict with her. There is no other way to treat people when they have been bad – is there, my dear husband?'

At the end of the letter she signed her name with affection.

'Lily.'

* * *

Midsummer was hot. Lily slept through the dripping afternoons, her dreams better than anything the day could offer. She fanned herself as she walked into the late-afternoon heat, screaming cicadas in the branches, to the courtyard of Minister Li's wife.

'The mistress is sick,' said Minister Li's wife's maidservant.

'How about her son?'

'Her son is sick as well.'

Lily tried to step past her but the servant pushed the door closed.

'Let me in!' Lily shouted, but her voice lacked conviction. She heard the bolt being drawn shut, stared at the door and almost laughed.

Lily tried to cheer herself up by ordering Eight Treasure Soup. When her maid came back Lily had her set the tray on the table in her hall, removed the earthenware lid, let the flavours steam up. She sat down eager and excited, but when she stirred it and lifted a spoonful to her lips she was disappointed. The taste was not the same. She still did not feel loved. She put the bowl down, left it to congeal and cool, watched the servants take it away again, uneaten.

The summer heat diminished with each falling leaf; autumn brought bleak and dreary rain, chill winds, the aura of death. It was nearly a year since Minister Li had left; the shrill of cicadas lessened as they fell from the trees and were swept up with the leaves and burnt. One year, Lily thought, unable to sleep.

The yard was full of the rustle of leaves; the chrysanthemums shed their last petals like tears, but the other flowers were dead and brittle, their petals crumbling when touched.

Each morning Aroma wagged her tail, barked and ran in circles, tried to cheer Lily up.

Lily picked her up and patted her. 'What would I do without you?' she asked Aroma, and Aroma jumped down from the bed, ran to her empty bowl and wagged her tail.

'You little piggy!' Lily said, as she ladled out a broth of rice and meat and kitchen scraps. 'Here's some Eight Treasure Soup!'

'Good? Yes!' she said as Aroma lay down on her lap.

Every day Lily fed the dog, and Aroma began to grow; her nipples became hard and distended.

'You naughty little slut!' Lily told her one morning, and refused to feed her. 'You little slut.'

Lily heard from her maid that Minister Li and Aroma were living in Changan again. She imagined them sitting in Moonlight Pavilion – as she had sat – and wished she had poisoned Aroma when she had had the chance.

Lily called her maid. 'Wine,' she said, went to find her cup.

'There's no more,' the girl said.

'Tell the steward I will fry his liver with garlic if he doesn't give you wine,' Lily said and sent the woman off.

A pot and a half later Lily sat down at her dressing-table and began another letter. 'Aroma is pregnant. I do not know who the father could be. She is such a slut – you can read it in her face: long ears, long tongue, a lecherous leer.'

Lily giggled as she sealed the letter.

'What is it?' Concubine Aroma would ask.

'Nothing,' he would say, and turn to kiss her on her piggy little snout, feed her kitchen scraps, sit up late to watch her lick herself.

* * *

Aroma went into labour one cold afternoon; let out a strange doggy moan each time the contractions came, lay on her side and panted.

'I know,' Lily said each time Aroma moaned. 'I know,' she said and poured more wine, trying not to think of the children she might have had, the life she might now be leading. Aroma walked behind the screen, panted, stood up, walked in tight circles, lay down again. Lily looked at the painted hermit eternally drinking wine with his concubine and saluted them. She danced a few steps, imagined that she was dancing for her husband, stopped still and held her pose like a painted dancer.

Aroma sounded as if she was growling. Lily balanced in the moment for as long as she could, then lowered her sleeves. Aroma was in a corner of the room, turning round and round in circles, contractions increasing till they were coming so often she lay down and panted, confused eyes looking at Lily as she gave birth to a bloody packet of puppy.

Lily bent down to watch Aroma chew through the umbilical cord, lick away the gore, devour the afterbirth. A few minutes later Aroma gave birth to the next. Two puppies; three; another five minutes to deliver and clean the fourth. It was brown, the others were black and spotted like their mother. Aroma sat on one of the puppies and it yelped a tiny helpless yelp; eyes shut, it searched for its mother, was silenced with love and licking and a nipple. Lily picked the brown pup up, and it yelped like the first. Aroma looked at her with pleading eyes and barked once.

'No,' Lily told her. 'You are a slut!' And carried the brown puppy outside. Aroma barked three times, unable to leave the others, unable to watch a puppy go. The door slammed shut behind her. The brown puppy yelped louder as it was carried out into the cold autumn evening. Hush,

267

hush, Lily soothed, cradled it close to her chest, still warm and slick with birth fluids. 'Hush,' she said as she lifted the well lid, held the puppy out by the scruff. Hush, she thought as the puppy let out another barely audible yelp. Hush, as she watched the comic scrambling of the puppy's legs, opened her fingers and watched it fall into the darkness – disappeared with barely a splash.

Aroma looked hopeful when she saw Lily come back inside, but Lily took the darkest puppy and dropped it down the well; then the other spotted puppies together, one in each hand, each one flailing into the darkness.

When she had the last puppy Lily kissed its black snout. 'You have had a good life,' she told it, and for a moment she considered keeping it, but then she thought of the loss she would feel when it was taken away from her, and threw the thing away. It bounced off the far lip of the well, flailed and disappeared, as the others had.

Aroma was frantic as Lily kept drinking, staring at the painted screen where a storm was about to break over the hermit and his concubine.

'No babies for Aroma,' Lily told her. 'Aroma is a slut!'

Aroma whimpered and whined. Dogs were so stupid. 'No babies for Lily, no babies for Aroma!' Lily said, and poured herself some wine, but Aroma sat and whined, ran round in circles and barked desperately. In the end Lily locked her in the side hall, bolted the door shut, but Aroma kept howling, and however much Lily scolded her she would not listen.

'You're a slut!' Lily screamed, and Aroma shrank back into the shadows as Lily kicked and shouted.

'Slut!' she shouted.

Aroma ran out into the courtyard and Lily ran after her, shut the gate, stalked the dog into a corner.

'You slut!' she screamed. 'You're a fucking slut!'

Aroma yelped when Lily grabbed her, kicked and whined as Lily carried her across the yard. Lily remembered kicking and struggling when Minister Li came to her that day. 'Want me to get off?' she asked as she held the dog over the well's wide-open mouth. Aroma was much heavier than her puppies. Her claws scratched Lily's arms. 'Want me to get off?' Lily demanded, but Aroma still struggled, drawing a red welt along Lily's forearm.

Lily did not remember letting go, but Aroma flailed, as her puppies had flailed, barked and hit the water with a loud splash.

Lily peered down. 'Aroma?' she called. 'Aroma?'

The splashing continued for some minutes, there was a whine. Lily sat by the well and listened to the sounds fade. When the splashing finally stilled she closed her eyes. There was no point struggling against fate.

The next day Lily's maid pulled up a bucket full of water with a drowned puppy in it and screamed.

'They were sick,' Lily explained to Grandmother Li. 'One of them had two heads.'

'I don't know how Aroma got in as well.' Lily seemed confused. 'Maybe she was sad.'

Grandmother Li sent Lily away. Sand was poured into the well, incense was burnt, the well lid sealed. Lily's days were quieter than ever. She sat on the well lid and wished she had Aroma back. At least the dog had loved her, she thought.

Three weeks after the incident with the well, Mid-Autumn Festival arrived. The full moon rose, fires were lit. Lily gazed into the fire, the blue flames twisting and untwisting till her eyes lost focus. In sixty years' time she would still be here, toothless and wrinkled like Grandmother Li, playing with the grandchildren of Minister Li. An abandoned concubine, now toothless, winter-haired.

The door to her courtyard creaked open and Lily looked away from the fire – but there were no visitors, only the north grasslands wind, passing through.

The morning after Mid-Autumn Festival, Lily was up early. There were grey clouds wandering over the hills, the trees swayed back and forth. She dressed simply, arranged her hair in a modest style, and walked to Grandmother Li's courtyard.

The old woman was sitting on her bed, eating a breakfast of mutton stew.

'Grandmother Li!' Lily said, kowtowing in the middle of the hall. 'Forgive me! I have treated your kindness with contempt, your household with disrespect, your grandson without the love and affection any woman should give her husband.'

Grandmother Li's gaze hardened, like cooked egg white. She slurped another spoonful of broth. 'I do not pretend that my grandson has behaved well,' Grandmother Li said after a pause, 'but you are a concubine, nothing more, nothing less. It is a hard fate to accept, but Heaven is not kind.'

Lily kowtowed. She went to Minister Li's wife's courtyard and was inside the gate before the servants could stop her.

'Sister,' she called at the open doorway. 'Can I come in?'

Minister Li's wife didn't know how to say no. She jumped up in a fluster and called her son to her, held his shoulders, just in case.

Lily began to kowtow.

'No – please!' Minister Li's wife said, tried to pull her up.

'You have treated me with honour and respect and I have given you nothing but contempt and disrespect in return.'

Minister Li's wife tried to pull her from the ground, but Lily was as stubborn as a garden weed. They struggled for a few moments. A tortoiseshell hairpin came loose and Lily's hair spilt free; both women fell over.

Minister Li's wife and Lily sat and talked through the morning. Lily apologised, and Minister Li's wife was so uneasy she smiled and laughed and touched Lily's arm as affectionately as if they were sisters.

Aroma was an easy target: large, fat and easy.

'She's a fox spirit!' they agreed.

'She's bewitched him!'

'You brought my husband back to me but she has taken him away again,' Minister Li's wife said.

At the end of the morning Minister Li's wife took Lily's hand. 'Sister,' she said, 'you cared too much for our husband. Loving someone who does not love you is like worshipping Buddha through the temple wall.'

Lily stood to leave, but her shoulders began to shake before the gate could be opened. Minister Li's wife squeezed her hand and Lily nodded, put the other over her mouth and ran out the gate, back to her own courtyard.

> Ripe plums are reserved for rich officials,
> but even the plain beech tree
> still yearns for the respect of common folk.

Peace returned to the Li Family Manor like a cautious crow. Servants and mistresses expected tantrums and swearing, but Lily rose at normal hours, slept after lunch, did not stay up into the night. She treated the servants with politeness, her relatives with honour, attended the daily sacrifices in the Ancestral Temple, bowing before the dead faces of ten generations that peered frozen from the walls. When Grandmother Li hired actors or storytellers Lily arrived on time, was polite and respectful.

'I have never heard anyone tell the story of the Monkey King with such vigour,' Lily told the storyteller. 'For a moment I really did think you were an ape, so impressive was your jumping and cavorting.'

The man bowed and thanked her for her generosity. 'My father was taught by my grandfather, who was educated in Changan,' he said.

'Have you been to Changan?'

'No, madam.'

'You should go,' Lily told him. 'The streets are very wide and busy, and there are more people and temples than you can imagine.'

When the evening was over Lily bowed. 'Goodnight, honoured Grandmother. Goodnight, Elder Sister.'

'Goodnight, Lily,' they said, and watched her walk silently away, her silhouette fading into the shadows.

A month later Lily heard from her maid that the magistrate was touring the countryside. She went to Grandmother Li and asked for permission to visit the Monastery of Massed Incense.

'I want to make sacrifices,' Lily said, 'to restore my good fortune.'

Grandmother Li gave her a cake and her servants poured Lily a cup of emerald tea. They sat and sipped together.

'I have written to my grandson,' she said, 'and told him how well you have become.'

'Thank you,' Lily said. They chewed thoughtfully. 'Did he say I could go to Changan to join him?'

'No,' Grandmother Li said. Lily ate her pastry and sipped

her tea. She looked out across the garden where the walls were always hemming them in and smiled. How pleasant!

That night Lily finished packing, early the next morning she left with a maidservant and two men from the manor leading her pony. As the gates of Li Family Manor shut behind her she felt as if a huge weight had been taken off her chest. She could stand up, look about her, draw in a deep breath.

> The first day I marvelled at how clear and broad the sky is. The second night there was thunder and a downpour, and the thatch above my bed leaked. Despite the discomfort, the fleas and the lice, I was happier last night than I have been for years. At one point we passed a beggar in the road, his open box filling with stones and rain. I gave him some coins and prayed for benevolence from Heaven. We stopped that evening at the inn where my husband and I stayed on our last night travelling down from the capital. I was sad for a little while and looked along the road that led towards the capital, and reluctantly turned away. I have determined never to be gloomy again.
>
> I stayed the last night at the house of Official Liu, whose wife and children were very charming. We talked of many things, including my husband, and in the morning he came to see me off and I left him a poem hanging from the door post.

On the fourth day Lily and the servants reached the monastery and the monks let them stay in one of the side rooms. Lily went and prayed, burnt sheaves of sandalwood incense, watched the smoke and prayers rise to Heaven. The next day she went down from the monastery and travelled to the local magistrate's yamen, walked inside and kowtowed in front of him.

'Lady Lily,' she was announced, 'concubine to Minister Li Zian.'

The magistrate asked her to stand.

She paid her respects to the magistrate, then began her petition.

'It is said that hair and skin and bodies are gifts from the ancestors,' Lily said. 'So it is with writings and histories that have come down to us from people who lived in these places before us. None is of greater merit than the Yellow Emperor, who taught the Chinese people to plough the fields, grow wheat and barley. He gave us laws by which we could govern ourselves, set out the triagrams by which our sages divine the future. The Yellow Emperor also wrote that a man should not marry more women than he could provide for,' Lily said, her breath coming more quickly, 'and since I have not slept with my husband for more than a year now, before you and these people I state that I wish to divorce him.'

The magistrate sat forward.

'I wish a divorce,' Lily repeated, 'from Minister Li Zian.'

There was silence. Someone tittered at the back and one of the scribes shushed them. The magistrate frowned and cleared his throat and nodded.

'There are five grounds for divorce in Tang Law,' he said, 'but these deal with a man divorcing a woman. There are no grounds for a woman to divorce a man.' He spoke as if he was explaining to a child.

'But—' Lily began, but the magistrate put up his hand to silence her.

'How old are you?'

274

'Nineteen,' Lily said.

The magistrate shook his head. 'What you are asking is beyond reason,' he said. 'Why, it would be as if in autumn the leaves had shed the tree.'

The bluntness of his argument made a few people laugh – but the magistrate scowled and Lily tried to speak again, but the magistrate cut her off: 'What you are asking is beyond nature!' he insisted.

In the time that Lily had been at the Li Family Manor, life had improved considerably for the Yu family. Scholar Yu had cashed in a few of the gold ingots Minister Li had given them, had had the thatch removed and replaced with expensive grey tiles. Theirs were one of the only houses in the ward to have a tiled roof: the local children had run alongside the carts, and the neighbours watched each tile being tossed up to the men on the roof, then carefully laid to rest.

At the same time Scholar Yu had bought himself new gowns, and given his wife three bolts of fine silk to make into clothes for herself.

'What do I want with gowns?' she said, and locked the cloth into the chest for safekeeping. On festivals Scholar Yu bought her small trinkets.

'What am I to do with these?' she asked, when he gave her two white jade hairpins. 'I'm too old for finery.' Her face looked almost wistful. 'I'd look like the chicken that dressed up as the phoenix.'

Scholar Yu tried to spend the money they had, but it seemed his wife wanted for nothing.

'I thought we might get a maid,' Scholar Yu said one day.

'Don't be silly,' his wife told him. 'What would we do with a servant?'

Scholar Yu didn't know what to say. 'Clean?' he suggested.

'What's wrong with my cleaning?' his wife demanded and he didn't know what to say. They sat in silence then he stood up with a sigh and went into the yard. Scholar Yu's wife waited for him to bring the matter of the servant up again but he never did. She didn't know what to do with the mountain of counter-arguments she had thought of, and they bounced inside her head, made her short and snappy.

A few days later Scholar Yu's wife was pulling up a bucket of water and thinking about the nights before they were married, when she had lain awake at night and waggled her fingers, imagining long twisted nails covered with gold foil. She dropped the clothes back into the bucket and looked at her hands, wrinkled with water, and dried them on the hem of her gown. It was not Scholar Yu's fault, she told herself, it was fate. Fate had decided to reward their efforts now, when they were alone and ageing. It would be ungrateful not to accept.

'Remember that idea you had?' Scholar Yu's wife said that night. 'About getting a servant? Well,' she said, 'I'm not against it.'

The first girl was too ugly; the second one was sly; the third was dishonest. When the fourth arrived Scholar Yu's wife didn't know what was wrong with her, but she was determined to find out.

Scholar Yu's wife stood over her, giving instructions. 'Rinse them first,' she snapped and the girl hung her head lower, slopped clothes from one bucket into another.

'You're spilling it all!' Scholar Yu's wife snapped again. 'Look – like this!'

She was showing the girl what to do when there was a bang at the door.

'You do it!' Scholar Yu's wife said, but the banging came again. 'Don't touch anything!'

At the gate was a man with a letter.

Scholar Yu's wife took it. 'Where's this from?' she asked, but the man couldn't read either. They both looked at the sealed scroll and wondered.

Scholar Yu's wife shut the gate behind her. 'You can go home,' she told the girl, who put her hands over her face.

'Please don't get rid of me,' she said. 'My family is poor. There are too many mouths to feed. If you get rid of me my family will sell me.'

Scholar Yu's wife gave the girl twenty copper cash.

'Off you go,' she said. 'Come back tomorrow.'

Granny Pig leant to the side to let out a fart, ignored Scholar Yu's wife as she put the letter on the bed, wrung out the clothes, hung them in the yard, chopped vegetables.

'Who's it from?' Granny Pig asked when Scholar Yu's wife at last sat down. They both looked at the letter.

'I don't know,' Scholar Yu's wife said.

When Scholar Yu came home his wife met him at the gate. 'There's a letter!' she said as she hurried him inside. 'It might be from Lily.'

Scholar Yu didn't like to be hurried, but his wife pulled him inside and let go of him only when he was standing with the letter in his hand.

'Husband!' she said. 'Is it her?'

Scholar Yu saw the seals and nodded, but when she started to speak he put his hand up. It remained up for a moment, then he cleared his throat and began to recount. 'She sends greetings,' he said. 'The weather is fine for this time of year. She is well and not to worry about her.'

There was a long silence.

'Don't stop!'

Scholar Yu frowned. 'She says that our son-in-law has abandoned her,' he said. 'He has abandoned her and she has moved to a monastery.'

'Which monastery?'

'I don't know,' he said.

When he had read and reread the letter they both sat down. Scholar Yu read the letter one more time and when he had finished they stared at the single sheet of paper, as if it were responsible for the terrible news.

'Burn it!' Granny Pig advised, and when Scholar Yu didn't move, his wife grabbed the paper and put it into the fire. The ink and paper and written characters crumbled to ash, but in their heads the words remained, going round and round like the crowds in the city market.

That night neither Scholar Yu nor his wife slept well. Scholar Yu eventually got up, took an ember from the stove, blew it to life and lit a candle. His wife's eyes glittered in the dim light; he sat down next to her.

'I can't sleep.'

'Nor can I.'

Neither spoke for a long time. 'Am I a bad man?'

'No,' she said.

'I thought it would be a good match.'

Scholar Yu's wife squeezed his hand. How could we know? This is Heaven's doing.

The next day Scholar Yu went into the side yard and tore down the scrolls he had bought for his daughter's classroom: all the words and wisdom and advice on living a harmonious and upright life. He carried them out into the yard, piled them up with her classroom books, put a flame to the corner of one scroll, left it to grow to a raging fire and watched sparks fly up into the morning, the flames faint blue in the bright daylight.

278

That evening Scholar Yu felt better; went to bed early and eventually slept.

It took him a week to find out where Minister Li was currently serving, and another week for Scholar Yu and his wife to agree on the exact wording of their letter.

Minister Li's response was polite and formal and correct.

I have only been a good and respectful husband to her. She has been treated very well, according to her station as concubine. My grandmother has shown her inestimable kindnesses. My first wife has welcomed her to her courtyard whenever she wants, without malice or deceit, yet none of this is enough. Your daughter breaks all the rules of propriety and her behaviour demands that she is first wife, mother, grandmother and father in my household.

Your daughter has destroyed the harmony of my house. I have shown great restraint and tolerance. When last I returned home she insisted on tormenting me and my family. My servants are frightened of her. My wife is wary. Contrary to what she has told you, I left her at home in the care of my family, with all the luxury and leisure she is accoustomed to. Dissatisfied, she has chosen to leave my household and apply for a divorce, in an attempt to bring my name into ridicule.

Minister Li ended his letter with a classical reference:

When Sage Meng's mother had a daughter she gave her a pot shard to play with so she knew that her place in life was lowly.

It seemed that her parents had failed to instruct her properly when she was young, his letter ended with his seal and the characters of his name.

'A pot shard!' Scholar Yu's wife spat. 'No wonder our daughter had to leave him. You should go and fetch her!' she shouted. 'Bring her home!'

'How can I go?' Scholar Yu said.

'If you loved our daughter you would go!'

'You're the one who spoilt her!'

There was no else to quarrel with so they argued back and forth, resurrecting old grievances. When their anger had burnt out, they sat exhausted. The next day Scholar Yu and his wife wrote to Lily, sent the letter through the Ministry of Roads and Transport, their concern and good wishes and advice carried by pony riders a thousand li north.

Lily read her parents' letter with a mixture of resignation and disbelief.

> Daughter, you and your husband's lives have been linked together by Heaven. You should return to his house and show him that you are a good and loyal concubine. When he understands that he will return and collect you.

Lily screwed up the letter and threw it across the room. She threw her stool at the door, saw the half-empty wine pot and lifted it over her head, watched it smash with cruel satisfaction.

AD 907

The morning after he had fallen, Minister Li's wife ordered servants to bring Minister Li's songbird from the pavilion. It chirped nervously and Minister Li's wife thought of the night that her mother had died, eaten up from the inside with disease. An owl had called that night.

Minister Li's wife kept Swallow with her all day, while she kept black eyes on her. Swallow swept the room, cleaned out the brazier, picked up a pair of red silk shoes to finish the embroidery.

'Girl,' Minister Li's wife said as Swallow plunged the needle though the silk, 'does the master ever touch you?'

Swallow blushed, didn't know what to say. He had tried to touch her once: old claws fumbling for her sash; stinking breath; hair as thin as winter grass. She had pushed him off and run from his courtyard.

'Don't be coy,' Minister Li's wife said. 'Has he fucked you?'

'No,' Swallow swore. 'Never.'

'Has he touched your breasts?'

'No, Mistress.'

* * *

When the sun began to set Swallow heard, very distantly, the sound of military drums being beaten, imagined ranks of soldiers rushing one way then another, imagined knocking on Fang's door and sneaking inside.

It seemed that life only existed in his room. Outside the world was cold and grey and lonely.

Swallow ran to Fang's room. There was no answer, so she lifted the latch, undressed, shivered at the cold embrace of the sheets.

It was over an hour later when Fang came back to his room after dinner, found Swallow asleep. He sat and looked down at her, then shook her shoulder gently.

'You can't stay here,' he whispered. 'The mistress is calling for you.'

Swallow nodded sleepily, hung her head as she dressed, but before she stepped back into the lacquer black night she stopped and kissed Fang, squeezed his hand.

'Where have you been?' the mistress demanded.

Swallow shut the door and hung her head and refused to answer.

'The minister is dying,' the mistress said. 'You will sleep with him tonight.'

Swallow swallowed, but the mistress's face was hard and set. Swallow began to undress, white body shivering. She imagined her night with Fang had left tell-tale marks of love and lust all over her body, blushed under the mistress's gaze, climbed in next to the sleeping minister, made a show of snuggling up to his old bones.

'You will be safe here,' the mistress said. Her voice betrayed no sense of irony. 'Call me,' she said, 'if anything happens.' Swallow understood, half nodded, half shivered.

Minister Li's wife bent over the candle, pursed her lips as if she were blowing a kiss goodbye.

The night swallowed the room in a single gulp. The old man's breath rattled his bones; he coughed and spluttered like a baby, seemed so weak that even a fart could kill him. Swallow kept thinking he would die there in her arms. She wanted to cry and wished she was with Fang; haunted herself as she imagined the old man's ghost trying to steal her life. She remembered the night before: making love to Fang. Sixteen was a good age to be married, she told herself. Maybe next year he would marry her.

Despite her fears Swallow fell asleep and dreamt of long ghost nails and white dead hair. She was being hunted, always hunted, the minister's old claws reaching out for her.

A warm touch. Swallow woke, gasped for breath and blinked as the candle flame moved close to her face.

'Mistress?' Swallow said.

'It's me,' a man's voice said.

Swallow reached out a hand, touched Fang's face.

'Please take me away.'

Fang blew out the candle, lifted Swallow naked from the bed. He let the door swing shut in the cold night breeze, the old man's life fluttering alone.

AD 863

As the year faded to autumn Scholar Yu wrote a number of letters begging Minister Li to think of the child his daughter had lost, to remember the happy times they had had together, all the things he had promised Scholar Yu and his wife.

Winter set in with a game of quote and counter-quote, precedent and ritual.

> Although the ancients laid down rules which govern the way both sexes should act, I beg you to remember that Lily is not just your concubine, but also my daughter. It is true that a concubine should seek her husband's love through devotion, but Sage Meng and Sage Kung also said that the husband should act with honour and kindness to his wives.

Spring Festival came early that year: the Yellow River was still blocked with ice, the monks shivered as they prayed. Lily threw more fuel into the grate of the kang, amused herself by writing the new numbers in her diary.

'First day, first moon, year 864,' she wrote, and the world

seemed so new and full of possibilities. I will be twenty this year, she told herself – then remembered that she was in the monastery and tried to cheer herself up by walking to the top of the hill and back. The new year did not bring any change in Lily's circumstances. She stayed at the Monastery of Massed Incense; Minister Li stayed in the capital; the monks went about their daily routines.

Sleep, food, prayer.

Sleep, food, prayer.

Monasteries were the natural homes of people adrift on the world, and the monks tolerated Lily as they did other paying guests. She did not disturb their routine, but spent most days in her room, which was small and bare – but the roof was solid and tiled with blue glazed tiles. The latrine was a thatched shed a little way down the hill; the monks brought water up themselves and when she was hungry all Lily had to do was go down to the kitchens and help herself.

On the way back she often stopped at the library, exchanged one book for another. The monastery had a few books of poetry, but many that dwelt on religious and historical matters. As she read their long-dead words, each writer seemed to spark briefly to life, die again as she turned the page. Some days the smallest things made Lily cry; at other times she sat and smiled or laughed out loud and wasn't sure why. Laughter was a rare and precious sound: she felt that she had almost forgotten what it was like.

When the cold finally lifted, the wheat seedlings began to show. Lily picked her way through them, watched the peasants hoe the fields; from the hillsides the woodcutter's axe sounded from somewhere deep in the forest, always thinning to let new trees grow.

It was a few weeks before Lily got bored of sitting alone.

The next day she wandered through the monastery, peering in as the monks held their esoteric debates, wished she could stop to listen. It was in the kitchen that one of the younger monks called to her and asked why she didn't go to the prayer hall to burn incense.

'The Buddha knew nothing of the customs and rituals of the Han people,' Lily said.

A few monks overheard their conversation and came to listen and join in.

'My father raised me to follow the advice of Sage Kung and Sage Meng,' Lily explained, and when they tried to tell her about the advice of the Buddha she shook her head. 'In Changan when people want to show their devotion they gouge out their eyes. How does it help the Buddha if a man gouges his eyes out?'

'He is unable to see temptation,' the monks chorused, and became earnest. They explained how the world was full of evil spirits tempting men away from virtue; how the key to happiness was learning to live without desire. Lily thought of a world without desire or emotion or excess of any kind and decided it would be robbed of beauty and intensity and violence. She wanted to live in a world where the grass was green, the summers hot and the winters cold and white and dead.

'That is the road to unhappiness,' the monks said with authority, but Lily laughed and they laughed as well and then none of them were so interested in religion any more.

That afternoon Lily climbed the hill and saw peach blossoms colouring the valleys red. She put her hands to her mouth and shouted, the hills and rocks and forested slopes echoing back her name.

'Lily!'

I've moved up here to live where the gods could live
flowers and groves flourish and bloom without a
    gardener's care
in the tree in the front yard I spread my clothes to dry
sit by the mountain stream and float my wine cup in
    the water
my covered walkways plunge silently deep into the
    bamboo trails
with my long silken clothes I wrap my heap of
    scattered books
carelessly drifting in the painted boat reciting poems
    to the glowing moon
trusting the night breeze to blow me back home

When the inevitable letter from Minister Li arrived, Lily
left it unopened for three days. She hoped it would leave,
but each day when she came back from her walks it was
still there, bristling with news. She told herself that she
didn't care, she wasn't interested; but at last she got drunk,
reached out to take it and then shut her eyes and walked
outside – the touch of the air on her face was like water,
refreshing and cool and calming.

The letter felt light as she lifted it up. I will not fall in
love with him, she told herself, one final time. I will never
fall in love with him again.

Lily broke the seal, unwrapped the message: a single
sheet, columns of characters, right to left, his name stamped
at the bottom. She tried to suppress the intimacy of the
handpainted words. Now I am twenty-nine, he wrote, I
have formally inherited my father's rank and salary as a
second-grade official.

Lily kept reading: he had been presented to the Emperor,
who had said some kind words about his father. He had
been appointed to an important position in the Bureau of

Iron and Salt. His characters were written in the fluid style, the words conversational and informal: she found herself warming to them.

'I remember our trip to the Temple of Divine Brilliance,' Minister Li wrote fondly. 'I have still not lost my ambition.'

Lily was not sure how he could write to her after all this time. At the end she laughed, screwed the paper up and threw it across the room. It landed at the foot of the wall. She stared at it for a long time, stood up and stamped on it, tore it into shreds and dropped them into the fire.

'It is good to hear from you, my dear.' Lily smiled as she wrote. 'Look after yourself. I think of you. I am waiting for you here.' She stopped before she signed her name, tried to think of the right words.

'I am still thinking of you. Love as always,' and then she wrote her name, as beautifully as she could: curvaceous and bold, free and full of spirit, heard the mountains and streams echo back.

Lily.

Lily gave the letter to a passing official, asked him to send it on to the capital, to the Bureau of Iron and Salt. She smiled to herself as she walked back up the hill, hoping her letter hit its mark.

'I have also been thinking of you,' Minister Li wrote in his reply. 'It is quiet here,' he told her. 'I do not have much work to do. It seems the higher a man rises the less he does. I think you should be back within the family,' he ventured, and Lily smiled.

'My darling husband,' she began, sent the letter off – sent another before he had had chance to reply.

* * *

'I have sent Aroma to the Li Family Manor. I am alone here in the capital and think you would be happier with me,' Minister Li wrote in his next letter.

Lily asked him what he meant: 'Don't ask me to come if you are feeling guilty. Only if you really want me to come,' she told him, and clapped her hands when his reply came. She tore it open and read voraciously.

'Come to the capital,' Minister Li said. 'I would like you to come to the capital. I have asked Grandmother to give you sufficient funds.'

Lily put the paper down on the table, sat down and stared at it, didn't know whether to weep or laugh or pray to Buddha to release her from the world's sufferings.

———————

It was the summer of 864 when Lily returned to Changan. She stepped through the magnificent gateways, heard the ram's-hide drums being beaten, and realised how deeply these streets and people and teahouses and palaces and pavilions and parks and markets of Changan were stamped into her. It had been four years since she had set off to the Li Family Manor, but it seemed that the capital had not forgotten one of its own. In every stranger's face she saw a friend; the wide bustling avenues were as familiar as family.

Lily hurried to her parents' house. Despite her excitement the place felt odd, as if she were looking down on her former life from a great height.

Her mother was alone.

'We haven't heard from you in such a long time,' Scholar Yu's wife said. 'You didn't write for such a long time. We have been so worried.'

'But I am here now.'

'You should respect your husband. He is your Heaven. Remember the classics: if you act like the mother of Sage Meng then you will be blameless. Remember,' Scholar Yu's wife said and Lily bit her lip and nodded. 'You'd better go before your father comes home,' Scholar Yu's wife said, bundled her daughter out of the door before she'd even had a chance to go and greet Granny Pig.

Lily paused outside the vermilion gates of Peach Blossom Palace. Inside, happy ghosts haunted those courtyards: watching the snow fall, running to fetch warm wine, sitting on the bed listening to the shouts from her wedding banquet. She did not know if she wanted to go in and disturb them, but perfection in love is always brief, she told herself, hung her head as she passed between the two pillars.

Peach Blossom Palace, to the right.

Minister Li Zian, second-grade official, son of Prime Minister Li Zifu, on the left.

Servants she half recognised took her packs to a court-yard that they had never used. She thought it was where the serving women had stayed during the wedding. The moss had been scraped away, the grille-work windows were carved with cranes and flowers; a silver lantern and thick red candles were in her room. The bed curtains had been folded back, the bedding neatly folded at the end of the mattress. Lily rested for a moment. She remembered the women's crude jokes with something like affection, looked out through the open doorway. Bright sunlight seemed too extreme for a day like this, she thought to herself, wished the world was veiled in thin mist.

'I'll have a bath,' she said when the maidservant arrived, and the girl brought buckets of warmed water and filled a green-glazed tub that four men carried behind the screen.

The miles of travel turned the water murky, but when

Lily had finished scrubbing her body she came out of the water feeling clean and pale and desirable.

'Minister Li will be back tomorrow,' the servants told her, bustling back and forth, and Lily went from room to room looking for evidence of Aroma – clothes, perfume, hairpins – but there was nothing, just her husband's casual gowns of blue and yellow silk, his deerskin boots, riding whip, paintings of Heavenly horses and misty southern landscapes.

Lily looked to see what he had been reading, found poems, history and biography – and at the bottom of the pile a book called *Visions of Spring*. The subtitle ran in a drizzle of characters down the front, *A Guide to the Traditional Sex Life*. On the inside flap there was a colour painting of a man and a woman fornicating in a garden, text to accompany the picture.

> It is spring, the scholar and concubine enjoy a delightful moment under the weeping willow. A pair of mandarin ducks turn their thoughts to the other. The object of her desire lies inside his trousers. She kisses him gently to ensure he is in the right mood, then leaves a puddle of silk at her feet, steps up on to him and guides him inside her. Both of them continue to watch the ducks as their bodies combine.

Lily turned the page.

> In summer the scholar plays his lute and peonies flower through all the garden. His spouse rushes in to tease him, and he leaves his studies and catches her from behind. Her trousers are dishevelled as they play, and he is aroused. Later the couple embrace in front of the open window. He caresses the most sensitive part of her body, then elicits a kiss from her cherry-red lips.

Autumn's picture showed a garden of chrysanthemums and a girl bent over a stool.

Winter showed a snowbound landscape, a pot of wine warming on a brazier, thick winter robes hiding their bodies, his hands disappearing into her clothing. The text said: 'Outside everything is frozen and covered with snow. The couple are warmly clad, but even with their clothes on they must listen to the call of love.'

Lily flicked through the pages. So this was how Aroma had kept him enthralled, she thought.

It was strange, wandering through her husband's life. Moonlight Pavilion had been freshly painted, but the name above the doorway was still as she had written it four years before. She looked at her writing, remembered the day she had arrived and she had punched his chest for making her cry.

'Don't you like it?' he'd asked and she remembered his smile, as if it had been a spell he had cast on her.

He didn't know you were coming today, a voice in her head told her as she walked across the room; heard her own footsteps echo from the alabaster floor. She tried not to think of the pillow book and the lurid illustrations. It is better not to be alone at night, she told herself, but when the servants came to bring her dinner she could not resist enquiring about Mistress Aroma.

'Oh, she left a few months ago,' the servant said.

'When exactly?'

The servant fumbled for the precise date and blushed. 'After Spring Festival,' she said, 'just after the baby was born.'

'Baby?'

'A daughter, mistress.'

So that is why he sent her away, the voice in her head said. That is why he summoned you back.

* * *

When Minister Li returned to his household he greeted Lily with kindness and respect.

'You look well,' he said. 'I hope the journey was not too tiring.'

'Not at all,' Lily said. 'Thank you.'

There was a moment of silence. Lily could feel her palms sweating.

'It is good to see you again.'

'Is it?'

'Yes,' he said.

Lily turned her back on him and looked at a vase of twirling dragons on the table in front of her.

'Did you miss me?'

He coughed to clear his throat.

'I did.'

Lily picked up the vase, felt its weight, the coolness of the stone, the twining dragons.

'When did that girl leave?'

'Which girl?'

Lily turned to face him. 'You know,' she said.

'After Spring Festival.'

'Why did she go?'

'I sent her away.'

'Why?'

'My wife wanted to raise the child. She did not want to be parted from her.'

'What was her name again?'

'Aroma.'

'My dog was called Aroma,' Lily said, after a pause.

'I remember.'

Lily put the vase down and thought of the letters she had sent.

'Did you leave the dog at the monastery?'

'Oh no,' Lily said sadly. 'It died.'

She had tried so many times to imagine her first night back, but this was quite unlike anything she had fantasised about. Minister Li did not crawl on his knees and confess undying devotion; instead of swooning she prickled defensively, and at the end of the night Minister Li yawned and said, 'I'm tired.'

Lily waited for him to take her hand, ask her to come to his room but he stood up and folded back his sleeves and said, 'I will be back tomorrow afternoon,' as goodnight.

'Then I will see you tomorrow,' Lily told him.

'Yes,' he said. 'Goodnight.'

Lily waited for him to follow her, but he did not: he left her alone with her pillow. She lay awake thinking of that book and Aroma, and the fact he had called her here because Aroma had given birth. He will abandon you, the voice said, do not fall in love with him again, remember how he treated you, remember that fat slut, remember the mother of Sage Meng.

On the second night Minister Li and Lily ate dinner in Moonlight Pavilion.

'Have you eaten here many times?'

'Not so many.'

'Didn't Aroma,' Lily stumbled despite herself, 'come out here and sing to you?'

'Her singing wasn't so good.'

'How about her poetry?'

'Not bad,' he said and poured them both a cup of wine. They drank them down, and Minister Li refilled her cup.

'I saw Wen Tingyun at Spring Festival.'

'How was he?'

'He asked after you,' Minister Li said. 'I told him you were at my family manor.'

'Did you tell him about Aroma?'

Minister Li poured them both more wine. 'Tell me,' he changed the subject, 'your dog called Aroma. How did she die?'

'I told you,' Lily said. 'She was sick.'

'I was told that you drowned her.'

'They would tell you that.'

He poured two more cups of wine.

'What else did they tell you?'

Minister Li lifted his cup and handed Lily hers. They drank their cups down again, and again he refilled them.

'It is good to have you back,' he said, and put his hand on her arm. 'I wish things had not turned out as they did.'

'I'm sure Aroma was quite content,' Lily said. Minister Li's jaw tensed and she smiled. 'I was teasing.'

At the end of the meal Minister Li refilled their cups.

'Long life!' he said.

'Happiness,' she replied.

At the end of the night, Minister Li stood up to walk Lily to her room. They said goodnight to each other as they had the night before, but as he turned to go Lily touched his hand with the tips of her finges. They stared at each other for a long moment. Minister Li took her hand, Lily turned away, let him lead her to his room, did not resist.

Without candles, clothes, pillow-books or words, they made love with furious passion, kept returning to the battle like two armies bent on each other's destruction. In the early hours of the morning they lay exhausted and spent. Lily's whole body tingled, sweat cooled on her back. She reached a hand across the sheets, found his and their fingers interlocked. Nothing else needed to be said.

* * *

Minister Li was supposed to be away for a few days on business, but on the second evening he galloped into their courtyard.

'Come!' he called down.

'I'm not dressed!' Lily said, but he would not give her time to powder her face or dress her hair.

'You look beautiful,' he told her, and lifted her on to the saddle.

Lily put one arm round him, could feel the soft fat of luxury beginning to belt his waist as they rode through the city to North Park, the guards nodding at Minister Li's robes.

'I'm allowed to ride in the royal park now I am a second-grade official,' he told her. They rode in silence; she pressed close to him. 'It is said I might be transferred to Hangzhou.'

'Heaven is above, but on earth there is Hangzhou,' Lily quoted, from the Han Dynasty poet Bai Chen.

Minister Li laughed. 'Would you like it there?' he asked, and she hugged him.

'Of course!'

They rode on for a little longer, thinking of a future in Hangzhou. 'Did you ever think of moving to Luoyang?' Lily asked at the top of a rise, looked down on the city walls and the drifting smoke of the cooking fires clawing its way up to Heaven.

'I did,' Minister Li said. 'Many times.'

The evening drumroll signalled that the city gates would soon be shut.

'I think we would be happy there,' Lily said.

Minister Li shouted, then spurred his horse down the slope and back to the city, and Lily held on to him as they rode towards the gates.

* * *

Minister Li was away again in the morning but he rode back before sunrise.

'You can't keep coming back like this,' Lily told him, but he did. Even on the fourth day, when the cold winds were blowing and autumn rains had begun to wash the green from the leaves, he rode in after curfew.

The next morning Minister Li did not get up to leave. 'Zian!' she said, when she woke. 'It's mid-morning!'

Minister Li pulled her down into a kiss.

'You have to leave!'

'No, I don't!'

'What do you mean?'

'I've finished the work.'

Lily laughed. 'I love you!' she told him, and they lay in bed all that morning, only got up for a hotpot lunch.

Late that afternoon Minister Li and Lily took a trip down to the Serpentine Lake. A black waterbird flapped to the other shore, the reflections of red and yellow trees set the misty waters aflame. Lily walked down to the lake's edge, tossed acorns to the carp, who churned the still water, disappeared beneath the surface.

Minister Li watched her walk back up the slope to where he was sitting, her embroidered gown catching the cold afternoon dew. She sat down next to him, looked out across the lake.

'What do you believe will happen to you after you die?'

'I don't know,' he said.

Lily threw an acorn down towards the lake, did not turn back towards him. She watched the daylight moon rise behind the hill, the sun cast long shadows, began to set, stretched the shadows of trees and fallen leaves.

'Why do you ask?'

'I don't know,' Lily said. She threw another acorn to the carp. It bobbed in the water; a fish jumped some way off.

After a long while Minister Li said, 'My name will be written on the ancestral tablets, and my sons and their sons will honour my ghost, sweep my grave and continue the sacrifices.'

'And what if they don't?'

Minister Li laughed at the idea.

'Of course they will,' he said.

On the Double Tenth festival the curfew sounded but Minister Li did not return.

Lily had dressed in a gown of Shaozhou red, waited alone with her lantern. When the lantern flame died, she waited in darkness, leant upon the carved railing and watched the fishing-hook moon rise over her wall. There must be a good reason, she told herself, maybe he has a banquet, as she spread her embroidered quilt across the bed and hummed 'Dream of the Southlands' as she undressed, then lay awake, watching the moon rise in her window.

The window was half dark when Lily heard her gate open. She pretended to be asleep as Minister Li shut the door behind him, stepped softly across to her bed.

'Darling!'

'Hmm.'

'Are you asleep?'

'Hmm,' she said, stretched as if she was waking. She could smell wine on his breath, rubbed her eyes. 'Where have you been?' she asked, as he climbed in.

It took him a moment to get comfortable. 'Remember Fast Yi?' he said.

'No.'

'Didn't you meet Fast Yi?'

'No.'

'Oh – well, he was appointed to be magistrate of Huaqing Prefecture.'

'Oh,' Lily said, as if that explained everything.

Minister Li was often out late, and though Lily disliked the fact, she did not say anything about it. On the last day of the year, she set out three dishes of delicious food in front of the picture of the Kitchen God and his wife, dabbed their lips with enough honey to keep them shut.

Whenever Minister Li went out, Lily went with him. She smiled as she poured Minister Li's wine, was polite and attentive, laughed at all his jokes, kept all the other women away. When Minister Li composed a poem, Lily clapped the loudest; when others asked her to compose she shyly declined.

'Why didn't you compose?'

'I don't feel like it,' she said.

'But your poems are better than all of ours.'

On the first day of the new year Lily woke and found three embroidered gowns cut in the latest style, ran to try them on, dressed her hair in the style of Yang Guifei falling off her horse. When she came out, hair artfully dishevelled, he clapped his hands.

'Does it fit?' she asked.

'You look like a fairie,' Minister Li said and she smiled because he had not called her that for a long time.

'I love you,' she said and kissed him.

'Come!' Minister Li said, taking her hand. 'We have a banquet!'

The officials had ten days' holiday at the beginning of the New Year, and Minister Li was so attentive and affectionate that it seemed that she and the minister were more in love than ever before. Each day they ate breakfast together, went to see the snow in Serpentine Park, climbed the Small Goose Pagoda, or he took her to the markets where antiquarian shops hoarded all kinds of treasures from the dynasties past.

'Here,' Minister Li said, and picked up a cauldron from the Three Dynasties.

Lily found a painting of peonies by the poet Xu Xi. The paper was yellowed and brittle, but the colours were still bright and vivid.

'How much?' Minister Li asked, and the proprietor peered closer to check which painting they were talking about.

'Twenty thousand cash,' he said, and Lily put the painting back, and a shadow hung over the rest of the afternoon.

The next day they sat in Moonlight Pavilion for their lunch, and when the servants came to take the dishes away, Minister Li walked Lily back to her room, where the painted peonies hung opposite the door.

'You shouldn't have,' Lily said, but she spent the next ten minutes moving the picture to different walls, decided to hang it next to the door. 'Thank you,' she said, and when the servants had gone she pulled him to her bed.

That night was the Lantern Festival. They walked through the streets, admiring the lanterns that hung from every branch, young lovers taking a walk together, faces fresh and excited.

'Do you think we look as happy as them?' Lily asked and Minister Li bent to kiss her.

'Definitely,' he said.

There is no other place to be for Spring Festival:
Changan is alive with lights and food and rosy cheeks.
We greeted complete strangers in the streets, wished
them Buddha's blessings for the year ahead.
　　Zian and I took his sedan out to view the lanterns.

They were as thick as fireflies, all different colours and shapes. The next day Zian played polo, and I wrote a poem to wish him good luck.

Laurel sticks clash, eager to compete,
riders pull free, chasing each other.
All over the pitch the riders gallop, sticks and hands
    all entwined.
Holding my breath, I'm waiting for a score.
When no one's in the way, take care with your shot.
When you're in the mêlée fight and jostle your way
    through.
You know the rules and how to score.
I wish you luck to take first place!

After Spring Festival Minister Li was given the task of travelling to Xiezhoufu and auditing the Salt Lake accounts.

Lily and Minister Li boarded a barge on Changbi Canal, drifted east for three days, saw palaces and gardens, like glimpses of Heaven. Each night they stopped at the house of a friend and each night they drank, wrote poetry and talked in the most beautiful surroundings.

On the third night their host was a thin man with a thin black beard and soft hands.

'I have heard that the concubine of Minister Li is a fine poet.'

'Which one?' Lily said, and the men all laughed.

'She is, but she is shy,' Minister Li told them, but this time, when the moment came to compose, Lily did not refuse, but sang a traditional poem about a wife waiting for her lover, to the tune 'Botthisatva Barbarian'. The images were classic, the theme was safe, and when she had finished all the men applauded.

'Very clever,' they said, as if an animal had performed a trick.

Their barge reached the Yellow River five days after leaving Changan, rose steadily, lock after lock, ready to brave the swirling waters. The Yellow River was swollen with spring floods: eddies and tree trunks raced past; the crew of the boat shouted and ran up and down the planks, poling to keep the boat steady, praying to the dragon of the river.

It took an hour to cross the Yellow River, and as they did so they passed a huge junk lashed to thick stakes. It was a Great Mother Ship, on its annual trip to the capital. There was a vegetable garden fore and aft; two hundred crew members ran and heaved at the ropes, used to the pitch of the ship on the waves.

'Why doesn't it sink?'

Minister Li had seen one of these monsters the year before, but never so close. 'They take a year to sail from Hangzhou to Changan and back again,' he said.

'They come from Hangzhou?'

Minister Li nodded. 'They carry more salt than twenty barges,' he said.

Lily stared at the Great Mother Ship struggling against the Yellow River, and wondered why anyone would want to leave Hangzhou. 'I should like to see Hangzhou before I die,' Lily said.

'We have plenty of time,' Minister Li laughed.

When they'd crossed the Yellow River they continued in an official's cart, pulled by four oxen.

Forests gave way to steep terraces that had been ploughed for more years than anyone could remember, generations of peasants working the fields beneath which their ancestors had been planted long ago. On the third day they passed through the town of Ruicheng, stopped at Yongle Temple to admire the paintings of Master Mao Fenshan, who had also painted the murals in the Imperial Palace. That night they ate with the local magistrate, and Lily chanted a poem about a wife sending her husband to the grasslands.

The next day they set off for Xiezhoufu. The closer they got, the worse the road was, its rammed earth facing worn through by the ceaseless traffic of salt wagons. Their cart reached the walls of Xiezhoufu as the sun began to set, the banner bearers pushed a way through the crowds, the cart lurched inside.

That evening the local head of the Bureau of Iron and Salt came to greet them dressed in official blue robes, his official cap on his head, pearls and beads dangling in front of his face. He brought them gifts of rice and tea and a bolt of silk and Minister Li gave him a packet of spices from Changan.

It took three days to conclude the official business. When it was over Minister Li and Lily set out to visit the tomb of the historian Sima Qian. The road was lined with statues: a pair of rams; a pair of lions; a pair of oxen, hard-working and stubborn and unchanging. There was a temple where Daoist priests took offerings and sacrifices in the historian's name. Minister Li gave them two strings of a thousand cash and they cooked a meal of pork and beans.

When the meal was finished the priests led Minister Li to the whitewashed wall of the side temple. 'Please, write something,' they begged, and gave him brush and ready-mixed ink.

Minister Li took a deep breath and composed.

Lily thought the poem not so good but clapped and talked with all the others. She waited for Minister Li to pass the brush to her, but he did not.

Zian continued on with his business and I returned to the capital.

It was so sad to see him leave. I wiped the tears on my sleeve, felt like I would never see him again. Looking across Han River I sent him this poem.

North and south
across the river
all we can do is stare.

A faint song lifts into the mist
as the ferry slips
out into the moonlight.

We remember soft words
and quiet moments
as we leave each other behind.

Minister Li stayed in Hedong Province longer than expected, but when he returned Lily held a welcome-back feast in the garden.

Minister Li had a few days' holiday, which they spent in a monastery in the hills south of the city, each day visiting the hot water springs that Emperor Xuanzong and Yang Guifei had made famous. They composed poems in the evening, and before he went inside for bed, Minister Li sat under the twilight blue sky, and wondered what could be better than trading poems with his favourite concubine.

When they were back at Peach Blossom Palace, Lily went through Minister Li's packs, instructing the servants in washing and folding. As the last clothes were folded in the red-lacquered armoires, she bent to put his shoes together. Something, bright pink, was half hidden under the gauze curtains. It looked like a crumpled handkerchief, the silk embroidered with turquoise lovebirds. Inside there was a faded chrysanthemum, the first blush of beauty almost lost in the discoloured petals.

Lily did not mention the handkerchief, tried to put it from her mind.

News came at the beginning of summer that Grandmother Li had died.

'Are you going to go home?' Lily asked.

Minister Li kissed her. 'No,' he said. 'I will write to the Li Clan. They will arrange it.'

It was not long after that that a letter came from Minister Li's wife, saying she wanted to bring the family to the capital.

'Your sons miss you so. I do not believe in families being separated,' she told him.

'She can't come here,' Lily said. 'She will bring that pig with her.'

Minister Li said nothing.

'Forbid her!' Lily said. 'Tell me you will forbid it. Otherwise I do not believe you.'

'Since when did a concubine decide what would happen in a family?' Minister Li asked. Lily turned away. When he put his arm round her she flinched.

'When she asks me to come, I will say no,' he told her.

'She is asking you there!'

Lily could not understand why he would not do as she wanted. She spent the afternoon in the Moonlight Pavilion. She hung Xu Xi's painting of peonies there, watched the sunset orange make the colours glow like embers.

That evening Minister Li came home late.

Lily was waiting for him.

'Where have you been?'

'There was a man who had been given promotion,' Minister Li explained, but Lily turned her back and in the morning she smelt his wine-stained clothes, convinced herself that they were flavoured with infidelity.

'Don't be silly,' Minister Li said, but Lily's white-powdered face flushed red. She remembered each time he had come home late and was certain that he was guilty. Everything she heard brought up another fact, which she added to the pile. It loomed over her, made each day seem dark and gloomy.

'How long does a man's life last?' she heard a servant humming. The line was a popular refrain of street songs, and Lily imagined Minister Li using it as an excuse. Women's lives were even shorter, she told herself, their beauty as brief as a tattered chrysanthemum.

It was a few weeks later when a servant came to her to say that there was a group of men at the door. Lily shut her painted fan, folded back her sleeves, followed the servant through the manor gardens. Outside the gate was a ragged group of people, dusty and tired from weeks of travel. Lily recognised the faces of men from the Li Family Manor.

Memories of that time were cold and hard like winter stones.

'What are you doing here?' she asked.

'We've brought the Minister's wife,' one of the men stammered.

'Where is she?'

'She is lodged outside the city. We came ahead to find the palace and let her rest.'

'Come inside,' she ordered, watched the nervous group file in. 'Steward!' she called. 'Have these men fed, then come to see me. I will be in the gardens.'

Lily paced up and down. I told you she'd come, she told herself. I told you.

When Minister Li came home Lily's anger had boiled into fury. 'I told you to forbid her!'

'How was I to know—' he started but Lily cut him off.

'I told you!' she screamed. 'I told you!'

Minister Li did not know how to talk to her. Lily sat down and put her face in her hands and her body shook. He tried to calm her down, but a dog started barking and he could hear the sound of shouting from the gate.

The commotion moved closer.

'What is it?' Minister Li shouted, but the servants were all running about and then his wife rushed into the court-yard and kowtowed in front of him.

'We have been abandoned!' she screeched. 'A father who does not love his son, a husband who cares not for the duties of a husband! You will send us back – at the mercy of robbers and bandits and evil spirits! Ayya-me!'

Minister Li tried to lift his wife from the ground but she shrieked as if he had hit her. It was only when Minister Li had said that his wife could stay the night and he would think on the matter that the commotion finally settled.

When he came to Lily's room he was surprised to find the door unbolted. Lily was standing in the far corner, staring at her painted screen.

'I'm not fucking you,' she told him as he closed the door behind him.

'Lily.'

'I am not fucking you with that woman in this house.'

'She's my wife,' he said, tried to put his arms round her – but she pushed him away.

'Lily!'

'I don't care if people hear! I don't care who hears!' Her voice rose in volume.

'Lily,' he said, but she pushed and struggled. 'Lily!' But nothing he said made any difference.

Minister Li's wife did not take long to make the household hers. All the servants understood that the wife had the authority to override a concubine. Lily argued every single point, but when Minister Li came home tired and exhausted, he refused to get involved.

'Since when did a concubine run a man's house?' he said, and his tone ended the conversation. That night he came to her courtyard and found her standing in the yard with packed bags piled up on the steps.

'If this is what you want,' he said at last.

Lily waited for him to leave. There was nothing else for her to do. She walked out of her courtyard, out of the gates of Peach Blossom Palace, into the dark curfew streets.

Lily hurried through the night-time streets to Scholar Yu's house.

'Who is it?' Scholar Yu shouted, but the banging continued without an answer. He opened the door and Lily pushed through, ran across the courtyard.

'Do you hear her?' Scholar Yu's wife asked.

'I do,' Scholar Yu said. 'I hear.'

'He's thrown her out!'

Scholar Yu didn't know what to say.

'What are you going to do about it?'

Scholar Yu didn't know. 'Minister Li is a good man,' he said, because there was nothing else he could think of, but his wife cradled Lily like an enormous baby, patted her back, rocking her back and forth.

Two days later they sat on the kang and Scholar Yu read the letter from Minister Li's wife aloud – but despite the protestations of affection, Lily refused to go back.

'She is a witch,' she said. 'She torments me.'

Granny Pig said nothing but Scholar Yu's wife sided with their daughter, and Scholar Yu slammed the door on his way out. That night he came home drunk. 'She is bringing shame on us!' he declared. 'She is making me look a fool!'

Scholar Yu's wife put her arm round her daughter. 'Shut up, you turtle!' she shouted. Scholar Yu tripped over a chair, fell flat on his face.

'Look at you!'

Scholar Yu tried to push himself up. 'Why are you shaming me?' he asked Lily and Lily stared at him and remembered the day she had been strapped to Old Fart's back, a kiss from her mother, a final look back at the Last Fort Under Heaven.

Scholar Yu and Minister Li met for lunch one day in the eighth month. The meal was slow and stilted. It was only when they were on to their second bottle of wine that the two men relaxed.

'I am sorry things turned out like this,' Scholar Yu said, and raised his cup.

'I am sorry too,' Minister Li said, and when he looked back at that moment, he wished he had said something different.

> no amount of wine
> can wash away
> the pain you left behind
>
> sadness when you come
> and again being left
> the clouds keep drifting

When Scholar Yu's wife told Lily that she was being sent to a monastery in the hills outside town, she nodded. It was like planting a peony and finding a willow had grown. All she wanted was to be living at Peach Blossom Palace, alone with the minister – but it seemed that such a small thing was impossible. If her husband had decided that she was to be put in a monastery then that was what she would do. Granny Pig refused to speak, but her disapproval was apparent.

'So they want to make a nun out of me now?' Lily said.

Scholar Yu's wife said nothing.

'Is Father paying for all this?'

'No,' Scholar Yu's wife said.

Lily laughed. 'So I'll be *his* nun, will I?'

Granny Pig was lying in the bed. She coughed and turned over; a moth began to flutter around the lantern.

After a long pause Lily cleared her throat. 'So,' she said. 'What's the place called?'

The Monastery of Boundless Contentment was set at the top of a hill, where the ridges curved to form a shallow bowl. It was about six hours' walk from the capital's west gates. Six hired men carried Lily's belongings up the steep climb to the monastery gates. When they got to the top the men's clothes were stuck to their backs. They dropped her possessions by the side of the road and squatted as a man in a cloak of kingfisher feathers greeted Lily.

Abbot Zhao was famous for his skill in herbs and elixirs and the use of qi. He had white hair and overgrown black eyebrows that gave his wrinkled face the look of a wise old monkey.

'Greetings, Sister Yu. I have heard much concerning you.'

'It is not true,' Lily said and the monkey smiled.

'You have an auspiciously shaped head,' the old man said.

'My husband did not think so.'

Abbot Zhao led Lily through the prayer halls and the library, where niches in the walls held scrolls and books and thick files of woodblock prints.

'If you like you may study here,' Abbot Zhao said. 'It is a modest collection, by the standards of the capital, but there are some fine books that scholars come to read.'

Lily smelt the air and remembered how books were friends in lonely times.

'Of course, as our guest we do not mind how you spend your time, but it would be a shame to waste your talents when so many others might enjoy your poetry. We often have guests from the capital. If you are interested,' he said, and Lily didn't know if it was a question or not.

On the path they passed a man with cropped grey hair who did not look like a novice or priest.

'Greetings, Brother Lin,' Abbot Zhao said. 'This is a new guest. Name Lily, surname Yu.'

Brother Lin did not smile, but bowed politely.

'He is quiet,' Abbot Zhao explained. 'He keeps himself to himself.'

'Why is he here?'

Abbot Zhao laughed. 'We do not ask why the stream flows, nor why the snow falls.' Lily saw a brief smile play over the abbot's lips. 'When we see the stream we wash our feet or quench our thirst. When the snow falls we sit and compose poems, do we not?'

Lily continued up the slope after him.

'So you don't know why I'm here?'

Abbot Zhao stopped and smiled. 'You are here to learn and study, and find peace with the world.'

AD 907

After his fall Minister Li's strength failed quickly. Each leaf that fell left him deeper in the clutch of ghosts and memories. 'Damn you,' he hissed through long black teeth, bony fingers clutching at his robes, his skull almost too heavy for his neck to lift. 'Damn you all,' he said, as they held him down and unfolded the heavy sheets on top of him, his threats turning to pleas. 'Don't leave me alone,' as the servants filed through the door.

'Who will stay with me?' he asked his wife, and each night she sent a servant to sit with him, sleep across the doorway. He watched their inert shapes and cautiously shut his eyes; blinked them open again; was finally too tired.

Minister Li's wife was horrified by the decline of her husband. She had Fang write to each of her sons to tell them to do their filial duty and send flesh for their father to eat.

Only the eldest responded with a sliver of flesh that he said had been cut from his own thigh. Minister Li's wife took the dried meat and hung it next to her mirror. The next day she sliced it into shreds, mixed them with diced pork and fried them in pork fat with a handful of green beans.

Minister Li swallowed painfully, let his skull fall back on to the pillow and rested.

'Where is the girl?' he asked, and Minister Li's wife had the wet nurse brought in. She was large and fat with short fingers and short arms, and her breasts were full and heavy, the nipples as long as grapes. Minister Li's wife watched as the woman lay next to the minister. He turned his face to the side to suckle the rich warm milk, tried to sustain the life inside him.

'Enough,' Minister Li's wife said after a few minutes.

'Don't leave me alone,' Minister Li said to her. 'Don't leave me in the dark.'

'I will never leave you,' she told him. 'I am your wife.'

Minister Li put his hand up and tried to speak, but his breathing was too weak. One hand wavered in her direction and she took his bony fingers and held them in both hands.

'I understand,' she said.

Minister Li tried to speak again, but instead of words there was coughing.

'There,' she soothed. 'I understand. You will never be alone.'

The coughs seemed strong enough to kill the old man, but when it relented he lay on his back and his chest heaved to draw breath, eyes stared at the plaster ceiling.

AD 866

Minister Li came out to visit Lily a number of times, but although the days he spent there seemed quiet and tranquil, a cold current flowed through their conversations.

'How is your wife?' Lily asked.

'She is well,' he said.

'How is the capital?'

'It is good,' he said, but the only thing they agreed on was the poor state of the empire. The latest Emperor was more interested in elixirs of immortality than the real world. Self-indulgence always resulted in the destruction of dynasties.

'You should work hard,' Lily told him, but she secretly wished that they could retire to a mountain home, live away from the cares of the world. Sometimes she hinted at returning to the capital. If he asks me to come back to Peach Blossom Palace I will go, Lily told herself in the weeks she waited for him, but when he was there her unhappiness surfaced and he never asked.

In the end she wrote to him and told him that she would prefer it if he never came at all. She hoped that he would ride out to see her, but instead he sent Xu Xi's painting of peonies, wrapped in a red silk sash. Lily hung it in her room and then took it down, put it into her wooden chest – all it brought were sad memories.

Lily tried to follow the example of the Daoist priests and ate nothing but rice and vegetables, pursued the teachings of Chuangzi. Each morning she sat on a woollen rug embroidered with a hundred linked swastikas, shut her eyes, concentrated on nothing. When sounds came to her she let them go; held up emotions and thoughts and reactions, let them fall away; emptied her mind; the world was impermanent.

She sat like this for nearly an hour, then drifted back to the surface, refilling her senses.

When she opened her eyes she saw lamp flames flicker left and right, bright burning yellow with a heart of black wick; the smell of sandalwood; felt the life inside her, pulsing and beating and precise, like a clock. She ran her fingers through her hair, shut her eyes again. The sudden intensity of the world was overwhelming. Almost out of habit she looked towards the capital, saw nothing.

> For several nights
> at the House of Qin
> he soothed my heart,
> till all at once
> my darling had to go.
>
> Sleeping alone
> there's no knowing
> which way the clouds journey.
> Around the old paper lantern
> a wild moth begins to flutter.

That evening Lily let out a sigh, walked to the doorway. The wind on her face was cold. She leant against the red door-post and watched iron grey clouds gather in the east. It looked like it was going to snow.

'He'll come,' Novice Yang called out.

'Who?'

'Your husband.'

'I don't want him to come!' Lily said, but they both watched the afternoon fade to evening grey, night black. When the first stars were showing, Novice Yang went inside, piled sticks of black charcoal on to the brazier and fanned them with the hem of her robe. Smoke spiralled up as the fire crackled with delight and sent sparks dancing into the darkness of the room. Lily spread her fingers and stared into the fire. A spark flew and landed on her jacket. She half stood and flicked it off: it had burnt a black-edged hole into the blue cotton; white cotton stuffing showed through. From the monastery hall the bell rang, a long low dong! drifting through the late-afternoon gloom.

'Well, he can't come today,' Lily said. 'I haven't washed.'

Inside her coat Novice Yang's white body shivered at the thought of washing in this weather, the cold kiss of the air, the warm splash of water that made toes and fingers tingle with fire.

'Do you remember,' Novice Yang said, 'the day in summer when we went down to Yellow Hill Falls?'

Lily nodded. They had picnicked under the long threads of water, dived into a waterfall pool, tried to touch the rocks at the back of the waterfall. Lily shut her eyes, felt the strong dark river flowing cold over her naked body. Fresh: feeling her skin tingle as she laughed and spluttered with water and kicked her legs. The current flipped her to the side; she took a deep breath and kicked again, laughing even though her mouth was shut and closed against the white foaming water, trying to touch the rock, bubbles churning around her and pushing her down and

316

she reached out a hand and kick-kick-kicking she touched the back of the waterfall. She stopped kicking and the current pushed her effortlessly back and she surfaced and let all that breath out.

'How was it?' Yang shouted from the bank.

'Slimy!' Lily had laughed.

Novice Yang shivered. 'When it's winter I can never imagine that the world will be green, and when it's summer I forget that it will all die and be black and crooked.'

The flames crackled.

'I liked that poem you wrote. Which one was it?'

Lily blinked and looked at the girl. 'I don't remember,' she said.

I waited to see if Zian would visit me, but the holiday passed and there was no news, so the next day Novice Yang and I set off before dawn. On the walk there Yang told me that she was given to the Monastery of Boundless Contentment as an offering to improve the fate of all her family. Her family were all peasants. They gathered round to watch their names being written and laughed out loud to see the different shapes. It seemed remarkable to them that they could be reduced to a few lines in the dust; easily drawn and easily rubbed away again.

One of Yang's brothers came with us to the Yellow Mountain Falls. We turned off the main road and stopped to eat on a ridge overlooking the river. I shut my eyes and breathed as lightly as the Immortals. That night we slept in an empty woodsman's hut. The next morning it was a short walk to the river. We took a narrow path down, through wet and clinging moss, the water flowing strongly. The falls were as magnificent as Yang had described. None of us was shy: we all took our clothes off and dived in; swam through the churning waters.

The next day Lily left the prayer hall and looked out towards the capital, saw three men on horses coming up the path. She watched for a long time. There was something about one of the men that made her mouth dry.

'Yang!' she shouted, as she began to run towards the house. 'Yang!'

The door opened.

'I think it's him!'

Yang was confused.

'Go and look!' Lily said and laughed at herself.

Yang held out her hands to say that they were dirty.

'It doesn't matter,' Lily told her.

Please don't let it be him, please don't let it be him! Lily thought as she sat on her bed and put her hands to her temples, pressed down hard on the bones beneath. And then she wondered what would happen if it was him, and had to take a deep breath to calm herself.

'I don't know their names,' Yang called through the door, 'but it wasn't him.'

'Are you sure?' Lily said, felt all the possibilities drop away again.

Novice Yang's head appeared under the lintel. 'Of course I'm sure.'

Drinking till evening, she recites to herself,
lines of love again this spring.
Another messenger sets out into the rain.

Still she waits under the window:
blinds raised so she can see the far mountains,
her sadness growing with the new grass.

The night he left she cleared their last meal away.
Their private parlour remains empty,
and the rafters have sprinkled it with a carpet of dust.

———————

As the summer failed Lily sat down to write an apology.
'My dear Zian'.
'My honourable husband.'
'Dear Zian.'
'Minister Li.'
'You.'
'My husband.'
Even, 'The Beloved Master of My Heart', but each of her sentences was loaded and aggressive. She took a deep breath, felt her lower lip tremble. The wind gusted again, the grasses whispered: do not go back, do not go back.

When autumn came, it piled rotting leaves in drifts by her door, picked off the cicadas, left silence and cold winds behind. Lily's spirit sagged: she sat for long hours in the gloom of the library hall, watching the statues of Sage Kung, Sage Meng and Lao Zi, the gold of their faces shimmering eternally in candlelight.

She tried to divert herself, but however much she prayed and meditated, there were Lilys inside her that seemed to come out only when she was with Minister Li.

I do not miss him, Lily told herself. I miss being the girl I am with him.

The winter of 866 was long and cold, but spring came as usual: bright and wet, with flowers on the bare hill slopes. The peasants unsealed the north windows, let air and warmth drift back into their lives, worked hard, thinking of all the fatness that summer would bring. Lily heard nothing from Minister Li. On the day of the Cold Food Festival she went down to Yang's village to help sweep the graves of the ancestors. There were no stones or markers: just a field with unploughed mounds, winter grasses still clinging to the soil.

Uncle Guhua, Cousin Pinlu – Novice Yang named each mound – Aunty Wang, Cousin Zhu. Novice Yang stopped at the next. 'This one is my father.' Lily looked at the swell of earth and watched Novice Yang tenderly pick off dead leaves, leave a plate of steamed bread and pickles. When they walked home Lily thought of the Nian, and how each year it returned, hungrier than the last.

That night Lily dreamt she was back with Minister Li, throwing acorns to the fish. His dream-self was so vivid that he stayed with her for the rest of the day, like a shadow. Lily looked west towards the capital and imagined him in the Hamlets, drinking with pretty girls, much younger than herself. Women's beauty was as brief as the morning dew; lives were spent in a single day; in a week everything we have known has died and crumbled away and all that remains are the words we leave – like imprints in the sand.

> The whole world's a dream
> of sorrow and joy.
> You've combined them
> In a single gift.

That evening Novice Yang and Lily returned to the monastery, picked up their old lives like discarded robes. Lily sat in her room and wiped the tears away, blew her nose till it was sore. The next morning she ground a little ink on to her stone, added wine till it was the right consistency, spread the white paper flat on the rough tabletop, wrote quickly. Before she could change her mind she caught one of the priests and gave him the letter.

'For the capital!' she panted. He put it into his basket and waved. Lily watched him diminish with each step, fade into the horizon, and wondered what Minister Li would do when he got her letter. What frightened her most of all was that he would come and visit her. She spent her days with a nervous eye on the road from the capital. When visitors came up the hill, she waited in her room in case one brought news for her.

On the fourth day back Lily was meditating when she heard the hut door open. The footsteps were too heavy to be Yang's.

'Hello?' a man's voice called.

Lily jumped off the bed and someone stepped through the doorway.

'It's me.'

Lily put her hand to her mouth but was too surprised to speak.

'Don't you recognise me?'

Lily laughed out loud. 'Official Wen!'

'No longer Official,' the man said, 'just Wen Tingyun.' A wine jug hung from a sash of torn blue silk. He looked like the wandering sage of poetic fantasies, each night sleeping exposed to the dew, almost beyond human cares.

Bad poets win public office.
Good poets hide in the hills.

321

Lily scratched her head to bring all her senses back and once she had got over the shock she remembered her manners. 'Tea?'

'No wine?'

Lily laughed again. Under the grey hair and beard, Tingyun was as ugly as he had ever been. 'Yang!' she called. 'Wine!'

Tingyun sat and warmed the wine on the brazier while Lily hurried down to the kitchens and came back with a plate of fried whitebait, tossed with red chilli, sesame oil and chopped spring onions. He poured two cups full to the brim, sat forward, chopsticks ready. As he took a bite of the steamed bread, Lily noticed that he had fewer teeth than when she had seen him last. When he caught her eye she blushed, and the old man took a sip of wine.

'How is Minister Li?' he asked.

'He hasn't sent you?'

'No.'

'Oh,' Lily said. She picked up a fish and put it into her mouth. 'Well, he was promoted to second grade. His grandmother died, and his wife came to Changan. She had another son.'

'A second?'

'Third,' Lily said, and stood up as she talked, spooned out some more pickle. She had spoken as if she and Minister Li had met just yesterday.

'How about your father?'

'He is well,' Lily said, but neither of them was interested and the conversation faded. They sipped their wine and helped themselves to the dishes. After a while Lily asked, 'So, if Minister Li didn't send you, how did you know I was here?'

322

'I was on the road below when I heard the farmers talking about a beautiful young poetess up in the monastery and had to investigate.'

Lily smiled as if he was flattering her. She picked up another fish and bit half of it off, spat a bone on to the floor. No one just happened along this road. 'Were you on your way somewhere?'

Tingyun put down his chopsticks. 'You want me to leave?'

That night Abbot Zhao hosted a meal in Tingyun's honour. The old poet recounted tale after tale: the amorous general Wei Shengkao, who had a secret appointment with a lady of the palace and waited under the arches of the Blue Bridge and drowned; the Dunhuang mystic, who saw a vision of ten thousand Buddhas and carved the first of ten thousand grottos; stories of Wen Tingyun's accumulated past, when he was young and stupid, and abused position and talent without care or thought.

'Then I wrote a poem about the Emperor Wenzong seeking immortality while people were starving,' Wen Tingyun admitted. 'Since then,' he looked around him as if looking for clues as to what he might have done next, 'I have been a wandering cloud.'

That night they went to their separate beds and the next morning Tingyun came to her hut.

'This is Wen Tingyun,' she said to Novice Yang, but the name meant nothing to the young girl. 'He's the most famous poet in the Empire.'

Novice Yang became flustered. 'I am poor and uneducated,' she said and hung her head and blushed.

That morning Tingyun delighted them with stories from younger days when his name was good through official circles. There was hardly anyone in high society he had not met and did not know some secret about. Tingyun reminded Lily of happier times. She laughed louder than she had for a year, laughed so hard her cheeks ached. With the wine and firelight it was easy to mistake shadows for real people, but each night she stood in her doorway and Tingyun lingered like the lone goose, waiting for migration.

Each day they talked poetry and politics, religion and history. Tingyun twined her dark hair into his verses, gave her quatrains that praised the lily as chief among the flowers.

Lily enjoyed the attention. It was good to have someone who cared whether she dressed her hair in the morning, listened to her poems, gave her praise and advice in equal measure. When Tingyun arrived she pulled up a stool, poured tea.

'Did you sleep well?'

'Very,' Tingyun said, and sipped his tea. 'You know, I am very happy here. At the monastery, I mean.'

'Really?'

'Yes.' Tingyun looked up into the roof and pursed his thick lips. 'It is so restful and quiet.'

Lily laughed. 'That's exactly why I hate it!'

After lunch Novice Yang came back from her studies and perched on a stool at the fringes of the conversation. It was hard for her to understand what Lily and Tingyun were talking about: it was all poetry, music and names of people she didn't know.

'Can I get anything?'

'Yes,' Lily said. 'How about some wine?'

Yang took the empty pots and brought them back full. The late-morning heat made the cool green wine twice as refreshing. They waited for the wine's glow before starting to write, composed linked poems on traditional themes: the seasons, landscapes, Daoism and the plight of conscripts sent to the grasslands.

'In ancient times they built a wall across the north,' Tingyun said.

'I saw it,' Lily said. 'There were ruins near the place where I was born. My father told me that the wall stretched over the mountain peaks all the way to the sea.' The memory surprised her because she could not tell if it was real or something she had imagined, but Tingyun faltered. How could he tell a story about the Great Wall when he was sitting with someone who had seen it?

'Yes, of course. It must have been a wall from the Jin Dynasty that you saw.'

Lily and Tingyun carried on drinking through the afternoon, ate a simple dinner of noodles with ground pork and spring onions and chilli. As the sun began to set Tingyun took out his flute and conjured up an air of thoughtful solitude. When he started playing the tune 'Water Clock', Lily smiled and tapped the irregular beat with her foot and waited for the moment to sing, took a deep breath for the last two lines:

> Pillow and bed are shivering cold.
> Another long night lies ahead.

'You sing so beautifully.'

'You wrote it,' Lily said, then touched his arm. 'Now, tell me the poem you wrote about the Emperor.'

'You'll get me into trouble.'

'There's no one to hear.'

'No?'

'No,' she said.

It seemed to Tingyum that their conversation had shifted emphasis.

'What about Novice Yang?'

'I sent her away.'

Tingyun stood up and shut the door, held Lily's gaze as he walked round the table, lifted her to her feet. His hands were sweaty, he moved towards her. Her lips were as full as the cherry, her cheeks as pure as jade. He shut his eyes and moved as if to kiss her, but Lily turned her face to the side, felt his stubble on her cheek. His breath was warm and foetid, as if the old man was rotting from the inside. Lily lowered her face like an evening flower.

'Please,' she said. 'Not like this.'

'But I love you,' Tingyun said.

'Do you?'

'Yes,' he said, voice hoarse.

For a moment Lily had to stop herself laughing. It took her a moment to consider her answer. 'If you love me,' she told him, 'you will take me away from here.'

It was a bright summer morning when Abbot Zhao waved Lily and Wen Tingyun on their way, wished them good winds.

'Good trip, Wandering Cloud.' He used Tingyun's literary name.

'Good trip, Xuanji,' he said to Lily.

As they made their way down to the road, Lily asked Tingyun what 'Xuanji' meant.

'It is difficult to explain,' Tingyun said. 'It means something like "Enigmatic Secret".'

'I like it,' Lily said and looked around at the fields and

mountains spread before her. 'It'll be my new literary name,' she declared. No longer Yu Yowei, who had been married to Minister Li, but Yu Xuanji who had lived in a monastery, wrote poetry and was on the way to see Hangzhou with the greatest poet of the age.

'Li Bai or Wang Wei might argue with that,' Tingyun said.

'Well, they're dead,' Lily said, as if that meant they no longer mattered.

Lily and Wen Tingyun travelled by barge to the Yellow River, two oxen pulling the boat through the willows' reflections. When three Great Mother Ships appeared on the horizon the barge's crew shouted and clapped and Wen Tingyun stood and acted as if he had arranged the whole spectacle.

'They carry salt and iron,' he said. 'The merchants buy licences to deal from the government – but there was a time when the mandarins did not need to rely on the merchants.' But Lily did not turn to him. The old man kept talking but the boats were more interesting than anything the old poet said.

Lily and Tingyun stopped for a week at Luoyang, and Lily remembered how she and Minister Li had come here on the way to the Li Family Manor. She seemed so young and naïve then, wondered if things might have been different if she had known a little more about life. They probably would, she thought to herself as they admired the peony gardens, but no one could change the past. When they stood at the same wharfs she and Minister Li had arrived at, Lily looked north towards the Li Family Manor as they took a salt barge south.

Each day the countryside along the Grand Canal became wilder and greener. Rice replaced wheat, paddyfields replaced mountains; scarves of mist wrapped around the limestone hills that stood weird and fantastic, from the emerald landscape. At night the mosquitoes were hungry, each morning Lily told herself how kind Tingyun had been, how thoughtful and considerate, but each time he came close she felt herself back away, when he looked at her too long she turned away and blushed.

At length the old man was unable to stem his feelings. 'I love you!' he said, almost like an accusation. Lily didn't know what to say. She looked at the grey water, where leaves now floated in pairs, and nodded.

> Our boat slants across the wide river
> to Wuchang city
> past Parrot Island,
> home to ten thousand households,
> and I dream myself a butterfly
> searching for a flower.

Lily and Tingyun rested for a few days at Hanjiang, then rented a boat to take them down the last of the Three Gorges.

At first I gazed back east and saw the far snowy mountains and dreamt of the fair country on the other side: Chengdu, Du Fu's poor hut, deep valleys, cold mountains. Very soon, though, the river became so wild and violent that we were both afraid of the heaving waters, towering cliffs and sharp rocks.

When we reached the far side the boatmen laughed at us as we thanked Heaven for our safe crossing. The next night we stayed at Washing Silk Temple, which is dedicated to Courtesan Xishi, of the Three Kingdoms Period.

But now there's just a place called Zhuji
along the banks of the Yangtze River.
In the shadow of the green mountains
only the name of her birthplace remains.

Lily and Tingyun spent a week in Yangzhou – city of
canals, palaces, gardens, boats and artists. In the mornings
they took painted pleasure-boats out along the canals; in
the afternoon heat they stayed inside and watched the
reflections sparkle on the ceilings; each night they teased
each other with linking poems. When it was time to sleep
Tingyun stood hopeful, like a hungry dog, but each night
they went to their separate beds.

On their last night they stayed at the house of a local
physician, called Pung, who invited all his friends and rich
patients for a banquet to meet the illustrious Wen Tingyun.
Tingyun greeted each man with well-worn modesty, but
Pung kept interrupting. Soon the two men were tussling
for attention. Tingyun tried to tell his stories, but Pung
insisted on recounting tales of disease and injury, and how
he had cured them. In the end Tingyun gave up and they
spent the evening complimenting their host on his fine
medical skills. Physician Pung went on at length to explain
the art of healing. 'Illness comes after each man's nature,'
he said. 'Understand a man's inner nature and you understand the cure.' When his guests started to yawn, Pung
said, 'I would be honoured if you would commemorate
my banquet with a poem.'

But Tingyun put up his hand. 'Alas, my head is too sore
for poetry. My spleen feels enlarged and my blood too
thin.'

'You say your spleen feels enlarged? And your blood
thin?' Pung pondered. 'Are you sure it might not be your
liver?'

'Master Physician, I know the difference between a spleen and a liver.'

A chuckle of amusement through the guests.

'It is just that thin blood and enlarged spleen are not normally seen together.'

'I have had this before,' Tingyun said, 'many times, and a doctor I know in the capital has the perfect medicine: egg white and arrowroot, mixed with powdered sandalwood and shredded mushroom.'

In the end Lily gave them a dull poem about a woman waiting for her lover to return; the men all protested admiration. She drank a few more cups and they begged her for another poem.

'You are too kind,' she told them, but they would have none of her modesty.

'She is very talented for a woman,' Physician Pung said to Tingyun and Tingyun nodded.

When all the guests had left, Lily and Wen Tingyun lingered like shades in the slanted shadows of the bamboo grove. As Tingyun leant forward to see, Lily saw how their shadows touched on the floor and felt oddly detached as she took his hand and kissed the palm. She opened the top of her gown and placed it over her left breast, shut her eyes as the old man touched her, opened her gown a little further. She imagined that it was Minister Li not Tingyun who bent his beard to one breast and then the other but when he tugged at her sash she started.

'What's wrong?'

'Not here,' she whispered. 'Let's go to my room.'

The next morning they got up early and their host lent them his sedan to take them to the wharfs. Tingyun was firm as he negotiated passage to Hangzhou, but Lily felt disconcerted and uncomfortable. She watched their possessions piled aft, and then a tent was erected where they could retire.

'Ready?' she said, and tried to hide her nerves.

'Ready,' Tingyun said, took her hand and helped her aboard.

That evening Tingyun fell asleep with his head on Lily's lap. He was better-looking asleep, Lily thought, and as she stroked his hair she imagined a messenger telling Minister Li that his concubine had run off. In her daydream Minister Li put his hand out to steady himself, pined like a concubine in a poem – unable to sleep, eat, drink or even get up from his bed.

You should no longer care about Minister Li, Lily told herself, through the open flap saw willow trees lining the bank and hummed a poem from long ago, in Changan.

> The lonely traveler fills his heart
> with a thousand lines of poetry.

Late on the second day their barge turned a corner and the pagodas of the West Lake drifted magnificently into view. Lily felt she had been there before: it was a landscape painted in a hundred poems. For a moment she could not believe that she was there.

'Thank you,' Lily said, and kissed Tingyun. 'It's so beautiful!'

The next morning they were up early to see the sights.
Lingering Snow on Breakoff Bridge.
Autumn Moon on Smooth Lake.
The Print of the Moon on the Three Pools.
Ice in a bowl of White Jade.
Settled Snow on Lone Hill.
Waves through the Pines for Nine Miles.

331

After lunch they walked over the half-moon bridge to Lone Hill Island; saw the grave of courtesan Su Xiaoxiao who had fallen in love with a rich young man, who loved her and used her and abandoned her. Lily felt that she and Xiaoxiao would have a lot to talk about.

Tingyun marked the occasion by standing with his face to the lake, chanting a poem, clapping his hands with each word. A little crowd gathered, and when they found out he was Wen Tingyun they asked him to repeat each couplet so that they could commit them to memory.

Lily sat in the shade of a rhododendron, a green sheen on the skin of her hand. She watched and smiled at the crowd around Tingyun, then picked up a stone and threw it towards the water.

That night they hired a painted pleasure-boat. Tingyun rowed; the boat's wake widened; Lily wondered where Minister Li was now – and whether he was sitting in a boat with a young beauty.

She turned to the moon and sang a poem to the tune of 'Water Clock'.

The dressmaker cut the sunset clouds
to get my gown so red.
Spraying a mist of perfume
I push past the tapestry curtain
and admire the lotus flowers.

Spring has dressed the hills and lakes
in a fine green cloth.
Wandering along, we stop,
listen to the birds, my heart soaring,
watch the crane flapping free from the open cage.

When she had finished Lily reached across the boat and kissed Tingyun on the lips. 'Thank you,' she said.

Today we saw three young girls riding past in a painted ox-cart. They seemed a strange group, and Tingyun enquired and found out that their parents had succumbed to illness. I sat and sighed and felt very sad, wrote this poem, titled 'For Three Beautiful Sisters: Orphaned Young':

It's dreadful to stand by the jasper water look in,
    and still see yourself a woman
fallen from Heaven into this world not able to act
    like a man.
It's with a sad gaze that I look and wonder where
    these girls will end up.
Drifting clouds return to the north then the clouds
    turn back south.

Autumn slipped casually into winter. The weather cooled, but so far south there were no dramatic winds or storms, just heavy clouds, mountain thunder and cold raindrops that splattered the lotus leaves to pieces.

Each day it seemed that Lily and Tingyun attended breakfast or lunchtime banquets, and while all the guests wanted Tingyun to perform, word soon spread about the young beauty who was with him.

'Master Poet Wen!' one man shouted. 'I think you have some competition here!'

Wen Tingyun smiled, but didn't like being in anyone's shade. One night Lily recited a poem about women being unable to take the civil service exams, and when they went home that night he was openly contemptuous: 'You can't write that.'

'Why?'

'Because it's worthless.'

'So I should continue with wilting beauties?'

'Yes!' Tingyun snapped, but after an hour he knocked on her door and apologised. 'I love you,' he said, but Lily lay in bed afterwards and felt that it was her body that he loved more. 'No,' he assured her, kissing her forehead. 'Not at all.'

Eventually Lily and Tingyun ran out of hosts. They walked through small towns and prefectures, lodged at the houses of educated men, and graced their quiet lives with poetry parties. But soon the towns ran out and the country became swampy: scattered villages perched on stilts; the occasional manor houses or yamens were too thinly spread. However much their hosts clapped and applauded, there was only so much praise an audience could give, and either Wen Tingyun or Lily went to bed feeling slighted.

While he could still make her laugh or smile, Lily no longer pretended to enjoy the old man's caresses.

'I don't want to sleep with you any more,' she said one day.

Tingyun didn't argue or protest: that night he lay down and slept on the floor. They travelled for a little longer, lodged in poor villages, guest-houses, hostels, all their words and education no more use than a wagon without an ox. Eventually Lily pawned a gown for ten strings of a thousand cash and Tingyun got drunk and paid fifty cash for a fighting cock, swore it would be the end of their misfortune.

'Get it out!' Lily told him, but the old man held the rooster head in profile. 'Look!' he said. 'That's a fighter!'

'I'm not sleeping with that in here,' Lily told him.

Wen Tingyun took his cockerel and sat on the doorstep.

When he came in he tried to touch Lily, but she pushed his hands away and the next morning she sat across the table from him. 'I'm going back to Changan,' she said.

'Do you want me to come?'

There was a long pause. 'No,' Lily said. 'I don't think so.'

The next day Wen Tingyun watched Lily walk away. He had the strange feeling that she had robbed him of his skill. He laughed when he thought of how he had seduced her, then shut the brushwood gate behind him and told himself that it was he who had been fooled.

AD 907

Old age devoured Minister Li as he slept; even his memories disappeared.

Fang was sent to prepare his coffin. He hurried through the abandoned courtyards to the barn. The brass lock was stiff and green with age. The sedan hadn't been used for years. It was draped with faded red paper that had decorated it when the last concubine had been brought to the house. Fang gave one of the poles a tug. It felt solid. He kicked the base: it was solid too. He started to pull the red paper off, kicked it one more time.

Fang marched back up to the house, listing the things that needed to be done. A bolt of silk to be taken to the town and sold; white paint to buy; provisions for the journey; the old curtains to be replaced with white; sandalwood planks for the coffin.

And he would have to get his clothes ready too, he thought, added it to the list.

Swallow lay and waited. A cold breeze stirred the curtains, gave a distant hint of winter.

* * *

Torches burnt all night as a team of workmen cleaned and scrubbed and painted the sedan. Fang calculated how long it would take them to finish the job. Faster, he thought, and shifted uneasily from foot to foot. Perhaps he could hire extra porters, and walk through the night – they might be waiting at the gates when they were opened at dawn.

That night Swallow came to Fang's room, undressed and slipped into the bed next to him. She put an arm round his shoulders, held him tight.

'He's going to die soon,' Fang said.

Swallow squeezed tighter.

'And then I'm going to leave.'

'Where will you go?' Swallow asked.

'I thought of going south,' Fang said, 'to Hangzhou or Suzhou.'

Swallow curled her toes. 'They live in boats!' she said, as if the people there were less than human. 'In the south-west they live on stilts,' she recited, 'in the south they live on boats, in the middle they live on Great Mother Ships, and in the north they live in caves in the ground.'

'Where did you learn that?' Fang laughed.

'I don't know,' Swallow said. 'I think I've always known it.'

They lay for a long time, Swallow pressing herself against Fang's body. 'Will you take me with you?'

Fang pulled her to him.

'Please don't leave me here,' Swallow said. She lay and thought about what she would do to be with Fang. 'We can live in a boat,' she offered.

Fang kissed her. 'Yes,' he smiled, 'we can live in a boat.'

AD 869

The highways and lanes are empty without friends.
Dusk comes, turns to dawn, fine silk gowns are
  pawned.
In my casket, the dusty mirror shows straggles of
  hair down my face.
The incense burner still gives off heat but now the
  smoke's grown thin.

When he heard that she was back, Abbot Zhao came to
Lily's hut to say that Minister Li had stopped paying the
stipend to the monastery.

'I read his letter,' Lily said, holding up the piece of paper
that stated he had divorced her on account of adultery.
He never came to see me anyway, she told herself, but that
night she buried her face in her pillow; woke in the morning and felt as if the door of her cage had been unlocked.
She peered through the open doorway, felt the breeze on
her face, was unsure how high she wanted to fly.

Lily stayed at the Monastery of Boundless Contentment for
little more than a week. She had met a number of officials

on her way home, and many had given her the addresses of friends in the capital who had said they would help her. Since her escapade with Wen Tingyun, her name had achieved a certain notoriety in official circles, but the young men and scholars who brought her gifts of food or wine or silk asked for nothing but conversation, company and a poem.

'And how was it meeting Wen Tingyun?' they inevitably asked and Lily had smiled and looked away, as if seeing a vision of the past through the open doorway. 'I learnt a lot from him.'

One night Lily had stayed at the house of a man called Zhao Lin. He was an educated man, but had never passed the civil service exams.

'I made my money from iron,' he said, quite openly, then introduced his concubine, who was grey and fat.

'Go to the Hamlets,' she advised. 'A pretty poet needs no husband.'

Lily couldn't remember the woman's name, but when she got back to the Monastery of Boundless Contentment she found a letter from her, reminding Lily of the advice she had given: a pretty poet needs no husband.

The next morning Lily wrote a poem in thanks.

Trying to fill the rented room,
I tear the letter open, admire your fine words.
Dawn finds me still reading your precious letter,
wrapped in my quilt I recite each word through dusk.
I should lock this gift in my sandalwood casket,
but keep it to hand, to touch your words again.

Abbot Zhao wished Lily good winds, wise choices and a welcome return; Novice Yang stayed up all night, was sitting crouched by the door when Lily left.

'Can I come?' she asked.

'No,' Lily said. 'Maybe next time.'

'When will you come back?'

'I don't know,' Lily said.

Novice Yang gave her a pair of shoes she had made: hemp with straw soles. 'They are a simple gift,' she said, wiped tears from the end of her nose.

On her first night in the capital Lily's admirers threw a banquet. Lily smiled prettily, thanked them for their kind words, felt thrilled and overwhelmed to be back. At the end of the evening she gave them a poem, and they clapped and cheered, and for a moment Lily felt as if they were cheering someone else who stood in her body.

The next day some of the young men came to the hostel where she was staying and begged her to come to Chongzong Temple.

'Have they posted the list?' she asked, and remembered all the times when she was a girl that her father had taken her to see the names of scholars who had passed the civil service exams. It took her half an hour to get ready: she dressed in a simple suit of red silk, carried a fan of peacock feathers, with her hair dressed in the style of Yang Guifei. When all was ready, Lily took a deep breath and stepped out into the world, without father or husband to steady her.

Or hold her down.

Chongzong Temple was in the south-west corner of Changan. They were still some distance away when they started to see hopeful young scholars with bands of friends and supporters. For a moment Lily felt she was like them: she felt the breeze move her hair, was carried forward with the enthusiasm of the men around her.

It was a press to get through the gates. Bodies crushed together and the young men tried to protect Lily, but despite their efforts her hair became dishevelled and one of her sleeves was torn.

'I feel as if I have fallen from my horse,' she said, and the young men burst out laughing.

'She has fallen from her horse,' they said to one another. 'Just like Yang Guifei!'

Lily spotted a young scholar called Pung An, whom she had met at the house of Physician Pung of Hangzhou. She waved to catch his attention, hurried through the press, and the young men hurried with her.

'Did you pass?'

'I did!' Pung An said, and the young men cheered.

'A banquet!' Lily said, and they found a restaurant a few minutes' walk south. A woman brought snacks of roast beef and chilli oil, jellied mutton and shredded coriander. They all drank three cups, toasted Pung An individually – so that soon he was red-faced and slurring.

'Poems!' he shouted and a crowd gathered to laugh at him. The other men helped drag him back into his seat, put their hands over his mouth when he tried to compose – but he was drunk and slippery with wine, and he managed to shout out a few lines before Lily stood on her stool, graceful as a crane.

'At the Chongzong Temple,' she announced, 'When I Saw the Lines Inscribed by Successful Candidates of the Civil Service Exams.'

There was a murmur of excitement and some in the crowd tried to quieten those behind, but Lily raised her sleeves, clapped out each line, as Tingyun had done.

> All around clouds shroud mountains
> then clear away in fine spring weather.
> Silver hooks grow from their fingers,
> displayed for all to see.

'What are silver hooks?' a boy in the crowd asked.

'It means beautiful calligraphy,' the boy's father whispered, and the man standing next to him smiled.

> These silk petticoats

The men at the back strained to see.

> hide my lines of poetry.

The little boy asked to be picked up.

> I can only look up and envy
> the list of successful scholars.

There was a moment's silence. One man shouted, 'More!' Lily chanted another poem and this time there was uproar. 'Fallen from Heaven into this world, not able to act like a man indeed!' The greybeards shook their heads and turned away in disgust – but the young and excited scholars pressed forward to see the pretty young woman who had said such a thing.

Over the next few days of fevered celebration, Lily was invited from banquet to banquet. Beauty was the least of her attributes, men said, and that year all the successful young scholars wanted her presence at their banquet. The excitement of the crowd elevated her beauty to the realm of fairies.

The owner of the hostel tried to keep them back from the door, but each time it opened the men pressed forward to see if Lily was there.

'Back!' the owner shouted, and took a broom to fend them off, but after two days he felt as if he was trying to stop the waters of the Yellow River. He threw the broom into the floor and marched to Lily's room, fell to his knees and wailed as if his mother had just died.

'People cannot get in or out,' he said, and pulled at his hair. 'If you stay any longer my business will be ruined. My children will be forced to beg in the streets. My wife will be forced to pick up scraps from the floor.'

There was one place a single young woman could make her home and that was in the Hamlets. Lily rented a whole court-yard in a ward next to the Southern Hamlet; she gave small presents to her neighbours. They came to inspect their new neighbour, the possessions she had, her depth of character.

'Are you that poet?' a short Korean girl called Fragrant Blossom asked.

Lily didn't know what to say. 'I think so.'

Fragrant Blossom shrugged. 'If you're living here you'll need a new kang.' She lit a fire in the bed grate: smoke seeped up through the cracks, made them all cough.

'I told the previous girl but she never did anything.'

'I'll get it repaired.'

'You can't repair a kang,' Fragrant Blossom said. 'You must rebuild it.'

'Can't they just fix the cracks?'

Fragrant Blossom did not cover her teeth as she laughed. 'You may be a poet,' she said, 'but you know nothing of kangs.'

The gateman of the ward found two men who said they would come on the first day of the ninth moon; their labour was cheap and they were punctual. They ate two fried buns before lifting their spades; ate two more when they had inspected the old kang; dug up enough earth to make a bed large enough for six to sit on and eat their dinner. On the second day the men mixed the earth with water and began

343

to fashion the foundations, laying out the place for the stove and all the vents that criss-crossed their way to the chimney.

'We've angled the flues back and forth to heat the whole bed. That will stop it cracking.'

Lily nodded as if it made sense. 'Good,' she said.

On the third day the bed was finished, smooth and damp, ready to dry. The workmen came back on the fifth day, grunted in satisfaction and lit a low flame in the grate. 'Keep it burning for three days,' they said. 'It'll heat the kang from within and dry it out properly.'

The next day was cold and damp. Lily came back from a banquet by the Serpentine Lake, fed the fire with fuel, used some of the embers to make Eight Treasure Soup.

When Scholar Yu and his wife heard that their daughter was living in the Hamlets, they sat at either side of the table, looked at the floor.

'I will go and talk to her,' Scholar Yu's wife said.

'No,' Scholar Yu told her. 'I will go.'

But when he knocked at Lily's door, Scholar Yu did not know what to say. 'Daughter.' He tried to sound pleased to see her.

'Father.'

'May I come in?'

Lily stepped back enough to let him inside.

'This is a fine place,' he said. 'Very different from a monastery.'

'How would you know?'

After a pot of green tea Scholar Yu broached the subject of returning to Minister Li's household. He and his wife had worked out a plan, he said. If she apologised, maybe Minister Li would take her back.

'Apologise!' Lily said.

Scholar Yu tried to talk over her but Lily kept shouting and he forgot all his words of reason and started to shout as well.

'I am your father and I order you to go back to your husband's house!'

'Who are you to tell me what to do?'

'We did not raise you to act like some common harlot.'

'You sold me as a concubine.'

'I am your father.'

'You have no right to claim kinship.'

'Your mother's heart will be broken when she hears of this!'

'Then don't tell her!'

'Is this all you want from life?'

'It's better than being sold for five ingots!'

'I should have beaten you as a child.' Scholar Yu's face was red. 'Then you might have learnt to respect your elders!'

'If you touch me I will walk out into the street and declare that the daughter of Scholar Yu, fourth-grade official of the Ministry of Roads and Transport, is a whore!'

Scholar Yu raised his hand, but instead of hitting her he seemed to crumple before her. 'Please do not punish an old man and his wife,' he said, clutching at her robe. 'Do not punish us for taking you into our home and treating you as our daughter. Do not shame us like this.'

Lily glared at him, but all she heard were the insults and threats; she spat on the floor at his feet.

All afternoon Lily paced up and down her courtyard, thinking of her father and Minister Li plotting together. The bastards, she thought and wondered how much her mother had had to do with it. The bastards! she said again in her head. Bastards.

'Oi!'

Lily looked up.

Fragrant Blossom was standing on a ladder overlooking her courtyard.

'We've got a pot of wine,' she called down. 'Come and join us.'

'I'm entertaining friends tonight,' Lily lied.

'Cancel!' Fragrant Blossom told her.

'I can't!'

'Of course you can! Tell the gatekeeper to say you're sick.'

'I don't feel like drinking,' Lily said.

'Why not?'

Lily didn't know what to say for a moment. 'My father came to see me today.'

Fragrant Blossom held up her hand. 'Stay there!' she shouted. 'I'm coming to get you.'

Fragrant Blossom climbed back into her courtyard, hurried round to Lily's gate. She took Lily inside. 'I want to know everything,' Fragrant Blossom said, as she put the pot of wine down, handed Lily the first cup. After half a pot they lay down on the bed and Fragrant Blossom stroked Lily's hair. She wiped Lily's cheeks. A smear of white face powder came away on her hand, revealing the skin underneath. Lily could hear birds singing outside; Fragrant Blossom took her hand and kissed it, then sat up. 'I have guests coming in an hour and you look a mess,' she said.

Lily gave her a pleading look but Fragrant Blossom insisted.

'Of course you must come,' she said. 'Dab water on your eyes. You can't wear those clothes. Borrow some of mine – I had them made last year. Oh, and tell the gatekeeper to stop letting all those excited young scholars in. You want men who will support you, not lovestruck scholars!'

* * *

Lily pawned gifts she had been given, had a number of gowns made in the latest style, bought a handful of gold and silver hairpins and one of pale green jade carved with an erotic scene of two lovers on a bed, limbs entwined.

In one shop Lily found an old statue of the gods of the boudoir.

'How much is this?'

'Two thousand cash.'

Lily looked at the six figures. At the centre was the God of Gowns, around him the other gods clutched everything a young woman would need: fragrant ointments, eyebrow paint, face powder, lip-rouge, and the last held out two pearl earrings.

'One thousand.'

'I can't go less than two thousand.'

'One thousand three hundred.'

The man waved his hand as if she were stealing from him, but took the money quite happily. On her way home Lily gave the ward gateman a gift of tea and asked him to stop the young men visiting her. When she got home she sent word to a few select madams and society matchmakers that she was available to attend banquets. She set the Boudoir Gods' statues on the dressing-table, flicked a little rosewater over them in return for their blessing, burnt a stick of incense to carry her thoughts to Heaven.

Requests began to arrive, singly at first, and after a month Lily's diary was crammed with appointments. She went from banquet to banquet, composing poetry and offering conversation. Word spread up through the strata of society about this charming young woman. Yu Xuanji, they said. The one who ran off with Wen Tingyun. Whose husband had to divorce her. Short, pretty; a little too thin, some men said, a little too fat, said others. The one who

wrote those poems about the plight of women, the girl
who was always with Fragrant Blossom.

'Xuanji,' one retired official said. 'That means "Enigmatic
Secret", does it not?'

'It does.' Lily smiled as she poured him more wine.

The old man patted her hand affectionately. 'What a
fitting name for a wild and passionate child like yourself.'

'Am I wild?'

'Oh, yes.' The greybeard's liver-spotted face creased into
a smile.

'I don't feel wild.'

The old man put a hand on her thigh and patted it affectionately.

'How old are you?'

'Twenty-three.'

'Exactly,' he said, his hand still on her thigh. 'When I
was twenty-two my father kept me locked in my study.'

As the year progressed Lily dropped the suitors she had
entertained in her first months, bought more gowns and
a fan of kingfisher feathers to waft away the summer heat.

Her fame continued to grow among the cultured of the
capital. Fragrant Blossom introduced her to other courtesans, with whom she formed a tight circle. Some of the
girls had formal patrons; most, like Lily, accepted a close
handful of lovers. But the only one she really cared for
was Pung An.

'If I were not married I would take you as my bride,'
he said to her one night, the lantern flame illuminating
their faces.

'I could be your concubine.'

'Would you like that?' His expression made Lily laugh.
She tilted her face forward, took his hand in hers.

'No,' she said. 'You do not want me as your concubine.'

Love and incense leave nothing but ashes, the old women said.

Love and incense, Lily reminded herself, when they took a pleasure-boat on Meipi Lake, kicked autumn leaves, watched the ducks swimming together.

Love and incense, as he refilled her cup with wine, smiled across the table, told her about his hometown near Chengdu.

Love and incense, as he took her to bed and kissed her tenderly.

Love and incense, Lily told herself, before she fell asleep, but as the night deepened around her, deep in the kang, hot embers still glowed.

Pung An came to visit me today and told me he was thinking of taking a concubine. I suggested Fragrant Blossom, and he said he would take both me and Fragrant Blossom and then we would be sisters. We laughed at this; and Fragrant Blossom said that if he did he would soon waste away to nothing. After drinking a few cups of wine we went to the Southern Hamlets and admired the pretty young flower girls in all their robes and make-up.

Lily took to wearing male clothes when she went to watch games of polo in the city parks. One time the young men asked her to play, and she and Fragrant Blossom giggled as they missed the ball, and the greybeards shook their heads and thought how little the world had improved in their lifetime.

One day Lily was returning from lunch in the Hamlets when she saw Minister Li.

'What's the matter?' Fragrant Blossom said.

349

'My husband!'

'Where?' Fragrant Blossom said, and turned to look, but it was hard to make him out and Lily kept pulling her along. It was not so much Minister Li she was afraid of, Lily told herself, but the memories of Li Family Manor. She took a deep breath and let them all go; told herself that she was fine.

A month Lily and Fragrant Blossom were lying on the bed.

'I heard that Minister Li has been promoted,' Fragrant Blossom said.

Lily didn't react. 'Who?'

'You know.'

'Know what?' Lily said but her cheeks flushed, and Fragrant Blossom pointed a sunflower seed at her and cackled. 'Who told you?' Lily asked.

'The gateman.'

'I didn't know he knew about *us*,' Lily said, but Fragrant Blossom laughed.

'Everyone knows!'

One of the men who sent discreet enquiries through Fragrant Blossom was Secretary Yen.

'Secretary Yen!' Lily said. 'He was my father's superior.'

Fragrant Blossom told Secretary Yen that his suit had been accepted, and he sent gifts of jade and silk. After a couple of banquets he sent a poem to Lily to ask her to come to a private meal. Lily accepted with a poem. That evening she stepped up into his sedan and folded her perfumed sleeves back over her wrists.

'Secretary Yen,' Lily smiled as he poured her wine.

'Yu Xuanji,' he said. 'I am most honoured to have you here tonight.'

Lily smiled, but she was surprised by how amusing the

secretary was, laughed several times. Clouds were beginning to obscure the moon when he suggested they go to his gardens.

'Tell me about Wen Tingyun,' Secretary Yen said as they floated wine cups on the water.

'He's an ugly old toad,' Lily said.

Secretary Yen shook with pleasure as she told intimate secrets of other men he knew. At the end of the evening there was one person she had not told him about. 'And Minister Li?' he said.

Lily turned to her cup: it bobbed on the ripples as if deciding which direction to take.

'We have our differences,' she said at last.

AD 870

After Spring Festival Minister Li summoned Aroma to the capital, but during her sojourn at the Li Family Manor she had grown unattractively plump. He slept with her on a couple of nights, then put her aside again. She lay around the manor house like a favourite cow, sentiment postponing slaughter.

Minister Li's wife became concerned at the amount of time her husband spent in the Hamlets, and interviewed a number of young women, chose one called Damson and paid two ingots of gold.

Damson was fifteen. She could sing, compose poetry and dance all the traditional sets. She arrived at Peach Blossom Palace on the back of a donkey, was shown through to Minister Li's wife's courtyard, where Minister Li's wife told her the rules of her household. She would not tolerate lateness for meals, disrespect to superiors, temper or tantrums.

Minister Li's wife presented her to Aroma. She was washed and her virginity was confirmed, and then she was presented to the ancestors. When all was done, Minister Li's wife took Damson to Minister Li's courtyard and sat her at the table that had been laid on the veranda.

'The minister will be home soon,' Minister Li's wife said. Damson seemed so small and neat, her skirts arranged around her slippers, a table for two laid ready for the master's return.

'I got rid of one concubine,' Minister Li's wife said. 'I will sell you to a whorehouse if you show disrespect. But honour your master and your future will be bright.'

Damson nodded to show she understood. Minister Li's wife shut the gate behind her.

Damson fitted well into the household. She always addressed Minister Li's wife and Aroma as Elder Sister; never spoke when Minister Li's wife was present; dedicated her life to pleasing the minister. Her affection cured Minister Li of his waywardness, but her conversation was too honest and unpolished for her to accompany him to literary evenings.

It was at one of these that he saw Fast Yi, a friend from his scholar days. His friend no longer went by the name they had given him but by the title the townsfolk of Huaqing Prefecture had bestowed upon him, 'Upright Magistrate'.

'I heard a magpie at breakfast this morning and knew I would see an old friend today,' the Upright Magistrate told him, and despite their official robes they clasped hands like brothers, sat down and talked as excitedly as young men. At one point the Upright Magistrate lowered his voice and spoke as one might speak of an illness: 'I heard about you and your concubine.'

Minister Li half laughed and nodded, didn't know what to say.

'Though I think I will have good news for you soon.'

Minister Li didn't know what he was talking about so the Upright Magistrate patted his hand.

'She lives under my jurisdiction,' he said.

That night Minister Li sent Damson away and could not

sleep. He tried to put the meeting with the Upright Magistrate from his mind, devoted himself to his work, diligently followed the strictest rules of filial piety as if there were a crime for which he must atone.

'Your father would have been proud,' an old mandarin said to him one day.

'You knew my father?'

'I did,' the old man said. His left hand wavered but his eyes were clear and bright and intelligent. 'He was a good and upright man.'

Minister Li lay in bed that night and imagined when he became old and infirm. He would retire, give up service of the country for the thatched hut, the mountain retreat, away from the cares of the world; drink wine, write poems about the futility of struggling in the world – but when he pictured himself sitting on a mountain ledge, admiring the view, it was not Damson or Aroma or even his wife sitting next to him. It was Lily.

Tonight we celebrated Pung An's appointment to the Ministry of Good Works on the East Side of the City as a sixth-grade official. Fragrant Blossom and I dressed him in his blue robes and hat of office, then took him to the Hamlets, where we drank many cups of wine, wrote many poems. Mine were of little value and my heart was not in it.

> When you're drunk and another cup
> is put before you:
> don't be disappointed.

> In life, the same mix
> of grief and joy
> is poured for everyone.

Inevitably the time came when Minister Li and Lily met: on the lawn at a cherry-blossom banquet in the Serpentine Park. Minister Li saw Lily first. She was dressed in a blue gown cut to show her bosom, white clouds swirling round the hem; her hair towered nearly a foot above her head, with more hairpins than he could count – some sparkled with jewels, others with dangling tails of pearls and beads. She looked too old and confident and stylish to be Lily, but there was no doubt. Her smile hadn't changed, and as she stopped to humour an old gentleman, Minister Li recognised the twinkle of suppressed amusement in her eyes.

'My love is like the West River water – day and night, eastwards it flows without thought of rest,' he remembered her telling him, and he shook his head and laughed. He did not know why but he felt proud of her, as if an untended flower bed had produced a peony of unsurpassed beauty.

Lily caught his eye and looked pleased to see him. He smiled back, waved, and the crowd between them seemed to part.

'My dear Zian,' Lily replied, 'how pleasant to meet you.'

'You look well,' he said, and her teeth sparkled like white jade. 'I hear you have made quite an impression with the young men of the city.'

It was meant as a compliment, but something in his tone made her wonder.

'And I hear your career is going well,' she said to him, and they talked for a little while about inconsequential matters. When Lily excused herself, she felt Minister Li's eyes follow her through the crowd.

Fragrant Blossom took Lily's sleeve and steered her to the side, flicked her fan open: raised it to hide their faces.

'And?'

'He looks very handsome,' Lily said.

Fragrant Blossom pinched her, but Lily laughed.

'He does!'

Fragrant Blossom lowered her fan but Lily squeezed her hand. 'Stop! He's looking.' And the fan went back up, the feathers shaking as she giggled. After a moment Fragrant Blossom peered out again. 'Very handsome!' she said and Minister Li seemed to sense them looking. Lily felt her pulse quicken, but Minister Li quickly turned away.

'He likes you,' Fragrant Blossom said, a note of distaste in her voice, and Lily looked again. He's embarrassed, she thought. His bashfulness made her think of holding his head, stroking the hair from his face. She imagined him asking her back, living at Peach Blossom Palace again, but then he started to make his way through the crowd towards her and she took Fragrant Blossom's arm and stood up, the two of them united in front of him.

'We were just leaving,' she announced abruptly, but Minister Li looked so disappointed that Lily could not resist calling back over her shoulder, 'Come visit me!'

Some of Minister Li's friends advised him to wait; others said he should not go at all. The Upright Magistrate took Minister Li aside.

'Do not get involved!' he insisted. 'I have been investigating moral standards and she has no idea what is proper behaviour.' He confided that his informers had seen Lily attend the kind of parties where clothes were an impediment to casual pleasure. 'There is no depravity to which her sort will not sink. Trust me, I judge these matters every day.'

Minister Li thanked his friend, but everything the Upright Magistrate said made the need for his visit seem more urgent. He would pluck her from the seediness of the Hamlets, Minister Li told himself, return her to Peach

Blossom Palace where he could tend her, nurture her talent, prune the excesses. He would design a garden especially for her, plant bamboo for resolve, pines for upright spirit, lotus flowers rising from the muddy waters for purity.

Nervousness held him back for a while, but each day that he put the visit off seemed like another day of danger. After three days he threw off his robes, dressed in a simple gown of black silk, ordered his horse to be saddled and galloped across town as if corporals were already being sent to bring her to the yamen.

'Minister Li,' Lily said as he passed the reins to her maid. 'How pleasant.'

Fragrant Blossom excused herself as Lily showed the minister round her courtyard. He was hot and sweaty, felt stiff and awkward, but Lily did not seem to mind his formal manner, insisted on showing him each painting that hung on her wall, even pointing out the small statue of the six Gods of the Boudoir.

'Isn't it charming,' she said.

When they had made a tour of the courtyard, Lily had her maid bring out hot water and whisks for their tea. They waited for the froth to settle; sipped loudly.

'Your home is very fine,' he said.

'Well, it's an improvement on the Monastery of Boundless Contentment.'

They sat for a while and chatted about Minister Li's wife and sons. Minister Li did not know what to say, but told himself he had to speak. 'I want you to return to Peach Blossom Palace,' he said at last.

Lily choked on her tea and had to put her cup down before she spoke.

'I'm not joking,' he said.

Lily imagined telling Fragrant Blossom and could hear her screech with hysteria. 'I'm afraid I can't,' she said.

357

'Lily,' Minister Li began but she cut him off.

'It's impossible.'

When Minister Li tried to bring the matter up again, Lily had to speak to him sternly.

'You've changed,' he said after another cup of tea.

Lily nodded. 'I think I have,' she said. 'Have you?'

In the early summer of 870 Secretary Yen invited Lily to a banquet to celebrate his promotion to Director of Astronomy. Each previous occasion on which he had invited her, there had been a group of his friends too, but this time there were no other guests, just a table by a pool and the clear moon reflection. Lily accepted his affection, and when the wine was half finished she let him lead her to his boudoir.

After they had made love Lily lay with her head on his shoulder, watching shadows playing on the window.

'You never told me you were Scholar Yu's daughter,' Secretary Yen said.

'No?'

'No,' he told her.

Secretary Yen and Lily continued their affair on and off throughout the summer. In the seventh month Emperor Wuzong died. White banners were draped from the palace gates, and in all the temples and monasteries pine branches were burnt, sending plumes of white smoke into the sky. An imperial edict was read: none of Wuzong's sons were of sufficient age so the eunuchs anointed Prince Li Chen, who had taken the name 'Xuanzong' – 'Proclaimed Ancestor'. From henceforth none of the characters that made up the Emperor's name might be used in conversation or in writing: replacement characters would be announced shortly.

For a month Secretary Yen was busy directing all the omens and portents for the new Emperor, but once the young man had been installed, he returned to his usual life of polo and banquets. Fragrant Blossom had fallen in love with a young poet, and Lily, unused to so much free time, spent several nights with Secretary Yen.

'Do you love me?' he asked her one night.

'Of course not!'

'Good,' he said. 'Then I think we might make a good couple.'

I saw Pung An today and he told me he had brought his wife to the capital and that she was pregnant. I felt sad thinking of his harmonious life. I met Fragrant Blossom's young poet. I do not like his poems. There was something about his manner that I disliked.

Minister Li visited Lily again, but his manner was formal and the conversation stilted. One afternoon in the eighth month, Lily arrived home to find Minister Li waiting at her gate. 'Don't be formal,' she said, couldn't resist adding, 'We're like old family.'

But Minister Li didn't smile. He took a pair of white jade hairpins from his sash and presented them to her as if he was a nervous scholar.

Lily twirled her head to make the hairpins sparkle. 'How do I look?'

'Like a fox fairie!'

'Thank you.' Lily called for wine, and after a few cups Minister Li relaxed. They laughed and chatted as if they had never been separated.

'I'm sorry,' Minister Li said suddenly and Lily raised her eyebrows.

'About what?' she prompted.

'About what happened between us.'

Lily blushed under her white face powder. 'So am I,' she said.

The garden seemed very still as they talked in low voices – but as Minister Li started to pour more wine Lily's laughter broke the stillness. 'Are you trying to get me drunk?'

'No,' he said, but kept on pouring.

Lily put out her hand. 'No more,' she said. 'I have to get changed soon.'

'Are you cold?'

'No. I have a dinner appointment.'

'Who with?'

'Friends.'

'What friends?'

'You're not my husband any more,' Lily said. She meant it as a joke, but her tone was hard.

'Lily, you must listen to me,' Minister Li began, but his audacity made her neck flush red.

'I'm not one of your flower-house whores. Two hair-pins do not buy *me* for a night.'

He managed to calm her down, and held out his hand, but when she took it he pulled her towards him. 'Zian,' she said, 'things are not as they were between us.' And he took his hand away.

'I want to change that.'

'How?' There was a warning note in Lily's voice. Minister Li's face went red; he tried to think of the words he had rehearsed but they would not come. He watched a tear slide down her cheek, and tried to clear his head. A second tear began the descent and Lily wiped it away with the back of a clenched fist.

'You're too late,' she said. 'It's all too late.'

Minister Li called to the servants to bring his horse, but

he stopped at the open gate. 'I'm going,' he called back to her. 'I'm going,' he called a second time, but she did not turn.

That night Minister Li went to bed early but he couldn't sleep. He had lanterns and food brought and paced up and down his courtyard. The air was cool, his gown was only loosely tied, gravel crunched underfoot. His mind kept up a constant conversation: what if I'd done this or that? What if? What if?

'Master,' Damson called, 'are you well?'

'Go away!' he shouted and shut his eyes. He remembered a night when Lily had asked him if any other couples could be so in love as they. Definitely not, he had told her. He put his hands behind his back and kept pacing. On impulse he dashed to the stables, woke the boy and told him he was going out. The bay horse snorted in the cool night air, its hoofs sounded on the flagstones in the front courtyard, a dog barked as the gates were shut behind him.

While the rest of the capital was dark and silent, the sky above the Hamlets had a faint yellow glow. Minister Li told himself that he would wait outside her house, greet her when she came back from her evening. No, he thought, that would seem as if he were a stranger. He would wait in her courtyard, have her maid prepare some food and a pot of warm wine, and they could sit under the stars again.

There was the twang of a bow-string, and a voice called, 'Who's abroad at this late hour?'

Minister Li announced his rank and name and the watchman let him pass. A few wards south of the Hamlets the sound of men's laughter or a fragment of song drifted through the night calm. He would treat her like a new bride, Minister Li told himself, honour her as he honoured

361

his ancestors, bury her fears under a heap of reassurances, silence her protests with a mountain of gifts.

Minister Li burst out laughing. He felt, once again, like a lovesick scholar. He was still chuckling when he reached Lily's red-painted door and took a deep breath. Maybe she is in bed, he thought. Maybe she's not home yet. Maybe she is in bed with another man. He knocked again, looked at the height of the door as if he could climb it, patted the neck of his horse. Then he banged harder because if she was in bed she should know that her husband was here to save her.

'Who is it?' a female voice called.

'Minister Li Zian!'

'Who?'

'Minister Li.' He had almost said 'husband', but the idea of a husband having to knock to get into his concubine's house was farcical. 'A friend of the Mistress Lily.'

'What do you want?'

Minister Li would remember to tell Lily about this later, he thought to himself. 'I want to come in to see your mistress.'

The door swung open. The maid rubbed sleep from her eyes, held up her lantern, threw shadows across her face. 'Mistress Lily is out,' she said.

'I will wait,' Minister Li said and spurred his horse into the courtyard.

'Bring food and wine for when the mistress gets back,' he said, 'and a brazier. We will sit under the stars and watch the moon rise.'

'The mistress is not coming back tonight,' the maid said.

Despite what she had told him, Minister Li strode up and down the courtyard to keep himself awake; each time he heard noises in the street he was convinced that Lily was returning: but the footsteps always passed by, faded away into silence. Minister Li's horse snorted. She must be coming home now, he told himself, when the eastern sky began to pale. The pre-dawn light re-established the world, turned darkness into colours and shadows into objects. No banquets went on so late, he thought. He remembered what the Upright Magistrate had told him about the things that went on in the Hamlets. The Upright Magistrate was part of a clique of traditionalists who had petitioned the Emperor against moral degeneracy. Minister Li imagined petitioning the Emperor on Lily's behalf.

She was wayward and passionate, he told the Son of Heaven. She had surrounded herself with people of bad character. Her nature was good and loyal and honourable.

The morning traffic was beginning when Minister Li set off home. The capital sky was a clear thin blue, kitchen smoke was starting the long climb to Heaven; a few clouds hung on the western horizon. When he returned to Peach Blossom Palace the gateman took the horse's reins, and Minister Li walked to his courtyard, lay down on his bed and put his hands over his face, tried to force out tears.

'You've been to see her,' Minister Li's wife said from the doorway. 'She's playing with you,' she said but he squeezed his eyes shut, wished that the years of grief could come out.

The next day Minister Li woke early, walked through his gardens, went to practise polo, sweated out all his frustration and nerves; returned home. It was natural that she had taken lovers, he told himself. How many women had he slept with since they had parted? She had taken lovers because she was lonely and frightened. When she understood how he felt towards her she would drop them, he told himself, tried not to think of her in bed with another man. She would drop them, he was convinced, as soon as she understood.

Minister Li took his sedan to her house but her maid said she was out. He went next door to see her friend, but Fragrant Blossom was sitting with a young man who had the beginnings of a beard.

'Where is she?' Minister Li demanded. 'She's here somewhere!'

He pushed past Fragrant Blossom but Lily was not in her courtyard. As he was leaving he saw the latrine hut and marched over there, but there was nothing but a well-swept hole and the stink of urine.

Minister Li cursed as his sedan pulled away. Damn the woman. Damn her to Hell! He felt like a shadow puppet, forced to dance for others' amusement.

'Take me to the Hamlets,' he told the sedan bearers, and they took him to a place called the House of Blossoming Petals, where he knew a girl who had once been a favourite of his.

'She's busy,' the madam told him, and he considered waiting, but then the woman said, 'I have another girl called Plum. More pretty. You will like her.'

Plum sang and Minister Li drank wine and the night seemed to thicken around them, like a scar. At last he took Plum's hand and pulled her upstairs, shut the door behind them. He remembered the sound of the latch falling, drew the bolt shut, blew out the candle.

Minister Li tried to imagine himself with Lily, but this girl smelt different, her breasts were larger, she moved differently. When they made love he was hard and brutal, but afterwards he lay with his arms round her and they slept without dreams.

The next morning Minister Li was lying alone, his clothes

neatly folded at the end of the bed. He dressed, left a few coins, stepped out into a bright fresh morning, felt lonelier than ever.

————

Prince Shen was a cultured young man with an interest in promoting the arts. He asked the officials to compile a list of Changan's top ten beauties and, despite the protests of the traditionalist clique, Lily's name was included. In the more refined teahouses of Changan, where jasmine flowers and rose petals were used to flavour the green infusions with the scent of morning or late afternoon, the young aristocrats agreed that to sit by the river in the Pavilion of Endless Sorrow in moonlight and hear Yu Xuanji sing 'The Lament of Greenslopes', to the strange music of a plucked zither, was worth more than a lifetime in Nirvana.

Lily's poems were written down and collected into a volume called *Fragments from a Northern Dreamland*. She visited the bookbinder's shop as they cut the woodblocks, printed a few hundred copies for avid collectors.

When she was presented to Prince Shen she kowtowed solemnly.

'I was born in the north,' she told him, 'at a place called the Last Fort Under Heaven . . . Yes, I was adopted. That does influence my work. How could it not?'

'My husband? I think of him often,' she said. 'We are still very close.

'How does my time in the Monastery of Boundless Contentment influence my work? Well,' Lily said, and pursed her lips, 'I think any artist needs a time of quiet and contemplation. Yes,' she said, 'there were many dark moments for me – and the greatest poetry is not just pretty language but *says* something.'

Minister Li tried to stop thinking about Lily, but the leaves were beginning to change colour and everywhere he went it seemed there was someone who had just been to a banquet and heard her composing. He spent long hours in the Bureau, trying to exhaust himself, but when he sat back at his desk and rubbed his forehead he remembered the feel of Lily's skin when she squeezed his hand, the press of her lips long ago, when she used to wait at home, remembered the love poems she had written on his pillow.

> Don't get waylaid, my love, by forest nymphs,
> but come back to me, back to the boatyard
> where I sit alone watching the mandarin ducks,
> where even the overhanging rock and its reflection
>   touch.

It seemed like a season since he had last seen Lily, but when he counted the days they added up to only a month and a half. The autumn leaves did not help, he told himself as he rode back from polo practice, but that night there was a letter from Lily. Minister Li's hand trembled as he picked it from the table, smelt rosewater and remembered younger days when he had been unsurprised by love.

He left that letter unopened, but a few days after the Mid Autumn Festival another letter came and this time he could not resist.

'I have not heard from you and you have not come to see me,' Lily wrote. 'I have missed you.' At the end of the letter she added, almost as an afterthought: 'I am alone this evening if you would like to come.'

Minister Li felt like singing and laughing and dancing and

running all at the same time. He hummed 'The Water Clock' as he combed his beard and picked out his most stylish gown, wrapped his head in a turban of the most modern style, inserted a peacock feather into the side. His stallion snorted as if it were one of the Heavenly horses, and he rode it through the streets as if he were the Emperor of All Under Heaven, an Immortal riding on clouds and rain.

When he got to Lily's house there were decks of red candles lighting the yard and braziers glowing red. A few maids hurried to lead the horse away, Lily greeted him as if he were an honoured guest. 'Zian,' she smiled and ushered him in. She had dressed her hair like butterfly wings; she wore a high-waisted gown of black with swirling white Heavenly clouds; her toes peeped from beneath her skirts. She led him to a table where a hotpot was bubbling, poured them both wine, asked him how he was.

'I am well,' he said. 'I have been busy.'

'Did you miss me?' she teased.

'I missed you very much,' he said, felt better for having spoken so honestly. Her eyes seemed to sparkle with candlelight.

'How is the hotpot?'

'Good,' he said. 'Very good. I hear you are friendly with the royal princesses.'

'I met them once,' Lily said. 'They wanted a team of beauties to play polo against.'

There was a knock at the main gate. The servant put down the pot of wine and hurried to answer it. Lily shook her head in mock disapproval. She saw her servant talking to someone outside but paid no attention until it became apparent that the person would not go away.

'Who is it?'

'It's Secretary Yen,' the girl called, flustered.

'Oh! Show him in!'

Minister Li cleared his throat and stood up. 'Wine?' he suggested, but Secretary Yen took the pot from his hand and poured them all a drink.

The two men seemed wary, so Lily talked to put them both at ease, addressed one and then the other. When she refilled their cups Secretary Yen shook his head. 'I cannot stay long. I have a banquet.' But he stayed for three more cups before he stood up and summoned his sedan.

When the gate was shut Minister Li cleared his throat. 'Who was that?' he asked.

'A friend of my father.'

'What's his name?'

'Yen,' she said. 'He's the Director of Astronomy.'

'He likes you,' Minister Li said.

Lily seemed amused. 'Does he?'

'Yes,' Minister Li said. He picked a piece of dofu out of the hotpot and dipped it into sesame oil. 'Is he the illiterate mandarin?'

'Yes,' Lily said. 'That's him.'

'I heard you and he were friends for a while.'

'We still are,' she said.

Minister Li stood up. Lily put down her chopsticks and waited for him to come back to the table.

He sat down with a loud sigh and she watched him with a hint of amusement.

'Why are we doing this?' she asked after a while.

'What?'

'This!'

Minister Li didn't know what she meant.

'Acting like we're still married.'

'We are married.'

'We *were* married,' Lily said. Neither spoke for a long while, until Lily said, 'I had hoped we could be friends, but maybe you shouldn't visit me any more.'

'What do you mean?'

'I don't think you should come here any more,' she said, and her tone was harsh. 'You're making me unhappy.'

'Lily,' Minister Li said, but she shook her head and stood up.

'Please leave me alone.'

Minister Li took a step towards her, saw that she was trembling. He took her hand to turn her round, put his hands to her cheeks and held her face as tenderly as if he were smelling a flower – but instead he bent close. She kissed him back. Her hands tensed on his shoulders; one hand slid to the back of his head and she pressed him down. They moved through the ranks of candles to her bedroom. The doors were open as they stripped the clothes from each other. The candles fluttered as they crushed together, made love with a fury and passion that neither of them had ever known before. Lily twisted the sheet in her hands, dug her heels into the bed. He moaned as if wounded and lay still, eyes closed, put his hand out to hold her – but Lily flinched.

'Lily?'

She turned her back to him.

'Are you crying?' he said, and her body began to shake. He held her so tightly she could hardly breathe; they lay for a long time, neither speaking. He remembered their first night when he had fed her duck tongues; remembered the first night he had ever seen her and he was convinced that she was a fox-spirit sent to bewitch him; he kissed her back, pressed his face against her.

'You should go,' Lily said as she struggled to sit up. She wiped herself clean, threw the cloth into the corner. 'Your wife will find out.'

When he got home Minister Li summoned his steward, told him what he had in mind.

'A banquet,' the steward repeated, 'for Mistress Yu.'

'Yes.' Minister Li clenched his fingers. 'I need you to organise the sedan and six bearers to bring her here, and my horse is to be saddled so that I can accompany her.' He spoke so quickly the steward had difficulty in keeping up.

'Duck might be hard to find,' the steward ventured.

'You must find it.' Minister Li's voice was unequivocal. 'Send a servant to get five pots of Toad Tumulus Wine. I want it warmed, but not too hot. Ivory chopsticks and the green-glazed porcelain. We will need someone to play music. Not Damson or Aroma. Talk to the mistress and get the name of a girl who can sing. Torches – I want the yard as bright as daylight. And lanterns. The blue lanterns. No – red. Red and blue and green.' He laughed as he talked, clapped his hands with delight. 'Now,' he said, 'repeat it back to me.'

Minister Li grinned as he walked to his yard. He felt like a young scholar again. He picked out his best deerskin riding boots, hummed to himself as he walked to the gateway, found the sedan and the bearers and his saddled horse waiting. But the nearer they got to Lily's ward the slower it seemed the bearers were going.

'Quick!' Minister Li said, as he trotted alongside them, but the banner bearer had difficulty keeping the banner upright and the sedan bearers were sweating, panting and beginning to trip. 'Quick!' he told them, but the sedan wobbled unsteadily and the men's faces were red. Minister Li was unable to resist: 'I'm going on ahead!' he shouted, dug his heels into his horse's flanks and galloped off.

After Minister Li had left, Lily lay down, but instead of sleep she fell a terrible fear, as if she teetered on the edge of a vast chasm. No tears left, she told herself, as she lay on her back and stared into the darkness, remembered an image of twirling red dragons, sucking each other down.

'Lily! Lily?' Minister Li's voice shouted over the wall. 'I have a sedan here!'

But his voice seemed to come from very far away and long ago. He wants to cage you again, the voice in her head said. Do not open the door. Do not let him cage you. Do not, do not, do not. She could not bring herself to open the door. The good memories were enough, she told herself, as if only so much happiness was apportioned to each man's lifetime.

'I want to take you home!' For a moment Minister Li's voice was clear and sharp.

Lily's lower lip trembled.

Do not, the voice reminded her.

Minister Li came back that evening when it was time for courtesans to go visiting. Fragrant Blossom saw his procession appear at the end of the street and ran to tell Lily.

'I can't see him,' Lily said, and jumped up in such a fluster that Fragrant Blossom ordered the maid to bar the gates and hid Lily in her courtyard. Lily grabbed her and would not let go.

'Don't let him find me,' she said. 'He can't find me!'

'He won't find you,' Fragrant Blossom spoke slowly so that Lily would understand. 'I promise he won't find you.'

'I've come to take your mistress,' Minister Li announced to Lily's maid.

'She's out.'

'Where has she gone?' Minister Li pushed past her into the courtyard. 'Lily?' he called and shoved the door of her boudoir open: found nothing but a bed and strewn clothes, on the dressing table an empty mirror reflecting open pots of make-up. 'Where is she?' he said but when the maid didn't answer he grabbed her by the throat and shook her so fiercely that she screamed.

Fragrant Blossom heard the commotion next door and thought that Minister Li was murdering Lily's maid. She began to fear for her life and Lily's as well. Lily's maid screamed again as Fragrant Blossom bundled Lily into her sedan chair and sent her out into the night.

'The house of the Director of Astronomy,' Fragrant Blossom hissed to the bearers. 'Go quickly!'

The sedan bearers hurried away, the sedan rocking like a camel. It had just passed round the corner when Minister Li came out of Lily's courtyard. His hair was dishevelled, Fragrant Blossom smiled politely, but he pushed past her into her courtyard. 'Where is she?'

Lily was shivering uncontrollably when she got to Secretary Yen's house. Her stomach hurt and her teeth rattled like dice in a pot. Secretary Yen sent for a doctor, had the maids warm plenty of water. They gave her a cup of wine to drink, sprinkled her bath with fragrant oils, and when they were finished the doctor gave her a massage that would help the circulation of qi through her liver and kidneys. When all was done she was wrapped in blankets. The ends of her hair were wet, the rest was dishevelled; her face was unpowdered.

Secretary Yen stood in front of her with his arms folded. 'Are you staying?'

'You do not want me to?'

'Of course I do,' Secretary Yen said, but something in his voice made her doubt him.

'Do you still love him?' Secretary Yen asked.

'I hate him,' she said.

* * *

Minister Li refused to go to the Bureau, refused to see any visitors. Whenever Damson tried to cheer him he shouted and swore and she ran back to her courtyard and slammed the door. After a week the girl was convinced that her beauty had faded. She came to Minister Li's wife's courtyard and kowtowed and asked if she would be allowed to retire to a nunnery where she could devote herself to worshipping the Lord Buddha.

'Don't be so stupid,' Minister Li's wife said. 'You were bought to serve the minister.'

Damson went again that evening, but the gates to Minister Li's courtyard were shut. She knocked, but his servant hissed at her to go away. However, Minister Li's wife refused to stay away and pushed her way into his room. 'She's made a fool of you,' she told him. 'The whole city is laughing at you.'

Minister Li pulled the pillow over his ears but she dragged it from him.

'They're all saying you're paying for what you used to have for nothing.'

Despite all the attentions of the women, Minister Li refused to eat, refused to get up. By the third day his cheek-bones protruded and his skin had turned a dull yellow. His wife came to him that night and held him. She tended him day and night, had the steward bring choice delicacies for him to eat, burnt incense in the temple, prayed for her husband's recovery.

One night Damson tried to kill herself by running into the wall of her courtyard. Her maid started screeching and all the servants hurried to hold her back, but she had split her scalp and blood splattered the soil like raindrops. A doctor was summoned, and prescribed herbs and rest.

No one spoke of the event to Minister Li, in case it should sadden him. When friends came to visit, Minister

Li's wife showed them into his room. Day by day he was weaned off his addictive sadness. When the Upright Magistrate came to him, he brought a packet of Longjing Tea and told the servants to draw water from the north well – it had the sweetest taste.

'Lily has bewitched you,' he told Minister Li. 'I will have her beaten.'

But Minister Li looked up. 'Please don't,' he said, and after that the Upright Magistrate avoided the topic. The year was nearly ended: they talked of the reforms of the new Emperor, the campaign to reassert control over the outlying provinces, the rice harvest.

After the Upright Magistrate had left, Minister Li asked for someone to sing to him and his wife summoned a sing-song girl from the Hamlets.

'Is Damson sick?'

'No,' Minister Li's wife said. 'She's no longer with the family.'

In the week before Spring Festival there were blue auroras in the night sky. The next day it snowed and then the snow melted and everyone wondered what this would mean for the year ahead.

A week later Minister Li went to his first banquet of the year, flirted with a courtesan and she flirted back. The next day he sent a poem and she sent one in reply, and on the fourth night after meeting he sent her a golden hairpin, was sent an invitation in return.

'Where did you go last night?' Minister Li's wife asked.

'I went to the House of Blossoming Petals.'

'Thank Heaven!' she said. 'I was so worried.'

When that affair failed, Minister Li began another. For the Double Second Festival, his wife bought another concubine called Peach, who was only thirteen years old. She was meek and mild and so young and pretty that Minister Li loved to show her off to all his friends. He took her to every banquet, and the men all praised her fragile beauty with poems – spring bud, morning dew, as brief as the winter frost.

When one man mentioned a poem of Lily's, Minister Li dismissed her. 'Lily? She's as wrinkly as old dofu.'

Whenever he heard her name Minister Li made another jibe. 'She's been nibbled by so many men there's nothing left of her.'

'It must be like riding an old mule – so many others have been there before!'

No one wanted to tell him what a fool he was making of himself, so Minister Li remained oblivious. 'Lily who?' he laughed.

Three young scholars came to visit me today and they reminded me of how long it had been since I last saw Pung An. Secretary Yen sent his sedan over for me and I stayed the night with him. How strange that we live in a world where a woman's beauty is over by the age of twenty. I turned twenty-four this year and felt like an autumn flower – dry and brittle.

One by one leaves fall with the dusk rain.
Plucking strings I sing to myself,
letting go of feelings for my thoughtless friend.
Contemplating life's bitter waves.

Rich carriages clatter up to my door,
but studying philosophy, books pile up on my pillows.
I'll keep wearing ragged clothes till I'm taken to
    heaven.
Blue water, green mountains when I've passed away.

Minister Li's taunts took a while to reach her, but eventually Lily heard them all – and worse: the ones he had never made.

'The dogfucker!' Lily said, with all the fury of spitting oil. She felt like some cheap slut tricked into bed with hollow promises, carefully put her peony vase back on its stand. That afternoon Lily and Fragrant Blossom dressed in men's turbans and trousers, led a few other courtesans out into the streets to see the cherry blossoms. A large crowd followed, staring at the women who did not have husbands or fathers to keep them at home as if they were fantastic animals – beautiful and expensive and available for hire.

'Oh – here is my old husband's house,' Lily called, and the flock of beauties stood around and laughed. The gates were shut – but they didn't have to be open for the neighbours to overhear. 'He has such unnatural desires,' Lily told them. 'I couldn't stay.'

'Is that why you ran away with the ugliest man in the empire?' Fragrant Blossom asked and all the girls laughed.

A few days later Minister Li received a heavy silk packet, scented with jasmine. He untied the ribbons that held it shut and pulled aside each flap of cloth; wondered if it was a gift from someone petitioning for official attention, told himself he would report them to the Upright Magistrate.

Inside there were two gold ingots.

My dear husband,
It was six years ago that you bought me as a concubine.
I have decided to buy my freedom. I advise you to treat your next concubine with more care. Why

plant a pretty flower in your garden to watch it wither and die? Better to leave them growing wild; they look so pretty on the mountainside, don't you think?

Lily knew that Minister Li would be unable to resist the temptation to have the last word, but it was not until the sunset drumroll that she heard a knock on her gate, her maid's voice, the sound of footsteps across the yard to her door and Lily felt a thrill of expectation – such as she had once felt when she was about to see him.

She snatched the letter from her maid, ripped it open.

Courtesan Yu Xuanji,
Daughter of Scholar Yu, fourth-grade official in the Ministry of Roads and Transport.
    I suggest you send the money to your parents. Two ingots of gold seems little recompense for the shame, disgust and dishonour you have caused them.

Regards,
Li Zian

Lily clapped her hands in malicious delight. The next day she and Fragrant Blossom were drunk and decided to take their sedans back to Minister Li's house. They drank more wine on the way; when their sedans had been set down in the street outside Peach Blossom Palace they picked up stones and clods of dirt and tossed them over his wall.

'Your concubine is here!' Lily shouted. 'Come and take your concubine! Come save her parents from shame and disgust!'

Minister Li was not at home that day, but his wife sat and listened to the noise outside as mud rained down into the front courtyard.

'Throw open the gates and have the bitch beaten,' she told the servants, but Lily threatened to steal their virility if they so much as touched her gown, and the men stood around, uncertain. Minister Li's wife took a broom but the steward kowtowed in front of her and begged her to stop.

'The neighbours will only laugh at you. Please do not go out there. She will curse us all!'

Minister Li's wife stayed inside and was speechless with fury. If I wasn't Minister Li's wife I would go outside and thrash her, she told herself, as an empty wine pot flew over the wall. She would make a complaint to the magistrates, have the woman's white buttocks beaten. The thick bamboo, she thought to herself, and sent a servant to Upright Magistrate's yamen, paid the neighbours to go and testify on her behalf.

The Upright Magistrate sent out his wardens to arrest Lily. They dragged her to the cells, left her there overnight to sober up. Fragrant Blossom came to the yamen and made such a commotion that they threatened to arrest her too.

Lily tried to keep herself warm by covering herself with straw, but by morning she had barely slept. Soon she was bound and dragged to the yamen. The Upright Magistrate regarded her like a beaten animal: tethered, toothless, cowed.

'There are no signs of delusion or insanity,' he dictated. 'The defendant is sound of hearing. Shows deep remorse.'

He proceeded with a casual air, thinking about the sentence he would give. There were many punishments available to the Upright Magistrate for public disorder: filling the ears with mud, hanging by the hair, pouring vinegar into the nostrils, inserting bamboo slivers under the fingernails – but he was aware of her powerful bene- factors, cleared his throat and announced, 'Conclusions!'

There was a hush of silence as the Upright Magistrate

read out the sentence: 'On account of all I have heard, I sentence Courtesan Yu Huilan, formerly concubine of Minister Li Zian, to ten strokes with the thin rod and three days in a cangue.'

Even though the officer of the bamboo did not use his whole strength, Lily screamed when the first blow landed on her bare thighs; her forehead started to drip sweat. When the ten blows had been counted out, Fragrant Blossom rushed across to help her stand. Lily almost fainted as the cangue was fitted round her neck and wrists, the heavy wooden board held her wrists at shoulder level. She had to be helped out of the yamen, but the guards would not let her climb into her sedan: they made her walk all the way home, the flesh on the back of her thighs striped with ten livid welts. Passers-by laughed and threw eggs, tomatoes and stones; a stream of children ran behind, trying to slap her legs to see if she would scream.

Fragrant Blossom beat them back but every so often one got through and Lily gasped with agony. Sometimes she stumbled and was unable to catch herself – she fell forward, the cangue jolting her neck.

While the welts cooled and stung less, the cangue was so large it made even the simplest tasks impossible. Lily's maid undressed and washed her, and cleaned the cangue as well; removed the dirt and vegetable filth from Lily's hair. She dabbed vinegar on the welts, combed her hair and dressed it for an evening out; helped her into a fine red gown of thick patterned silk.

'Are you sure you want to go out?' Fragrant Blossom asked.

'Oh yes,' Lily said. 'I want you to write something for me.'

Fragrant Blossom wrote out a placard 'Concubine of Minister Li Zian', and then Lily went out with her maid in tow, parading herself through the Northern and Southern Hamlets. People she had never met invited Lily to their banquets.

'My husband,' she told them all, 'needs the magistrates to punish his naughty concubine!'

But he had divorced her, Minister Li's friends desperately asserted, but no one listened: when there was scandal, no one cared about the truth.

———————

Lily had the gates of her courtyard thrown open and continued her life as if nothing had happened. On the third day she could sit without pain; friends and admirers came to visit, and laughed as Lily showed them she could balance a wine cup on the edge of the cangue and tilt it to her mouth without the help of her maid. They took it in turns to feed her. She even treated Secretary Yen to a night of pleasure, playing games of submission: naughty concubine, locked in a cangue, unable to resist.

'It seems you have made a public spectacle of yourself,' the Upright Magistrate lectured when she went to have the cangue removed. 'If you continue like this I will have you beaten and deformed.'

The Upright Magistrate had a man he had punished brought into the room to show her what he meant. The man's ears and nose had been cut off to reveal two gaping nostrils. Even though the eyes blinked and he breathed through the holes in his face, Lily had the strange feeling that she was looking at a skull.

* * *

Lily did not go to Minister Li's house again, confined her activities to her household and the Hamlets. Even so, it was impossible for her not to comment when the name of Minister Li came up in conversation.

'Ignore her,' the Upright Magistrate advised Minister Li again, and Minister Li nodded. 'Robbers don't just get meat, they also get punished,' the Upright Magistrate assured him.

'I feel everyone is laughing at me.'

'Not now,' the Upright Magistrate told him. 'Now they respect you.'

Despite her notoriety, it was only three weeks after her beating that Lily was invited to a breakfast banquet at the house of Du Muli, the Sage of Poets.

'What should I wear?' she asked Fragrant Blossom, and picked out a lotus-green gown.

'That's no good,' Fragrant Blossom said, and Lily found another one, adjusted her hairpins, but Fragrant Blossom still frowned. 'They're too gaudy,' she said. 'You're going to write poems, not be the evening's decoration.'

Lily pouted at herself in the mirror, and Fragrant Blossom recombed and dressed her hair in a simple style, reminiscent of the virgin knots unmarried women wore. 'There!' she said. 'How could anyone resist you now?'

Lily hired a sedan for the afternoon to take her to the house of the Sage of Poets. She told the men the name of the street, but they walked along there and saw nothing that might be the house of anyone of note, sage or not.

'Sage of Poets?' a passer-by said. 'Never heard of him.'

They went a little further and stopped again.

'Are you sure he lives in this ward?' another man asked.

They repeated the directions they were given.

'You mean Du Muli?' he said. 'He lives down there. Third house on the west, with the thatched roof.'

Lily told her bearers to follow the man's directions, but when she stopped to check with another passer-by they said the same thing: 'Du Muli, in the thatched cottage.'

The house in question had no courtyard: the front door opened directly on to the street.

Lily stepped out of the sedan and hoped that it was not too ostentatious. She knocked and pushed inside. The door creaked shut behind her. The room was empty, except for a kang, a stove and a worn bookshelf with panels of lacquer.

There were voices from the backyard so Lily stepped outside into a small garden, four plots divided by a raised walkway. In one melons sprouted; another had lines of seedlings, and there were what looked like miniature bak choy in another – but the soil of the fourth had been recently hoed and a table had been set up, at which five old men sat talking and laughing.

'Du Muli?' Lily asked, and one of the old men nodded. Lily raised her skirts and tiptoed between the seedlings.

'Please,' the sage said, 'take a seat. We were just discussing whether poetry had any value or not.' He did not seem to be joking.

'It is one of the most important things in life,' Lily frowned.

The sage raised his white eyebrows, surprised. 'Is it?' he said.

'Yes,' Lily said, and found herself blushing.

'Why do you think so?' a man with a thin wrinkled face asked.

'Because . . .' Lily began, and didn't know how to finish.

'I suppose it gives one a voice,' a man said.

'It does,' Lily said.

'And marks moments for posterity.'

Lily looked from one man to another as they spoke, wondered if this was some strange test. When they had all offered suggestions they turned back to her. 'It is stronger than any Daoist elixir,' she said. The Sage of Poets tilted his head, as if none of his guests had ever claimed such a value. 'Any man's life is mapped out by the poems he writes,' she said, 'as stars make up a constellation.'

No one reacted and Lily began to feel stupid. 'There was a screen I used to own,' she tried again, 'on which a hermit and his concubine sat drinking in a hut while a storm was about to overwhelm them. Not only does poetry mark moments between friends or lovers, like that painting, it captures in words the essence of life.'

The men nodded politely. Then the Sage of Poets poured them all a cup of wine. 'We must thank Mistress Lily for her observations,' one of the old men said. Lily smiled so hard her face stiffened.

'Poetry, my dear,' the sage said, and Lily remembered the old man who had put his hand on her thigh. 'These vegetables are poetry. This leaking thatched roof is poetry – even,' he smiled, 'this cup of wine.'

The men laughed and congratulated him as if he had told some great joke, and Lily forced a brief laugh. She was nervous throughout the meal, ate little, made conversation with the man next to her.

After the meal had been cleared away and everyone had drunk enough wine to remove inhibition, the sage announced that it was time to compose.

Lily felt a trickle of sweat run down the small of her back.

'The topic tonight is "Selling Peonies".'

Lily thought of the painting by Xu Xi. When it was her turn the men's faces were kind and encouraging. She began to chant:

Facing the wind I sigh
as the petals keep falling,
their perfume fading
with the passing spring.

Flowers like these should command
a high price, but there's no one to buy them.
Their perfume is so rich,
it even scares the butterflies.

These exquisite buds
will only open in the palace.
Green foliage like theirs
would be ruined by the dusty roads.

But noble lords, if you wait for these flowers
to be transplanted to the Imperial Gardens
even you will come to regret
that you have no way to buy them.

There was silence when she finished. Lily lowered her
eyes and saw a slug crawling under a lettuce leaf.

When the banquet was over and Lily got up to leave,
Du Muli shook her hand and thanked her.

'I think you might not like my kind of poetry,' she said,
but he kept hold of her hand.

'We do not invent poetry, it invents us,' he told her.

When she had heard the whole story, Fragrant Blossom
told Lily how well she had done.

'But no one said anything.'

'They were master poets,' she told Lily. 'They were
not going to stand and clap like the drunks out in the
Hamlets.'

Lily was unconvinced, and when the Double Fifth Festival came without another invitation from the Sage of Poets, she sank into a gloom that the bright spring rain could not lift.

It was a week after the Double Fifth that Lily realised she had not had her period. She didn't know whether to be nervous or excited, remembered what had happened to her last pregnancy, told herself that she was not to imagine the baby till it was born. Another period passed, and when Fragrant Blossom gave her a bowl of pork broth, Lily smelt mushrooms and was unable to eat.

'They're only small,' Fragrant Blossom said and picked them all out, but Lily's appetite had gone.

'I'm pregnant,' she said at last.

'You're not!'

'I am!'

'Who's the father?'

'Secretary Yen.'

'You're sure?'

'Of course,' Lily said. 'Who else could it be?'

'You know!'

'I wouldn't give him the pleasure.'

When Lily told Secretary Yen that she was pregnant he clapped his hands and sent his servants running for food and wine. That night Scholar Yu was in the Hamlets with some other men from the Ministry of Roads and Transport when he saw Lily at a table with Secretary Yen and some other aristocrats. He barely recognised her at first, tried not to draw his friends' attention, but such was the crowd that had gathered to hear her compose it was impossible.

385

'Who is that over there?' one of his friends asked.

'Secretary Yen,' another man said, 'with Abbot Wang and Prince Gudu.'

Scholar Yu poured them all another cup of wine and they sat and talked Ministry of Roads and Transport business for a little longer. Then there was a burst of applause and the men with him turned to look and one of the men asked a servant,

'What's happening over there?'

'It's Yu Xuanji,' he said. 'She's composing.'

'Let's go and listen!' one man said, and only Scholar Yu held back.

'I'm tired,' he said.

'You're getting old.'

'I do feel it,' Scholar Yu admitted. He walked to the door, and turned for a moment to hear his daughter compose, before a hushed crowd, on the theme of autumn and soldiers sent to the grasslands:

> On the mountain slopes
> young chrysanthemums
> are drenched in red
> by the sunset light.
>
> A chill wind
> shivers the green trees
> and plaintive music
> is played on the red strings.
>
> A lonely wife makes
> winter clothes
> for the conscript soldier
> beyond the Wall.

Wild geese fly,
fish swim through water:
and carry their thoughts
across the miles.

Scholar Yu shut the door behind him as the men clapped and shouted. The noise was muffled as he turned for home: he remembered Diyi, the day he had taken a mule to Wang Family Village, paid Old Fart thirty strings of cash.

'That's not a very pretty name,' he'd said to her that day, and the little girl had swung her shoulders from side to side.

'I'll call you Little Flower,' he had said, and Little Flower had nodded.

———

In the summer of 871, there was news of a rebellion in the south, which was quickly crushed: the leaders were executed, the supporters scattered. Elsewhere peasants plucked mulberry leaves, ploughed the fields, herded their sheep into the hills. In the planting and ploughing season Heaven was kind: the rains were generous.

Lily listened to the distant rumble of devastation as if it were nothing more than gossip in the marketplace. Her stomach swelled, the nausea passed, the sleepiness lifted. Secretary Yen treated her with the utmost respect and honour and Lily told herself that honour and respect were worth more than passion.

They were sitting in the afternoon shade when a servant came to say that there was a visitor at the door.

'A male visitor,' the girl said.

'Who is it?'

The servant came back flustered. 'He says his name is Wen Tingyun.'

'Show him in,' Lily said. 'Can we please have him shown in?'

Secretary Yen paused for a moment and Lily touched his shoulder.

'It was only a little affair,' she said, 'and I only want to see how ugly he has become.'

Lily waddled forward to welcome Tingyun. There was a livid red scar on his left cheek, and a piece of his right ear appeared to have been bitten off.

'Well, they certainly made a mess of your face,' the secretary said, pouring the old poet some wine.

Tingyun drank three cups and tried to summon up some amusing stories, but Lily's pregnant belly seemed to distract him.

At long last Secretary Yen shook his head. 'You are wasting your life,' he said. 'I am nothing but a stupid, illiterate man, but you are clever and talented, and have wasted the gifts that Heaven has given you.'

Tingyun did not respond, but soon afterwards he got up to leave. The farewells were short. Lily watched him walk away with relief, wondering if she'd ever see him again.

It was a few days later that she heard Wen Tingyun had been arrested by the Upright Magistrate for abusing the Emperor. She called her maid and set off with food and provisions, took a deep breath when she remembered the last time she had been to the yamen. The closer she got, the more the memory of the man deformed by the Upright Magistrate troubled her. She wished that she had worn a veil or a scarf to hide her face, asked the sedan bearers to stop a little way off.

Lily watched the yamen gates: people came and went, and after some time she saw the Upright Magistrate's wagon come out and turn north along the avenue. The sedan bearers took her on to the gates.

'I've brought some food for Wen Tingyun,' Lily said to the guards.

'Wen Tingyun?' the man said, and turned to his list. 'He's gone.'

'Are you sure?'

'Left this morning.'

'Where to?'

'He's been exiled to his hometown.'

'I've brought him food and clothes,' she said.

The man didn't know what he could do.

'Can I give it to the others?' Lily asked.

Lily went along the line of cells, handing food through the bamboo bars. 'Ten thousand blessings!' one man said, an old woman pressed her face against the bamboo bars and clutching hands reached out and tried to grab Lily as she passed.

'Daughter!' she hissed. 'Are you my daughter?!'

'No,' Lily said, and tried to hold in her revulsion as the grimy fingers grasped her clothing.

'Where have you been?' the woman's voice called after her. 'I waited for you.'

'I'm not your daughter,' Lily said, but the woman kept calling to her.

Lily stopped for a moment and went back. The woman was lying on the floor of the cell. She stank of sweat and urine, but Lily stepped closer.

'Mother Hua?' she called. The woman did not move. Lily tried again, but the old woman did not move.

————

Wen Tingyun's hometown was a thousand li away, near Taiyuanfu. A government goader was sent to accompany

389

the criminal to the Magistrate of Taiyuanfu's jurisdiction. He had just come back from a year's walk to Yunnan and back. He swore and cursed as he collected the appropriate papers, couldn't believe that he was being sent to the other end of the empire. He collected the prisoner, bound and gagged, with a sign round his neck that the goader could not read.

'Come on!' he ordered, but Wen Tingyun came on too slowly and was cuffed around the back of the head. 'I'm not in a good mood!' the goader warned Tingyun, made him kneel by the side of the road as a tinker sharpened the point of his walking-stick.

When he had bargained over the cost of the job, the goader waved the sharp point under Tingyun's nose. 'Just in case you give me any difficulties,' he said, and prodded Tingyun like a farmyard animal. 'Ya!' he joked, and the people in the street laughed. 'Ya! Ya!' he repeated, and grinned at the crowd. Man-in-charge-of-prisoner! It was good to be in control. As long as you didn't mind the walking, he told himself, and he had grown up on a barge, so he was used to it. He missed the smell of the water sometimes, missed the unsteady wobble of the boat. 'Ya!' he shouted, and waved to the soldiers as he passed through the city gate. 'Ya! Ya!'

Tingyun couldn't even get his hands together to clap out a poem; when he tried to tell the man a story he was prodded. 'Prisoner is not to speak!' the man commanded, and when Tingyun tried to tell him a joke the goader used the sash of his belt to gag him. 'I can tell you're going to be trouble,' he said to the silent prisoner, as he tied the knot at the back of his head. As he admired the gag it occurred to him that he could add to his joke by making it look like a halter. He imagined putting a ring through the prisoner's nose and pulling him along like a bull. Maybe he'd save that for later in the trip: that would be funny! Prisoner with nose-ring! He's ugly enough for a nose-ring, the goader thought.

On the second day Tingyun was exhausted: his arms ached, his mouth was dry, his tongue swollen. His legs ached where he had been stabbed with the end of the stick. When he tried to lie down he was prodded and kicked; when he tried running he was caught and prodded and kicked.

In the end Tingyun tried weeping, but the goader shouted, 'Ya! Ya!' to get him moving. Tingyun rolled around in the dirt unable to avoid the thrusts of the stick. He tried to kowtow and beg for the smallest kindness. 'I am Wen Tingyun,' he wanted to say, 'former chief examiner of the civil service exams. We could sleep in every manor house from here to Taiyuanfu. Untie me!' he begged. 'Untie me – let me talk to you.' But all the goader heard were muffled noises; all he saw was a beast that refused to get up and walk.

'Ya!' he shouted, hit and prodded, wrenched the halter so violently that the beast stood up and stumbled forward.

It was within sight of the Yellow River that Tingyun lay down and refused to move any further. The goader prodded his legs and feet, kicked and punched him. 'I don't want to walk to Taiyuanfu any more than you,' he shouted, 'but you're going to even if I have to drag you.' He prodded harder and harder till the end of his stick was stained. At one point his stick went in so deep he had to stop and pull it out. Tingyun wailed and screamed into his gag, but the goader kept prodding even after the old man's trousers were slick with blood and he had stopped yelping. When Tingyun stopped moving the goader kicked him.

'Get up!' he shouted. 'Get up, you ugly old bastard!'

I am an ugly old bastard, Tingyun thought, as he drifted in and out of consciousness. I *am* an ugly old bastard! I am Wen Tingyun! a voice in his head said. I am Wen Tingyun! The voice laughed, still laughing and laughing. It was so good to not be chained and gagged in pain. I am Wen Tingyun the poet, the ugly poet, the voice laughed, till a kick twisted his head to an unnatural angle and the muffled moaning stopped.

The death of Wen Tingyun did not surprise anyone. He had long since slipped from being famous for his poetry to being famous for his lifestyle and ugliness.

Wen Tingyun dead? they thought, turned to more interesting gossip.

The night Lily heard she could not sleep, but imagined one last meal with him, when he told all his funniest stories; afterwards he played the flute and she sang all his most famous poems.

The same night Minister Li was with Peach in the Southern Hamlet. He looked out of the open window to the lantern-lit street and raised his cup in silent tribute. Tingyun, he thought, and drank the wine in one long gulp.

As that summer slipped into memory the leaves curled up and died. The first were lamented with lines of poetry, but after a while people stopped caring. There were thousands of dead leaves littering the streets, floating in the canal water, drifting into doorways. No one could write a poem for each of them.

Lily's waters broke on a cold winter's afternoon. Her labour lasted seven hours and by nightfall the room stank of hot blood; her low moans mixed with quiet encouragement and at last the sound of a baby's first choking breath.

'I'm going to call him Joyful Hope,' Lily told Fragrant Blossom.

Fragrant Blossom watched the baby suckling from Lily's breast and squeezed her hand.

'Do you think Minister Li knows?'

'I don't know,' Fragrant Blossom said.

The days and weeks after the birth of Joyful Hope were filled with feeding and bathing and burping and putting to sleep. Joyful Hope broke each night's sleep, and Lily spent more and more time alone at her house; Secretary Yen came during the day to see his son.

'He looks like you,' he said to Lily.

'You think so?'

But when the sun began to set Secretary Yen always had some appointment.

Secretary Yen came to visit today and we sat and drank many cups of wine. Fragrant Blossom came round with another pot. I remember the days when there was nothing to do but drink and laugh; and now I am a mother and all I seem to do is clean and bathe and feed my baby. I thought I would miss my younger days, but I would never go back. I am happier now than I have ever been.

When Pung An was in the capital he came to visit Lily, and was surprised by how much prettier she was than he had remembered her. They drank a few cups of wine, talked of his life and of hers.

I showed him Joyful Hope. He was asleep, but as we stood and watched he opened his eyes and stretched out his arms. Pung An nicknamed him Old Buddha since he seemed so wise and calm, and Joyful Hope stretched out his hand to Uncle An, held his finger

393

very tight. I gave him a poem I had written for him in the summer. He tried to give me an ounce of silver but I refused it.

He said he had heard about me from many of his friends, who laughed when they thought that they had known me before I became famous. I do not care for fame any more; all I wish for in life is content-ment.

> Dashing red and purple,
> the clatter of official carriages
> fills the streets.
>
> Walking behind
> my crude wicker gate
> I chance upon a poem:
>
> these white flowers,
> so undeserving
> of my poor verses.
>
> In my tender life,
> the thirst for company
> has passed,
>
> pine trees are content
> to live their lives
> on high mountain slopes.

AD 907

Minister Li did not recover consciousness again.

Minister Li's wife clung to her prayer beads when she saw him lying in bed, thin neck, bony head. Gloom hung over the household, even though the spring sunlight cast sharp dark shadows across the courtyards and gardens.

That night Fang and Swallow lay in bed together and watched the moon rise in their window. The breeze cast strange shadows, made the gates creak and rattle.

'Did you hear that?' Swallow hissed.

'It's just the wind,' Fang said, but Swallow's nails dug into his arm.

'No, it was something else.'

Fang kept stroking her hair, but only after they had made love did Swallow sleep. She dreamt of a bridal procession, three steps forward and one back, the bride sitting upright and still, her hair coiled tightly round her head, her skin rotted away, the sockets rotten and black and empty where once eyes had smiled.

AD *872*

In the ninth month of the year 872, Court Astronomer Wang walked out into his yard to breathe the cool evening air, noticed something strange in the south-eastern sky. At first he thought it was the glare of a fire, but as it rose higher he saw it was eggshell-white.

Court Astronomer Wang stood on tiptoe and heard his wife's laughter as she cleared the dishes. One of his daughters started singing. He heard his wife shushing her as he put a hand to the pear tree to steady himself. The bark was rough. It left a green-brown smear on his palm.

As the star rose it dragged a sword-shaped tail behind it: there was no mistaking that it had a tail. Astronomer Wang blinked and peered again. No mistaking it at all, he thought as he bit his lip and tugged at his beard, twisted the hairs of his moustache into a braid. No mistaking it at all.

Astronomer Wang estimated the length of the tail and the direction in which it was pointed, then fluttered out of his gate to the Temple of the Bamboo Sages, gathering his robes behind him. Stay calm, he told himself, repeating the measurements he had made in case he forgot them; it wasn't far.

Wang saw a colleague running down the street ahead of him and called, but the other man didn't hear. He was sweating as he turned into the courtyard, went to look for the Director of Astronomy – but he was nowhere to be seen. He looked for the Vice-Director, the Inscriber of Imperial Fortunes – but none of them was there.

Court Astronomer Wang felt he should assume responsibility: he could hear Secretary Yen shouting in his ear, 'Stupid donkey! Educated fool! What do you mean you didn't know the comet was supposed to rise?' A bead of sweat tickled as it ran down from his armpit over the soft skin on his side. It felt like a snake curling down his ribs towards his trousers. He rubbed his arm against himself to wipe it away.

'Fellow scholars!' Wang called out, and the feverish debates silenced. Thirty faces turned to listen. 'Fellow scholars,' he began again, 'we must find a precedent here. We must examine the records and find a precedent.'

Order seemed to assert itself and the men hurried to the rear courtyard where a library of stones stood in silent ranks. The stones were carved with the records of previous dynasties, each as tall as a man.

Candles were lit and handed round. The light was ghostly inside the white paper lanterns. Shadows danced, strange and lurid. The stones seemed to exhale cool cave air. Astronomer Wang's breath puffed like smoke before his face, but under his robes he was still sweating as he rubbed lichen from an old cracked stone, and consulted the words of long-dead men. Not that one, he thought, and moved to another, holding his lantern up so that he could see. Not that one, not that one either, as he counted his way along the line. At the

397

fifth stone he bent low towards his own shadow and peered at the words.

'This is it!' someone shouted, sounding almost surprised to have found the right stone. 'From the reign of Han Emperor Guang Wudi,' the man called. '"On Celestial Phenomena".'

Astronomer Wang winced as he stood up and hurried over. Yes, it was the relevant stone. They huddled round it to read the description of the star and the events that it had foretold. When they extrapolated all this information to the present day they consulted the charts, wrote down their forecast in vermilion ink and rushed it over to the palace. Despite the curfew, the city guard did not try to stop them.

The palace lay at the northern end of the Avenue of Heaven. The high walls stretched away to left and right as far as they could see, no breeze to fill the banners, torches set at regular intervals. The astronomers stood around in a nervous and guilty crowd. No one wanted responsibility for bringing bad news. In front of them the brass-studded gates were closed, the walls silent. They knocked and shouted. At last a doorway in the gate opened and a hair-less hand thrust out of the shadows; made Court Astronomer Wang jump. He put the scroll into the hand, then the door shut.

The astronomers didn't know if they were supposed to wait. Was that it? Had they all come here for no reason?

'Hello?' one called, but the walls were silent. They knocked again: nothing, so they hurried away across the street to watch from the shadows.

While they waited the younger men heard singing: it sounded like a fairy from Heaven, and Court Astronomer Wang imagined one of the Emperor's fairies: hair like clouds, willow-waisted, as beautiful as Yang Guifei. The

398

singing stopped and a woman laughed: sharp, dangerous shards of laughter. It made them all flinch – even the old men. Heaven is not kind.

'It's cold,' Court Astronomer Wang said, stamping his feet and rubbing his hands.

Just before dawn, the palace gates opened and Court Astronomer Wang woke with a start, as if he had been plunged into cold water. He tried to stand but his knees were stiff and he winced as one gave way beneath him, tumbling him to the ground. He propped himself up with one hand as a single horseman, dressed in imperial robes, rode out of the palace gates.

'What shall we do?' one man asked when the sound of hoofs had faded from earshot.

They all looked to Court Astronomer Wang. 'We should go home and wait for news.'

'Shouldn't one of us stay here?' one man asked.

'No,' Wang said, 'we should all go home.'

They bent their beards to each other in a respectful bow and set off on their individual paths home – but Court Astronomer Wang went to Secretary Yen's house, knocked and waited.

Secretary Yen summoned the astronomer inside, did not shout, asked him to explain how the predictions were misread.

'I do not know,' Astronomer Wang told him. 'We took all the signs. We referenced all the records.'

Secretary Yen dismissed the man. The predictions had been corrected; there was no damage done.

That might have been the end of the matter if torrential rains had not destroyed the wheat crop in Hexi and Hedong Province. Wheat that was not battered flat rotted in the fields, and the administration creaked as vast quantities of rice were shipped to the north to alleviate famine. But even though the rains stopped, the waters of the Yellow River kept rising, swirling and hungry. Orders were sent out to raise the dykes, but years of corruption and neglect had taken their toll: the dykes could not keep the river in the skies for ever. The thick water swamped the land, washed villages and towns away. Of the cities of Pingli and Zuzhou, it was said that only the brick pagodas remained.

The spring of 873 began with a terrible storm from the north, bringing snow and cold in the middle of spring. In all the forts of the north the soldiers hid in their guard rooms, let the winds fly south.

It was said that the winds carried all the ghosts of conscripts sent to the grasslands. Prayers were said and incense was burnt but there had been so many wars, so many unburied ghosts, so many years of expansion that not all of them could be assuaged. They tossed the heavy grey tiles up into the air, threw them down into the street; tore off branches; bent trees to the ground. Even the Emperor in his palace was unable to sleep. He listened to the wind and heard voices taunt and provoke him. 'Come out and play,' they jeered. 'Come out and play with those who fought your wars!'

The Emperor could not face insubordination from the ghosts of his soldiers. He leapt out of bed, threw open his doors and started shouting and swearing. 'Sons of turtles!' he screamed into the winds. 'Sons of turtles! Just wait till I appear in Heaven,' he shouted, words lost in the storm. 'You will all be punished!'

The ghosts took no notice of either prayers or insults. And the ghost of a long-dead marshal led his men through the gardens of the palace, danced with the willows, waving their arms, shaking their hair and whistling with pleasure.

The people of the capital did not dare leave their houses till the storm had exhausted itself. Then they pushed open their doors and walked about the city, counting the uprooted cherry and plum trees. The storm damage was severe, but the mandarins were in control; the Emperor was safe.

The next day the air was deathly still; a thick mist rose from the canals and walked through the streets of the capital unopposed. It curled curious tendrils down the streets; it swallowed the stars and turned the night milky black. Windows were shut, bolts drawn, and behind closed windows an evening meal of rumours was served up: the passes were still open; the Emperor was dying; the Emperor was dead.

Lily sat alone in her courtyard with Joyful Hope, under the waves of mist, thought back to her meal with the Sage of Poets.

Secretary Yen had fallen in love with a girl he had seen in the Hamlets, and was entertaining her at his manor.

Scholar Yu and his wife lay in bed; Scholar Yu's wife kept thinking of the comet, of all the evil omens it predicted, not worrying for the empire as much as for her daughter and Joyful Hope.

Scholar Yu dreamt he was standing on the Large Wild Goose Pagoda watching the moon rise over the capital gates. He then seemed to shift position and watched the moon and its reflection meet at the far edge of the waters of the North Lake, sinking into each other and disappearing completely. There was a strange succession of images: the Emperor's sandalwood barge floating low in the water; a pair of cranes standing side by side; two mandarin ducks floating together. Scholar Yu woke for a moment and wondered if he was having some kind of prophetic dream. The cranes and ducks meant fidelity; he wasn't sure what the rest of it meant. With fidelity in mind he wrapped his arms round his wife.

As they slept, the moon rose and set. Night crawled back under the stones, and the mist shrank back to the canals. The dawn light found barges of rice floating fat on their reflections. They had made their way north despite the storm, and now they sat low in the water, tied nose to tail like mountain donkeys. Their masters slept on the decks as a thunder roll from Drum Tower declared the next day had arrived. As it ended, the gates of the palace creaked open and an imperial runner dashed out into the half-dark.

The Upright Magistrate was at his desk early. He leafed through a few documents and sat back. There was another letter about the provinces of Hebei and Shannan: the governors refused to pay their taxes to the government. His eyes flicked across a few lines, then he put a hand to his head and massaged his temples.

The Upright Magistrate tried to enjoy the quiet, but the minute the yamen doors were reopened his troubles returned. Getting in early gave him time to work; time and peace and quiet. He heard the back door of the hall open, footsteps came closer. His manservant shuffled out of the gloom.

'Your Honour,' the man said, put a scroll on the desk in front of him. It bore the imperial seal: nine dragons all intertwined.

The Upright Magistrate looked at the scroll and the draught goosepimpled his arms. 'Go back to bed,' he told his servant, who yawned as he shuffled back to the door.

The Upright Magistrate took a deep breath, shook his head. Another one, he thought, and pushed back his sleeves over his wrists and up his arms.

The Upright Magistrate turned the scroll over in his hands, ran a thumb down the crease and unrolled it. 'Notice of the fourteenth day of the ninth moon of the fourth year of the Emperor Wuzong by the Commissioner of Good Works on the Streets of the West Side, Liu Chen,' the subscript read. The wording was familiar so the Upright Magistrate's eyes flicked down, looking for the name. Hmm! He smiled and picked a piece of meat from between his front teeth. It would make Minister Li happy: the stamps were all in order. He started to yawn; reread the arrest warrant; gave it life with his scarlet seal; left it on his desk; reached for his bell. His secretary could handle the rest.

Secretary Yen slept well that night. If he had any dreams he did not remember them, but woke with a full bladder and a half-erection. He held it in his hand as he grunted and climbed out of bed and walked to the chamber pot in the corner of the room. His new girl murmured something as he came back to bed – she held out her hand for him. He took it as he climbed in, enclosed her in his arms.

Secretary Yen and his girl dozed, all arms and legs and groin and buttocks. They were lying together when the doors of the hall flew open. All Secretary Yen saw were the puffing faces of the Imperial Wrestlers. Time twisted like a rope: everything happened in slow motion and he couldn't move to stop it. He heard the girl moan: it struck him as a strange sound to make. A thousand reasons and questions all argued in his head. The Wrestlers grabbed him, lifted him up as he was, half naked. They grabbed the girl as well. He was shouting and she was screaming. Everything was happening very fast now. Secretary Yen swore at them. His bluster had no effect but he kept shouting: it felt better than being silent.

* * *

403

The Imperial Wrestlers continued ransacking Secretary Yen's palace till a large crowd had gathered at the gates. The city guard held them back with lashes of their bamboo canes. The Wrestlers gathered up their loads and marched back through the streets, bundles in their hairy arms: a rolled carpet, a kicking girl, an expensive vase, a bundle of scrolls.

When they reached the hall of the Upright Magistrate each item was placed carefully in the courtyard and diligently listed. Each Wrestler was paid and the prisoners were carried to the Palace for Supreme Justice, where the doors of the prisons stood open and hungry and waiting. Any missing male relatives of the Secretary were harvested from the streets. Secretary Yen was taken for questioning.

As soon as Scholar Yu heard what had happened he rushed to the Palace for Supreme Justice and looked for Lily. The place was full of people rushing back and forth, but he was certain she had not been brought in so he lifted his gown and hurried across the city to her house, puffing and panting.

The streets were still quiet with early-morning business. Her ward gate stood open; men played chess by the side of the road. Scholar Yu was not as young as he had been and he had grown fatter with the years. His silk robes were too heavy and he wished he was wearing a simple scholar's robe instead.

The closer he got to Lily's house the slower Scholar Yu walked, and at the last bend he slowed down to a dignified pace. There was a crowd outside her house. He was Scholar Yu, fourth-grade official of the Ministry of Roads and Transport, he told himself to bolster his courage.

When he had pushed through the crowd he found Lily's gates open and her courtyard empty. Inside, her room was quiet and strange: all the furniture and people had been removed.

'They took her away this morning,' one of the neighbours told him. 'Imperial Wrestlers came and took everything. Yes, the baby as well.'

Scholar Yu hurried all the way home. His eyes were set on the end of the street that led to his house. 'Wife!' he called when he got there. 'Wife!'

Scholar Yu's wife was sitting on the doorstep, helping the maid wash cabbage leaves. She was pushing a stray strand of hair from her forehead.

'What is it?' she said, but her husband was so out of breath she couldn't understand a word he said.

'Our daughter!' he managed at last. 'She's been arrested. So has Secretary Yen. They've all been arrested.'

———————

Secretary Yen had not had a good morning. He had been carried half naked through the streets, beaten and questioned. At the end of it all he felt gratitude to the man who eventually handed him a brush. He took a deep breath and steadied his hand, carved his signature at the end of a full and frank confession. His office had incorrectly predicted the fiery star; he had failed to perform minor duties to the best of his ability; he had sometimes been less than conscientious; he had mistreated and abused his staff; occasionally he had even taken bribes from minor officials to influence the stars to a small degree. Nothing serious.

When there was nothing else he could think of or invent, Secretary Yen reached for his seal and almost laughed at himself. Of course it wasn't here! He was in prison. He wondered when they would let him go; whether they'd exile him; and, if they did, where they would send him. He hoped it wouldn't be the far south: he'd rather be sent north into the grasslands. Anywhere but the south. He painted his left thumb black and thought that he'd probably become a village scribe somewhere barbaric, put the pen down and stamped his thumbprint at the bottom of the paper. There!

The confession of Secretary Yen was taken to the Palace of Supreme Justice, right up to the seat of the Upright Magistrate. It was held up to his list of offences and a few items were ticked off. Unfortunately all the important crimes were those he had yet to confess to. The man's signature was so rudimentary the Upright Magistrate felt as if he was trying a child. He let out a sigh and shook his head. Some people made life so difficult.

The Upright Magistrate ordered that Secretary Yen be brought to his hall. When he arrived he made a wretched figure. The Upright Magistrate watched impassively as the bedraggled old bully limped up the steps, stood shivering between the cedarwood columns.

'Give him some clothes,' the Upright Magistrate said. His officials scurried to find a robe. The Upright Magistrate watched them. A robe was found. It was rushed across the room, pulled down over Secretary Yen's head. He had difficulty in raising his arms so they gave it a stiff jerk. Secretary Yen yelped with pain. The officials ignored him and fussed to straighten the robe. Red stains began to appear on his shoulders.

The Upright Magistrate looked at the accused, gave him a long and unnerving smile. He had tried many people: from bandits to traitors to rebellious peasants. He knew what to look for in a guilty man: blushing of both cheeks, breathlessness, erratic heaving of the man's lungs. He ticked them all off: sure signs of guilt.

The Upright Magistrate picked up the confession and read it aloud, followed up with pertinent questions, then moved on. At one point Secretary Yen tried to elaborate on the issue of the fiery star, but the Upright Magistrate cut him off.

'Please limit yourself to answering the questions as efficiently as possible,' he said in an exasperated tone. 'I am a busy man.'

Secretary Yen stopped mid-sentence, behaved as everyone wanted him to. At the end of the questioning the Upright Magistrate sat back in silence, reread the confession. Everyone waited. The accused looked to his shoulder where the red patch had grown, like spilt wine, through the linen. He wondered if he would be reassigned somewhere. There were worse ways to spend a life, he supposed. He had many friends and relatives. They would look after him.

When the Upright Magistrate was ready he cleared his throat and sat back in his chair. Everyone turned to listen.

'There are contradictions,' the Upright Magistrate began. 'Contradictions!' he announced to the whole room. 'Contradictions!' he said again, and waited for the echoes to fade before he picked out the accused's falsehoods, holding them up between his fingers for them all to admire. As he recounted the evidence the court murmured in appreciation; there was a patter of applause.

In the middle of the room Secretary Yen bowed his head. He had realised that he wasn't at the centre of this act, but the dead body at the end of the play.

The Upright Magistrate turned to Secretary Yen.

'Come closer.'

Secretary Yen shuffled forward. The Upright Magistrate looked him full in the eye, turned to the scribe.

'The accused's hearing is sound, his eyes are clear. There are no signs of delusion or insanity.' He turned back to Secretary Yen. 'What have you to say to the charge of treason?'

Secretary Yen was unable to answer: he knew nothing of treason.

'The accused is unwilling to admit to his crimes,' the Upright Magistrate noted, as a casual aside. 'He shows no remorse, no will to reform.'

The scribe dipped his brush into the ink, and beautifully noted this unwillingness to reform. He dipped his brush again, dabbed away the excess, wrote 'Conclusions' with a delicate swirl, held the brush off the paper and waited expectantly, head cocked sideways, like a thrush.

The Upright Magistrate began in a practised tone: 'Conclusions,' he began, 'are that the prisoner should be taken away and beaten until he is willing to confess.'

The scribe noted this down.

'Officer!' the Upright Magistrate called, and the chief officer stepped forward. 'When you have it, add his admission for the records.'

He turned to Secretary Yen and pursed his lips in careful consideration. 'For your own benefit may I advise,' he sat forward a little, 'a simple confession.' He spoke confidentially: 'It would be easier for everyone, including your family. I will make sure of that.'

The condemned nodded. He was taken away and beaten with the thick bamboo pole; thrashed till the skin on the back of his thighs split open and the blood started out; thrashed till he put up his hand, agreed to sign.

The brush shivered in his hand as he wrote his name.

The following days were a nervous time for anyone who knew Secretary Yen.

Scholar Yu's wife was out in the streets, jostling with crowds and traffic, when she happened to pass by the Palace of Supreme Justice for the fourth time that day. A pair of guardsmen stopped anyone going in. They were dressed in the yellow uniform of the Army of Divine Strategy. They looked disgruntled and bored. She walked up and stopped a little way from them, peered in through the gate as if she was looking for someone she knew.

'Any news?'

'Yes,' one of the footmen said. 'Good news.'

'Oh?'

'They're going to execute him.'

'Oh!' Scholar Yu's wife said, and put her hand to her mouth to cover her alarm. 'When?'

'Soon. Before the anniversary of the Emperor's accession.'

'And what,' she asked, as if in passing, 'about the courtesan who was arrested with him?'

'No idea.'

Scholar Yu's wife wrung her hands. 'She's my daughter!' she said, all pretence gone. 'I want to know where she is. She's my daughter. I don't want her to come to any harm. She has been bad, but she was led astray. She was always good when she was a girl.'

The man saw her distress. 'Listen,' he said. 'I'm just a guard. There's nothing I can do. If you have friends you should use them – otherwise . . .' He pulled a finger across his throat.

Scholar Yu's wife turned away. She had tears in her eyes as she hurried down the street. She found Scholar Yu still sitting under the pear tree, face red, slurring his words.

'They're going to kill her!' she hissed at him.

Scholar Yu was too drunk to stand, so she took hold of his beard and held him steady. 'Our daughter,' Scholar Yu's wife shouted, anger fanned by powerlessness. 'They're going to kill her.'

Scholar Yu groaned. His wife slapped his face. Damn you, you old fool! Damn you and damn that marriage, and damn your ancestors for giving birth to you.

Scholar Yu's wife refused to let Scholar Yu in that night, but he was apologetic and insistent and after some time she was too exhausted and lonely to resist his pleas. He still smelt of wine but his footsteps were steady and when he spoke he seemed sincere.

'Tomorrow I will go and talk to people,' he said. 'I will look after her. She is my daughter too. She doesn't belong only to you.'

Scholar Yu's wife was too tired to care now. They could kill her daughter. She didn't care. They could kill her and her husband and her grandson. Scholar Yu's wife had stopped believing in the future.

The stars faded from view. Secretary Yen knelt close to the bars of the prison and watched them go, disappearing as quickly as the days of his life. He had heard it said that day by day there is less of the future to fear, but as his shrank the more precious it became to him. What is there in life when there is no more future left? he wondered, and leant against the wooden bars.

When the morning star rose, Secretary Yen could see his fingers, white on the bars, then even that was lost from view and the sun rose out of the Eastern Sea. He had never been so unhappy to see the sun rise. Even so, he stared at its beauty, bent his head and prayed. He prayed aimlessly at first: a babble of thoughts on the last day of his life, then he tried to aim his prayers, thought of a god who might help him now.

In life a man serves Sage Kung, the saying went, 'in retirement he searches for the Daoist elixir, and only on his deathbed does he turn at last to Buddha. Secretary Yen wished he could have had the chance to seek the elixir of immortality, but he was glad to have found the Lord Buddha before it was too late. The compassionate face of the Buddha came to mind, and he felt as if the god had put an arm around his shoulders. He was not alone. 'I am with you,' the Buddha said. 'Come here, my son, and touch my robe.' Secretary Yen shut his eyes and stretched out his arms. He could feel the divine presence all around him. It meant more to him than he could ever say.

'Bring me back as a moth,' Secretary Yen prayed, 'so I can study the stars better. Bring me back as a moth or a bat or a peasant man so I can avoid the pitfalls of success. I do not want to be a successful man again. Bring me back as a peasant or a monk. I do not want to inherit position. I do not want to have so many lives dependent on mine, or my confessions. I did not want any of this.'

It was customary to kill the male members of a family when one was sentenced to death and all boys and men between six and seventy-six were taken out to the Western Market and throttled. Throttling was a late concession, kinder than beheading, which would shame a man before his ancestors. The body was a gift from your parents, and it was important to keep it in one piece.

The swordsman was up early that morning, watching the same sunrise. He used a rough stone to smooth out nicks the last spine had left, soothed his sword, talked to it quietly. 'This one will be easy,' he whispered. 'Officials always are. They have women's souls, women's bones.'

After a breakfast of mutton broth the soldiers walked to the prison and signed for the prisoner: a constellation of thumbprints at the bottom of the paper. They wheeled him through the straight streets, his head sticking out of the top of the box-cart, decorated with a banner with the imperial edict ordering his execution, listing his crimes. Secretary Yen's mouth was bound shut, a wooden ball in it. He had nothing to say about his crimes; nothing he could say could even begin to express what he felt inside.

They wheeled him to the Western Market, where axes and saddles and cloth were bought and sold, and where the Persian bazaar overflowed with vendors of gruel and sweet congee. This morning it was also where the corpses of his brothers and sons and uncles lay in the dust. Around them gathered a confused audience of cows, on the way to their own slaughter.

When the cows had been moved away, they continued to the execution ground, just beyond the Pond for Releasing the Living where the religious and superstitious were queuing to buy live fish from the buckets of the fishmongers, then paying the priests to let them go into their pond. It gave them extra merit towards their next reincarnation.

Secretary Yen was salivating uncontrollably. He tried to swallow but with the wooden ball in his mouth it was too difficult. He started drooling like a hungry dog, shook his head to detach the threads that hung from his mouth, but they stayed where they were.

Secretary Yen looked at the clear waters of the pool and wished he had eaten less fish in his day. Less fish and lamb and beef and mutton and shrimp and squid and pork. He wished he had never worn silk, that he had prayed more often. Now that he was about to die he felt the suffering

412

he had caused in his lifetime. All the men he had beaten or driven from office. All the men he had insulted because he refused to be intimidated by their learning. Through it all he heard the mooing of nearby cattle. The sound seemed very vivid – as if the human business of buying and selling and making a profit was for that moment entirely insignificant, but the market continued to bustle as soldiers led Secretary Yen to the willow tree that grew on the banks of the pond. He lagged behind, trying to draw out his last minutes, struggling to not keep up with the guards. But they were in a hurry for home and lunch. They pulled him forward like a farm animal.

Under the tresses of the bending willow tree the Buddhist monks bowed their heads and prayed for compassion. They looked away as Secretary Yen was forced to kneel. The sword was sharpened again, a fish splashed up in the pond, bringing a ripple of amusement in the crowd. Secretary Yen was forced to bow forward. His hair was yanked tight, his head pulled forward, his neck stretched out like a chicken's. The monks did not look up. Their eyes were shut, but they could still hear the scrape of steel, the kicking and whimpering as Secretary Yen struggled for a few more seconds of life. They heard the swordsman clear his throat and spit, the hush of the crowd as the sword was raised, then the single solid thud: like a butcher's cleaver chopping into a carcass.

There was a moment of profound silence.

The monks took deep, compassionate breaths. The market swirl faltered for a few seconds as people stopped to look. Secretary Yen's blood pumped from the stump, then trickled and dripped. A fly buzzed in the executioner's ear. He swatted it away, cleaned his sword in the pond water, then picked up the head.

The guards felt hungry. They walked back to their

barracks, and sat down to a lunch of pork flavoured with green chilli and with rice. The headless body lay still as the market picked up speed again, swirled as before. Eventually the monks opened their eyes, resumed taking people's money. The fish that had been saved from the lunch plate splashed playfully in the pond.

After the execution the women of Secretary Yen's family were locked into the Side Court of the Palace – a whole village of women whose husbands and fathers had transgressed against the law. There were officials' wives and daughters, foreign princesses, the concubines of noblemen, the sisters of the condemned, a thousand wasted lives. They wove and washed for the needs of the palace, lamenting their fate and the crimes of their families that had led them to slavery. Almost unnoticed in the harem of misfortune Secretary Yen's widow sat alone, weaving in silence. She fed the spindle through the skeleton of threads, turned her grief into a plain length of purple silk. It grew by three feet each day, till within a month there was a bolt so heavy it took two men to lift it. But she felt no lighter. Without looking up she picked up a new thread. Started again.

———

Each night Lily stared at the moon rising over the roofs of the capital and hoped that Joyful Hope could see it too. The clothes she had been wearing were now dirty and lice-ridden; when her breasts leaked milk she missed her son most.

Lily remembered the morning of her arrest with scattered images and a clutching fear that made her palms sweat and her heart race. A herd of Imperial Wrestlers, like bullocks in the dawn light, standing all eager and excited.

They seemed very clear to her for a moment: their fat faces, heavy nostrils, breath steaming in the cold morning air. She took a deep breath, shut her eyes and felt the fear and terror and detached bemusement as she was picked up and carried through the streets. She didn't know if she screamed or not. She didn't scream. She thought of her son. Please take me away from here, she thought. And then came the memory of her mother, and sweeping the courtyard in childhood – now she was helping her mother make dumplings. They kneaded the ground pork and spring onions and fragrant chives, sprinkled a little soy sauce, a little sesame oil, then mixed in roughly chopped wood-ear fungus to add crunch. The pork was a white pink: nice and fatty, good for keeping you warm. They let the stuffing settle as they mixed the flour and salt, then massaged it all together, rolled it out into thin strips, cut away little balls of dough and rolled them flat. Lily wiped her hair, filled each dumpling with pork, then sealed the dough. But the arms still held her, the bullocks were all around; faces of the people who were watching the parade. She could tell that they didn't like to look her in the eyes. They were afraid or embarrassed. She could tell that they saw their own death in her eyes. She kicked and struggled and one of the Wrestlers laughed. She shut her eyes, tried to will the sight of death to go away.

They threw Lily into a cell at the back of the Upright Magistrate's yamen: bamboo bars restricting her view, straw on the floor, a wooden bucket in the corner in which to piss and shit.

Joyful Hope was taken from her on the first morning and Lily screamed and cursed and had to be beaten to let go. She could not understand the cruelty of taking her son.

'Stop screaming!' the guards hissed. 'He will be safe! Stop screaming or you will get us all into trouble!'

Lily believed them at first, then she began to think it was a trick and she shouted for her son.

One of the guards came in and beat her with his stick. 'He's with a friend,' the man said. 'He is safe.'

Such was the venom with which the guard spoke that Lily spent the rest of the first day in terror of being taken out and disfigured. She had watched Secretary Yen being led away and had been too frightened to call out to him. But each passing day lessened that initial fear. Now she pretended she was a poetess in a mountain valley, living the hermit's life in a thatched hut, like Du Fu and Wang Wei. She missed her son, missed him too much. If it wasn't for him, she could keep up this fantasy, but each day she slumped in the corner of the room and shivered with cold.

No one seemed to know which prison Lily was in, but after days of searching Scholar Yu's wife found the right one, came to her door.

'Lily?' she said, because she wasn't quite sure that the slumped and dirty figure was her daughter.

Lily looked at her but she was so deep in her fantasy that she had to hear her name called three times before she realised that she was being spoken to, that it was her mother and that her mother had brought food.

'Joyful Hope's with us,' Scholar Yu's wife told her. 'Fragrant Blossom bribed the guards. She brought him to us. He is with us,' she repeated until Lily understood. 'He is safe but he misses you so much.'

After a while the guards herded the visitors away. Lily took her mother's hand and kissed it. 'Tell him his mother loves him.'

* * *

416

Scholar Yu's wife went out each morning with more things for her daughter. On the second day she took Joyful Hope, but he howled as soon as he was brought near to the prison, kept crying as his mother talked to him through the wooden grille, stroked his head and took his little hands in hers.

Each day Scholar Yu went out to take gifts to all his friends and to ask them if they would be prepared to intervene on his daughter's behalf.

'Do you know the Upright Magistrate?' he asked each man. Any who did laughed at the idea that they might be able to sway the Upright Magistrate.

'Your daughter is an affront to traditional Chinese values,' the hard-hearted said.

'He's a friend of Minister Li,' others said.

'You know who you have to go and see,' Scholar Yu's wife told him that night and Scholar Yu poured himself another cup of wine and pushed his grey hair off his head.

'I will go tomorrow.'

———————

Minister Li heard about the arrest of Secretary Yen with a prickle of alarm. His palms sweated and goose pimples started up on his forearms. He sent out his servant, who came back with the news that Lily had been arrested as well.

'Quiet,' he told his thoughts, as he paced up and down. 'Quiet!'

Minister Li went home that night and considered inviting friends over to talk to them, but ended up walking up and down in his gardens. There was the contorted rock he and Lily had set up, Moonlight Pavilion, all the places where she used to sit.

Everywhere he went he saw Lily, heard her or heard his fantasies of them both: old, happy and content. He told himself that he was better off with her dead, told himself that his life would be easier now. He imagined her in her cell, writing a letter to him, begging him to forgive her, asking to be taken back. He had nightmares of Lily being given the sentence of death by a thousand cuts: saw her pretty eyes in a flayed skull, her dead mouth hanging stupidly open.

Minister Li lay in bed for hours, but still he could not sleep: each way he turned a labyrinth of thoughts wound in, over and around themselves, like a bucket of worms. When he eventually slept, Minister Li dreamt that he was lying in prison watching the moon rise when he felt a soft woman behind him in the dark. He stretched out in his sleep, rolled into her arms.

'You've come,' she said. 'I knew you'd come.'

Minister Li wanted to visit the Upright Magistrate but didn't know what he would say. I will leave it to Heaven, he told himself. If it is fated to happen, it will happen. I have no control. It is all decided in Heaven.

Each day was a trial of temptation, but each time he felt like breaking he took a deep breath, closed his eyes and let the anxiety go.

On the fifth morning Minister Li was binding a turban round his head when a servant appeared.

'Master,' the servant said, 'there is a visitor.'

'Who?'

'Scholar Yu,' the man said.

'Greetings,' Minister Li said, when Scholar Yu entered, but the scholar's face was tense and drawn.

He dropped to his knees.

'Forgive me my pride and the foolishness of an old man

418

who loves his only daughter! Help me – help us – have mercy on us!' Scholar Yu prayed. 'He's going to kill her. I know she has behaved badly – we were too indulgent with her when she was a child. Her behaviour is unacceptable – you promised to treat her like a wife and in the interests of your family's honour and a mother and father's old age, please, have mercy on her!'

'Please, stand up,' Minister Li said, but only when he had lifted Scholar Yu to his feet did the old man stop babbling.

———————

The Upright Magistrate had a pleasant morning in which he condemned one man to death, and sentenced two others to beatings with the thick bamboo. After the execution of Secretary Yen he had broken the thin bamboo over his knee. It was a statement of severity: from now on he only sentenced people to the thick bamboo.

After lunch the Upright Magistrate was due to consider the case of Yu Xuanji. He finished his steamed bun, swilled the shreds of fatty pork from his teeth, cleared his throat and spat.

'Ah, my friend,' the Upright Magistrate said, as he got up and saw Minister Li entering the back court of the yamen. 'I thought I would see you today.'

Minister Li was cautious. He listened to the case against Lily, nodded gravely. Without a doubt Lily had flouted the laws and customs of the empire and the ancestors.

'The reason the empire is in such a sorry state,' the Upright Magistrate said, punctuating each word with his finger on the table, 'is because no one cares for society and ritual and custom.'

I know, Minister Li's expression said. I know.

'If I set this woman free, what message will that send?'

Minister Li kept nodding his agreement.

When the Upright Magistrate had exhausted his conviction, Minister Li poured him more tea, leant in close.

'You know, I have been a bad husband and I have let this concubine behave poorly. I am as responsible as she is. If you punish her, you should punish me.'

The Upright Magistrate took a deep breath and shook his head, but Minister Li would not let him say no. They spent the whole afternoon negotiating Lily's release. At the end of the day neither man was entirely happy.

Minister Li sent a message to Scholar Yu and the next day he went to visit their house. It was the first time he had been there for nearly eight years. It was odd to think that this was where Lily had grown up.

Scholar Yu and his wife welcomed Minister Li, and the three of them sat together like conspirators. Scholar Yu and his wife listened and nodded and agreed to all the binding stipulations on their daughter's behalf.

Minister Li politely refused to stay for dinner, and when Scholar Yu tried to press a gold ingot into his hand, he refused.

'Many bad things have happened between our families,' he said, 'and I hope that this is the beginning of better relations.'

The old couple agreed, their wrinkled faces eager. To sustain a marriage is like carrying rocks on your shoulders, to ruin one as easy as eating. All they wanted was better relations between Lily and Minister Li. That was all they had ever wanted: for the world to be at peace, and for their daughter and her husband living in harmony.

For the first time in a fortnight Scholar Yu was not troubled by dreams; his wife did not lie awake worrying. Joyful Hope lay between them as his mother had once done, and Scholar Yu's wife thought of Lily locked in the cell and how soon she would be released.

When Lily was told the conditions of her release she kicked the bamboo bars of her cell. Joyful Hope started to wail and Scholar Yu's wife felt tears well up.

'Lily!' Scholar Yu's wife said. 'They were going to kill you!'

'I have done nothing wrong!' Lily insisted, but her mother tried to hush her.

'I would rather they killed me!'

Scholar Yu's wife started to screech that they would all be killed.

That night Lily cursed her parents' name. Joyful Hope had nothing to do with Minister Li. She struggled to remember her mother's face, her *real* mother, the grasslands, the childish happiness at the Last Fort Under Heaven, remembered a day when she had come out of the snow and her mother had warmed her hands in hers.

Lily was six years old again. She stood by her mother's shoulder. 'What do you think I should do?'

Her mother was stitching shoes with tiger faces for her.

'It is better to see a child grow than die of pride,' she said. When she was finished she gave the shoes to her. 'These are for Joyful Hope,' she said.

The next day Scholar Yu went to the Hamlets, found Lily's friends, begged them to appeal to her to accept Minister Li's offer, but she refused to listen to any of them.

'Kill me,' she said. 'I will go with pride to see my ancestors.'

Even Fragrant Blossom had difficulty. 'Listen to me!' she said. 'He is protecting the child. Sister, please listen to me. Lily! The Upright Magistrate has killed all Secretary

Yen's children. Just think what he would do to you.'

Fragrant Blossom left without changing Lily's mind. Lily swore that she would return as a ghost and murder them all. She would rather murder her son than see him grow up in Minister Li's household. She kicked over the bucket, shouted curses into the night – but there was no one there to listen.

When Lily had exhausted herself she lay down, thought of Joyful Hope and dried her eyes on the hem of her sleeve. Perhaps Minister Li wasn't trying to control her, she reasoned. Perhaps he really wanted to help her – had not forgotten the promises he had made when they were young.

She took a deep breath, as if shedding a great load that had been crushing her.

'Very well,' she said, when Scholar Yu's wife came to see her the next morning. 'I accept.'

AD 873

Abbot Zhao had died in the years that Lily had been in the capital. She went to his grave mound and spoke to him, asking him for advice, but the winter grasses hissed in the wind and the mound of earth did not even shake.

I miss Joyful Hope more than I can say and wrote five letters to Minister Li today asking him to bring my son to me. The Buddhists say that to be in a position of power and to not help others is like returning from a treasure hill empty-handed. Please show benevolence.

I sat and wrote letters to all the people I knew, asking for help, but so few of them write to me now.

From where I sit I can see the slopes
of Wang Wu Mountain
where we went exploring together.

I keep thinking of the rainy evenings
we sat at the table
to eat together.

Now the lane
to my secluded house
remains silent.

Every spring
the river traffic is so busy
along the Qu River.

Novice Yang had grown in the two years that Lily had
been away. Her hair was still dressed in virgin knots; her
body was so broad and solid that it was hard to decide
whether she was a priest or a nun.

You shouldn't have left, her attitude seemed to say. Aloud
she said, 'Poor child. Poor orphan child.'

It took a moment for Lily to realise that Novice Yang
did not mean her when she said that, but her son.

'Your husband is very understanding,' Novice Yang said.

Lily refused to play.

'You must have hurt him,' Novice Yang said. 'Poor
man.'

Lily clenched her fists with frustration and when Novice
Yang came and stood over her Lily screamed, 'Leave me
alone. Get away from me!'

Novice Yang blinked but refused to look away. 'No
wonder you have ended up like this. You have a child now,
you know. You have a husband. You should apologise and
go back to him. That's what I would do if I was you.'

'How do you know so much about my husband?' Lily
said and Novice Yang blushed. 'Have you been talking to
him?' Lily demanded.

'No!'

Lily was convinced that Novice Yang was being paid by
Minister Li. She walked up to the top of the hill and
screamed to the clouds: 'Fuck Heaven. Shit on the Buddha!

Piss in the mouth of Sage Kung! Shit on the face of Sage Meng's mother!'

But Heaven refused to strike her dead.

Pung An came to visit me today. He told me he had received all my letters and poems but that an official at the Ministry for Good Works on the East Side of the City had warned him not to come. In the end his conscience would not let him rest and he rode out to see me.

I thanked him for his visit, and he promised to take the shoes I made to Joyful Hope. I told him where Minister Li's manor is. He promised to see the child and to write to me to tell me how he looks.

I cannot bear to think of my son growing, changing and learning without me there.

As soon as Pung An's letter arrived, Lily ran up the hill to her room, slammed the door. Before she had finished the first paragraph she was fighting back tears; by the end of the second she was unable to see clearly.

He had grown. Without her to see it. Minister Li was treating him like a son. She hated him for his kindness and benevolence. It was easy to be benevolent when you held all the power.

That night Lily packed a bag of clothes and was up early the next morning to walk to the city. At the monastery gate, the gateman stopped her.

'I'm afraid you cannot leave,' he said.

Lily shouted and screamed, and in the end the gateman and his two sons had to carry her back to her house. Novice Yang stood guard, and Lily glared at her.

'You shouldn't have tried to leave,' Novice Yang said. 'You'll get us all into trouble.'

From then on Novice Yang followed Lily wherever she went; a shade with a shadow: always trying to escape.

Again Lily read the letter that Pung An had sent her: reading and sniffling and reading again. All she wanted was her son. She didn't care if that meant she had to live with Minister Li. He could sleep with her if he wanted. She didn't care.

That afternoon Lily stood in the doorway; stared out towards the capital. A persistent wind shepherded the blind storm south. The land beneath it was dark; Lily couldn't tell if it was raining – it looked more like dust whipped from the ground by angry demons. It was like a storm building inside her. The wind on the mountainside blew in sympathy. Lily saw someone riding out to the monastery and wished that he might bring news, but the rider passed the path up to the monastery and Lily felt the terrible hurt growing inside her.

'Your husband won't come,' Novice Yang said when Lily came back inside. 'You'll have to write to him. Apologise.'

Lily blinked to calm herself. She could feel her muscles bursting with energy. Concentrating hard, she lay down on her bed, but the feeling would not go away.

Lily lay awake all night, staring at the ceiling. Dawn came, as always, with birdsong, but Lily felt more firmly caged than ever before. Eventually she heard Novice Yang wake and cough, piss in the chamber pot, then footsteps around the room before the door latch clicked and she went out. When she came back Lily listened to the clatter of bowls, chopsticks being laid out on the table.

'Breakfast!' Novice Yang called.

Lily pulled herself up from the bed. She walked slowly

as if in a daze. On the table was a simple meal of noodles and pickled cabbage. There was no meat. She was sick of eating this filth.

'You should eat,' Novice Yang said, but Lily stared at the food, didn't respond.

'You don't want it? Then I'll have it.'

Lily did not stop staring, so Novice Yang pulled the bowl across the table and shovelled in more noodles.

Lily could not bear to watch Novice Yang eat. Across the room she saw her sandalwood casket lying open.

Novice Yang belched and watched as Lily stood up and walked across the room.

The casket was empty. 'Where is my letter?' she demanded.

Novice Yang belched.

'Where is my letter?'

'Which letter?'

'The letter about my son!'

'It isn't good for you.'

'Where is my letter?' Lily's voice was shrill again.

'I burnt it.'

'You did what?'

Novice Yang's face was earnest. 'It only made you sad,' she told Lily. 'I threw it away.'

Lily started picking through the glowing embers as if they were pebbles on the shore.

'Mistress!' Novice Yang said, as she heard the hiss of burning skin, but Lily was trying to lift the flakes of ash that had once been that letter, but each time she grasped at it the ash crumbled and left a smudge of black on her fingers.

'Stop this!' Novice Yang told her, but Lily fought her until Novice Yang held her tight. 'I'm trying to help you,' Novice Yang said.

Lily was stiff in her arms.

'You know that, don't you?' Novice Yang said and at last Lily nodded.

You are trying to help me, she thought, as she stood and walked back to the casket.

Novice Yang tried to persuade her to sit down, tried to put medicine on her burnt fingertips, but Lily would not let her. At last Novice Yang went back to her noodles, ate them cold.

Novice Yang was hunched over the table, shovelling food in, when Lily lifted the empty casket. It only took three short steps and she was standing behind Novice Yang. Lily lifted the casket above her head, as she had once lifted Joyful Hope, brought it down on the back of Novice Yang's head. The blow was so hard that Novice Yang's face hit the table. Blood spurted from her nose. Lily brought the box down again, then a third time. She lost count of how many times she hit Novice Yang, but suddenly she was staring at a pool of blood and Novice Yang's head was lying sideways on the table.

The wind howled outside and the door rattled, as if someone was trying to get in. Lily screamed and threw the box across the room, threw anything that came to hand – sandals, a stack of bowls, one of the books Novice Yang had been reading, her pot of tea, a bamboo tray. The door kept rattling. Lily backed away till she was pressed against the wall and the door had stopped rattling.

Novice Yang's eye had a fish's glassy stare. It was staring straight at her. Lily slid down the wall till she was sitting amid the scattered debris. In her hand was a piece of broken porcelain. She dropped it on to the floor and started to laugh.

* * *

Minister Li agreed to pay compensation to the family of Novice Yang and to her monastery; paid for the Monastery of Boundless Contentment's statue of the Emperor of Heaven to be covered in gold foil. Society was not surprised at the news that Yu Xuanji the concubine had murdered her maid. Lily was sentenced to execution by beheading. The Upright Magistrate shook his head: if he had had her killed two months ago this need not have happened.

Scholar Yu did not go to the trial. He did not even go to work. The death sentence did not surprise him, but it robbed him of any hope he had had left in the world. Only Scholar Yu's wife was there. She collapsed when the sentence was read out: the blood drained from her face and legs and she fell into a heap on the floor; the pain in her guts was as sharp as if she had carried Lily inside her.

Scholar Yu's wife blamed her husband. He had not loved their daughter as much as she had. He had always been more interested in his career than in his family. If only he had been a better father. She thought of a handful of instances when he had been harsh or cruel or uncaring. That night he had beaten her. The nights he had stayed away. The way he had handled her education.

'You were too hard on her,' she moaned the night before Lily was due to be killed. Scholar Yu poured himself another cup of wine, did not react. This was beyond him. He did not know what he could have done.

Minister Li refused to go to the trial or the execution; when Lily sent him a poem from her cell he refused to read it. There was nothing he could do, he told himself.

When his hopelessness overwhelmed him, Minister Li went to the wet-nurse's courtyard and walked Joyful Hope around the yard. The wet-nurse tiptoed away, left them alone. Minister Li picked the baby up as if he were a prize vase and held him to his chest. The child looked at him and seemed to tell him that he understood.

The night before Lily's execution the wet-nurse was stitching tiny cloth shoes for Joyful Hope, with tiger faces to scare away evil ghosts.

'He's asleep,' she whispered, and nodded towards the kang.

Minister Li pulled back the covers and lifted the baby out of the bed.

'I'm taking him away for a few hours,' he said. 'May I?'

The wet-nurse nodded, confused that the master of the house should ask her.

'Good,' he said. She gave him a blanket to wrap the baby in, and he bent low to pass out of the doorway.

> The well beside the tree echoes with autumn rain
> under the window-ledge
> dawn blows softly in

Minister Li's sedan was waiting for him in the courtyard and he climbed in, bundle in arms.

The bearers lifted the chair to their shoulders; the gates opened; Joyful Hope remained sleeping as they made their way out of the ward and into the great wide silent avenues of the capital. None of the guard dared to stop a second-grade official; the guards at the Palace of Supreme Justice did not dare to refuse him entry.

The gates swung open, the file of lanterns and banner-bearers marched in, the sedan chair following.

Minister Li's bearers waited in the front courtyard while Minister Li carried Joyful Hope out. One man tried to stop him going to see the condemned criminals, but his sedan bearers bustled him into the shadows and beat him into a bloody and brutal silence.

'Lily?' Minister Li called to the row of cells. His voice broke and he cleared his throat, his breath coming out in plumes.

'Lily?'

When Lily first heard her name she opened her eyes, assumed that she had been dreaming, but the call came again.

'Lily?'

Lily pressed her face to the wooden bars. 'Yes?'

She heard the grinding of grit as someone came closer. Minister Li stood a little way off. 'It's me,' he said. He could see her face dimly lit by the moon behind the bars. Her eyes were black and glossy. They seemed very wide in her full-moon face.

'Zian,' she said.

'I have brought your son,' he said.

From the darkness between the bamboo bars two hands reached out, unnaturally pallid in the moonlight. He gave Lily her child. Her fingers ran over his head and mouth, and Joyful Hope woke. 'Hush,' Lily whispered, tried to give him a lifetime's worth of kisses, handed him back through the bars. 'Hush. Go with Zian now. Go on.'

Minister Li jiggled the baby to soothe him.

'I'm sorry things have turned out like this,' he said. When he tried to speak again Lily reached out, put a cold hand over his lips.

'Last night I dreamt that there was a painting of us in Changan,' she said. 'We are sitting happy together as a storm is about to break.'

Minister Li nodded. 'Who will throw clods over my wall?' he said, even though it wasn't really what he wanted to say,

Lily laughed and pursed her lips. They stared at each other for a moment and then he turned and walked away.

'Look after my son!' Lily called after him, pressed up against the bars, struggling not to lose sight of them.

———

Minister Li shied away from public engagements, but one day he was caught in the street and a man from his office stopped to congratulate him.

'I heard she was killed – at the Western Market.'

Minister Li smiled and nodded. 'Thank you,' he said, and hurried away. He felt as if a deep well had opened up and devoured all manner of possibilities and expectations. When he shut his eyes all he could see was Lily's outstretched hand, pallid in the moonlight.

———

On the morning of her execution, dawn came cold and misty, blurring the division between night and day.

You always knew that you would die, Lily tried to calm herself, but she had never thought that death would come so soon. When she heard the scrape of steel on stone she shut her eyes and slowed her breathing, remained calm.

There was the desolate splatter of footsteps.

'It's time,' the guards called.

In the Western Market near the Pond for Releasing the Living, the monks were selling fish for the devout to buy and save from the fishmonger's knife.

The busy bustle paused as the crowd watched to see who it would be today. They saw a woman standing under the willow tree. A gust disturbed the tree. Lily put her hand to her face and smoothed back her hair. The red drums beat as the steel was pulled from its scabbard.

The sword swung.

The snow fell.

AD 907

There was no geomancer, no procession for Minister Li's funeral. A few peasants dug a wide hole in the stubbled field, where a few worms wriggled excitedly. Minister Li's widow went to see him before they shut the coffin. Minister Li's eyes had shrunk a little but his face was no more wrinkled than the day he had died. She touched his cheek, her old fingers gently brushing the wrinkles around his eyes. She let her hand fall to his cheekbone.

'I gave you sons, maintained your household, picked out concubines. I was a good wife to you,' she told the sunken eyes; told herself she had done all that was expected.

It took five men to carry the nailed coffin to the sedan, another five to bear it out. They lowered it into the hole, and it slipped to the side, lay awkwardly at the bottom. Minister Li's widow burnt incense, threw coins into the grave to bribe the officials of Heaven, then cleared her throat and nodded to herself, as if in some private conversation, walked slowly back to her chambers.

When Minister Li's widow got back to her room there was a faint smell of old incense hanging in the air. In her

434

husband's room was a pile of old papers. Even though she was illiterate, she knew whose they were.

Lily had not made him happy, Minister Li's widow told herself. She had not made anyone happy. Even less herself.

Minister Li's widow bent stiffly, picked out all the letters from the bottom of her husband's chest, fed the old dry papers to the brazier. She held the last bundle over the flames for a moment, then relented, left them on the table.

Early the next morning Swallow and Fang had their sacks packed and slung from both ends of their carrying poles. Minister Li's widow met them at the open gateway, gave Fang a tightly wrapped packet.

'This is for you,' she said, watched them walk out into the world, their youth still armour against bitterness and regret.

Swallow and Fang tramped country roads, avoided all hint of war, even avoiding cottage smoke until they felt well away from raiding horsemen. On the fifth night the weather turned cold and they stopped at a tavern, bought warm wine, ate a dinner of smoked pork shredded with cabbage.

Inside Fang's pack was the packet that Minister Li's widow had given him. He unwrapped the faded silk cloth, found a bundle of papers, the sheets old and brittle, disorganised and tattered. Fang flicked through them; found an entry about a visit to Yellow Hill Falls, fluidly written characters descending in columns.

'What is it?' Swallow asked but Fang shook his head.

It was a literary diary, poems intersecting the text. He sipped his wine and Swallow pressed herself into him. There were dates here and there.

'I know these poems,' he said, leafed through the pages, found poem after poem that he had recited to the minister. The last page was dated the second day of the twelfth month 873.

The last page was a letter.

'What can a mother say to a son she will never know?' Lily took a deep breath as she wrote; saw the dawn light was bleaching the sky. It was green in the east; violet in the west.

'Please forgive me for not being there with you. Know that I love you and think of you.'

Fang put his cup down. Swallow held his arm.

'My son – it is such a beautiful sunrise.' Lily stopped.

'My son. When you see the sun rise, or the moon in the willow, or when you are alone and afraid, I will be there with you.'

Footsteps came across the yard and stopped outside Lily's cell door. She signed her name and put down her brush. There was a knock at the door.

'Mistress,' the guards called. 'It's time.'

'What does it say?' Swallow asked.

Fang folded the page, took a deep breath and reached for his cup. 'Nothing,' he said.

After a while Swallow stood up and went to the door. 'It's snowing,' she said, and tugged his arm. 'Let's go out to see the snow falling!'

Fang drank his wine and let her pull him up from the floor. Large flakes were falling softly and silently, filling in all their footsteps, the whole world turned to winter. Fang and Swallow stood in the doorway, facing the night.

'It's cold,' she said and shivered.

'It is,' Fang said, and put his arm around Swallow's shoulder.

Author's Note

The cultural life of Tang Dynasty China was a time of feverish creative energy and diversity. Tang Dynasty poets were the pop stars of the age. Of the female poets of that time, Yu Xuanji's is the most interesting and unconventional voice, but outside her poems, almost nothing is known about her life.

The story of Yu Xuanji's execution was first written twelve years after her death in a tabloid-style journal, *The Little Tablet from the Three Rivers*. The forty-nine poems, many of which were written to mark an event or moment with friends, are undoubtedly a fraction of what she produced in her lifetime.

Her poems were published during her lifetime in a collection called *Fragments of a Northern Dreamland*, which has been lost. Her forty-nine surviving poems were included in an anthology during the Song Dynasty (when female freedoms were sharply curtailed and foot-binding was becoming widespread) mainly for their 'freak' value. The anthology also listed poems by ghosts, monks, priests, foreigners and women, 'and others whose efforts might provide amusement'.*

* *Indiana Companion to Traditional Chinese Literature*, William H. Nienhauser (ed.) (Bloomington: Indiana University Press, 1986).

The Tang Dynasty was a time in which East Asian women enjoyed a level of personal freedom greater than at any time before the twentieth century. In her short life Yu Xuanji experimented with three of the roles in which women could blur and break gender distinctions: concubine, Daoist 'nun' and courtesan. Despite the manner of her death, she is also considered to be the most prominent Tang female poet.

This novel started as a collection of translations of Yu Xuanji's poems, which formed the skeleton on which the rest of the book has grown. Her poems remain grains of truth, embedded in my fiction.

Apart from Lily, the other characters in this book – Minister Li, Abbot Zhao Lianshi, the Upright Magistrate and Official Liu – were all real people to whom Yu Xuanji addressed poems on topics as varied as playing polo, welcome, and in response to their own poems. A number of poems directly address Wen Tingyun, who was the first distinctive writer of literary song lyrics, and was as famous for his debauched lifestyle as for his poetry.

I would like to thank Emma Xiaofang for her monumental effort in helping me translate Yu Xuanji's entire collection into English.

Thanks also to Alan Chiswick and Charles Mindenhall for their comments on various stages of the manuscript. I would also like to thank Hannah and James Boxshall, and Melissa Morrisey and Daniel Beaulieu for their generous hospitality while I was wrestling with this narrative. I would also like to thank Zhang Songqing for his calligraphy.

Note on Translations

Here, for readers who may be interested, are the titles that I have given to my translations of the forty-nine extant poems. If a translation of a poem appears in this book, in full or in part, there is a page reference. Some of these translations have appeared in the periodical *Equinox*, to which I am grateful.

1. 'River Edge Willows' p.128
2. 'For the Girl Next Door'
3. 'A Poem for Guoxiang'
4. 'Tribute to Master Alchemist Liu' pp.194, 332
5. 'Sent to Official Liu'
6. 'Washing Silk Temple' p.329
7. 'Selling Tattered Peonies' pp.181, 384
8. 'Thank Minister Li for the Gift of a Bamboo Mat' p.166
9. 'A Love Letter for Li Zian' p.430
10. 'Boudoir Resentment' p.161
11. 'My Spring Feelings for Li Zian' p.220
12. 'Watching a Game of Polo' p.301
13. 'Late Spring: I Think of You'
14. 'On a Winter's Night I Wrote this Poem for Wen Tingyun'
15. 'A Poem for Li Ying*: to Match his "Summer's Day Fishing"'
16. 'Matching Poem for my New Neighbour to the West, Inviting Him over for Wine'
17. 'A Poem for a Close Friend: Matching his Style' p.339

* Minister Li's literary name